Mary Elizabeth Braddon

In High Places

Mary Elizabeth Braddon

In High Places

ISBN/EAN: 9783744777582

Printed in Europe, USA, Canada, Australia, Japan

Cover: Foto ©Andreas Hilbeck / pixelio.de

More available books at **www.hansebooks.com**

IN HIGH PLACES

In High Places

By M. E. BRADDON, Author of
" London Pride," etc., etc.

London: HUTCHINSON & CO.
Paternoster Row, E.C.
1898

Printed by Hazell, Watson, & Viney, Ld., London and Aylesbury.

CONTENTS

CHAP.   PAGE

   I. FELLOW TRAVELLERS 1

  II. WAS THIS A ROMAN SPIRIT? 16

 III. A FRIENDLY GENTLEMAN 23

 IV. FROM CHILDHOOD TO MANHOOD . . . 34

  V. FAIR FACES AND NOBLE HEARTS . . . 50

 VI. "TO WIN HER PRAISE" 68

VII. "PUT NOT YOUR TRUST IN PRINCES" . . 80

VIII. "SO RUNS THE WORLD AWAY" . . . 93

 IX. "AH! BITTER SWEET" 110

  X. THE WOMAN'S REIGN 130

 XI. SPLENDID PATRONAGE 152

XII. DANGER FOR SOMEBODY 172

XIII. TO PREVENT MURDER 191

XIV. TAKEN BY STORM 217

XV. NOT TO BE BOUGHT 233

Contents

CHAP.		PAGE
XVI.	EBBS AND FLOWS OF FORTUNE	251
XVII.	FOR A WOMAN'S SAKE	263
XVIII.	BETWEEN LIFE AND DEATH	286
XIX.	"LIKE A STAR FIXED"	316
XX.	A RETROSPECT	351
EPILOGUE		367

IN HIGH PLACES

CHAPTER I.

FELLOW TRAVELLERS.

A SHORT, thick-set man, with a dark complexion and a gloomy countenance, came slowly through the mists of a summer dawn, on the Portsmouth Road, a few miles west of Godalming.

The man walked wearily, like one who had walked far ; and indeed the gait and manner of the wayfarer, the weather-stains upon his cloth jerkin, the dust and dew upon his boots, suggested that he had been tramping all through the summer night. The sun was creeping up behind Leith Hill as he left Godalming and trudged along the great high-road between wide wastes of marsh and common. A long stretch of wild, uninhabited land lay between him and the great hill of Hindhead ; but he hoped to pass the Devil's Punch Bowl before noon.

Every door in Godalming had been inhospitably shut against him—even the doors of the inn, where coach and post-horses stopped. The High Street had not yet opened door or window to the morning freshness ; not a single smoke-wreath rose in the grey air ; and even at the forge, wont to be early astir, there was no glow of fire, or clinking of metal upon metal.

He was dead beat, and could not even wait till the

dew was off the grass before he threw his weary limbs
down to rest ; but he looked about him for a hillock
where the ground was driest, and, having made his
choice, sank in a heap, with his back against a furze
bush, flinging his oaken staff aside as he sat.

The stout oak sapling struck something alive, something that gave a shrill cry of pain, at which John
Felton started to his feet, and looked into the bush
behind him.

A small boy—a mere child—lifted himself slowly
from the furze as Felton rose, and looked at him
piteously.

"Why did you hit me, sir?" he asked. "Indeed I
was doing no ill, and I have no other place to sleep in."

"I hit thee by mischance, child, not evil intention.
Are you so poor? Have you neither father nor mother,
home nor shelter?"

"No, sir, I have nobody. Daddy is dead of the fever,
and Mammy has gone away with the baby, and bade
me walk to the farmers' houses, and ask them to let me
mind their cattle. But there was none that would let
me ; and some called me a beggar, and gave me a clout
on the head ; and one kind woman gave me some bread
and meat ; but they all told me I was too little ; and
they all bade me begone."

"What is your name?"

"Jarge."

"Jarge! Do you mean George?" cried Felton, with
a start, all his face hardening, and the light of an angry
resolve kindling in his tired eyes.

"Yes, sir. It's all as one. Mammy called me Jarge
—the gentleman that came to see me sometimes called
me George—like you do."

He was a pretty boy. His clothes hung about him
in rags. He had not started shoeless on his quest of
fortune, but his shoes were worn with walking over
rough ground, and his feet were cruelly scratched and
blistered. He could not tell his age when questioned.
For his size he might have been six or seven years old,
but for intelligence might pass for eight or nine. He

had fine features, strongly marked for so young a face, yet delicate. His hair was dishevelled and dusty, but he had washed his face in a running stream over-night, and had waded for a mile to cool and cleanse his feet. He was cleaner than most urchins of his age would have been under such adverse conditions.

" Are you hungry ? " Felton asked abruptly.

" Yes, sir. It was the day before yesterday that the woman gave me some bread and bacon."

" And thou hast fasted forty-eight hours, belike. Well, I'll share a crust with you. Yes, I have that much charity," he added slowly, as he opened the wallet, and gave the lad a hunch of bread. His left hand was crippled by an old wound, and he used it with a feeble clumsiness. " I'll share a crust with you ! " he repeated, in his sullen, muttering voice, " though your name is George."

" Is it a wicked name, sir ? "

" It belongs to the wickedest man in England ; but it's a good augury, perhaps, that the only creature I've spoken to since I left London should bear his name. George ! Are you telling truth, boy ? Is that verily your name ? "

" Verily and indeed, sir. But I have another name. You may see the first letter of it on my breast, if you can read letters."

The little lad pulled open his ragged shirt, and Felton saw the letter V tattooed on his breast.

It was not the first time he had seen such marks ; for he might have remembered a certain hairy-breasted sailor on the voyage to Cadiz, tattooed with sun, moon, and stars, crown and anchor, and the initials of more than one sweetheart's name : but to-day, to Felton's over-heated brain, the Viper-sign on the boy's tender flesh seemed to smack of sorcery, the black magic which that arrogant upstart the Countess of Buckingham, the mother of the man he hated, was said to practise. By what lesser art, in sooth, could she have brought her son to rule the hearts of two kings to the perdition of the kingdom ?

"Why, this is Satan's work!" he cried, gripping the boy's skinny shoulder with his strong right hand, throwing him upon his back among the furze, and glaring down at him with eyes that threatened murder. "And you are one of his imps! This is devilry! And the voice that has been in my ears is Satan's lure, and not God's bidding. Is it the devil? Do you come from hell, you starving whelp? Are you but weak, hungry, footsore human flesh; or are you an imp of the Prince of Darkness, that doth but simulate distress, and could spread dragon's wings and fly away—or vanish in a flash of fire, did thy master call thee, and leave but the stench of brimstone in this furze-bush? Art thou natural and mortal; or aerial and Satanic?"

The boy's tears and look of childish terror were assuredly as true to nature as any human expression could be. But the devil and his imps, when they act a part, must needs act better than mortal players; and Felton, seeing that Viper-brand, the initial of a name which an angry fire had burnt deep into his brain, began to believe himself the dupe of Satan.

An inspiration had come to him, tossing on a sleepless bed, in his lonely lodging, but a few nights ago. A resolve, desperate, deadly, fatal to himself and others, had slowly shaped itself in his fevered brain. Suggestions, which he had believed to come from on High, had been breathed into his mind. A mission had been given to him, as pure in its unselfish purpose as the impulse which guided the sword of Judith, or nerved the hand of Jael.

But now on a sudden he began to question the source of that inspiration—whether from Heaven or hell; since here, in this appearance of an accursed initial upon the boy's flesh, there seemed evidence of demoniac influences. It was surely witchcraft, if not the handiwork of Satan.

Yes, there must at least be witchcraft in it! This whimpering wretch might be human, a shivering, scared little mortal, weeping real tears; but that initial which seemed to grow under the skin, a dark, ineradicable stain, had been written there by one of hell's agents, inscribed there for a purpose, and that the ruin of his, John Felton's, soul.

"Oh, sir, don't kill me ! Sure I have done no ill !"

"Who put Villiers' initial on your breast, and when ?" the man asked fiercely.

"It was the snowy winter when I dursn't go into the fields, and the starlings came in at the window, and pecked my supper out of my hand," prattled the boy, "and Mammy's brother, the sailor, came from Portsmouth—and then the strange gentleman came, a-horseback, and he could scarce get through the snow, and he saw the letters on Mammy's brother's breast, and bade him mark mine with a V.—'which stands for a viper or a villain,' says he. Mammy's brother hurt me a-doing it, but I was brave and did not cry—and the strange gentleman gave me a crown-piece. Mammy used to kiss the mark sometimes when she put me to bed, but that was before the baby came—and when I had my velvet coat—but afterwards she was not so kind. And then Daddy died of the fever—and wicked men came and drove us out of the house, and off the farm, and Mammy told me I was a beggar, and she was a beggar, and the baby too, and we must needs starve, unless folks would give us food. But there was only one woman who gave me some bacon and some bread, the day before yesterday."

"Was there never a witch came to your mother's house ?" Felton asked, looking up out of a deep abstraction in which he had heard no syllable of the child's discourse.

"No, sir. There was a witch lived in the lane on the Guildford Road, but Mother would never have let her cross our doorstep. Daddy and I used to call after her when we saw her gathering sticks on the common ; but we was all afeared of her at night, when it was dark. Mammy said she would come in at the window if I was an ill boy, and fly away with me. We saw her steal a stake out of a hedge one evening, and carry it home with her, and Daddy told me she wanted it to ride about upon, after dark, in the sky. But belike she burnt the stick, to boil her kettle, for I never saw her in the sky," he added reflectively, " though I've often looked out of the window to see. It was a very little window, and there was an owl in the ivy that used to frighten me, and I used to bump my head against the ceiling, for the roof was so low I could touch it with my hand as I lay abed."

The intelligent voice went prattling on, pouring its little confidences into unheeding ears. Felton had gnawed his crust with a ravenous impatience, forcing his dry throat to swallow that untempting food ; and now he was sitting with his elbows on his knees, and his chin in his hands, brooding upon the tragic mission that lay before him, and upon the wrongs which lay behind.

Fortune had used him badly ; fortune and that man who for the last ten years had ruled Fortune, who had made fair weather and foul for the common herd, such as this poverty-stricken foot-soldier with his maimed hand, cheated of promotion, starving discontentedly upon a lieutenant's scanty pay.

Bad luck had been his companion through life—bad luck which perhaps may have been another name for bad temper. He had not conciliated friends or wooed fortune, being of a saturnian nature, given to much brooding upon small injuries, at war with life. He was a man of good birth—of the blood of the Arundels—and good education, who felt that the world owed him something—a man of truth and honour, the " honest Jack " of the barrack-room ; but an unlucky quarrel with Sir Henry Hungate on the Cadiz voyage had blasted his fortunes ; for Hungate was the Favourite's favourite, and to be ill with Hungate was to be in the Duke's bad books.

Twice had he applied for the command of a company, while last year's expedition for the relief of Rochelle was on foot, and he had been twice refused, though well recommended. A personal appeal to the Duke of Buckingham, in which he pleaded that without promotion he could not live, had been treated with contempt ; and he had to idle and starve in England, while men he deemed his inferiors were favoured.

The fatal result of that ill-advised siege of St. Martin, the ignominious flight from Rhé, tragical in its waste of noble lives, had provoked a tempest of anger, scorn, ridicule, the abuse of the envious, and the malignant exultation of prophets who had prophesied the disasters their envious hearts desired. George Villiers, Earl, Marquis, Duke, Lord High Admiral and Commander-in-Chief, Warden of the Cinque Ports, bosom friend, chosen companion, and alleged murderer of the late King James, trusted and idolised friend of King Charles —George Villiers, that splendid failure, a fine gentleman of thirty summers, entrusted with the Nation's honour and the succour of England's Protestant allies,—stood as the mark of every stone the meanest hands could fling at an unsuccessful leader. All the literature in London, or all that any Londoner cared to read, was to be found in ballads and libels, broadsides and pamphlets, reeking with foulest abuse of the man the King loved and honoured.

A breast aching with private wrongs is the surest hot-bed for indignation against a public enemy. Felton thought that he had forgotten his own particular injuries —that he had sunk his own petty sufferings in the sum-total of England's shame. Where was ever deeper shame than ours when we set out with a great show and clamour, and cost and boasting, to succour and support those heroes and martyrs of Rochelle—and so miserably failed to help them—all our arrogant pledges ending in futile endeavour, and the massacre of English soldiers upon the sands of Rhé?

The figure of the Duke no longer haunted Felton in daily reveries and nightly dreams, as his personal foe. That form had assumed a grander shape, and wore the aspect of the public enemy, Moloch, Beelzebub,—a destroying fiend, whose inordinate ambition, greed, vanity, and incapacity, had brought the pride and honour of England under the great Cardinal's velvet shoe.

Still those martyrs of Rochelle were crying to King Charles for help. They apologised for their importunity. Starving men, they pleaded, must be pardoned if they were too pressing. This third expedition had hung fire since the beginning of the year, but was at last on the eve of departure; and again the Arch-enemy of the English people, the gilded idol of England's King, was to challenge failure, and was again to prove himself useless as a bubble painted by the sun, a beautiful, empty shape floating in sunlit air, a splendid phantasm, unsubstantial as the breath of flatterers.

Felton had heard of the farewell masque and supper, given at York House a few nights ago, and of the allegory in which the Duke had appeared, followed by Envy, with her dogs yelping round her, to symbolise the barkings of the people; while after these came Truth and Fame; a costly pageant, on which Charles Stuart had looked complacently, and which the mob had heard of with disgust. Neither the mob nor John Felton knew those proud words which the Duke had spoken to his secretary: "Gerbier, if God please, I will go, and be the first man who shall set his foot on the dyke before Rochelle, to die or do the work." Nor had Felton heard of those auguries which had threatened the Favourite—how a woman had dreamed a prophetic dream, and a picture had fallen, and the anxious spirit of a long-dead father had appeared to a faithful follower of the Duke's, and had spoken words of warning, and how Villiers had defied Fate.

"There are no Roman spirits left," he exclaimed, when his friends talked of assassination; and so he who was said to have a "terrible courage" under his silken gentleness, went with proud front on the expedition which was to win back that empty breath he loved so dearly, the praise of his fellow-men. Was it of his own loss and gain he thought most, the bitterness of being the best-abused man in England, the target for every hired scribbler's venomed shaft, the mark of every man's hate; he who but three years ago, when he came home from Madrid, flushed with having flouted the Spaniards, had been the most popular man in England? Was it of this so transient affection, the capricious favour of the ignorant vulgar, he thought most, when he swore to conquer or die? Or did he think of that city of enduring souls, willing to perish by inches for their religion and their liberties? "There are no Roman spirits left," he had said, while Felton was buying his tenpenny knife at the cutler's on Tower Hill, or leaving his name at the church by the Conduit in Fleet Street, to be prayed for next Sunday, as a man disordered and discontented in mind. "There are no Roman spirits left!" How should George Villiers apprehend a Roman spirit in that dark-browed, thick-set, lieutenant of foot, who had pestered him last year for place or pay—one of the herd of supplicants, stiffer and less fawning than the common type of beggar, but not otherwise to be remembered.

A grim companion for a child of seven summers, this dark-browed patriot, with the dagger-knife sewn in his right-hand pocket, and all his thoughts fixed on that knife, and the deed it was to do. But the child had suffered the shapeless fears that haunt dark nights and solitary places, the vague terrors of a newly awakened mind that had been peopled with witches and demons, and filled with the dim horrors of the unreal. The scowling, melancholic stranger, who suffered him to run at his side, seemed a friendly presence to little George, as compared with that dark, bulky creature, with fiery breath, and shining eyes, and strange, uncouth movements, that had started up from behind the gorse-bushes in the dead of night, and which was, doubtless, the foul fiend, though it changed anon into a black horse, and galloped away with a great noise, and vanished into the summer fog. In the broad daylight little George was of a bold spirit, and feared neither man nor beast; but at night, when fiends and witches were abroad, he knew what it was to feel the coward's cold sweat and fast-beating heart; and as he thought that he would have to wander about the country, and sleep on commons and in woods, for the rest of his life, he was very glad to find a friend in this short, dark gentleman, whose eyes looked at him so strangely, now and then, while he prattled—looked, and saw him not. Sometimes at such a moment, gazing awe-stricken at those unseeing eyes, a sickly fear came upon the boy, lest the foul fiend who last night took the form of a horse, might not to-day have changed to this dark man.

But the day passed, and the traveller revealed no demoniac instincts. He suffered the child's company, and gave him a share of his humble meal at a roadside inn, and, when he got a lift in a tilted waggon between Hazlemere and Petersfield, asked leave for the stray child to ride with him. And so, for the first time in his life, George knew the bliss of a moving landscape, trees and hills, streams and fields, that passed and changed to other trees and other fields before his wondering eyes.

Childhood lives in the present and the immediate future; it knows no longer interval than from sunrise to sundown, and can scarcely grasp the notion of to-morrow; whereby the disappointment of to-day means despair. This boy had known only the simplest pleasures; but he had not known that his life was hard while there was porridge or rye bread for break-fast and a mess of pottage for supper, while Daddy sang or whistled at his plough, and while Mammy had a smile and a hug for him.

All that little world of his childhood had vanished into space; the pleasant homestead, the deep chimney, where he sat on Daddy's knee in the red light of the burning logs, his little bed in the corner under the sloping thatch, out of which strange insect life dropped upon him, while the grey swallows, with soft white breasts, twittered and chattered under the eaves, and flashed across the open casement, darkening the sun-light with wide-spread wings;—that narrow world upon which his consciousness had awakened, the smiling meadows of early June, with a depth of buttercups, in which he lost himself as in a golden labyrinth, the white fogs of his first remembered autumn, when he had clung to his Daddy in vague fear, shrinking from the mystery of things hidden—the wonder of standing barley, taller than himself, waving with a mighty sound in the summer wind, and, stranger still, and how much dearer, the wonder of newly born animals, the litter of black pigs, the foal, the brown-and-white calf, so small and gentle and approachable that he could hardly believe in its relationship to the great horned cow which he ran from in fear and trembling. The thirty-acre farm, which, with a mile or two of high-road and a cluster of cottages, had been his universe, the farmer and farmer's wife who had peopled it, were gone ; and the child nestled at this dark-browed soldier's knee, and watched the sunlit road, and babbled with delight at the wonder of this wider world.

"May I stay with you, and will you be my Daddy ? " he asked his silent companion ; for this new kind of life in the corner of a hay-scented waggon was so pleasant that the little lad wished it might go on for ever.

"Stay with me ! " echoed Felton. "Thou poor little devil ! To grant that would be to promise thee ruin and a bloody grave ! "

" Will you not ride in a cart like this always ? "

" Nay : I may ride in a cart—fettered and bound— when the iron shall enter into my flesh. I have nothing to do with thee, thou innocent imp of Satan, that bearest the Viper-sign on thy tender breast. Go or stay as thou wilt, child : ride or walk with me for to-day, and to-morrow, if thou canst ; but be on the look-out for another friend. To-morrow night we must part company."

The boy began to cry, with a vague sorrow, dimly conscious of his helplessness. The landscape lost its charm, blurred by the tears through which he saw it. He nestled closer against Felton's knee, and sobbed himself to sleep ; and when he woke it was night, and the waggon had stopped. Felton was standing in the road, and the waggoner dropped the sleepy child into his arms, and the two sat down on a bench in front of an ale-house, and had their supper of bread and ale in the summer darkness, and then tramped on into the deep of night, till they found a barn with an open door, a barn as big as a church, into which they crept, and where they lay on a heap of straw, and fell asleep to the sound of the rats rustling and nibbling among the corn, happily too well supplied to attack the sleepers.

They slept till late into the day, Felton worn out by a journey in which he had spent his strength with a prodigal rashness, so that he had been half dead when he made his offer of a shilling to the waggoner. The long sleep made a new man of him, and he set out in the coolness of sundown with the boy trudging bravely at his side, but ever on the alert for the sound of wheels behind them, and still hopeful of another friendly waggoner, and a ride in the starlight. Beguiled by this hope, he almost forgot the pain of his wounded feet, and the childish hunger which their rare meals had left unsatisfied.

Fifty miles of Felton's journey had been accomplished before they laid themselves down in the barn ; and now there was the cool night before them in which to accomplish the remaining twenty miles between them and Portsmouth.

So far as he was capable of thinking of anything except the deadly purpose that gave strength to his sinews, and dyed all the world of one blood-red hue, Felton thought, and with kindness, of the little clinging child ; and he thought that it might be for the child's welfare to be taken on to the busy sea-port, rather than to be left to the scant population of the rural road, where his chances of kindness and shelter would be of the smallest. In the town somebody would be found to succour him. A little human being, beautiful as a pictured seraph, and gentle of speech, would surely meet with kindness in a town where even a cur dog would scarce wander all day without finding a friend.

So, with this charitable impulse moving him, Felton let the child tramp beside him, slackening his own pace to suit that shorter step of the boy, who strode along valiantly on the dewy road, his worn-out shoes white with summer dust, his little hand in the automatic grasp of that deep-thinking companion, who, for the greater part of the time, was no more conscious of his presence than a meditative man is of the dog that follows him.

Presently, however, feeling the childish feet begin to lag, the childish hand hanging heavier, Felton awoke from his dream of blood, and stopped to consider the meaning of this companionship.

They had walked nearly three miles since they left the barn, and the child was tired. How about the seventeen miles to be travelled before morning? For the small wayfarer such a journey was obviously impossible. What was to be done? Leave the child in helpless distress upon this lonely road? There was not a cottage door within sight. They were in the midst of an undulating country, heather-clad hills that rose and fell in picturesque variety, patches of broken common-land, valleys through which here and there ran a streamlet—showing thin and fine as a silver ribbon where the moonlight touched it. The Hog's Back lay far behind them. They had crossed Hindhead, and around them stretched wild hills crowned with pine-woods, black against the horizon. No; he could not leave the child to die of fright in this summer solitude; nor could he suffer the delay which it must cost him to let the boy drag along at his side. He must find a shelter for the child at the next village, hard as it would be to appeal to the charity of some rough cottager, angry at being awakened from well-earned slumbers.

Felton stopped on the moonlit road to deliberate, greatly embarrassed by the burden of this small existence —a child whose innocent face, framed in loose golden hair, appealed to him with an irresistible pathos, and who might be, notwithstanding, an imp of Satan, a diabolical appearance, a vision of his own distempered brain. The nearest village might be two or three miles distant; and in his burning impatience, with that necessity of rapid movement which ever goes with agitated thought, Felton chafed at the idea of crawling along at a pace to suit those tired feet.

"I would thou hadst not fastened thyself to me, little wretch," said Felton, "for we are sorry companions; and I doubt thou wilt be half dead before we can reach a shelter."

"We could lie down there," said the boy, pointing to the common beside the road, where there were hollows among the gorse that looked like comfortable nests for slumber.

"Nay, child! there is no more rest for me till my work is done. I must be in Portsmouth to-morrow morning; and I would like to take you there with me, George, if I could; for in a town you might chance upon a friend, or, at the worst, there are places where a pauper child would find shelter. Hark! There are wheels as well as horses' hoofs! It may be a waggon like the one that carried us yesterday; and if it be bound for Portsmouth, you shall ride there."

The boy answered with a rapturous little laugh. "I love to ride in waggons," he said.

It was a waggon, and a heavier and more important vehicle than the tilted waggon that had carried them yesterday. A baggage-waggon, the last belated item in the halting progress of preparation for the expedition to Rochelle, came slowly along the road. Felton stood aside, till the wheels were nearly on a level with him, when he preferred his prayer to a soldier who walked beside the horses. Here was a destitute waif, picked up on the common near Godalming, for whom a lift to Portsmouth would be a charity.

The request was curtly refused.

"Don't try to father your by-blow on us, fellow!"

But on Felton describing himself as a lieutenant in Sir Edward Cecil's regiment, the soldier's tone changed, the driver drew up his horses, and a sergeant in authority consented to give the child a corner among the crates and boxes in the waggon.

"What are we to do with him when we get to Portsmouth?"

"Your charity will tell you what to do. His father is dead, and his mother has deserted him. His pretty looks may win him a friendly shelter, if you put him in the right way—but he will be better off left upon a tradesman's doorstep, than if I abandoned him on this lonely road."

" Do you want a lift for yourself, Captain ? "

" No ; I would rather walk."

The boy, who had held back his tears hitherto, with Heaven knows how big an effort, burst out crying at being parted from his friend, and was lifted into the waggon against his will, but soon cried himself to sleep in his corner, between two huge ammunition-cases, dazed and deafened by the reverberation of the great wheels, and the rattle of iron and steel. And so George the nameless, cast like a withered leaf upon the great, busy world, fared towards the end of his first conscious journey.

CHAPTER II.

WAS THIS A ROMAN SPIRIT?

THE boy was sound asleep when the waggon horses were pulled up on a causeway by the sea. The sudden stoppage awakened him, and looking eagerly out of the waggon, hoping to see his dark-visaged friend, his wondering eyes beheld, for the first time, the morning sunbeams shining on the crisp morning tide, the plash and dance of waves that made the pebbles leap and glitter on the edge of the strand, many-hued and beautiful. But he was somewhat scared at the strange faces round him when the sergeant lifted him out of the waggon and set him on his feet on the beach, while the soldiers began their work of shifting the baggage to a couple of open boats, with considerable energy, and no little noise.

"Now, my mannikin, here is half my morning rations of bread, and if that won't fill your little maw, here's a penny to buy a cake in the town, presently," said the sergeant, addressing the child as gravely as if they had been on an equality of years and reason; "and that's all we can do for you. So you had best ask the first charitable person you can find to take you into his service in kitchen or stable. You are handy enough to scrape trenchers, or clean harness, belike, baby as you are."

George looked at the sergeant in pure bewilderment, hearing words that had no meaning for him. These rough, strong men, sailors and recruits, shoving and shouting; the blue expanse of water, alive with boats;

—all things were new to the child, reared in the loneliness of a pasture farm. It was like some vivid dream, and the little creature stood there alone, still staring helplessly, when the oars were dipping and the boats growing small in the distance, and the lumbering waggon was standing a little way off, in charge of a man in rough clothes. There was an inn near the beach, and he could hear coarse, loud voices through the open windows, and could see a woman sweeping the doorstep.

Scared by the strange world around him, he turned his back on the sea and wandered into the town ; and the vague terrors that had made it so hard a struggle to hold back his tears gradually gave way to that all-absorbing wonder with which he looked at streets and churches and shops and hucksters' stalls, for the first time. It was not yet nine o'clock, but Portsmouth was astir, and the active life of the town was in full swing ; earlier than usual, doubtless, and with much more of bustle and noise and movement than usual, for the ships were lying ready to sail for Rochelle, and belated preparations were still in progress under the personal supervision of the Lord High Admiral the Duke of Buckingham, who had spent his life during this month of August in journeying between London and Portsmouth, trying to expedite those dilatory purveyors on whom the munitions of war depended, and whose delays and lying excuses had well-nigh driven him distracted.

The King was a guest in Sir Daniel Norton's mansion of Southwick, in the neighbourhood of the port ; but the Duke, with his wife and sister-in-law, was lodging at Captain Mason's spacious house in the High Street. The townsfolk were moved and fluttered by the residence of such magnificent guests in the heart of their town, with the frequent apparition of noble messengers from Southwick, where the Venetian Ambassador was to meet Buckingham in a conference with the King in the afternoon of this twenty-third of August. The streets were alive with unusual traffic. Women were looking out of their windows, or standing on their doorsteps, cumbered with inquisitive children, that hung upon their skirts. Men were grouped at street-corners, talking of the coming expedition, and repeating the various and contradictory rumours of which every man claimed a particular knowledge, and whose source no man could name. And, interwoven with every topic, the dark, deep undercurrent in that rambling river of talk, was the people's hatred of the King's bosom friend, that all-accomplished gentleman in whom a " terrible courage " had been useless, for lack of the experience or the genius which makes a great soldier. His military career had been one dismal story of mistake and failure, one un-deviating record of bad luck ; and yet this unlucky commander was to direct the new enterprise, this fatal marsh fire was to be the guiding star of a new army, and was to lead more men to ignominious death. A sullen anger breathed in every man's speech when Buckingham's name was the subject ; and of whom else could they talk, now that he was housed in their midst, in almost royal pomp, his kindred, his satellites, depen-dents, and flatterers, around and about him, a little Court moving at his heels ? Who cared to mark the anxious brow ? Who cared to remember how recklessly the man who was careless of other lives had ever hazarded his own ; or to consider how often his in-experience had been abused by the ill-advice of veterans ; or to know that this splendid parasite, whose greed of gain was on every man's lip, had poured his gold and jewels into the empty treasury, and would have made himself a pauper could his last coin have bought oblivion of Eliot's scathing indictment : " Treasures exhausted, crown-lands sold, royal jewels pawned, tax-payers oppressed, provisions wasted, ships and men destroyed ; the country never so deep sunk in ruin, never so hopeless of recovery ! " ?

To win again the esteem and adulation of that bril-liant season when the man who had outraged Spain was the idol of the populace ! That desire must have been stronger even than his pity for the famishing Huguenots hemmed round by Richelieu's troops, cut off from succour by land and sea—a company of martyrs, dying for their religion and their liberties—a little Republic in the midst of an absolute monarchy, with creed, privilege, and independence, at stake.

How galling, how intolerable, to a man of Buckingham's ardent nature, must have been that revulsion of feeling which had made him the best-hated man in England, held answerable for every disaster and every disgrace that had overshadowed his sovereign's brief reign, the Sejanus of angry patriots, the man whose name only hinted at in the House of Commons could change the gravity of debate to storm and fury. Stung by the injustice of public opinion, who could wonder at this man's scorn of portents and omens, dreams and ghosts that prophesied death ; a falling picture, symbolical of his own fall ; his wife's tears ; his friends' entreaties that he would wear a coat of mail under his velvet and gold. Death ! The assassin's dagger—the mine under the room where he sat—the fate of Rizzio —or Darnley—of the Guises—of Henry the Great! Could death have any terrors for him whose brief life had comprised all that life knows of triumph and splendour, who had looked on his fellow-men from so giddy a pinnacle that he might well forget that he, too, was mortal ; and who now, still in the flower of manhood, knew himself the mark for a kingdom's detestation, knew himself more solitary in the depth of his fall than he had been in his isolation as the favourite whose only equal was his King? Charles loved him still. Charles was faithful to an affection that had begun in boyhood. But how long might the sovereign's fidelity hold out against bad luck and unrelenting foes? Ballad and pamphlet, lampoon and epigram, scurrility in every form that venal pens can devise, had been but the scum on the top of the cauldron. Under that foul surface there hissed the hell-broth of private malignity. Every Court parasite who had failed to better his fortunes since the page, George Villiers, stood behind King James' chair, had his stone to throw at the fallen idol. Beautiful as

Olympian gods are beautiful, gifted, generous, frank and sweet of speech, brave as a lion—all these ; and yet fatal to England and England's king.

He knew that for the man whom the people hate there is ever the peril of assassination : and lightly as he put aside omens and warnings, with a grave smile at the credulity of loving women, the shadow fell darkly over his last days in London ; and in parting with Laud he put in a plea for his wife and children. "I look to your lordship to keep the King in mind of those dear creatures, if I come not back," he said. "Some adventure may kill me as well as another man."

Only yesterday, the twenty-second of August, he had seen a fresh proof of his unpopularity in the fury of a mob of mutinous sailors, bent on the rescue of a comrade who had insulted him, and had been tried by court-martial and condemned to death. The Duchess had begged for the offender's life, and her prayer would have saved him, but for that bloody fight and attempted rescue, in which Buckingham had risked his person, accompanying the procession to the gibbet, in the vindication of outraged authority, and from which painful scene he had returned to his lodgings guarded by a circle of officers who apprehended the worst from the angry crowd. Those savage faces, those strident yells, had haunted his restless slumbers through the sultry night ; and now, at nine o'clock, he was breakfasting at the house in the High Street, in company with the Duc de Soubise and the deputies from Rochelle, messengers coming and going, in a fever of movement and talk, a letter from the King open on the table at his side.

While they were still at table came the news that Rochelle had been relieved ; news which, if true, would bring a sudden turn of Fortune's wheel, a speedy peace with France, and would set English ships and English soldiers free to fight for the King of Denmark and the Protestant cause. But the Frenchmen protested vehemently against any credence being given to rumours that must inevitably prove false ; and the meal ended in the midst of a loud and angry discussion.

Little George, following the human current at random, had come to this focus of the town's excitement, the heart of the High Street, to which all idlers gravitated. He stood watching the finely dressed gentlemen going in and out of the great house opposite; the mounted soldiers, the shining arms, the horses being led up and down the street by grooms whose livery was more sumptuous than George had imagined the attire of princes. Every moving thing in that busy street astonished and interested him. He forgot fear, hunger, fatigue, forgot to weep for his abandoned condition, and had scarcely any more care for the future than the sparrows have. He lived only, in this brief hour, to see and admire. Gold! jewels! His daddy had told him that there were such things in London. Kings and princes wore them. But imagination had never conceived such figures as these gentlemen in velvet coats and plumed hats, whose jewelled sword-belts flashed in the morning sun, whose spurs made music on the paving-stones. Every now and then the sound of drum and trumpet sent a thrill through the child's heart and nerves. How beautiful life seemed to those young eyes! how exquisite this splendour of sunlight and jewels to that newly awakening reason!

Suddenly, in the midst of this pleasurable bewilderment the child espied a familiar figure, the squat figure of the man with the dark face. The man crossed the street hurriedly, threading his way through loiterers and passers-by, and entered the house where all the traffic of the town tended. Little George followed, but could not cross the road as quickly as his dark friend, being hustled by a group of sailors, and nearly run over by a man on horseback riding sharply up to the door through which Felton had vanished. He lost a minute, or a minute and a half, perhaps, by those hindrances, time so brief as to be scarce noticeable on the dial of the town clock yonder, yet long enough for a tragedy that might change the fate of England and Rochelle.

A clamour of voices filled the house when the child came to the door—deep voices of men; and then, cleaving that muffled thunder, there rang the agonised cry of a woman, loud and shrill, repeated and repeated again, as the child peered in at the tumultuous crowd, a chorus of intolerable woe.

While he stood gazing, scared by those tragic sounds, a man forced his way through the crowd and caught him by the hand. It was his old friend with the swarthy face—lead-coloured now—and the face of one distraught, but not brutal or cruel, illumined rather by the inspired look that martyrs have, who give their lives for their religion.

"Run, boy," he cried, with his strong right hand grasping George's arm. "Away with you—to the other end of the town—or they will tear you to pieces—as they may do me. Go! go!"

He pushed the child down the broad stone steps, thrusting him away with vehement action, and then turned at the sound of voices from within. A cry had been raised in the crowd: "'Twas a Frenchman!"—meaning the murderer. Felton thought it was his name that was called, and pushed his way back into the hall.

"I am the man," he said. "I am here!"

CHAPTER III.

A FRIENDLY GENTLEMAN.

GEORGE stood among the crowd outside, scared and trembling, watching the house to which every eye was turned. He heard men talking of murder ; God's righteous judgment ; some pitying the murdered man ; some with a tear for the wife who loved him, the heart-broken woman whose wild shrieks had pealed out above all the tumult within. He heard much distracted talk, understanding nothing ; and watched till those of the crowd who had pushed their way into the house poured out again in a solid mass, his dark-faced friend, bare-headed, in the midst, all walking away at a quick pace, scattered groups of idlers following them. They were gone, and he found himself standing alone in an empty street. The change from all that tumult and horror, crowd and clamour, to a deathlike silence and blankness, was almost as sudden as if all that the child had heard and looked upon had been the transient shapes and sounds of a dream.

More terrified at this desolation than at the tumult that had gone before, the child stood staring at the great house, with its open door, within which something strange had happened, something which filled his half-awakened mind with an awe-stricken curiosity. Slowly, falteringly, he went up the steps, and crossed that fatal threshold, awed by the silence, yet emboldened by the solitude.

The hall was empty of all life and movement. On a long table in the midst lay a figure over which a velvet cloak had been thrown, like a pall; but flung so carelessly in the confusion following on the catastrophe, that the face of the dead had been left uncovered, and George saw for the first time in his brief life the countenance on which the King of Terrors has set his seal. Never to be forgotten was the aspect of those noble features, in all the awfulness of recent dissolution, the horror of sudden death still visible in the wide-open eyes and fallen jaw.

The boy stood like a figure of stone, afraid to move, almost afraid to breathe, in that dread presence. Heaven knows how the agonised wife and sister had been withdrawn from that tragic scene, conscious or insensible, consentient or reluctant; but they were gone. The Duke was lying alone and unattended, he whose state had been royal, whose servants had been reckoned by the score. Not on the desert sands of Arabia could death have seemed more lonely.

Upon *this* act of the tragedy the curtain had fallen. Friends, retainers, foes, the indifferent yet eager crowd, had all hurried to the Court-house to see the next act played out.

The child uttered a sudden sobbing cry, like one awaking from a nightmare dream, and turned and fled from the deserted hall, back to the empty street. He remembered what Felton had told him, and rushed along the street at his topmost speed, with the horror of death's aspect still before his eyes, the measured drip of blood on the polished floor still sounding in his ears. He tried to find his way back to the water-side from which he had come, with a faint, vague hope of finding the waggon there, and a friendly soldier. The sense of desolation—those old terrors of the lonely heath two days ago, had come back upon him, and his only thought was of finding the sergeant, his confidence being unbounded in any creature who had shown him kindness, were it ever so little.

He drifted away from the direction he aimed at, being afraid to question any one of the few people he met in his wanderings, and at last halted, weary and miserable, on a grassy platform where there was a row of guns that had turned their black muzzles seawards as they did now when Elizabeth was Queen and the Armada was a thing of yesterday. There was the sea, the strangely beautiful expanse of blue and white, the wavelets dancing under the fierce noonday sun. He could not take his eyes from the wonder of it, though he was afraid, and footsore, and hungry, his penny still in his pocket, his crust of bread eaten long ago, and all the unknown world and the long struggle called life staring him in the face.

He knew not, in his childish helplessness, of any possible shelter, save the chance of a waggon or a barn, like the waggon and barn of last night and the night before. All he could foresee in life was a repetition of the life he knew. His tears fell fast as he sat in the sun ; they fell upon his hands and his ragged sleeves ; and then, for the first time, he saw that one hand and one sleeve were dyed with a red stain which his tears moistened, and which he knew for blood. Child as he was, he shrank instinctively from those stains. They had been left there by the dark-faced man. The gory print of his hand showed red on the neutral grey of the sleeve. How came that blood upon the man's hand— the man whom he had seen quietly crossing the street two minutes before they met ? He remembered how, before he fell asleep in the barn, he had heard the man muttering to himself about a knife in his right-hand pocket ; how, being awake himself in the early dawn, he had seen his companion lying on his back fast asleep, with a convulsed countenance, groaning and murmuring in a faint, far-away voice, "Blood—the blood of Holofernes ! the blood of Sisera !"

Was it Sisera's blood that stained the sleeve on which the boy's tearful eyes looked with instinctive disgust ? That hateful stain intensified his unhappiness, his discomfort, his fear. Even the bright water in front of him, the busy harbour in the distance, all the freshness of an unknown world, took the colour of his weary body and frightened heart, and he flung himself face downward on the dusty grass, and sobbed aloud in such blind, hopeless grief as only little children feel when they think themselves abandoned by all human love and care.

A brisk step and the jingle of sword and spur sounded on the common behind him, as a well-built *débonnaire* figure came with buoyant pace over the hillocks ; but George was too lost in grief to hear the *débonnaire* gentleman's approach, and knew not that relief was coming to his loneliness, till a powerful hand clutched the top of his jacket and lifted him into the air, as easily as if he had been a well-bred puppy dog with a loose skin to his neck.

" What art howling for, thou baseborn whelp ? " asked a strong baritone voice, with a jovial note in it which must needs inspire confidence in child or dog. " Hast thou nothing better to do when the devil is dead than to lie in the dust and bewail thyself ? "

The stranger set the boy on his feet as he spoke, and stood looking down at him with a friendly grin. A pleasant-looking stranger, this one—very unlike that black man on the common by Godalming, who might at any moment have developed horns and hoofs and declared himself Old Nick in person.

In his friendlessness the boy had clung to the swart-faced traveller ; but there had still been a lurking distrust. His heart went out with a leap to this merry gentleman, who had light brown hair and beard, and laughing blue eyes under thick brown brows, and who wore his wine-stained velvet and tarnished gold lace as if they had been the purple and ermine of kings.

" Is the devil dead ? " George asked, awe-stricken ; " and is this the devil's blood ? "

The stranger laughed aloud at the question, thinking that the boy's nose had been bleeding perhaps, and the little wretch was precocious enough to venture a jest.

" Nay, thou atomy, thou wert not standing by to see the greatest man in the kingdom die by a stab from a tenpenny knife—he who wanted to play the Roman, to expire in a blaze of glory, in all the pomp of a dear-bought victory, or to mount skyward amidst the ruins of Rochelle, to soar to the gods he has mimicked with his monkey sovereignty, and to be remembered for ever as Villiers the glorious, who, when he could not save the city and the souls that famished there, put torch to touch-hole and went up to heaven with a republic of martyrs. Did he not swear that he would conquer or die upon the mole before Rochelle? Vain braggart! The tenpenny knife was a-grinding for him while he boasted. Omens have not lied; ghosts have not walked for nothing; dreamers have dreamed true; and George Villiers is as dead as his sycophant and parasite Dr. Lambe the astrologer."

Evidently a man who loved the sound of his own ripe, round voice, and facile turn of a sentence; since there was small chance that the little boy, whose tearful eyes gazed at him in blank wonder, could follow the sense of this rhapsody; a man who had spent many a summer afternoon in the playhouses, a man who had drunk and spouted at many taverns, and knew where the best ales were sold and where the best company might be met.

He flung himself down upon the coarse turf, and seated George beside him, and dried the child's tears with the cuff of his tawdry coat, and made him happy and at his ease in the space of a few minutes. Indeed, it were hard for a helpless brat, who ten minutes ago had fancied himself abandoned of all mankind, not to feel cheered by the kindness of a man whose face and voice brimmed over with good-humour, and who was usually in the condition of one who sees the world through a rosy glow of strong wine—not drunk, but warmed to the core by good liquor.

To this new friend George freely told his simple story: the farm—Daddy and Mammy—and the strange gentleman in a black suit who had appeared on rare occasions, and who had caused those purple marks to be made upon his breast. He told of his adventures on the road: the lonely night on the common, when he had been frighted by a great black beast with fiery breath, which he took for the devil, till it started up out of a bush and changed into a horse; the black man who had been kind to him; the night in the barn, and those mutterings of murder.

"I'll wager thy travelling comrade was the black-a-visaged soldier who killed the Duke. Thou wert lucky he did not stab thee to get his hand in. Well, they have thy friend safe under lock and key—so now what wilt thou do?"

"The soldier bade me seek a gentleman who would let me scrape his trenchers; but I know not where to find such."

"Thou art a pretty guileless creature, with a voice like a silver bell. I have a mind to adopt thee as my page and armourer, till I can find thee a richer master!"

"Oh, sir, I would like to stay with you. I am not afeared of you, as I was of the black gentleman. Yet he was kind. Will they kill him because he killed the Duke?"

"Faith, if John Eliot and some others at Westminster could have their way they would reward him with a handsome pension for having lightened England of the heaviest incubus she ever carried. But law is law, and I'm afraid his guerdon will be a hempen necklace. So you would like to be my little page, and tramp the highway with me when I have no money to pay for a ride; and lie in a corner of my garret, and wake me when I see ugly shapes in my dreams; and fetch me my liquor from the nearest tavern, and brush my coat; till I can get you into some fine lady's household. I have rich and powerful friends, child, though you might not think it!"

"I would rather live with you always, sir. I like you better than anybody, except Daddy."

The friendly gentleman sat on the grass, looking dreamily seaward, with the child nestling against him. The boy's simplicity, his pretty face, and sweet little piping voice, had appealed somehow to this jovial citizen of the world, and he could not find it in his heart

to leave the desolate imp to wander and starve on
Southsea Common. To a man who lived from hand to
mouth the taking of a penniless brat on his shoulders
mattered little. Responsibility there could be none
where there were no means. And this man had lived at
odds with Fortune for the last seven years, and defied
Fate to use him worse than she had done, unless he put
himself in her power by some foul crime of his own,
which he had no mind to do, having indeed no criminal
instincts. He drank hard, and loved all games of
chance and skill, but he had never stooped to the
sharper's tricks with marked cards or cogged dice, or
filled his purse by sharking a boon companion.

A rich man might have hardened his heart against
the child's pitiable case, lest he should take upon himself
an encumbrance that it would be difficult to shake off,
and incur lifelong liability; but what would it matter
to this man that another depended on him? He could
but give the child a share in the ups and downs of a life
of adventure, to feast to-day at somebody else's expense,
and to starve to-morrow if cast upon his own resources.
He was young himself, and pitied all young creatures—
colt, puppy, kitten, or callow bird. He had a heart that
the world had not hardened, roughly as it had used the
owner.

So when he had sat in the sun for half an hour,
watching the great war-ships at anchor in the offing—
where flags drooped mournfully half-mast high in the
summer calm—and listening to the child's prattle, he
took little George by the hand, and set out for the town
to buy a dinner with one of the few silver coins in his
pocket. George asked no questions about the future,
happy with a new and complete sense of being cared for
and protected. Here truly was a friend who replaced
his lost Daddy, the kindly peasant farmer whose loss he
had mourned with many tears, but of whom, having
been kept remote from the aspect of death, he had
thought as of one gone on a long journey, whose honest
countenance might beam upon him suddenly at any
turn of life's highway.

And so these two adventurers began their wanderings together. Francis Mountain—the surname was not his own, but it served—in his twenty-fifth year, George Nameless, age unknown, but from his stature he might be reckoned between six and eight, while speech and intelligence were in advance of his size. So they started on a life-journey, the child charmed with his protector, the man pleased to exercise so pleasant a patronage—so cheaply to buy love and confidence, and the trustful upward look of innocent eyes, and the warm touch of a little clinging hand. Here was something to exorcise those blue devils, those curious impertinent imps and insects from the invisible world, which made themselves so diabolically real to this man after one of his glorious nights at the Dagger or the Windmill. He was not so steeped and seasoned in liquor as the men he drank with, being in most cases considerably their junior ; and it might be that he had a more vivid imagination, and nerves strung to a sharper pitch.

Francis Mountain and his child-comrade were in London three days after that eventful twenty-third of August. They found the city jubilant with a cruel exultation at the tragical doom of one who had never been cruel even to an enemy. The brilliant intelligence, the warm impulsive heart, were cut short in the very prime of their powers, by a fanatic's knife ; and that London which, after the breaking of the Spanish match, and the Duke's bold defiance of Spain, had run with wine and blazed with bonfires in honour of George Villiers, was now loud in its vilification of the untimely dead.

From the pinnacle of public favour Villiers had sunk to the lowest depth of public contempt. The Gazette that told his death was but a bare record of fact. There were no party journals to defame or to defend ; there was no sifting of evidence for and against ; there were no friendly casuists to excuse failure, to make a bad cause good. The influence that governed opinion was subtle as the poison in the veins of the snake-bitten. It ran through the whole system of the State, swift as some powerful drug in a sick man's body. The word had gone forth that Buckingham was the kingdom's bane; and thousands, who had never looked upon his face, never sunned themselves in his smile, or heard the music of his voice, had made up their minds that the Duke of Buckingham was a monster—a modern copy of that base Roman Minister to whom Eliot had likened him in the licence of a fiery debate, the boon companion and counsellor of the tyrant Tiberius, whose mutilated carcase was dragged Tiber-wards through the city gutters in a tempest of execration.

To liken Villiers to Sejanus was by implication to liken Charles to Tiberius, as the King himself averred; but the patriot, in his passion, had not halted at discourtesy to his Sovereign.

The Favourite's hated figure bulked large, and overshadowed the King, who had no will save that of his bosom friend. Had he not, for love of this man, put such an affront upon the representatives of the people as no former sovereign had ever ventured? Had he not been obstinately blind and deaf to iniquitous proceedings which should have made Villiers and that vile murderess, Lady Buckingham, loathsome in his sight?—for who could doubt that the late King had been done to death by the Favourite's mother, in the interest of her son. The bookstalls and taverns were strewed with pamphlets that charged the Countess of Buckingham with that foul crime. Every doctor in London knew the story of the poisoned plaster which had changed a chronic sickness into a fatal disorder, and carried off King James just as his eyes were opening to the worthlessness of his long-cherished favourite. Disenchantment had meant death. The mother, for her son's sake, or mother and son in agreement together, had made a sudden end of the wavering monarch, had allowed no time for change in the King's feelings to bring about change in the Duke's fortunes. Not one of those tavern orators doubted that James had been murdered, or took the trouble to consider upon what scanty evidence that atrocious charge was made.

For the mad monk Jacques Clement, who slew Henry III. of France, there had been swift justice, hacked to death, almost in the presence of his victim, by furious courtiers; for Ravaillac, murderer of Henry the Great and Good, no torture had been deemed too terrible, no infamy too lasting or too deep, his very name becoming a word of reproach; but "honest Jack" met with a curious indulgence, and found himself the idol of the mob before the blood upon his garments was dry.

John Felton's journey to London was a triumph. A cry of exultation rang loud in the towns through which he and his gaolers passed. Old women praised him, little children were held up to see him go by; one old dame, moved by a scriptural zeal, called out, "God bless thee, little David!" as the dark, squat figure, with bent and gloomy brow, came in sight. The public enthusiasm knew no restraint of policy or fear. Men were fined and imprisoned for drinking the assassin's health. John Milton's schoolmaster, Gill, junior, narrowly escaped the loss of his ears, which had been sentenced to pay for the licence of his tongue, and were only spared by the intervention of a friendly Bishop.

Alas for the patriot whose knife had gratified the people's rage! He shared not in the public exultation, thrilled with no pride at old women's blessings, or the piping praise of innocent children. The murder done, his eyes had been opened to the cruelty of that deed. Perhaps in those brief moments when Buckingham turned upon the assassin, and the eyes of murdered and murderer met, the imperial beauty of that perfect face, the splendour of that dauntless mien, struck the half-crazed fanatic with a remorseful awe, and he felt as if he had slain a god. Or it might be that the wild shriek of the new-made widow never ceased to ring in his ears till death dulled them. Certain is it that all his after conduct evidenced the profoundest sorrow for the thing he had done. He met his ignominious doom as one who felt that no sentence could be too severe, no detail in the hangman's office too humiliating. What remorse, what consciousness of crime could be deeper than his,

who had pasted in his hat so bold an assertion of the
patriot's right to slay his country's foe, and who now
sued for pardon to his victim's scullion-boy, and stretched
out his guilty arm in the open court, offering it to the
executioner's knife ?

CHAPTER IV

FROM CHILDHOOD TO MANHOOD.

IT was a strange fancy on the part of a strong man perhaps, but Frank Mountain's notion that the child-companion would save him from the spectral shapes that haunt a drunkard's pillow exercised a stronger influence upon his conduct than he himself was aware. Had he not even contemplated wedlock with some light companion of his orgies, as an escape from the unspeakable horrors of those long burning nights when millions of devils danced and rioted in his delirious brain? And behold, instead of an impudent hussy who might soon become a worse horror to him than even the frogs and flies of Egypt and the fiends of hell, here was a little innocent imp who would sit beside his pillow and prattle to him, and bathe his temples with vinegar and water, and keep all the populace of dis-tempered fancy at a distance.

As time went on, and these two soldiers of fortune marched together, now in France, and now beyond the Alps, anon in Germany, or in the sober, humdrum Netherlands, finding rough and smooth, kindness and unkindness, bad and good weather, and bad and good luck, the cure that Mountain had anticipated worked on somewhat different lines from those he had laid down. He had fancied that he was to drink as deep as of old, and that little George was to lighten the drink-delirium by his loving company ; but as his liking for the child ripened into a warm affection, almost like that of a father for his first-born, Francis found himself spending less, and leaving the Tavern earlier, till by-and-bye, upon meeting those jovial roysterers with whom he had so often sprinkled the night with wine, he felt half ashamed of his sobriety.

The boy loved his master as children love indulgent fathers, and loved to serve him.　Never had grand seigneur page more devoted ; never were threadbare garments more sedulously brushed and cleaned, nor was the gilt handle of a cheap rapier ever made to look more like gold.　Francis taught him to read and write, and he picked up the useful current coin of foreign tongues, the three or four hundred words which suffice for a traveller's daily needs, as they fared from country to country, the child being quick and eager, as all healthy young creatures are, questioning his companion about everything he saw or heard, until he was able to read for his own enlightenment.

When once possessed of this incomparable art, he fancied he had the key to universal knowledge, and was more greedy for books than for food or rest after a long day's tramp on a dusty road.

Alas that books should be so dear !　George read his little library over and over again.　It consisted but of a handful of well-known books which Mountain had bought for him from the colporteurs by whose side they often walked for miles at a stretch.　Sir Thomas Malory's " History of King Arthur " ; the " Praise of Folly," by Erasmus, in the original easy Latin, which his master taught George to construe as they sat under a hedge in the noontide, resting after a meal ; Luther's " Table Talk," in the same learned language ; and, most precious of all, Spenser's " Faëry Queen," and the immortal story of Don Quixote.

Later there came Romantic literature, in French and Italian.　The lad had ever a well-thumbed volume in his pocket, and had begun to long for the life he read of ; for the first germs of youthful ambition are mostly found between the leaves of a romance ; and more boys have been made soldiers by the story of " Palmerin of England," or " The Seven Champions of

Christendom," than by the sight of a troop of cavalry, or the blare of trumpets and beat of drums.

For the boy bred in a humble farmhouse, abandoned in the helplessness of childhood, this wandering life, with its varieties of fortune, seemed entirely happy ; but it needed all Francis Mountain's philosophy to enable him to dine contentedly on dry bread, and sleep on a truss of hay, since the first eighteen years of his life had been spent in an almost regal luxury.

It was not until many years after their meeting on Southsea Common that George was admitted to the secret of his protector's name and story ; for albeit this kindly, light-hearted young man had but venial sins of his own to blush for, he was sensitively alive to the stain upon his name, and to the humiliating experiences of his eighteenth year.

He was the son and heir of that richly favoured monopolist, Sir Giles Mompesson, who enjoyed the monoply of inn-licences, and of the trade in gold and silver lace—two privileges which could hardly have been held by the most honourable of men without the hazard of unconscious favouritism and unwilling injustice, but which Mompesson had used as a means to the vilest traffic, selling his licences to inns that were nests of robbers and dens of depravity, and permitting wholesale adulteration in those costly manufactures which his own respectability was supposed to guarantee.

Looking back upon his luxurious childhood and boyhood, Francis Mountain recalled a noble mansion on the banks of the Thames ; a chaplain-tutor who pandered to his boyish pleasures, and encouraged him to despise the learning whose elements the tutor was paid to teach ; idleness and extravagance at Oxford, where he might have been Master of Arts at seventeen years of age, had he afforded official servility only a reasonable excuse for giving him his degree, but from which University his follies had banished him under a cloud of disgrace, the thinnest and silveriest of clouds as compared with the Egyptian darkness which wrapped the exit of his boon companions, lads of meaner birth and lighter purses.

Escaped from the easy jurisdiction of the University while still in the flush of boyhood, and with all boyhood's bent towards folly, he found himself the pet and plaything of a profligate Court, in palaces where life was a continual masquerade, sitting at banquets that began in solemn magnificence, with a dignity and beauty that Veronese would have loved to paint, and which ended in the wallowing of human swine in a trough ; revels that recalled Circe's swinish courtiers, or the companions of Comus, the gluttony and riot of men transformed into beasts. The handsome boy, clad in white velvet and gold, in rose damask and silver, inferior only to the Villiers brood in the sumptuousness of his apparel, passed not unscathed through that burning ordeal in which mind and senses were alike tried and tempted. The memory of that time was no spotless page which the graver eyes of manhood might contemplate with satisfaction. There were women whose favour then had seemed a crown of glory, whose lightest caress Francis Mountain now recalled with an abhorrent shudder. He had lived and loved while the down upon his lip was soft as the velvet on a peach ; the praised of wrinkled she-libertines, the favoured of high-born wantons ; only escaping utter pollution by a rugged strength of character, and preference for decency, which made him scorn the smiles of painted faces, the flattery of lascivious tongues.

A sudden exposure of nefarious dealings, an outcry that rang through the country, a trial famous among State trials—and Mompesson, the lord of inns and ale-houses, the man of gold and silver, whose money-bags had bought the favour of the Court and the subservience of the City, was a fugitive beyond sea ; and the Palace, rising stately above Bermondsey's fairest gardens, had melted away like one of the fairy temples in those magnificent masques of which Francis had seen so mauy.

A hasty letter scrawled by Sir Giles in the hour of his flight bade the young man make his way to Rotterdam, where he, Sir Giles, would look for him at the Golden Lion Inn on the Quay ; or, if he had too proud a stomach

to join fortunes with a disgraced father, he might stop
to beg his bread in the streets of London.

Francis did neither, but offered himself, and was
accepted, for Sir Horace Vere's expedition to the Palatinate, with a company of Volunteers, the only aid which
King James allowed Protestant England to send to
the Protestant Union. The lad volunteered for foreign
service, almost hoping that some flying bullet would
find its billet in his heart or brain. The revelations at
the trial of the two monopolists, Mompesson and Michel,
had sickened him. He loathed the memory of those
idle wanton years, of the gold he had squandered. He
hated himself for the boyish arrogance which had pro-
cured him a score of enemies, and had lost him the
worthiest among his friends. The youth, who was per-
sonally known to Vere, was permitted to enlist under
a feigned name ; and it was as Francis Mountain that
Sir Giles Mompesson's only son began his new and
harder life.

The little company arrived on the scene of war too
late to succour the Elector Palatine. Spinola and his
Spanish battalions were moving up the Rhine ; and the
Thirty Years' War had begun.

When he shook the dust of London off his boots,
Francis shook off the husk of his former self, and faced
life with a bold front. He had thews and sinews, a
sure aim with gun or pistol, a skill in fence surpassed
by few swordsmen of his years. He could speak
French and Italian, and could ride the great horse. He
had a handsome face, bold and candid, and strongly
featured as Henry of Navarre's aquiline visage. He
had a full baritone voice and a jovial laugh, and a
happy-go-lucky disposition that revelled in the sunshine, and took foul fortunes and foul weather lightly.
He joined the Palatine Prince's troops, and was a
favourite with the men, and a welcome guest under the
tents of their officers. He had the unmistakable air and
accent of a man who had lived in courts and eaten off
gold and silver. He had the gift of mimicry ; and

his imitations of the two bishops, Williams and Laud, of Bacon and Cecil; of the Scottish parvenu, Somerset; of King James mouthing his drink, with the red wine slobbering over his thick lips and spattering his ruff; and even of the late Queen Anne, royally gracious, but somewhat overcome with wine, were so true to the life as to vouch for his having lived with the personages he caricatured. He had, in brief, the gifts that make a young man particularly acceptable in worthless company. He was at his best after supper, when the wine had flowed freely; or, if his friends were not men of long purses, he could be merry upon a tankard of ale. He was a general favourite, but most appreciated by acquaintances whose favour could be of very little use to him; and so, serving under one banner or another, Huguenot or Papist, he had drifted to the town of Portsmouth, out at elbows, and with but a handful of silver between him and starvation, meaning to volunteer for the Rochelle expedition, when Buckingham's tragical death, and the encounter with a nameless waif on Southsea Common, brought a new and reforming influence to bear upon this featherhead's career.

The nameless waif influenced Francis Mountain's fortunes in more ways than one. He grew less fond of soldiering, and was less careless about random bullets, now that this little life depended upon his. He fell into a roving, gipsy-like existence, and began to turn his talents to account as a civilian; and, falling in from time to time with old friends in positions of authority and power, he by-and-bye got himself employed upon irregular diplomatic missions, in that secret service between high-born intriguers in England and France, which offered a living in the present, and the chance of promotion in the future.

Wherever Mountain went, or on howsoever grave or secret a business, his boy went with him; albeit at the beginning of his diplomatic career the fact of so shabby an adventurer being attended by his page had not escaped ridicule. With the coming of more prosperous days, and the growth of the child to a tall stripling, his attendance seemed a natural appendage to the unofficial messenger between Court and Court, and Embassy and Embassy. Once when they were in Paris on a secret mission that old intriguer, Bassompierre, was taken with the lad's handsome looks, and wanted to steal him.

"The boy has a countenance that haunts me like a half-remembered dream," he said; "he recalls a face I have known. 'Tis not Mazarin—though he has the Italian's features without his crafty expression—'tis some other face I have known long ago. He is too pretty a page for your rough work. In my service he would have little to do but sprawl on a velvet cushion, and play with my Italian greyhounds. His hardest work would be to carry a *billet-doux* to a lady who would cram him with sweetmeats and line his pockets with gold, for love of the writer."

"I would as soon cut off my sword-arm, Monsieur le Maréchal, as part with my comrade. We have lived together in sunshine and cloud; and the black welkin has no thunder that could sever us."

George was mostly silent in fine company, but he lifted his face from the book over which it was ever bent in his leisure hours, and smiled at his protector; and in the smile there was a promise of life-long fidelity.

Bassompierre was in the Bastille a few days afterwards, so his patronage would not have led to high fortune.

The boy's service had lasted a dozen years, and the sunny-haired child picked up on Southsea Common now stood shoulder to shoulder with his patron, and, judged by the manly lines of his figure, might have been taken for five-and-twenty as easily as for eighteen. But the delicate red and white of his complexion, the lucid azure of his eyes, the slenderness of his limbs, and the supple grace of his movements, marked the adolescent in the first freshness of life's morning; and, with all the desire to ruffle and hold his own among strong men, George was still only a handsome boy.

Mountain and his page were in London in the late

summer of the year 1640,—that fatal year in which the air was full of the low mutterings of a muffled thunder, forerunner of the storm that wrecked Strafford, and left an indelible stain upon his master's name.

The three weeks' Parliament of the spring was almost forgotten in the dead calm of an uneventful summer; but the forewarning thunder of which that thoughtful and pious lady, Colonel Hutchinson's wife, took notice, was felt by all who knew the mind of the English people. Oppressive restrictions, forbidding the natural expansion of London, enforced by heavy fines, had exasperated the city, and had changed that stronghold of loyalty into the focus of discontent. It was but a few years since a little band of Nonconformists, all of humble origin and fortunes, had sailed away from the world they loved, to make themselves a home and a Church in the wilderness; and now there were men of mark, among the noblest of the land, who turned their faces to the unknown West, to the new places with the old familiar names, sick of Archbishop Laud's trivial tyranny, and of the fines, imprisonments, banishments, whippings, gags, pillories, and mutilations, by which the Star Chamber dealt with cases of conscience; sick, too, of the petty oppressions of monopolists, licensed to supply the vilest goods at the highest prices; disgusted at all those wrongs, which in the coming year were to be massed in one stupendous indictment of the Commons against their King.

The "taste of happiness" which Charles Stuart had given his people during eleven years of personal rule had left an exceedingly bitter flavour in the people's mouth; and Francis Mountain and his page heard almost as much complaining against an arbitrary government in the White Lion tavern at Westminster as they had heard at the Pine Apple in the narrow street near the Louvre, where deep damnation was drunk to Richelieu and his lieutenant, Joseph the Priest, in the rough red wine of the Gironde, which left stains upon the tables like blood.

Talk ran riot in London taverns, while silence reigned

in the Parliament House yonder, and while patriots
were moving about the country, with John Pym for
their leader, rousing the spirit of the electors, in preparation for that new Parliament, which the King was
so loth to summon. The late Parliament had owed its
existence to the sovereign's necessities, and on the
Lower House refusing an immediate grant of twelve
subsidies, had been dissolved in a huff, by His Majesty's
angry order. "Better so," said the forward-looking
spirits, "for this Parliament was of too yielding a temper.
We want iron men, and iron measures, if England is to
remain a country that free men can dwell in."

Neither Francis Mountain nor his companion was
concerned at the violence of party-feeling or the muffled
thunder in the air. They had lived under too many
governments to be keenly interested in any. King or
Kaiser, Stadtholder or Doge, mattered but little to these
cosmopolitans, so long as they had food and lodging,
clothes to keep them warm, and boots that kept out the
water. Mountain had prospered of late, and he and his
protégé wore doublet and cloak of the newest mode, and
were able to afford respectable lodgings in a small
retired house in Milbank Lane, hard by the great water-
way, which in this brilliant summer season George
thought almost as beautiful as the Grand Canal at
Venice.

"I have wandered over half the Continent of Europe
out at elbows and in broken boots," Mountain told the
boy, "but you may note that I waited for a full purse
and a sound suit of clothes before I showed myself in
this pettifogging island, save as a bird of passage. I
have a sturdy British pride that forbids me to live as a
pauper in the city where I was reared like a prince."

"Was your father some great nobleman, like the
Prince de Condé or the Duc de Bouillon?" George
asked simply.

"My father was a prince of the blood royal of Plutus,
George. He was rich enough to buy the favour of
princes, and the smiles of women who played as deep
as the men, and drank as deep, some of them, and had

such stringent need of money that they would sell their souls to Satan for a loan of a thousand or so at a crisis. My father was a rogue, but he was a magnificent rogue, and scattered his ill-gotten wealth with a hand as lavish as Francis Bacon's, who let his servants rob him before his face—and had a head too high in the clouds to take note of how his own fortune came."

"It's a pity one so rich in wit and wisdom should be so careless of honour."

"Tush, lad. Bacon was of his age. 'Twas a glorious age for men of spirit and brains; for the pettifogging distinctions and wire-drawn border-lines between honesty and dishonesty, which make sneaks of us, had not come into fashion. King James squeezed his subjects dry to fatten his favourites, and was a well-spring of gold to the men he loved; but I doubt if man or woman at Whitehall—save only painters and architects—has been a hundred pounds the better for any of those exactions that have cost King Charles the love of his people. You heard last night that for every thousand that finds its way to the Royal Treasury other two thousand are swallowed by collectors and purveyors, præfectors and clerks of the market."

"'Tis a dishonest world, sir, in which such things can be."

"'Tis a curious world, and changes its shapes and colours almost as fast as the clouds change in the sunset sky; but 'tis a pleasant world for a man like me, whose pulses beat strong, and whose sinews are iron; and for a lad like you, who have all the chances of life before you. God's truth! but I believe your star is a lucky one, George; for I know my own life has travelled in smoother grooves since I found you on Southsea Common, snivelling in the sunshine."

"Is it lucky to have neither father nor mother, nor even to know my father's name?" George asked bitterly.

"Better such ignorance than to bear a name that you would be ashamed to speak. You have never heard my father's name, George; and perhaps you never will, from my lips."

London was changed since Sir Giles Mompesson's son had known it in the flower of his youth. Great lights that were shining then had gone out. Ben Jonson was dead, full of years and wine and gout, but cherished and admired to the last, a power and a delight to those who loved him, an eloquent voice sounding in the deep of night in the great room at the Devil Tavern, by Temple Bar, the Apollo room, where the old Elizabethan held a kind of club, and where his loving disciples were sealed "sons of Ben."

Jonson was dead; the bricklayer's son, who had upheld the dignity of letters, in his drunken, impecunious way; Jonson, whose friends had been kings, and chancellors, and bishops, and privy counsellors, and who had boasted that he "never esteemed of a man for the name of a lord."

Mountain loved to talk of old Ben, and those nights at the Devil Tavern; those feasts of reason and of wit at which he had assisted in his ignorant youth, fresh from a neglected curriculum at Oxford, knowing more about bear-baiting, and hawks and hounds, than of those classic authors which Jonson quoted upon every subject, with an air of supposing that other people loved and remembered them as well as he did.

Master and page were sitting at ease in a roomy skiff, while a couple of watermen bent their stout backs to the oar, the boat going with a strong tide up stream and carrying them towards their destination at Isleworth, where Mountain had to deliver a packet of letters to Lord Llanbister, a nobleman who had figured with distinction at the Court of Elizabeth, and had taken a leading part in international politics under James. He had retired from public life, but he had still strong alliances on the other side of the Channel, notably with one brilliant, adventurous lady, who lived only to conspire, and conspired only to fail.

"Of all my father's fair-weather friends, Llanbister is the one man who has held out the hand of kindness to me since my misfortunes. Many a meal you have shared with me has been at his expense, George. But

do not suppose that I would ride a free horse to death—
I only appealed to him when our case was desperate.
He was in Florence that time you were dying of fever.
I ran against him on the Ponte Vecchio, coming from
the Pitti Palace, where he had been dining with princes ;
and it was as if I had met an angel. His purse was
open to me on the instant. Manna and quails in the
desert could scarce have been liker to a miracle. He
is a good man ; and his wife, who for her years might
be his daughter, is a good woman, though she has spent
a decade at Queen Henrietta's court, where virtue is
not the chief quality admired in women—as witness
that splendid sinner, Buckingham's niece, who had the
courage to save her seducer at the cost of her own
reputation, and the generosity to decline a husband
commanded to the altar by his king."

"There are some wrongs that cannot be righted,"
said George, who took life more seriously than his
senior. "What happiness could that poor lady have
hoped for with such a man as Jermyn, married to her
against his will ?"

"Faith, I believe he would have secured her a place
in heaven by making her a martyr upon earth. Jermyn
aims high. He has a queen for his bosom friend ; and
if—well—if our royal master were to die of the plague,
I think I know where his widow would look for
consolation."

"Another of your tavern scandals, sir. I wonder you
can lend an ear to them."

"Nay, do not think I believe *all* I hear of the Queen,
or of her sister-in-law at the Louvre, or of her mother
at Brussels, or of any woman in this world, high or low.
Men had need be kind to women by their acts, for they
are devils to them with their tongues, and will puff
away a matron's character to spice a tankard of mulled
wine, or calumniate a virtuous widow for the chance
of cutting a verbal caper."

George had seen many rivers in the course of his
peripatetic boyhood ; and to eyes that had looked upon

Danube and Rhine, Rhone and Seine, this gentle stream, flowing between the daisied meads of Fulham and Barnes, past village churches and cottage roofs, each little settlement curiously repeating the last, in the same picturesque grouping of flowery gable-ends, clustered chimneys, square church-tower, and glistening vane—must needs seem a world in miniature, small and fine and prim and precise as landscape and buildings in the background of a triptych by Memling or Van Eyck. Yet, perhaps by some predisposition in English blood, this rural scenery and placid river pleased the lad's fancy better than many a grander scene had done. So small, so placid, so full of variety and colour, was this gentle Thames, as it flashed and sparkled in the July sunshine, so brightly glowed the deep-toned red of Tudor barns and homesteads, through their rich veil of greenery,—that as he watched that moving picture he could but think he had come to a happier country than he had ever seen in his wanderings.

There were stately mansions along the river banks, as well as farmhouses and thatched cottages, mansions which lacked the massive towers, aerial turrets, conical roofs, long ranges of lofty windows, flying balconies, and florid decoration, which were familiar to him in the *châteaux* that rise far apart along the monotonous plains between Avignon and Paris, where George and his master had journeyed so often on foot or on horseback, through the summer dust and winter snow—hardy travellers, a kind of civilised gipsies, content to fare as gipsies fare, and to sleep under Jove's starry canopy when needs must.

Beautiful as the scene was—shining river, bending willows that dipped in the stream, meadows enamelled with orchis and daisy—a shadow of melancholy lay over all things to-day, like a dim grey veil spread between the eyes of the adolescent and the scene they looked upon. A new sense had awakened in this homeless youth since he had trodden his native soil, a sense of loneliness, desolation, shame even. It was not that he loved his kind master less, or was ungrateful for the love that had sheltered him, sharing all the best that Fortune could give as freely as the hard fare of earlier days. It was perhaps the natural growth of an intellect in advance of its years, the natural awakening of ambitious longings in a lofty soul, the natural yearning for a deeper and holier love than this rough-and-ready soldier of fortune could give him. Even in that loose-lived company which Francis Mountain liked best there were men who were not ashamed to reveal their love for mothers and sisters, their regretful memory of a vanished home, or their pleasant anticipations of a day when they would go back with mended fortunes to the fireside, where there was always a place kept for them. George had heard godless reprobates talk of parents and kindred across wine cups and flagon ; boast of a sister's modest loveliness ; brag of a father's honesty ; or speak with a tearful eye and a faltering voice of the long-dead mother whose face had been the light of the home.

No such memories lay in George's heart ; no mother's face haunted his dreams. As he grew in knowledge of life he made up his mind that the weather-beaten face he recalled was not the face of his mother ; that the rough cottage he remembered was not the home of his father. Through the mists of bygone years he could picture scenes and recall speeches that to his later judgment were proof positive of some secret behind the commonplace of the peasant's hearth and the peasant's fare. The memory of a thoughtful child will retain words which carried but little significance when they were spoken.

To-day, in the sunlit idleness of that water-journey, George looked back upon the picture of a March evening in his first home ; the hearth-glow reflected on the great oaken beam that spanned the ceiling, himself squatting among the wood-ashes in the chimney-corner, which was more than half as big as the room ; those whom he called Daddy and Mammy sitting side by side upon the settle opposite him ; and, standing straight and tall in front of the sloping chimney, a man clad in black from throat to foot, and wearing neither sword nor spurs—a pale, stern-featured gentleman, whose light grey eyes had a searching look that frightened him.

"Yes, he is to lead the life you lead, eat and drink like you, sleep on as hard a bed, wear grogram or Norwich drugget. God knows 'tis the happiest life for him who has known no other, and brings with it less of trouble and vexation. Treat him like your own; love him like your own—if you can."

"Us do that a'ready. It have a-come easy," grunted Daddy from his seat in the chimney-corner. "Us don't want to be paid for *that*."

"So much the better for all of you. You will be paid for his bite and sup; fairly, but not generously—I am too poor a man to be lavish—till he is old enough to earn his own bread. When that day comes, if he be grown strong and stalwart, honest, God-fearing, and a member of the Church of England—I will have him no Puritan, mind you, stuffed with the rank blasphemies of a Calvinistic lecturer;—if by his eighteenth birthday you can show him to me an honest English peasant, true to Church and King, I will give you that which will help to make your old age easy."

The slow, deliberate speech had sunk deep in the childish memory—for those were the last words he ever heard from the tall gentleman in black. In the summer that followed Daddy was laid in the rural grave-yard in the shadow of the church, where George had so often slept on Daddy's knee through a drowsy afternoon sermon. Daddy was dead; and Mammy—who perhaps had never known the black gentleman, save as a stately visitor, nameless and secret—was without a home; and he, George, was a wanderer on the face of the earth.

The vision of the sailor who made that Viper-sign upon his breast lay further back in the dim long-ago, and the pictured scene was less definite. Again he recalled the changeful light and shadow; the light so ruddy and warm; the shadow so black and deep, and full of frightening things; again the tall, dark figure and stern countenance of the stranger, in such marked contrast to the rubicund face of the sailor, grinning and shining in the glare of the logs, with the twinkle of laughing eyes and the flash of broad white teeth ; again the slow, distinct speech which he seemed to hear across the distance of years, and which gave him the same cold thrill to-day that it had given him then, when he stood between the sailor's broad knees, his head leaning back against the sailor's breast as he looked up at the stranger. He remembered the fire-glow flickering upon black velvet doublet and trunks, and high black boots, and he saw again the thoughtful eyes looking down at the sailor's bare arm, stretched out to catch the fitful light on those strange, purple signs upon the sunburnt flesh.

Then had come a tedious operation upon his own tender skin, watched by the stranger who had ordered it to be done.

Was it for sheer caprice or even cruelty that he had been subjected to this process ? Or was it because the man in black desired to brand him as cattle are branded, with a mark that he would carry all his life ? Yet what need so to distinguish one who was to be a peasant, something only a little higher than the beasts of the field, earning his bread in the sweat of his brow ? What need so to mark one of that common herd—since the days of serfdom were past in England, and he could be no man's chattel, wear no master's iron collar ? Brooding thus in the light of his experience of life he was disposed to think that the stranger had been governed only by a capricious cruelty, wanting perhaps to test the courage and endurance of a wretched little mortal whose destiny was in his power, and to whom he had allotted the labourer's dull round of drudgery.

CHAPTER V.

FAIR FACES AND NOBLE HEARTS.

FROM that long reverie of slow, sad thoughts, in tune with the lullaby of the river, George looked up at his friend and protector with a sudden affectionate glance. To him he owed the happy-go-lucky years which had made his boyhood one long romance ; not without its dark pages, its nights of fear, and days of hunger : but so full of movement, that to look back upon it was like turning the leaves of one of those chivalrous novels he loved so well. To him he owed the knowledge of foreign lands and foreign tongues, and that far-reaching, many-sided intellect which is the natural growth of constant friction among men of divers nations and divers professions. There were few callings of which George had not some experience. He had slept in the tents of Bohemia, and heard strange songs in the Romany tongue, and sat in the college halls of German and Flemish cities, to listen to grave priests or fiery students arguing upon the deepest mysteries of the Catholic Faith in their dry scholastic Latin. He had been patronised by princes and ambassadors, and had carried a friendly colporteur's bag along the dusty roads of Flanders and of France. He had been nursed through a fever in the Carthusian Monastery near Florence, and had eluded the importunities of the monks, who would have had him enter upon his novitiate when he rose from his sick-bed. Francis Mountain professed himself ever of the local religion, and was a staunch Papist between Calais and Naples, a sturdy Calvinist in the low countries, and a virulent high-Churchman and champion of the Book of Sports in London.

"If the Puritans get the upper hand I may begin to see the cloven foot under Laud's cassock," he told George, "and may come round to love sour faces and Geneva gowns, and sermons that outlast the sand in the hour-glass. But I confess to a liking for handsome vestments, and an altar set altar-wise, with candles and crucifix, as I remember them in my father's private chapel. Yet the spectacle of respectable citizens flogged, and pilloried, and mutilated, and pining in prison, because they refuse to bow to the altar and prefer a conventicle to a church, shows like midsummer madness to a man who loves life and liberty ; to bask in the sun at noon under a hedge, like a beggar ; or to feast at midnight with princes in a tapestried banquetting-hall ; and who has never cudgelled his brains to discover the why or the wherefore of things."

At eighteen years of age George's thoughts were deeper than Mountain's thoughts at eight-and-thirty. He was one of those who are born thinkers, and his childish mind, under that cottage roof in Surrey, had been full of far-reaching wonder. It was good for him to live in Mountain's joyous company, and even to sit on a tavern bench till midnight, and hear the talk of men whose eloquence was warmed with strong drink, and whose random cleverness missed as often as it hit the mark. Amidst the foolishness of fiery argument there were occasional flashes of wisdom, and wandering gleams of truth, together with much wit and poetry, struck off in the heat of talk that seemed ever to brighten as the night wore on. The boy was too diffident to join in such discourses, and was content to sit silent, in the shadow of his master's bulkier form, and to absorb the wisdom, while he smiled at the folly, of his seniors.

"Is Lord Llanbister one of the Queen's friends ? " George asked, when they were nearing their destination, having the ugly, straggling street of Brentford on their right hand, the rushes and willows of a long narrow eyot on their left.

"A staunch friend. But it is her ladyship who most affects Queen Henrietta. She was one of Her Majesty's maids-of-honour fifteen years ago, in the bloom of her beauty ; and there was no lovelier face at Whitehall. She married a man old enough to be her father : yet they seem to live happily together ; and not the foulest libeller in London has ever wasted printer's ink upon Lady Llanbister. It would be like slandering the evening star to assail virtue so stainless."

"I hope his lordship's age has not made him a harsh husband."

"Harsh ! Why, he adores his wife, as Laud worships the saints. If a beautiful young woman wants to secure a willing slave, and to exercise imperial sway at home and abroad, she had better marry, as Mrs. Redgrave married, a lover whose beard has a sprinkling of grey, and who has seen enough of Court wantons to know the value of a virtuous wife. I would wager this head of mine that there is no more affectionate couple in England than Lord and Lady Llanbister."

They passed the broad lawns of Syon, and the rowers pulled their boat alongside a low wooden landing-stage, a little farther west. A terrace walk, bordered with flowers, lay along the bank of the river, and across a broad sweep of velvet turf George saw a grey stone mansion of the Tudor period, with crow-step gables, and diamond-paned casements, set in massive mullions. A dry moat divided the lawn from an old-fashioned garden in front of the house, where peacocks, cut in yew, and close-clipped hedges of ilex and hornbeam testified to the industry of his lordship's gardeners. The water in a wide stone basin in the centre of this prim *parterre* had the dark lustre of a bronze shield, save where the gold fish, with which it was crowded, glittered across the darkness.

Moving with sauntering step along a grass walk by the moat George saw a man with white hair and beard, and stalwart figure, broad-shouldered, and of commanding height, by whose side there moved the tall and slender shape of a woman whose graceful bearing was not without a touch of pride. The poise of the beautifully shaped head suggested scorn of common things; the leisurely walk had an imperial air, as of one who moved not with the press and hurry of the world's commerce. Flitting over the grass on the nearer side of the moat a young and supple figure, with wind-blown hair, disported in a solitary game of battledore and shuttlecock, the girlish form set off by a gown of primrose brocade, upon which the gold of the flying hair showed brighter than the silken fabric.

"His lordship's orphan granddaughter—a romp, a beauty, and an heiress," explained Mountain. "Lord Llanbister spoils the child. Her father was his only son. He commanded a company of foot in Buckingham's army, and was massacred on the bridge of Rhé. The slightest word that recalls that shameful disaster will blanch the old man's cheek, and kindle a savage fire in his eye. If he were not a Christian gentleman his arm might have been as ready as your fellow traveller's to fit George Villiers for a bloody shroud."

"The young lady can scarce remember her father, I doubt."

"She can remember neither parent; for she was but two years old when her father fell, and that poor lady, her mother, sank to an apathy of sadness after the fatal news from Rochelle, and died before the blacks on her chamber walls had been taken down. She was Lord Lindisfarne's daughter—a most accomplished young lady. Llanbister loves to talk of his troubles, and of those two precious lives lost to him through the malice of events rather than by the will of Heaven."

"She is an orphan like me, and can remember neither father nor mother," said George musingly; "but there ends the likeness. She knows they were honourable and well-born. She can be proud of their names; she can love their shadows. She has their portraits perhaps, and can conjure them back to life by gazing at their pictured faces."

They crossed the moat by a stone bridge, and Lord Llanbister left his wife's side and came to meet them.

He greeted Mountain with the frank cordiality of a man whose exalted station is a part of himself, and needs no assertion.

"I have been waiting and longing for you all day, friend Francis," he said. "Your news is of the tardiest. Is the lady at Brussels too busy to answer our letters?"

"No, my lord, there has been no neglect. A north-west wind which blew the smack my friend travelled in back to Flushing is answerable for the delay."

"And this is your *protégé*-page, the young waiter upon Fortune of whom you have told me such fine things?" said the old man, surveying George from head to foot with kindly eyes, a look that was at once friendly and jocular. "Well, the nameless wight you picked up has a countenance that commends him to my liking, and which ought to win him favour in any company. Go get you a battledore, youngster—there are some in yonder summer-house—and play a match with Mrs. Geraldine, my grandchild, while I talk with your master."

George made a leg, and ran to the summer-house, an octagonal building of dark red brick, open on four sides to the sun and the river. He lost not a minute in selecting his battledore, and sped fleet as an arrow across the smooth grass till he brought himself to the young lady's side.

"His lordship bids me play a match with you, sweet mistress," he said, with his lowest obeisance.

She had her battledore in the air as he spoke, ready to hit the flying cork, but started at his voice, and let the shuttlecock drop at her feet.

"See what you have done, Sir Vehement! That was the ninety-third stroke, and in a minute or so I should have made a hundred; for which his lordship was to give me a pair of Spanish gloves. Madame de Chevreuse was to order them for me at Brussels."

"I doubt that accomplished lady is too busy to think of gloves. Will you not play a match, Mistress Geraldine, and take your revenge upon me for having spoilt your hundred ?"

"Nay, I'll wager you play better than I. You come from France, belike, where they are ever at their *jeu du volant.*"

"I come from everywhere. I belong to the wandering tribes."

"But what is the country of your birth ?"

"I would not say for sure, since I cannot remember the day I was born."

"I dare swear not ; but you know the house in which you first saw the light."

"Nay, sweet lady. The wandering tribes have no roof but the sky, or a canvas tent for hard weather. I know nothing save that I have one good friend, and that the world is a pleasant place for the young and free. And now will you give me a taste of your skill, madam, and prove that a lady's arm may be as strong, and her eye as true, as a man's ?"

"As a man's," she echoed, measuring him from top to toe, with a most bewitching laugh, that sparkled in the darkness of her eyes, and dazzled him. "Where are we to find boys for our pages, if you take rank as a man ? You can scarcely be three years older than I, who am always being flouted as a child."

"I am forty years older than your ladyship in experience."

"I am no ladyship. His Majesty would have made me a Baroness in my own right, after my mother's death —to make amends for the slaughter of my father and her broken heart. It was the Duke of Buckingham urged King Charles to offer that honour, which my grandfather refused for me with the scorn it merited."

"And you doubtless regret his lordship's refusal, now that you are old enough to know the value of rank and title."

"Regret ! Why, I could scarce have lived under the burden of a favour from Buckingham, now that I know it was by his blundering folly my father lost his life. A man without military training trusted with the command of his betters! I am angry whenever I think of that fond preference which gave such power to an ignorant youth. The King might as well choose a lad like you to lead an army!"

George was startled at the change in her as she broke into this angry speech. From a child, joyous, insolent, charming, she had become a woman, her face pale with scorn, her eyes flashing, her lips trembling. But while he gazed at her in mute wonder her mood changed, and she was again the happy sylph he had accosted five minutes before. She was taller than most women, strongly built too, her head gracefully set upon a perfect throat and shoulders, the figure of a wood nymph. Her dress was of a sumptuous simplicity, a yellow brocade gown and broad lawn collar, over which her golden hair fell in large loose curls, below her waist. She had the frankest outlook, eyes bright and daring as an eagle's, a delicate aquiline nose, an air of one prepared to fight for supremacy over the stronger sex.

"I did wrong to speak of Buckingham or the King," she said; "their names always anger me."

"Are you so disloyal a subject as to be angry with your King for a tragedy in which he had no share?"

"No share! Had he no tried veteran to whom he could have trusted the relief of Rochelle?"

"He had tried his tried veterans, and they proved not always fortunate. There are some who swear that George Villiers was not to blame for the losses at Rhé."

"Now you are going to make me furious again," she cried, shaking her finger at him.

"That will I not, fairest Miss, for what was Buckingham to me that I should venerate his name? Sure I never saw him living, though I was within a few paces of him when he fell, and looked upon his face in the majesty of death."

She looked at him intently, thrilling with sudden interest.

"You were at Portsmouth when he was murdered?" she exclaimed. "Tell me—tell me. Let us walk to the river—I shall play no more to-day. Tell me about

Buckingham's death! Poor wretch! I hate him; but I do not love murder. There are some who call Felton a saint and a martyr; but I have been taught better. 'Vengeance is Mine, I will repay, saith the Lord.'"

They strolled side by side to the broad grass walk by the landing stage, from which the ground dipped towards the water, where sedges and lilies, and such wild flowers as love a river, grew along the slope with the lavish bloom of midsummer. All the air was filled with the delicate scents of herbs and flowers that grow as God made them. A company of swans and their grey cygnets moved slowly down the stream, in a stillness broken only by the light ripple of the tide, and the hum of those invisible myriads that live in leaf and flower, sedge and sward.

"Now," she said, "tell me how you came to be at Portsmouth when Felton killed the Duke? I was but three years old, yet I can remember hearing my *gouvernante* and my nurse talk of the tragedy. How old were you when it happened?"

"Old enough to have a long memory," he answered curtly; and then he described the scene: the crowded streets; mounted messengers riding to and fro; the sparkle of gold and colour; soldiers, sailors; women at the doors and windows; trumpets blaring, drums beating; merry jests, broad faces smiling in the morning sun. And then he painted the sudden change to tumult and horror; men groaning; women screaming; and Felton walking in the midst of a mad crowd, with blood upon his hands and clothes, an ashen-faced spectre. "He gave himself up at once. I doubt he was distraught from the first inception of the crime, and repented on the instant. There is so wide an abyss between the deed contemplated and the deed done."

They sauntered by the rushes for some minutes in a grave silence; and then George began to talk to her of the river, and of other rivers he had seen—wider—swifter—nobler—but not more beautiful. She had never crossed the Channel, and could only tell him of the castle near Shrewsbury where she had spent those portions of her life that had not been spent in London or by the Thames.

"My grandfather has a house in Aldersgate Street, but we love this place better," she told him; "for there are too many sea-coal fires in that part of London, though I look over fields and woods from my chamber window. London has grown such a monstrous city since his lordship was a boy, and he has grown to hate it, and thinks His Majesty wise for inflicting heavy fines on the people who build new houses, and even making them pull down their old ones, where the press of buildings shuts out God's sky from the poor pale children that live in them. My great-aunt has a mansion and garden in Shoe Lane, but the street behind her orchard is so narrow that those who occupy the upper rooms can shake hands from window to window. I wonder that any one can like to live in the heart of a great city."

"Yet the great city is the heart of England, and all the best blood of the country flows to it. Statesmen and poets, churchmen and playwrights, painters, actors, inventors, all love the great city. I have heard more wisdom and more wit in London and Paris in a night than one could hear in a year of country life."

"Who cares for wit or wisdom when one can watch the sunshine on the river, and that sunlit haze behind the rushes yonder that looks like molten gold; and when every morning brings new flowers, and the summer nights are full of music? Wisdom and wit are well enough by the winter fire. In summer I am content to live among dunces. Yet I have heard great men and poets talk, Mr. Page. I have sat at table with Lord Strafford; and I can remember old Mr. Jonson, a great, rolling man, with a coarse, lumpy face, and eyes that burnt like red-hot coals. My grandfather loved him, and he came to supper in Aldersgate Street, when he could scarcely walk for the gout, and would sit drinking and talking till long after I had been sent to bed. I could hear his great deep voice as I lay abed on a summer night, when all the windows were open, rising and falling like the sea, in everlasting talk. They say it was the cleverest talk in the world, and had but one fault, that he would too often brag of his own genius. I am proud to remember that he has patted my curls, and composed an epigram for my birthday."

"Did he compare you with the butterflies, or call you living sunshine?"

"No; his lines were neither foolish nor fantastical, or he would scarce have pleased my grandfather, and won so heavy a purse of gold as I saw him toss laughing in the air. He was a pleasant old gentleman; but my lady says he drank too deep to be good company for women."

They sauntered by the river, heeding neither time, which has no measure for the happy, nor distance, which the feet of youth know not. The low western sky had a splendour of light and colour that set Geraldine at finding out fiery palaces and jewelled streets among those vermilion and amber clouds moving slowly on a vast opal sea. The river seemed a burnished floor that almost tempted them to walk upon it; and every reed and every waterside flower had a slender, aerial look against that brightness, as of things unreal, splendour seen in a dream. And when, within sight of Twickenham Church tower, they stopped to listen to the curfew bell, above the lessening glory of the reflected sunset over Richmond Hill there trembled the faint silver of a crescent moon.

"'Tis the first time I have seen her," George cried exultantly; "and I may win my wish, if Phœbe be but kind."

"But if you tell your wish you will not win it."

"Were it not so, it is a wish I dare not tell," he answered, smiling at her; and then he dropped one knee upon the sweet-scented herbage, doffed his hat, and whispered his prayer to the moon.

"You greet Diana as if she were a mortal queen," said the girl. "You have quite the Court air. I doubt you have been at Whitehall, and seen our gracious Henrietta?"

"Not yet. My master and I are but wayfarers in a world that is too busy to heed us. And what should a waif without rank or name do at Court?"

"Oh, but it is a lad like you, with nothing to lose, who wins fame and fortune," Geraldine answered gaily. "I have seen the house near Exmouth where Raleigh was born. 'Tis a poor place. His father was an obscure country gentleman; and what a name *he* has left! And a greater than Raleigh—Columbus—was the son of a weaver. No man need be ashamed of beginning low. It is keeping low, or sinking low, that should shame him."

Her sapphire eyes shone with young enthusiasm. She had read Hakluyt's voyages, and thought there were no heroes like those who discovered new worlds. She had wept for Raleigh as if he had been of her own kindred. A girl must have gods and heroes when she casts off her dolls. Hero-worship follows close on babyish plays. It is the first dim dawn of passion, perhaps, this adoration of the heroic dead.

They talked of many things: of the world he had seen, and of that narrower world of hers; the castle in Shropshire; the house in Aldersgate Street, with its large, walled garden, between the town mansions of the Earls of Thanet and Kingston; the plays she had seen by the Queen's players at the Phœnix, in Drury Lane. She questioned him about his Latin and Greek, and the books he had read in both languages, and whether he loved Virgil's Æneid, which was the only romance she had been allowed to read.

"My grandfather will have me taught Latin and the mathematics like a boy, or like Lady Jane Grey and Queen Bess," she said. "I am forbid to learn Italian—and I see my lady sighing over Tasso or Petrarch, and hate myself because I cannot read poetry as she does. Her father taught her, who was a Bishop, and one of the first scholars of his day. But I am to be reared like a man."

"And you like not that?" questioned George, since there was a touch of disgust in her tone.

"Oh, I like and do not like! I love to play boyish games; I hate to have so little pains taken with my music; and to be forbid to waste time on embroidery. I want to do all the best things men and women do— to run and ride like a man, and dance like a woman— to make pillow-lace, and to row a boat—to construe Virgil, and to paint flowers on velvet. But I have to obey his lordship. In that matter he has made a woman of me. Obedience is my portion."

They lingered on the bank till the last touch of vivid colour had faded from sky and river, and sombre shadows had crept over the willows and sedges along the bank. These are the hours old men and women look back at, across the waste of years; moments that came and went so lightly, that had no before or after, but which are remembered with a sick longing half a century later, when life is dull and grey, and the diminishing sands can almost be counted as they drop through the glass. George never forgot that evening, and the proud, high-bred face, the sparkling manner, the charms and graces of girlhood unacquainted with care.

It was supper-time when George and his companion went into the house; and Lord and Lady Llanbister and Mr. Mountain were already seated at table in a low-ceiled dining parlour, panelled with oak, and beautified by a monumental mantelpiece of coloured marbles, which Lord Llanbister had brought from Florence. Her ladyship was somewhat reproachful at Geraldine's tardy appearance.

"Nay, my lady, let her roam while the days are long," pleaded his lordship. "She is no parlour-miss, with a back that has grown round over a 'broidery frame. She has been bred in fields and gardens, and stifles under our low ceilings. You see, Mountain, she is all the issue I have, male or female—all that Fate and Villiers spared me of child and heir—and I have reared her to be as worthy an heir as manly breeding can make her. If she cannot fight for her King, she can think for her King; and that is more than our baby-faced Court beauties can do, who think of nothing but lovers and fine clothes, the last masque or the next ballet, and know not that while they are dressing and dancing the world they live in is crumbling about their ears. Sit down, Mr. Page. There is a stool reserved for you next my lady. We are in the country here, and have no degrees of rank—no below the salt. This is friend Mountain's young comrade, Viola, for whom I entreat your kindness."

Lady Llanbister gave the lad a smile and a gentle inclination of the head; a recognition which had in it as much of hauteur as of kindness, George thought. She was a beautiful woman, in all the splendour of mature womanhood. Her features were classic in their regularity, her profile delicate as the engraving of a Greek gem. George looked at her with reverential admiration, but with a sinking of his spirits, as when a mortal gazes on a goddess. So might Diana have appeared to Endymion, a creature afar off, isolated in an awful beauty.

It was not a jovial supper-party. Mistress Geraldine's audacity was dashed by the presence of her elders, and she spoke only when spoken to; Lord Llanbister and Mountain conversed in undertones; while George sat mute, and ate sparingly of the ample cheer which was administered by four lackeys in sombre but sumptuous liveries of brown velvet and gold. His lordship took only the plainest food; but Mountain contrived, even while deep in most serious converse, to ply an active knife and fork, and to do justice to a dish of spiced carp, a capon pasty, and a tankard of choice Burgundy.

"One can get no such aroma of violets t'other side the Channel," he said, passing a brimmer of the perfumed wine under his nostrils. "They send all the choicest growth of the Côte d'Or to the English market."

George bent his face over his trencher to hide a smile, remembering in what wayside inns, along the country roads, and in what dingy drinking-shops in Paris he and his patron had enjoyed their chief experience of French wines. True that once in a way Mountain and his boyish squire had been entertained at rich men's tables; but the palate across which so many a gallon of rough new wine had been flung could scarcely be of the texture to appreciate nice differences of flavour.

The moon was high when they rose from the supper-table, and they all strolled into the garden, where the sultry warmth of a still evening was perfumed with roses and stocks, honeysuckle and jasmine. This time George found himself walking at Lady Llanbister's side, while Mistress Geraldine hung on her grandfather's arm, skipping in her walk every now and then, for sheer exuberance of spirits.

"You are new to England, I think," said her ladyship. "You speak our language with a foreign accent. Are you of French birth?"

"Nay, madam, so far as I know myself I am English born. My first memories are of English lanes and hedgerows."

"Indeed! But is your history so mysterious that you must needs speak with uncertainty? Do you not know the place of your birth?"

"I have no certain knowledge—except of the place where I began to see and hear and wonder."

"What was the name of the place?"

"Indeed, I know not if it had a name."

"How do you know, then, that it was in England?"

"Because I know it was within a child's three days' wandering from the Portsmouth Road."

There was an interval of some minutes while they strolled along the gravel walk, before the lady continued her questioning; and then she said carelessly,—

"The Portsmouth Road is seventy miles long, sir, and begins a mile or so out of London. If you have no nearer knowledge of the locality, it will never help you to revisit your childhood's home."

"Indeed, I have no wish to see the spot, madam. I have none belonging to me that live there. I look back upon my childhood as a dream that I dreamt. It has left me no more of substance than a dream leaves."

"Poor waif! I heard your master tell his lordship

something of your story, but I did not gather that it was in England he found you. I am ever interested in orphan children—perhaps because I have no child of my own."

He could see her face clearly in the silvery light. She was looking at him with a grave interest, and he thought now that melancholy, not pride, was its most marked characteristic. She gave him her hand presently, when they parted, midway between the house and the moat, and he dropped on one knee as he might have done to the Queen.

" It will be morning before you see Westminster, though you will have the tide with you all the way," Lord Llanbister said, as they were going away, and insisted on lending them a couple of boat-cloaks, lest the night should be cold.

Their boatmen had been feasted on beef and beer, and were primed for their work ; and under a sky crowded with stars, river and landscape were lovelier than by day. Mountain was in a genial mood, and trolled out one of Ben's joyous songs, as the boat swept swiftly onward, to the rhythm of dipping oars :—

> " The faery beam upon you,
>   The stars to glister on you ;
>   A moon of light,
>   In the noon of night,
>   Till the fire-drake hath o'ergone you !
>   The wheel of fortune guide you,
>   The boy with the bow beside you ;
>   Run aye in the way,
>   Till the bird of day
>   And the luckier lot betide you ! "

" Would you not think that my Lord Llanbister, in his prosperous case, with estates in three counties, land which he reckons by the thousand acres, would be content to let Pope and Bishops go their own way," Mountain said thoughtfully, after a silence that had been longer than his wont, "and would be the last to waste his fortune, and risk his head, by dabbling in

Jesuit schemes, and trying to bring back the religion which lit London and Oxford with martyrs, as Nero lighted Rome ? "

Mountain had dropped into the French language, lest the watermen should catch a compromising word, albeit the two stolid faces bending over the oars had not a look of dangerous intelligence. Who could tell behind what dull countenance the spy's keen wits might hide ?

" I thought Lord Llanbister would be a staunch Protestant, since his son lost his life in trying to rescue the Rochellese," George said, also in French.

" You had good reason to think as much—but there is a woman's influence here, as there is at Whitehall— and women are ever on the side of the priests. My lady was bred a Protestant—ostensibly at least—though 'tis said her father, the late Bishop of Southminster, was at heart a more zealous Papist than Laud. She turned Catholic some years after her marriage, drawn that way by an elder brother—pervert and Jesuit—a member of the Roman College of the Propaganda— who has all the fierce fervour of a renegade, and who, unluckily for his lordship, had unbounded influence over her when he was last in England. I doubt the good old man is no fanatic, and would fain leave his country- men free to worship, each after his own fashion ; but he has let himself be drawn into his brother-in-law's scheme, which is nothing less than to have England and the Pope reconciled as they were under Bloody Mary, with a like result in fire and flame at Smithfield and at Oxford, I'll warrant, though her gentle ladyship does not foresee it."

" Is Madame de Chevreuse concerned in the in- trigue ? "

" Why, next the Jesuit, that brave, beautiful devil is the head and front of it ; fetches and carries between Whitehall and the Escurial ; and is deep in all the French Queen Dowager's undermining plans."

" I heard them talking the other night of a likely union between the two Churches—each to concede some points to the other ; so that, while all that is holiest in the old Faith should be restored, none of the old abuses should be revived."

"A dream, George, and of a misguided dreamer! The Roman Church knows not how to yield! She is founded on the rock of stubbornness. She is rooted in the stiff soil of ancient superstition—she has no more yielding in her than Judah has—and thou knowest the Jews cook their meat to-day in Muscovy as they cooked it thousands of years ago under Syria's burning sun. Rome moves not with time any more than Israel. If the Papal power is to be restored it will bring back every rite and impose every doctrine that England suffered before the Reformation; but I doubt the stretched-out arm of the Vatican will never again reach across the Straits of Dover. The Puritans are too strong to be put down; and, take my word for it, George, it is they who will have the upper hand before your head is grey. Every fresh act of persecution, every pair of ears sawn off, every conventicle tyrannously closed, gives new vigour to the cause. If King Charles wanted to keep the Nonconformists harmless he ought to have let them alone!"

George was not deeply concerned in theological questions. He had not been trained in pious paths; and he had thought little upon serious subjects. Of the two creeds he preferred the Roman, with its glow of colour and picturesque ceremonial. Such moments of religious emotion as he had felt had been under the vaulted roofs of Continental cathedrals, where he had wandered in to look at a picture or a statue, and where some sublime strain of organ-music, some sudden sense of a sanctuary isolated from common life and common things, some unexpected influence of the beauty of holiness, had caught and held him for a brief space, and he had sunk upon his knees in the dusk of a side-chapel, and had poured out his young soul in prayer to his Saviour: "Oh, Thou who wast so pure amidst the world's impurity, separate me and keep me from the wickedness of this life!"

Holy thoughts were in his mind to-night while

Mountain sat smoking his pipe in silence, and while the river-banks and quiet villages glided by, mute and peaceful as a moving picture. Some pure and elevating influence seemed to have been breathed into him during his brief converse with Lady Llanbister. Her face haunted him in the summer stillness, and was more vividly present to his mental sight than that so much younger face which had flashed its vivacious loveliness upon him amidst the splendour of sunset. Perhaps it was the unknown history, the closed volume of sad secrets, which he divined behind the austere beauty of the matron, that so much impressed him. He admired the girl with all a lad's admiration of peerless girlhood, ready to kindle into passionate love ; but he mused upon the woman's words and the woman's countenance with a romantic wonder : and to-night, in his exalted mood, he felt that life could have no happier close than to fling itself away in her defence, in the furtherance of her dearest desire—in any manner, for her sake.

To-morrow night, amid the wit and satire of that riotous crew in the Apollo, he might see all things in a different aspect, and would be ready, perhaps, to admit that the beautiful Lady Llanbister, with a husband thirty years her senior, might furnish no spotless page of woman's history when the great book of secrets is flung open. He was young enough to take the colour of his thoughts from external influences, to be chameleon-hued in mind and feelings.

CHAPTER VI.

"TO WIN HER PRAISE."

GEORGE was in attendance on his master at the Queen's private chapel during Mass next morning. Henrietta came in late, with a train of ladies, courtiers, and pages, and sank to her knees on a crimson velvet *prie-dieu* in front of the altar, amidst a burst of triumphant chords on the organ, which had been discoursing softly in a dreamy Agnus Dei during a prolonged period of waiting for this august worshipper. The ceremonial, once started, was conducted at a brisk pace ; and it was less than half an hour from that opening Jubilate to the *Ite, missa est.*

When the congregation had dispersed, a groom of the chambers conducted Mountain and his page to one of the private apartments of Denmark House, where George found himself in the presence of that Royal lady whose mignon features and flashing black eyes he had hitherto seen only from his place among the crowd in the street, or in the pit of the theatre. He had ample leisure to study the Queen's countenance this morning, standing aloof in a distant window, where he had been bidden to wait while she conversed with his master. He saw her take a letter from Mountain and give him two, which he placed in his breast pocket, with an ostentatious solicitude that badly matched with his casual handling of such documents in the retirement of his lodgings.

Watching the Royal lady from that distance, George noted a curious mixture of pride and familiarity in her manner to Mountain—now with her small head flung back at a scornful angle, her eyelids drooping, and her

speech short and disdainful ; now inclining her ear, with
the costly pearl solitaire, towards his bearded lips, her
eyes sparkling, her little white teeth exhibited in frank
laughter. He saw in that quarter of an hour all the
indications of the proud, impetuous, dauntless nature
which would have made a fine character under the
guidance of a wiser mate than Charles Stuart, but
which, in its fluctuating strength, was the worst possible
ally for his weakness ; strong enough to influence him,
but not wise enough to guide him ; turning all that
was best and noblest in his character as a man to his
disadvantage as a king.

The waiting-woman stood beside George in the deep
embrasure of the window, a window which commanded
the shining water-way, crowded with pleasure-boats and
barges, and looked south-eastward across the river to
Bankside, where some of the Court gallants had their
bachelor lodgings in a row of houses almost hidden by
the trees that grew in front of them. The lady fanned
herself in a haughty silence, scorning to make conversation with Mr. Mountain's page, yet not too proud to
admire the lad's handsome face, and to stare him out
of countenance in an arrogant inspection which could
not have been more deliberate had he been one of the
mechanical figures in the Italian puppet show. He
gave her back her look with interest presently, stung
by her discourtesy.

"Indeed, madam, I am alive, though you take me for
a piece of machinery," he said. "My wooden features
and dull complexion are to blame for your ladyship's
mistake."

"You are neither wooden-featured nor dull-com-
plexioned, wretch ; but you are as insolent as you are
high, and your master should know better than to bring
such a malapert monkey into her Majesty's presence,"
the lady retorted, surprised but not displeased at his
assurance. "Come, I forgive your ill manners. I hate
a fool so much that I would sooner suffer audacity than
dulness. Where do you come from, and what are
you ? Some rural squire's son, who thinks a handsome

face should make his fortune at Court—not knowing that we have got beyond the day of handsome faces, and want only long heads and deep purses. If you are poor, come not to the Court to mend your fortunes. There is scarce a more necessitous lady in his Majesty's dominions than she who should be the richest. These ragged window-curtains, which go so ill with yonder Flemish tapestry, may tell you as much."

"It is no purpose of my own that brings me here, madam. I go where I am bidden, and follow my master's fortunes."

"And who is your master?"

"That question is for him to answer, madam, or your mistress, who honours him with her confidence, and in so doing stamps him worthy of your respect."

"Oh, you are very close and very artful, and presume intolerably upon a Greek nose and a brilliant eye," cried the waiting-woman, as she turned her back upon him, and leant out of an open casement, affecting to be wholly absorbed in watching the river traffic.

The conversation between the greatest lady in the land and the soldier of fortune lasted much longer than George had thought likely; but from the Queen's laughter, and Mountain's *débonnaire* bearing, and the rollicking sound of his voice when it rose above the confidential pitch, the page could but think that the subject of their discourse had dropped from the lofty region of ecclesiastical intrigue to the lower level of amusing anecdote. He knew his master for an accomplished *raconteur*, with an almost unlimited repertory of good stories, some among which, perhaps one in ten, were not wholly unfit for a lady's ear.

This was the first of many private conferences that Henrietta Maria held with George's master; at which the young man was present, but out of hearing, if the room were large enough, or in attendance outside the door, if the chamber were smaller.

These meetings took place at considerable intervals, at various hours, and in various places—at Whitehall, at Denmark House, at Greenwich, at Oatlands, at Hampton Court. George and his master rode many a dusty mile under a scorching sun to wait upon her Majesty, when the river journey was too slow to serve her turn. The Queen's life at this time was full of wild schemes and far-reaching plots; for her keen wit had divined the darkening of the Royal sky, and she was painfully conscious of the storm clouds that gathered and blackened, day by day. But while Henrietta Maria was shrewd enough to see that her husband's fortunes were sinking, the King remained stubbornly blind to the obvious aspect of things; stubbornly deaf to that tremendous voice of the English people, which had been growing louder and more menacing with every year of Thorough; stubbornly self-assured as to his own capacity to govern England after his own fashion, however he might fail in the attempt to rule that ruder kingdom of Scotland, with which he was even now coming to a compromise.

“Root and branch” had been triumphant beyond the Tweed. The second deliberate attempt to impose Episcopacy on Scotland at the point of the sword—the so-called Bishops' War—had just exploded in disaster at Newburn, near Newcastle, where Leslie's guns and Leslie's cavalry had routed Conway's royalists at the first encounter—a skirmish which was to prove the ignominious close of an ineffectual war.

The bad news from Scotland came to George's knowledge in the peaceful gardens between Syon Park and Isleworth Church, where he was now a frequent visitor, walking or sitting with Lady Llanbister and Geraldine —or sometimes alone with the elder lady—while his lordship and Mountain conferred apart, and while Mistress Geraldine sat at her daily task with the chaplain, construing Virgil, or composing execrable Latin verses. Those quiet afternoons and evenings by the river seemed to George the golden hours of his life, hours that brought him for the first time within the influence of a pure and high-bred woman. He had met good women before, and had received kindness from them, and had been grateful: but they had been of the hard-working, rough-handed races. He had seen ladies before to-day, but they had been proud and unapproachable, or of a brazen familiarity that sickened him. This lady was a creature apart. Every tone of her low, calm voice—so exquisitely modulated, yet so strong ;—every movement of her gracious hands, or turn of the small head—round which the plaited hair was coiled in a style that suggested a portrait by Giorgione rather than the airy modern fashion ;—seemed to him the perfection of womanly grace and dignity. He admired Geraldine's bright beauty, with all the warmth of adoring youth. He loved to be teased and jibed at by her ; to quarrel and make friends ; to fetch and carry for her ; to help her with her Latin composition, or " the mathematics " ; to spend hours in the City trying to match a skein of silk, or at the Holy Lamb or the Three Bibles on London Bridge, searching for a novel she wanted to read ; to be praised, scorned, scolded by her. But he knew that she was very human. There was nothing upward-looking in the devotion which he gave her. If Lady Llanbister had had a daughter, she would have been a being of a vastly different mould, he thought ; and he scarcely wondered that there seemed so little of sympathy between my lady and her husband's heiress.

To him Lady Llanbister was especially kind. She had had youthful worshippers by the score, and was indeed sated with the adulation which had been given to beauty, wealth, and high place ; but it may be that she discovered in this nameless waif—whose story she had heard from Mountain—more sincere affection, and a stronger character, than she had ever met with before in a lad of nineteen. She compassionated his lonely situation, his dependence on a reckless adventurer like Mountain—a man who courted danger, and loved the game in which the stakes are heads, and who was never happier than when buzzing hither and thither athwart the web of a political intrigue. She went so far one day, when George had gained the footing of a friend, as to talk to him of the life he led in the present, and of his aspirations for the future.

"You are wasting yourself, I fear, in Mr. Mountain's service," she told him. "He is clever, and has powerful friends; but the work he does for them is dangerous work, and I tremble to think what the end of it may be. You have talents; and though you have had no collegiate training, Father Calhoun tells me you have a very handsome knowledge of the classics and mathematics. Have you no desire for a nobler career than Mr. Mountain's service can open for you?"

"No, madam. Francis Mountain is the maker of my fortunes, such as they are; and I must sink or swim with him, live or die with him. Apart from him I am nothing."

"Then you have no ambition?"

"I have no-name to ennoble or to disgrace, madam, no kindred to please by my prosperity. No one would be the prouder for my fame—or the richer for my fortune. For me the thirst of glory would be but self-love. Ambition would ill become George Nameless."

She rose from the garden-bench in sudden agitation that took away his breath, her countenance first flushing crimson, and then fading to a marble whiteness.

"I will not hear you call yourself by that hateful title! Nameless? You! Young, handsome, brave, generous, clever! Genius and courage shine in your eyes. Great names are made in a day, sir. Why, Archbishop Abbot and Lawyer Selden were the sons of peasants. I could reckon a dozen famous gentlemen at this hour who were born in labourers' cottages."

"True, madam; but they had parents for whom it was sweet to toil. I have no one. I am not whining at my ill-fortune. Fate has been not altogether unkind. I love a roving life—I love my master—I have no quarrel with Destiny or the world I live in; but I will not hazard my one friend's favour to court Fame—which would bring me little joy—or fortune, which I can do without."

He had risen as she rose, and walked at her side as she sauntered along the terrace by the moat. Her agitation had passed like a gust of the light autumn wind that blew the fallen leaves about her feet, and her face was now grave and thoughtful.

" Be sure that fame and fortune will come to you, and that whatever name you choose for yourself ; and you must have a name——"

" Let me be George Mountain, then. I have as good a right to that name as my master, who confesses it is none of his."

" Whatever name you take, it will be in your power to make it honourable and esteemed."

" Be it so, dear lady. While you are kind to me I have at least one spur to endeavour, the desire to be worthier your kindness ; " and then he quoted four lines written by a man whose youthful poetry was well-nigh forgotten in the virulence of his polemical prose, a bitter republican pamphleteer, one John Milton, who, in his youth, among the level meads and shady Buckingham-shire copses about the village of Horton, had sung so sweetly of the city tournament, and its

> " Store of ladies, whose bright eyes
> Rain influence, and judge the prize
> To wit or arms, while both contend
> To win her praise whom all commend."

He repeated the last line, dwelling fondly on the words.

" Oh, madam, you know not what harm you may do me. At a word from you, ambition kindles its consum-ing fire in my breast. What would not a nameless youth attempt to win your praise—to be worthy of your liking ? "

" You have that without painful endeavour. You won my esteem before I had any ground for thinking you deserved it ; for a foolish reason perhaps. You remind me of some one I knew when I was young."

" And who no longer lives, madam. The sad music of your voice tells me that."

" One who has long been dead. Well, I must talk to Mountain. He is an honest, warm-hearted being, and will not, I think, wittingly bring you into danger or disgrace."

" Let me be your ladyship's knight-errant. Let me wear your colours," he cried, emboldened by her kindness, and lightly touching the knot of rose-coloured ribbon which relieved the sombre grey of her velvet sleeve. With your badge hidden in my breast disgrace cannot come near me. I shall move in a rarer atmosphere than common men breathe."

" Nay, I am past the age of ribbons and badges," she answered, smiling at his boyish boldness, curious in him who not very long ago had been dumb and awestruck in her presence. "But you shall wear my colours," she added gravely, looking long and fixedly at a single sapphire plainly set in a band of gold—a ring which he had noticed, for she wore it always on the forefinger of her left hand, whatever change she made in her other rings, which were chosen to match her mantua ; rubies when she wore crimson ; emeralds with green ; diamonds with the sable velvet or satin which she most affected.

" Look at this deep blue, like the vault of heaven in a summer midnight. The ring was given to me under such a sky. This is my colour, George, this unfathomable blue, in which I once thought I could read the story of my future life. You may wear it, if you will, and think of me sometimes when you look at it among strange scenes, far away from this tranquil place. Let it be your amulet, a charm to guard you from sinful thoughts and sinful acts. Danger no man can escape, who has a man's courage to dare and do ; but any man can avoid sin if he will. Every lad begins life with the power to leave his name as stainless as King Arthur's— as noble as Bayard's. You say you would like to be my knight-errant. Will you try to lead a good life, George—for my sake? That is better than to ride in the lists, and to win golden spurs."

" There is nothing I would not try for your sake, dear lady; but indeed I cannot take your sapphire. I have noted it so often on your finger, and I have marked how the whiteness of the hand sets off the colour of the gem."

He argued earnestly against the acceptance of so rich

a gift; but she would not be denied. She held his left hand with a gentle force, while she put the ring on his finger.

"You have a finely shaped hand, George—almost as handsome as Wentworth's, about which her Majesty raves."

"If by the magic of this jewel—symbolic of your dear favour—I could ever climb as high as he has mounted!"

"Oh, do not speak of it! He is a great man, I grant you, a great wicked man—with the finest brain and the hardest heart in England. I have seen some of his letters to the Archbishop—such cruel letters—always in the same strain, always suggesting, not lenitives, but corrosives for the cure of the nation's malady; always urging 'Thorough.' Do you know what 'thorough' means, George?"

"Indeed, madam, the word has been bandied about stormily enough in my hearing. With the King's friends it is a word of grace, and they hold him fortunate in having so bold and able a minister as the Earl of Strafford; but for Nonconformists and Puritans it stands for a tyranny as implacable as Nero's."

"'Thorough,' as Wentworth intends the word, means callous indifference to individual rights and individual suffering, in the furtherance of an iron policy which would make the King's rule absolute for good or evil, and would dispense with parliaments for ever. The grass would grow in Palace Yard, and the cobwebs hang thick over the windows of both Houses, if Wentworth had his way. He would rule England as he has ruled Ireland."

"And the little finger of Prerogative would be heavier than the loins of the Law. Is not that what Lord Strafford said, madam?"

"I have heard that he turned the sentence the other way, and meant to indicate his Majesty's indulgence as compared with the Law's cruelty. Indeed, the King was ever a kind master—mistaken often, his will yielding too easily to injudicious advisers—but a tyrant never!"

"Not when he kept Eliot in prison—to languish and

die in the prime of manhood—because his petition for release was not humble enough? Was that tyranny the result of injudicious advice, madam? or of a jealous regard for his own importance—a sullen pride that could not forget the orator's attack, or brook the statesman's superiority?"

"I cannot argue about my Sovereign, George. I have known and loved him. He has qualities that appeal to all hearts. He has faults that may wreck England. And his best hope is in Wentworth, whom the country hates, but who is perhaps the greatest man England holds, and the one man who might yet make England great—for this country has fallen very low, George. Richelieu laughs at us; Spain tricks us; Venice wonders at our folly. Strafford might make us honoured and feared; but, alas! at what a cost!—the axe, the torture-chamber—means lawful or unlawful to keep the Houses closed and dumb; to bring the people into subjection, and make the King of this free country as absolute as Baber."

"Were Charles as wise as Baber, England might thrive under an absolute government," argued George, to whom Eastern history had been as delightful as the "Arabian Nights" to lads of a later age. "Well, there is an unquiet spirit abroad in London, and a growing sullen anger against the great Earl, which I fear will burst in thunder by-and-bye. I thought, when I was in Paris, that the hatred of tavern politicians could not be fiercer than that of Frenchmen for Richelieu; but there is a something deeper and more purposeful in the tone of the City Puritans when Strafford is their theme—nor is their talk much kinder of his ally and counsellor, Laud."

"The poor Archbishop—so well meaning; so inevitably wrong! You must forget what I told you of Wentworth's letters, George. I did ill to speak of them, for they were shown to his lordship and me in confidence."

"I will be dumb, madam. No words of yours shall ever be repeated by these lips. But once more I would

entreat you to resume your ring. I know you value it
—above most others."

" Above every other ornament I possess ; and it is
for that reason I give it to you. And—I will trust you
with a secret known to none but my husband and one
other. It will but be a few years, I fear, before I shall
have done with all such ornaments."

He looked at her, speechless, for the moment, with a
sudden fear.

" God help us, dear lady," he faltered, "do you apprehend some mortal malady preying upon so precious a
life ? "

" Not *my* life, George—that is not threatened. But
my dear lord is older than you may think him, since his
fine carriage and handsome countenance might become
a man twenty years younger. Lord Llanbister is in
his seventy-fifth year. May God lengthen his days, and
make them full of such quiet comfort as he and I have
enjoyed since we retired from the Court. But at the
happiest I cannot hope to enjoy his dear company many
years. And when that bond is loosened, I shall be free
from all earthly ties—a childless widow—quite alone in
a world of which I have long been weary. I think you
can guess to what calm retirement I shall take my
loneliness."

" You will enter a convent, madam ? "

" Yes. I have friends in the Benedictine Convent of
Val de Grace ; and there the remnant of my days might
be passed in a placid retirement, which would be happier
than to linger in a world that had lost its interest. You,
who are a Protestant, picture a dungeon when you hear
of a convent, and imagine the sacrifice of every hope
and every comfort. If you could see the faces I have
seen in the Benedictine parlour, the sweet serenity, the
loving pity for the sorrows of weak human nature, you
would not look aghast at the prospect of a childless
widow ending her days within the convent gate."

" Oh, madam, you are the best judge of what is wise
and right ; but the wickeder the world becomes the
more there is need of good women moving about among

the sinners, free to come and go, to speak and to act,
owning no director save God and their own noble hearts.
And, sure, for one good work a nun can do within an
enclosed convent, a pious woman at liberty in the busy
world could do twenty. Nay, madam, I will not presume
upon your indulgence by daring to question your wisdom.
I pray Heaven that his dear lordship may be the Nestor
of his age, and that the occasion of that sad sacrifice
you contemplate may be long postponed."

CHAPTER VII.

"PUT NOT YOUR TRUST IN PRINCES."

WHEN November came, Strafford was in the Tower. The black storm-cloud had burst in a rain of fire. Thomas Wentworth, the renegade, Strafford, the advocate of despotic rule, was the point of attack for the new patriotism, the one bold sinner who was to be held responsible for every abuse of kingly power under which the country had groaned while the voices of the people were silent.

Strafford! Prejudice, passion, fear, swelled the accusing clamour. Men had neither speech nor thought for any other offender against their rights or their liberties. To impeach Strafford was Pym's master-stroke. From that hour the plain country squire, "the man in Gray's Inn Lane," became "King Pym."

While these grave issues were pending, George was a daily guest in the great house in Aldersgate Street, where the deep-set windows, low, heavily timbered ceilings, ponderous furniture, and dark tapestries, all conduced to shadow and gloom rather than to light and gaiety. Yet, when curtains were drawn, and candles lighted, the old low rooms were full of cheerfulness—or in the friendly winter twilight, when the logs blazed, and reflected flames danced upon the smooth darkness of mirrors, and on the polished silver of tankards and the parcel-gilt surface of rose-water dishes, hung like great golden shields against the black oak panelling. The house had been built under the first Tudor king, by the first Lord Llanbister, a famous lawyer, in an age when the legal profession was recruited chiefly from patrician families, and when blue blood was common at the Bar. Holbein's portrait of Lord Justice Llanbister, painted towards the close of his life, filled the place of honour in the picture-gallery, where a long row of family portraits hung above a choice selection of Italian and Flemish art.

To have made himself a welcome visitor in this peaceful and dignified home—nay, to be admitted there almost as a member of the family—seemed to George the highest privilege youthful ambition could desire. It was her ladyship's indulgent tenderness which had given him this privilege. She had an inexhaustible tenderness for the orphaned and the widowed; for helpless childhood; for all who were in need of a friend. Whatever there might be of imprudence in bringing a handsome and gifted youth into daily association with Lord Llanbister's young heiress, her ladyship disregarded. To her mind Geraldine was little more than a child, and light and shallow as a child. That there could be future sorrow for her *protégé*, or for the girl, in this friendly association of careless youth with youth, had never entered into Lady Llanbister's thoughts; nor was Geraldine's grandfather any more on the alert to discover peril in a boy-and-girl friendship. To him, even more than to his wife, Geraldine appeared still a child—a child who had outgrown her petticoats, but who was not the less a child in heart and intellect because of that rapid growth which had brought her fair young face above the level of his shoulder, the face which but a little while ago, as it seemed to him, had scarce reached his sword-hilt. Child as he deemed her, he had already begun to make plans for her establishment, and had pondered over the merits of more than one young nobleman among the most loyal of his Majesty's servants. His matrimonial views for his granddaughter were of the loftiest; and the gulf between his aspirations and an alliance with a nameless adventurer was too wide to allow of his suspecting danger when he saw the boy and girl happy in each other's company. George was teaching Geraldine French, a language of which she had at present only a rudimentary knowledge; for Lord Llanbister had educated her as if she had been that male heir whose non-existence he deplored. She had been taught Latin and Greek, and had advanced further in the exact sciences than many a lad of her age at Christchurch or Trinity, soon to write Master of Arts after his name.

" Yes, she has a pretty face, I grant you; but it is for finer qualities than an oval cheek and a melting eye that I value her. Having neither son nor grandson, you see, sir, I have done my best to make Mistress Geraldine a man in learning and courage, and frank, manly temper," the old man told his friends exultingly, when his heiress had been praised for youthful grace and beauty. " She can handle the foils as dexterously as her father did at her age, and could pink her antagonist, were she called upon to defend herself. She can ride the great-horse, and knows more about falconry than many a grown man. And she is better at Homer and Virgil than half the undergraduates at Oxford."

French, Italian, and the lighter accomplishments, had been neglected, and it was just these accomplishments which the wanderer George possessed. French had long been as his native language; he knew Italian almost as well, and was but little less familiar with Spanish: for the people among whom he had mostly lived were Cosmopolitan, an ever-mixed and ever-changing race— soldiers, peasants, priests, gipsies, diplomats, the high and low of many nations.

He and Geraldine read French and Italian together in the winter afternoons, when her formal lessons were over, and the weather was too foul for those long walks or rides which she loved. They had her ladyship's parlour for these recreative studies, a room looking into a large garden, beyond which, across buttressed walls, one caught glimpses of other gardens, those of Thanet House and Peter House, the residences of the Earls of Thanet and Kingston. The room had been beautified

with choice pictures, and Rouen china, when his lordship's second wife was brought home as a bride to this
old-world mansion in the East end of the town, from
which fashion was passing away to the Earl of Bedford's
palatial houses at Covent Garden.   Lady Llanbister
had never valued fashion, and the house in Aldersgate
Street was very dear to her, its only objection being
the long coach ride to Whitehall—or even to Denmark
House in the Strand, where she went daily while in
London, to wait upon her Queen.

She was more devoted to Henrietta Maria than ever
now, since that poor lady was in bitter trouble, assailed
by the malice of a populace that loved her not, the
butterfly existence having ended as summer ends, as it
were in a breath, when the first autumnal gusts sweep
the first dead leaves from the chestnuts, and the flowers
in the once gay borders shiver and droop, and all the
skies are grey.   All was grey in the Queen's life now.
She was full of sickening apprehensions and of heroic
resolves ; was now an angry lioness, and now a lamenting
dove.   She heard the angry voices under her palace
windows, and heard them again in her dreams, and saw
strange dream-pictures of the dull winter streets of
gloomy old London, mixed and jumbled with the bright
avenue beside the Seine, the gilded galleries of the
Louvre, Paris, the city of her girlhood, smiling like a
flower garden in the clear light and buoyant air.
Here, in this day of dread, the atmosphere seemed to
press upon her aching brow like a band of iron ; the
church bells seemed for ever tolling the knell of happier
days ; and when men and women were not talking of
Strafford and the Bishops, they were talking of the
small-pox and the Plague, both of which scourges were
on the increase.

Henrietta Maria remembered that evil year, 1625,
when the Plague had devastated London, and the Court
had taken refuge at Oxford.   She looked back and
remembered what it was to be a Queen in those days
—how absolute the power of the young King at her
side ; how strong his hold upon his subjects' minds and

hearts ; how firm his hold upon the sceptre. She remembered the love, the adulation, that had been lavished upon the Mignonne Lady from over the narrow sea, and how life, despite the pestilence that was filling graves in London, had seemed a triumphal procession along a lane of well-dressed people and kind faces. And now she heard the angry clamour of the populace, and sometimes the clash of steel, under her palace windows ; and her husband's brow was clouded, and his speech slower and more perplexed than of old ; and a hundred resolutions were made in a day ; and the wildest schemes were debated ; and she, the Queen, knew not whether to go back to France, or fly to Holland, or stay and face her enemies.

Mistress Geraldine never went unattended, either at her studies at home, or in her walks abroad. She had an old nurse whom she used exceeding ill and exceeding well, atoning by much tenderness and generosity for the little tyrannies and impertinences of a spoilt child. George was often reminded of Juliet and her nurse—in the tragedy he had seen at the Fortune Theatre—when he watched the petulance of the elderly dame and the playfulness of the girl. Mrs. Hillyer had been nurse to her young charge's mother, and was wont to praise that deceased lady, to the disparagement of her wayward mistress ; and it would have been hard to say whether the old servant or the young lady took most liberties, or had been most spoilt by indulgence.

Geraldine was too well accustomed to the company of this nurse-*gouvernante* to object to her presence ; and Mrs. Hillyer, at five-and-fifty, being as active and as hardy as a girl, proved no hindrance to the young people in their rambles in the fields and copses between Aldersgate Street and Highgate, where Geraldine loved to roam, attended by her nurse, and by a young woman who dressed her and helped with her tapestry and other fancy work, and who, being the daughter of a Shropshire vicar, was treated as a companion rather than as a waiting-maid. The young lady had also her own footman, who walked before her and her duenna whenever they ventured into the City streets, which happened rarely without George being also in attendance upon them.

It will be seen therefore that although these young people were allowed all the freedom of an old friendship, and spent many hours of each day together, they were seldom alone, and had but little scope for sentimental talk. Only in the high-flown language of the novels of the new French school, which they read together, had George any opportunity of telling his lovely companion that she was adored ; and in that stilted, heroical style of compliment, Love wore his most harmless aspect, a Cupid of the Court and the drawing-room, whose bow was filigree silver and his arrow feathered with thistle-down.

George still lodged at Westminster, but, save to sleep and dress there, spent little time at his lodgings, where he would have been passing lonely, since his friend and comrade Mountain was abroad, oscillating between Brussels and Paris, and very reticent in his occasional letters about the business that occupied him in either city. Indeed, George began to doubt his present or future usefulness to his master, and to feel despondent about a position which savoured of dependence. He would have fretted more, perhaps, at his dejected condition, without profession or fixed employment, had it not been for Lady Llanbister's goodness, who assured him that his services as teacher of modern languages to Geraldine were invaluable, and a sufficient return for any kindness or hospitality that was given to him in Aldersgate Street.

" It is we who must for ever remain in your debt," she told him, " since his lordship tells me you will accept no more substantial recompense than our thanks for the use of your talents."

During that long ordeal of the fallen minister (an agony which began on March 23rd, with Pym's formal capitulation of the charges connected with Strafford's government in Ireland, and which was to end on May 9th, with the King's despairing abandonment of his minister, amidst the clamour of a savage mob), George was a frequent witness of the proceedings, standing in the throng of eager spectators who crowded the narrow benches on those tiers of scaffolding which lined the Great Hall at Westminster, eleven stages high ; a most portentous spectacle, a scene never to be forgotten—the mere shadow of which thrills and awes us after two hundred and fifty years. A throne had been erected midway along the West Wall, and remained empty throughout the trial—symbol of a vanished sovereignty ; while the King and Queen occupied seats screened with a lattice, like a box at a theatre, but from which the King's impatient hand tore down the screen—possibly in order to hear and see better himself, or possibly with the hope that his presence might overawe the turbulent brood which had usurped an authority greater than his own, and against the thunder of whose voices, multiplied ten thousand-fold by those other voices of the outside rabble, Crown and Sceptre were but impotent baubles.

Who shall sound the depths of Charles Stuart's despair during that protracted trial, while the Great Hall was lined from floor to roof with a careless multitude, intent on this fight for life as on a gladiatorial show, the man with the net, the Christian among the lions ? For that indifferent rabble the trial was a vast picnic. Bottles passed from hand to hand ; men ate and drank, and were merry ; and the hubbub of voices rose loud in every interval of the proceedings ; nor was silence to be obtained, even when the foredoomed orator was pleading—not even for the pathos of that closing speech in which he spoke of his children—" the pledges that a saint in heaven left me "—and then, melted by the memory of love and loss in a life still in its prime, burst into tears.

Throughout that memorable scene, while the spring days lengthened, and the spring sunshine brightened, the King was in his place in the Great Hall, to watch and listen, to hope where all was hopeless, perhaps, being ever of a sanguine temper, and loth to grasp hard facts : to sicken with despair sometimes, when that inexorable accuser, John Pym, was pressing his charges home, seeking to establish a cumulative treason where no separate act was treasonable. Day after day that weary prisoner, broken in health, a martyr to the searching tortures of an inward malady, was brought along the smiling river, from his narrow cell in the Tower to the vast, crowded Hall, to be carried back to that fatal fortress at sunset, harassed, exhausted, and knowing that the ordeal was to begin again to-morrow. Once only, in a crisis of the trial, he pleaded for a brief respite in order to prepare his defence, which was grudgingly yielded.

George was deeply moved by this public tragedy, and contrived to be present day after day, not among the passers to and fro of bottles and venison pasties, but a silent spectator, wedged in the best place he could find for seeing and hearing, earnest and intent; and to his mind this long-drawn-out battle of one against many was more tragical than any play he had ever seen at Burbage's theatre, or the Red Bull at Clerkenwell. It was the reality of it all that thrilled him. A host of murders, the stage strewn with corpses, half a gallon of the property-man's rose-pink blood, could not move him like the pallid aspect of the King yonder—peering from his place, the long, oval face half in shadow and half in light, the taper fingers drumming on the front of the box, the stammering lips moving in piteous speech to those about him, the melancholy brow too early furrowed with care; and the Queen, ever restless and agitated, now admiring Strafford's hand as it moved in haughty gesticulation, now flinging herself back in angry despair while the elder Vane was being examined as to that fatal advice of Wentworth's at the Privy Council, that treasonable suggestion of bringing an Irish army into England to overawe an English Parliament.

George's feelings were all on the side of the prisoner, first because he was a great, brave, gifted man caught like a wild stag in the toils—the first illustrious victim to the cause of progress, the first sacrifice to this new Spirit of Liberty, which after all was but a narrow-minded and one-sided spirit, and as ready to deal unjustly with its opponents, being victorious, as it was to revolt against injustice. He was on Strafford's side of his own instinct; and also for the sake of those kind friends in Aldersgate Street, Lord Llanbister being one of that small minority of peers who voted in the fallen minister's favour—most of all for that dear lady who spent many a confidential hour with the Queen during this unhappy season, and who ever returned from Whitehall or Denmark House full of sorrow for all she had seen and heard there.

He knew afterwards that there had been a plot on hand to rescue the prisoner—that a vessel had been lying at anchor in the Pool of London, waiting to carry him to exile and safety, could but his custodians be bribed or propitiated. But the attempt to obtain possession of the Tower, by a certain Captain Billingsley, with a hundred armed followers, on an order from the King, had ignominiously failed; and the failure had lost Strafford his last chance of a lenient sentence. The King's ill-considered efforts had produced as direful an effect as if the headsman's axe had been flung into the fatal scale while the balance yet trembled betwixt life and death.

Never to be forgotten was that golden evening in the second week of May, when the whole household, down to the trencher-scrapers, were too much perturbed by the public agitations to settle to their usual Sunday calm, and when George and Geraldine, with the young lady's little court of two, had rambled as far as Islington, and had come back to Aldersgate by the light of the May moon, laden with hawthorn-blossom and meadow-flowers, to find his lordship waiting supper, by the dim light of a pair of candles, in his library, a spacious apartment adjoining the *salle-à-manger*.

"You are late, children," he said, as Geraldine flung down the May flowers on the table by which he sat, and bent her fair young face over the grey head that drooped upon his folded arms. "I doubt you must have rambled far."

"Far enough to make my old bones ache," grumbled the nurse.

" Haply to reduce your unwieldiness by a superfluous ounce or two," said the mistress.

" But every one is restless to-day," pursued Llanbister. "The city streets are full of anxious faces. Hark ! Sure that was my lady's step in the hall," he cried, starting up to welcome her whose absence ever left him melancholy.

Lady Llanbister entered while he was speaking, pale and agitated, her eyelids swollen by much weeping. They knew that she had come straight from Whitehall. Her coach had taken her to Mass at the Queen's Chapel in the morning ; and she had spent the day at the palace, in close company with that distracted lady. She sank down upon a chair which George brought for her, and suffered Geraldine to remove her mantle and hood, while he stood near them, with his anxious looks intent upon the beautiful, sad face, and while Nurse Hillyer and young Mistress Betty, the waiting-woman, stood agape, full of a dismal curiosity.

"Thy face foretells thou bringest no new hope !" said his lordship.

"Alas, no ! All is lost. He has yielded."

" Well, sweetheart, did not all the world know that he would yield ? Charles Stuart was ever like the Muscovite in his sledge—let the wolves press near enough, and howl loud enough, and he will fling them his dearest."

" It was of her he thought—of the Queen ; not of his own peril. He would have given them his life, could it have bought Strafford's pardon. Indeed, Llanbister, could you have seen that drawn countenance, those tortured looks, as I did to-day, in that brief glimpse I had of his Majesty when he passed through the Queen's closet, you would pity him."

" Pity !" cried the old man, in a voice that trembled with indignation. " A king should need no man's pity —or should accept none. Pity him ! Kings should be superior to pity, save in their subjection to disease and death. Their *acts* should give no scope for compassion.

From the hour of Strafford's impeachment, every action of the King in his minister's behalf has been ill-considered, feeble, disastrous, subversive of his own dignity, ruinous to the cause he championed. And this is the King who would stand or fall by Prerogative; who deemed Prerogative a word to conjure with; who was too strong to need the support of Parliaments; who would stand alone and show the people how happy he could make them! Prerogative! The Prerogative of an anointed King who surrenders to the clamour of a handful of yeomen-squires, and the howling of a mob that scarce knows what it howls for, and will catch any cry—'Down with Church and Bishops!' 'Down with Strafford!'—to excuse a riot, and afford the chance of plundered shops, and a taste of blood."

"My lady looks as if she would swoon," interposed Geraldine. "I'll warrant she has eaten nothing all this bitter day. Had we not best go in to supper, sir?"

"Wisely urged, wench! The world must go to supper, though we have a poltroon for our King, and though the wisest head in the kingdom must fall."

"Oh, sir, degrade him not by such a name. Let not him who has never seen his wife and children in peril, and has never been told that by one act alone he can save them, despise his Majesty's weakness of this day. We might all prove wanting, were we tried in the same fire," Lady Llanbister urged sadly.

"He had given his word—a King's word—for Strafford's life and honour; he bade him come to London when he was safe among friends in the North, and knew there was peril in coming; he swore that not a hair of that noble head should be harmed," cried Llanbister, on fire with indignation. "But Charles Stuart was ever thus. He has neither heart nor memory, save for the companions of the hour, who can hang upon him and shed their tears upon his breast. He is all tenderness to a wife; but what has he ever been to a friend? I was in the chapel at Porchester when the news was brought him of Buckingham's death. His cheek whitened, but he bade the chaplain go on with his prayers. Was it a sublime fortitude, think you, the calmness of a martyr, or coldness of heart, the inability to love deeply and truly? I say the latter. Why, from the first hour of trouble he has turned a cold shoulder upon Strafford. The attack upon his minister is no sooner made than this champion of Prerogative is grovelling in the dust before Pym and his followers. 'I grant Wentworth a criminal,' he cries, 'a tyrant—a traitor, whatever my faithful Commons please to call him. Let him never again be trusted with the meanest office in the state; let him never more approach my person; let him rot in the Tower, if it please your honourable House; but I pray you for my sake spare his miserable life.' Do you think Thomas Wentworth set a high price upon such advocacy? Why, there is more magnanimity in Strafford's late letter to the King than in any act of his Majesty's life. I say again, Viola, and again, and again, if need be, Charles Stuart has stamped himself a poltroon."

"You know not the struggle between conscience and policy."

"What avails the struggle if the upshot be surrender?"

"He consulted the Bishops. He had them with him yesterday—and again to-day."

"And were they for conscience or policy?"

"Bishop Juxon bade him refuse his assent to the Bill, had he but a shadow of a doubt that 'twas a righteous sentence. Dr. Williams took another view."

"And turned the scale upon the side of policy, I'll wager. He was always the most politic of clerics; a lawyer in lawn sleeves."

"He bade his Majesty remember that he has a public and a private conscience—and that in this question his affection for Strafford as a man must give way to his duty as a King, which is to regard the welfare of his people, and to stem that rebellious tide of anger and terror which has risen flood-high throughout the kingdom —caused by the misgovernment of him whose blood the people clamour for."

"Did the King remember another people who

clamoured for innocent blood—or that Roman judge who yielded to their importunity? Nay, I touch upon blasphemy when I compare *that* victim with this. Strafford is not guiltless. There are some of his dealings in Ireland which justice must condemn ; but there was also much of wisdom and generosity in his government of that troublesome people. And to the King he was of all servants the most devoted. Well, Charles obeyed the worldly guide—rather than the heavenly one? Strafford's blood will appease the rebellious spirits, and restore peace. Yet think you, wife, now that Parliament and mob know what a flexible reed is the sceptre that rules them they will not for evermore take the upper hand ? "

It was a melancholy meal to which they sat down presently in the adjacent dining parlour.

Lord and Lady Llanbister supped in a stately solitude at the chief table, while George sat at Mrs. Hillyer's table, with Mistress Betty, and Geraldine, who, being still in a state of pupilage, was allowed to preside over her little court, and to be as gay and as trivial as she liked, at a respectful distance from her grandfather.

CHAPTER VIII.

"SO RUNS THE WORLD AWAY."

NEVER could George forget those three days of an awful suspense, in which the household in Aldersgate Street waited, sick at heart, for Strafford's doom. To George, as to his patroness, it seemed impossible but that kingly power should intervene to save the truest servant that ever spent brains, and estate, and health, and life, in his Sovereign's service. Could those yelping curs in the City scare the monarch who had bragged of Prerogative, and hound a great man to death? and could the King, who had sworn that not a hair of his servant's head should be harmed, with his own royal hand condemn that head to the block? Not long would Strafford's life have lasted had the capital sentence been annulled; for a mortal disease was upon him, and his name was written in the register of untimely death. But the life-history of Charles Stuart would have been saved from that one ineffaceable stain for which even his admirers and apologists can find no excuse.

The days hurried by; at Whitehall hesitations, vague schemes, wavering to and fro, the King and his friends made irresolute by their fear of the rabble outside, a new and unknown danger, which might presage a palace in flames, a Queen and her children murdered; in the City blind fury, unreasoning malignity, the cry for Strafford's head; as if, with that wise brain lying in the dust, the millennium would be at hand.

The days did not pass without one feeble intercession

on the part of Majesty. The King sent his son, the youthful Prince of Wales, with a message to the Lords, praying for a mitigation of Strafford's sentence—from death to close imprisonment for life—clemency which would afford an unspeakable contentment to him, their King. Such unspeakable contentment was not granted him ; and Thomas Wentworth was spared that mockery of mercy which would have mewed his fiery spirit in a prison-cell, crushed and killed him, as his once ally Sir John Eliot was killed, by the heart-sickness of captivity. The axe made an easier end of his troubles.

The summer followed quickly on that tragical May, and George and his young pupil found the golden afternoons all too short, as they roamed along the flowery banks between Isleworth and Hampton, or took longer journeys in the capacious wherry which, with two sturdy watermen, was reserved for Mistress Geraldine's use. This young lady was Queen Regnant at Isleworth, and had grooms, horses, falcons, dogs, and boats at her sovereign disposal. The watermen were her own servants, and wore her livery of brown and orange, with her paternal arms in gold embroidery upon their collars, when in state attire, but wore lighter jackets of thin kersey when they bent over their oars. She was very imperious with them in her childish arrogance, having grounded her manner to the lower *classis* on the traditions of Queen Elizabeth ; but she was lavish of gifts and of kindly services to their wives and children, and their cottages and gardens were the prettiest in the village of Isleworth, where her grandfather owned all the property not owned by the Lord of Syon House.

Before the family migrated from the City to their summer retreat, Lady Llanbister insisted that George's position should be put on a better footing. Mountain had now been away from England for nearly half a year, and the young man had been left to his own devices, with a garret in the lodging-house at Westminster, and an occasional remittance of money from his master,

who wrote of himself as both busy and prospering.
Lady Llanbister saw the danger of bad company in
taverns, and dancing gardens, and bear-pits, and other
public resorts, for so young a man as George, who had
his evenings free, and nothing to do but amuse himself.
Nor was it right, she reminded her husband, that her
protégé should continue to do a tutor's work without a
tutor's pay.

"It is no longer friendly, casual instruction which he
gives Geraldine," she said. "He is teaching her three
languages, and expounding the best books in each.
You know what a troublesome pupil she is——"

"I know she is a high-spirited wench, and loves to
ride her horse and fly her peregrine better than to sit
all a summer morning with her nose in a book," interrupted his lordship, who was too fond of his granddaughter to allow the faintest hint that she fell short
of feminine perfection. "Well, she will make a better
wife for an ambassador if she can jabber in a babel of
tongues, and bandy lying compliments with an *olla
podrida* of secretaries. As for this boy of yours, of course
he must be paid for his services, and so much the higher
wages if she boxes his ears, or throws an accidence-book
at him when his lesson plagues her."

"I should not forgive her for any such boorish
incivility. No, Llanbister, your granddaughter is a
lady——"

"Albeit a fiery jade."

"And George Mountain is a gentleman, although you
speak of him so slightingly."

"Did I slight him, *ma douce*? Nay, thou knowest
I would not slight any favourite of thine, on four legs,
or on two. I would no sooner belittle thy paragon page
than kick the spot dog that follows thy coach. But as
for gentleman quotha, that depends on the meaning
you give the word. Friend Mountain is no hidalgo;
and the stray imp he adopted as a follower could
scarce brag of blue blood. But Master George is a
very pretty fellow, and I prythee give him handsome
wages."

"And, if your lordship had no objection, I would have him live with us altogether, rather than let him be tempted by his loneliness to waste his evenings in a tavern."

"Aye ; our taverns are no longer the resort of harmless wits and playwrights, the Sons of Apollo, as in old Jonson's time. They are the hot-beds of sedition, the nurseries of rebels."

Thus it came that George had his own chamber and study at Isleworth, a little suite of rooms in the roof, with deep-set dormers shadowed by heavily timbered gables. His lattices commanded a fine reach of the river, eastward to the village of Kew, westward to the wooded hill of Richmond, where the king's new park had given offence to many proprietors whose ground had been taken from them in a high-handed fashion to map out the line of wall according to his Majesty's taste.

The summer of 1641 passed like a golden dream for the young pedagogue and his wayward but not ungrateful pupil. Strange that such joyous days could be gliding by, in such a peaceful and gracious scene ; a river smoothly flowing between grassy banks tapestried with flowers, and under dipping willows from whose shade the dragon-fly's emerald wings flashed out like living light. All through England, perhaps, by meadow and stream, there were unconscious lovers as happy as George and his pupil, young hearts beating as high, young eyes looking forward to a radiant future. And yet it was a year of unexampled terror and trouble ; the year of the Irish Rebellion ; the year of that great indictment against the Sovereign, in which every evil of Charles Stuart's reign, every act of oppression, every encroachment upon the liberty of the subject, wrongs redressed as well as wrongs unredressed, were massed together in one tremendous charge, and published through the length and breadth of the land.

It was a year of bitter strife between Prelacy and Nonconformity, Laud, the Primate, lying in the Tower through all the bright summer-time, through the slow fading of the year, without much hope of release, a weary captive in that cell from whose barred window his feeble old hands had been stretched out to bless and absolve the murdered Strafford. It was such a year as the Church had not seen since the Reformation. Never, perhaps, had an established Church encountered such public enmity, since the first Christian church was founded. A clergyman of the High Church party, or suspected, by his appearance, to belong to that detested body, could hardly walk the streets of London and escape insult ; for it was ten to one he would have a rabble mob at his heels before he reached his own door, jeering at him as a Jesuit—a Baal's priest, an Abbey-lubber, a Canterbury whelp.

But these troubles were only heard of at Isleworth from an occasional visitor—and Lord Llanbister, having given his adhesion to the older faith, took little heed of these religious animosities among Protestants. Advancing age had in no wise blunted the keenness of his mind, but it had brought with it those larger and more tolerant views, that serenity of temper and generous indulgence for the errors of other people, which in some rare and noble natures make the decline of life resemble the pensive close of a summer evening.

The growing virulence of the quarrel between Prelacy and a Free Church, with all the vulgar brawling and bad blood that went along with it, made her ladyship so much the more intent upon those secret efforts, tending towards the restoration of the old Faith, which the Queen and her spiritual directors had at heart. It would seem that in the disruption of the heretic Church and the persecution of heretic Bishops, Rome's opportunity must be at hand ; and there were Papal agents in London to help in the work, agents with whom Francis Mountain had friendly or business relations, and for whom, or for Queen Henrietta, he crossed the Channel almost as often as a Queen's messenger of the present day, making meteoric appearances in Aldersgate Street or at Isleworth, and ever seeming warmly attached to his squire-page or adopted son.

" Thou art better off in this snug nest than gipsying with me, George," he said ; " but remember, if ever your great friends cast you off, or you begin to pine for adventure, whatever roof covers my head shall shelter yours."

Lady Llanbister had talked often and earnestly with George of that Church which held so vast a place in her thoughts ; but she had not been over-zealous to convert him from his lax notions of spiritual things to the most exacting of all creeds.

" I love to talk with you of the one true faith," she told him, as they walked alone by the moat one August evening ; " but I will never urge you to act against your convictions. I wait for the hour when your own heart will speak, and you will come for strength and comfort to that eternal and invincible Church of which I am a so humble member."

There was one visitor at Isleworth—who appeared at long intervals during the summer and autumn of 1641 and 1642—whose presence was a subject of curiosity and even distrust to George, who had never caught so much as a glimpse of his face, though from the window of the oak parlour where Geraldine worked at her lessons he had once seen the gentleman leaving the house—a tallish man, of a lean figure, and an almost Puritanical plainness of attire. He was the same man, George thought, that he had seen in the dusk of an April evening, creeping up the great staircase in Aldersgate Street ; and he remembered how on that particular evening Lady Llanbister had been absent from the family sitting-room till long after nine o'clock, when she made her tardy appearance at the supper-table, looking anxious and weary. There was a kind of jealousy, perhaps, in George's dislike of this unknown gentleman, whom he took for a crypto Jesuit, one of those missionary priests who had been rife in London of late years, and probably an ally of her ladyship's brother at Rome.

The King was again in the north, where the situation had been ameliorated by his concessions ; but it was while the pacification of Scotland was tending towards a sense of security that terror and amazement ran through the nation at the news of that savage slaughter of the Protestant population in Ireland, more horrible in its relentless cruelty than the dark story of the Sicilian Vespers, or the massacre of Saint Bartholomew's Eve.

With the late autumn Lord Llanbister and his family removed to Aldersgate Street, travelling by way of Brentford and Kensington in two capacious coaches, while their baggage and servants were conveyed down the river to the Old Swan Stairs, west of London Bridge, in his lordship's barge, which then returned to Isleworth, to be laid up there for the winter. George went with them, riding a well-bred hackney that had been assigned to his use, and which he loved as if the beast had been his brother. He was so fine a rider as to win his lordship's approval, who thirty years before had been no less accomplished a horseman than his friend, the famous Lord Herbert of Cherbury. George had learnt to handle a horse in schools so various that it would have been strange had he ridden ill. From the half-broken Arabs of Andalusia, through all the varieties of hackneys bred in Provence and Dauphiny, to the rough percherons of Brittany and Normandy, and the blood horses of the Parisian riding-school, experience had taught him what a horse could do and how he could best be governed ; with what artifices to counter the tricks of the beast—when to soothe, when to threaten, and when to punish. His hap-hazard life with a man of adventurous spirit and dauntless pluck had given him advantages which no home-bred youth enjoys ; and the old nobleman, prejudiced against a lad who could show no claim to gentle ancestors, was fain to confess that this youngster equalled the highest born among his contemporaries in good looks, good manners, and manly exercises.

"I begin to think your crow is something of a swan after all, dear wife," he said, as he watched his granddaughter's tutor riding beside her coach through the pale November mists that hung over Knightsbridge and Hyde Park. "'Twas clever of you to discover such accomplishments in scatterbrain Mountain's dependent."

"'Tis a sorry fate to be a dependent even upon us," sighed her ladyship; "but 'twas dreadful to think of him as a hanger-on of Mountain's, who is a blind follower of that perilous woman, Madame de Chevreuse."

"Nay, my heart, I will not hear thee belie poor Marie de Rohan. I grant you she has been ever unfortunate —harassed—in debt—separated from daughter and husband——"

"They all three support *that* affliction with exemplary patience," said Lady Llanbister, with ineffable scorn, "but Madame de Chevreuse is ever ready to use it as a tragical plea, when she teases the Cardinal to let her go back to Paris."

"I doubt you are like other lovely women, dearest, and can brook no rival; and you hate poor Marie because she is handsome."

"Nay, Llanbister, you know better than to think so meanly of me. I despise her for having misused her beauty."

"That depends on what we call misuse, child. I doubt if Helen of Troy made more clatter in the world with her god-born charms than Marie de Rohan has caused with hers. Was it a waste of beauty to ride across the Pyrenees in doublet and hose, the admiration of everybody she met, since never had so handsome a cavalier, or so fine a leg and foot been seen 'twixt Paris and Madrid? 'Twas an escapade to exalt her into a heroine for ever. But I grant you she is reckless, and will not stand on punctilio with Francis Mountain, should it suit her to make him carry compromising papers, or jeopardise his neck any other way in her service. But you have to remember how good a Papist she is, and how zealous for the true Church; and you may be sure there will be ready absolution for any private peccadilloes she has to confess."

They were in London in time to witness the sumptuous reception which the City offered to the King on his return from Scotland. They saw the narrow streets hung with tapestry, the conduits running "claret wine," and Moorgate adorned with a splendid tent, in which Lord Mayor Gournay waited his Sovereign's coming. They saw the King step from his coach, smiling and *débonnaire*, and mount his horse, and ride through the decorated streets, attended by a cavalcade of loyal citizens in gala dress, while joy-bells rang, and all the populace shouted for joy, and trumpets sounded the passing of the King from station to station, and the choristers of St. Paul's stood on the steps of the Cathedral singing an anthem of welcome. And as the early November dust crept through the narrow ways, and darkness dropped a veil on the City, though 'twas not long after the festival dinner, torches flared along the streets, and lights shone from every window, till the winter night grew glorious as summer noon. And the heart of the King beat high at this festal greeting,—and he knew not how transient was this outburst of cordial feeling, which seemed so rich in the promise of peace, nor that Lord Mayor Gournay would expiate his loyalty by-and-bye in the Tower, surrendering the civic chain to a citizen of republican principles.

This ebullition of love from Lord Mayor and Aldermen and Common Council was still in the air, and their Majesties' hearts were still aglow with gratitude, while that terrible indictment against Charles Stuart, that cold-blooded recapitulation and solemn summing up of all the evils and iniquities, injustices and cruelties, of his reign, of which he, or his servants for him, had been guilty, was being debated, article by article, at Westminster, the most memorable assault upon kingly authority ever imagined by a nation's representatives, and destined to stand out from the level page of Parliamentary history for evermore, as the Grand

Remonstrance. For this were the Commons sitting fourteen hours at a stretch ; for this men beheld the hitherto unknown spectacle of candles brought into the House at dusk, during a debate which continued through the small hours of the winter morning, in light that was but Milton's "darkness visible." For this hot blood raged and swords were drawn, and men's hands were at each other's throats.

And again, as in the crisis of Strafford's fate, the King paltered with the situation—complained and complied—protested and submitted—threatened and flattered —saw the imminence of the danger, and saw it not— would have Whitehall fortified—would fling himself into the arms of his dear people—blew hot—blew cold—and hastened the ruin of his rights and his prestige.

Was it born with him, this helpless hesitancy of mind as of speech, this instability of purpose that seemed akin to the feeble limbs of his infancy, too weak to carry their frail burden till the sickly prince was seven years old ?   Had some pre-natal curse hung heavy upon him from his cradle ?

As over all the life of James there had fallen the dark shadow of one dreadful night at Holyrood, might not the conspiracy at Gowrie House, that darker and more mysterious tragedy of the two slaughtered brothers, have set its deadly mark upon the character of his son, born immediately after the fatal date ? There were those who said that James's Queen was an unhappy woman, if not a false wife, and that Alexander Gowrie, slain in the flower of his youth, was dearer to her than her husband.   There was so much that was noble in the man Charles Stuart—so much of Royal largeness of mind and knightly instinct to mark the descendant of eight centuries of kings, that it would seem as if some latent strain of feminine apprehension and despondency, born with him, could alone account for all that was weak, false, and cowardly in his conduct as a king.

Troubles abroad had but little disturbing influence

upon the peaceful days and happy evenings in Aldersgate House. In his studious home in the same street, John Milton was on fire with lofty aspirations and eager interest in the conflict between King and Commons, Prelacy and Presbyterianism; but those who sat by the fireside in my lady's panelled parlour heard the rising of the storm as something afar off, in which their part was only to pity their Sovereign's misfortunes, and to pray for the return of peace. Lord Llanbister was too old to serve his King in the field, and had of late been but little at Court, all that he had ever offered of counsel being heard with a smiling politeness on his Majesty's part, and making no more impression than the light spray of the fountain made on the marble margin it sprinkled, in that pleasant semi-circular garden at Hampton Court, where Llanbister walked bareheaded at Charles's side. He knew that there was but one counsellor whose advice—accentuated by all the notes in the gamut of womanly passion—was ever taken, and that fatal counsellor was the Queen.

"I might govern England at this hour, old as I am, and sitting in this arm-chair," he told George, "were I of an aspiring temper, and my wife subservient to my ambition; for she, who has the stronger intellect, can do what she likes with Henrietta; and Henrietta rules the King. Indeed, since a woman's will *is* to rule—'twere better for the nation if that wayward will were guided by an old man's experience. 'Tis ill for England, perhaps, that I am not adapted for underhand policy. But there is a young man lately come to Court, one Edward Hyde, a Wiltshire squire's son, who is as deep as Machiavel, and ought to be of use in his Majesty's difficulties."

The beginning of the end had come in the attempted arrest of the Five Members, an act so ill-judged that they who knew the King guessed at once that it had been urged upon him by his wife. A failure so ignominious was indeed inspired by one woman, and betrayed by another, her confidante: for it was Lady Carlisle's warning to Pym—whom the uncharitable called her lover—which made the attempted arrest so futile an assault upon the privileges of the House, and so piteous a humiliation for him who had essayed the despot's part without the despot's power.

That fatal aggression raised such a storm as neither the King nor his feminine counsellor had imagined possible. London was in arms; and Charles and Henrietta left Whitehall in the dark wintry weather, for the desolate and bloomless gardens and groves of Hampton Court—left as fugitives in all but the name; and from Hampton Court, where their enemies had them within too easy reach, they speedily retired to Windsor, leaving the Parliament master of the field, and the City, which had so lately welcomed the Sovereign, now boisterously acclaiming the triumph of the Five Members, carried by water to Westminster, upon a river covered with boats and barges, while guns thundered, and streamers waved, and all along the shore trumpets and drums swelled the triumph, and trained bands and mob rolled westward in frantic jubilation, yelling their party cries against Bishops and Papist lords, and jeering at the absent King and his cavaliers.

Lady Llanbister's chief anxiety during this time of trouble was to keep her husband out of the fray. She knew upon how thin a thread that waning life depended; for his lordship's physician had warned her that any fever of mind, any paroxysm of anger, the sudden flame of a fiery soul, might be fatal. Her constant care was to avert distress from the devoted husband who had given her so many years of unalterable affection, a love that had deepened as the years went on. Love and praise, such chivalrous homage as poets sing of in a golden age—all had been hers from the husband who in years might have been her father. She was paying him in some wise for that romantic love by an affectionate watchfulness that gave her leisure for but little thought of anybody else in the world.

And thus it happened that George and Geraldine were almost as free to follow their own devices as our first parents in the Garden of Eden, before the snake surprised them there. Here there was no serpent. There was only a growing love, of which one was still unconscious, and which the other hardly acknowledged in his own secret thoughts. Geraldine, in spite of her Elizabethan arrogance, her audacity in advancing her own opinions and contradicting her elders, was so childish and simple in all her feelings and inclinations, that for a man to talk to her of love would have been a kind of profanation. Here was no daughter of romantic Italy, ready to tell the moon her passion for the stranger who had held her hand and whispered in her ear in the brief contact of a stately dance; but a high-bred English girl, who would have deemed the worship of years, and the character of King Arthur, only enough to deserve her favour—and whose pride would have been quick to take alarm had she known that the delight she took in her tutor's company, and in teasing him, was the dawning of love.

George kept a watch upon himself, and grew more stately as he grew more fond, trusting to his power of self-control to retain the dear girl's friendship and enjoy her society, and keep the secret of his passion till the end of time. He was very sure that his love was hopeless; for he rather exaggerated than lessened the gulf between his obscurity and the nobly born heiress. He listened with an iron calm when Lord Llanbister enlarged upon the virtues and dignities of that *preux-chevalier*, Mistress Geraldine's future husband, as yet unnamed and unknown; though every word the old man said seemed like the dropping of ice-cold water on an aching wound.

"God knows when I shall find a mate for my pretty bird, now that all the young noblemen who love their King, and all who hate him, are cutting each other's throats," he said, sauntering with George by the river in the late October of 1642, after the battle of Edgehill; "but once this war ended—as it must end, haply, before very long, by the triumph of his Majesty and the good cause—I shall seek such an alliance for my granddaughter as shall give me the security of her happiness in this life : and then I can say '*Nunc Dimittis*,' and go to join my murdered son in that Paradise of Rest where poor ill-used Dr. Laud tells us the dead await their uprising at the Last Judgment."

George listened, not once only, but on many occasions, while his lordship enlarged upon his matrimonial views, and criticised his granddaughter's character. He listened assentingly, with an outward calm which indicated heroic patience, since every day he lived in Geraldine's company made the prospect of the inevitable parting, and the thought of that thrice-blessed lover who was to woo and win her, more intolerable.

" I am grateful to you, friend, for your capable teaching," the old man told him, brimming over with benevolence, and assured that his praise must make his dependent happy. " The child read a chapter of ' Don Quixote ' to me last night, while you were helping my lady with her house accounts. I was a fair Spanish scholar in my youth, and I read that admirable book so often as to imprint certain chapters on my memory, whereby the language is still familiar, and comes back to me as the child pronounces it. You have taught her well."

" I am proud that you should think so, sir."

" Nay, the pedagogue's is an ungracious office ; and I doubt she hates you for all the pains you have taken with her. So 'twere hard if I stinted commendation that is your due. Her manners are a trifle more sober, too, which improvement I also credit to your account. Not that I would see her otherwise than gay ; but she was at times too boisterous a hoyden for a young woman of high rank."

Through all the troublous year that saw the King's repulse by Hotham at Hull ; the raising of the standard at Nottingham, in the teeth of the tempest, a royal flag set up only to be thrown down ; from the bloody opening of the war at Edgehill, which lost the King his faithful Earl of Lindsey, and many another gallant soldier, but which proved at least that the Sovereign who was so weak to govern was brave to recklessness in the field ; through battles and rumours of battles, and many false reports as to the conquering side—a fight won by the King announced by some hard-riding premature messenger, bursting breathless into the startled senate-house, as a triumph for the Parliament ; or a field won by Essex and his orange scarfs heralded as another victory for the King—through all the agitating events of that tragical time, the domestic life at Isleworth and at Aldersgate Street knew little change. The battle and sacking of Brentford brought the sound of war within a mile of his lordship's waterside house, but by good fortune at a season when the family were in London ; and in London the streets were barred with iron chains, and the citizens were in a fever of apprehension during that February of 1642-43, a period when there were still many among the best and wisest of the nation who longed for reconciliation and concord, and would have done much to secure a quiet ending to the struggle, together with the assurance of their privileges and liberties. That assurance his Majesty was just as far from yielding to his lieges as he had been before the war began.

He had endured great hardships, and had seen his subjects wasting their lives for him, Englishman against Englishman, brother against brother sometimes. He had tasted the bitter pain of severance from wife and children. He had been dinnerless and roofless. He had suffered discomforts and reverses that would have broken the spirit of many a stronger man ; but he was still the same Charles Stuart who went down to the House of Commons with a casual rabble at his heels, to arrest the five most powerful members of that House ; and he would have taken as ill-judged a step to-morrow had occasion offered.

While the royal fortunes waxed and waned, Geraldine bloomed into early womanhood, with such gradual

unfolding of new charms and graces that her elders
remained almost unconscious of the fact that the mad-
cap child was becoming a woman, with a woman's heart
to love and suffer, and to break, perhaps, if love proved
unhappy.

Lord Llanbister had not been indifferent to his
Sovereign's misfortunes, though it might be that long
experience of the King's tactics, in Scotland and in
England, had made him less enthusiastic than younger
members of the Cavalier party. But he was not the
less loyal ; and while apologising for length of years
and feeble limbs, which forbade his carrying sword and
petronel, and riding down the crop-eared Parliament-
arians, he provided more than his share of the sinews
of war, and had given the strongest testimony to his
fidelity by a journey to Beverley in the early summer,
at which loyal little town he found Majesty poorly
accommodated, and sadly out-at-elbows, though the
King's deprivations and inconveniences of that time were
small as compared with the hardships which he suffered
with such heroic fortitude during the progress of the
war. Indeed, it may be said that from this time
forward Charles Stuart knew no more of royal splendour,
till that too brief season on the threshold of doom when
he found himself once again at Windsor, once more
pacing those noble rooms which his taste had beautified
with all that is most perfect in the painter's art—
rejoicing in those art treasures, in that stately palace,
in the deference paid to royalty, but a lonely man, and
pining for the wife and children he loved. But those
halcyon days at Windsor were still far off in the un-
foreseen future, and the fortunes of war still favoured
the King rather than that curious mixed rabble of
'prentice lads, crop-eared Nonconformists, and German
mercenaries, who made up the greater part of Essex's
army.

And at this time there were some lookers-on, and
some in the thick of the fray, who asked whether Essex
really wanted to beat the King? Even the Parliament
was beginning to question its General's whole-hearted-

ness, and to ask whether he had seized his opportunities,
and made the most of his advantages—or whether he
was not at heart a believer in the divine right of an
anointed king, anxious to bring about a reconciliation
between the Sovereign and his people, rather than to
compass the liberty of the subject and the downfall of
absolute monarchy in one bloody field?

CHAPTER IX.

"AH! BITTER SWEET."

GEORGE had seen three yule logs burning upon the hearth in Aldersgate Street, the hearth of that spacious panelled parlour with its four deep-set windows, each provided with a cushioned seat, and its convenient recesses and roomy ingle-nook, where, on cold winter nights, Lord Llanbister sat on an oak bench and smoked his after-supper pipe. This panelled parlour was the family resort and meeting-place. Here my lady had her chamber organ, which she touched so sweetly; and here Geraldine had her pair of virginals, her lute and theorbo; and here an Italian lady came thrice a week to give her a music-lesson. They were as musical in the tranquil hour after supper as Mr. John Milton and his pupils lower down the street, that pedantic gentleman whose handsome features and smooth hair Geraldine knew so well, and of whom she was inclined to make mock—first because he was a schoolmaster, and walked abroad with half a dozen raw-boned hobble-de-hoys at his heels; and next because his hair was straight.

Thrice had George kept Christmas with this kind family, making a solemn and a happy festival of that "Youle" which sectaries denounced and fanaticism banished; and when the third Christmas came round, it seemed to him as if he had lived with them and belonged to them always, and as if all his adventurous youth with Francis Mountain was the story of another life, which he had read, and which he remembered and looked back upon with a curious impersonal interest.

How strangely different the rough-and-tumble of those roving years from the repose of this aristocratic household!—so simple and unpretentious in its quiet stateliness; the little army of servants moving about their work with a calm regularity, never demonstratively busy, yet never idle; her ladyship's mind directing everything, harmonising everything, and contriving that all who served her should be at ease and happy. There were none but smiling faces in the household, save when ill news of some near kinsman fighting for the King or the Commons caused tears and anxious looks; and then the kind mistress was ready with comforting, hopeful words, and contrived to get the earliest possible news of the soldier, wherever, or on whichever side, he might be engaged.

Three times the great Yule log had sent its flames up the black gulf of chimney—flames that seemed to dance and leap for pride and joyousness; three times the huge limb of oak had flamed and roared and crackled and spluttered; wasting itself in a fierce fever of impatience, like the ardour of youthful hopes and loves, George thought; and burning its heart out for very wantonness, only to slacken its fires, and fade slowly to a faint pale grey, and crumble to ashes and nothingness, like age, thought George. Two summers, and three winters, he had lived under Lord Llanbister's roof, and had been to her Ladyship almost as a son, helping her in her alms-giving, her patronage of struggling poets and painters, and her household accounts, which involved much labour, as Lord Llanbister had of late delegated all financial management to his clever and capable wife. The house steward's office had become almost a sinecure; but as he was an old man, and adored his mistress, there were no complainings.

With so much money going out to the King, it was needful to keep a wary eye upon all other outgoings, and in February 1643, the second year of the civil war, Lady Llanbister resolved upon a step which distressed her, but which she felt it incumbent upon her to take. She reduced her establishment to little more than half its customary number, dismissing most of the young servants, who would be able to get fresh places ; or at the worst the men could find employment with the army, and would be doing well by fighting for their king. So curtailed, there was still a sober dignity in the spacious, rambling house at Isleworth, the old servants moving about slowly and quietly, and doing everything well, but taking an unconscionable time about it. Neither master nor mistress was permitted to feel a lessened state.

When Lady Day came round, George resolutely refused the little packet of gold which her ladyship handed him for his quarterly wage.

"Let me help the King by at least so much as that, dear lady. I have a well-stocked wardrobe, and a gala suit just home from the tailor's. I want nothing, and have no more need of money in this house than if it were Eden before the Fall."

To him it was Eden ; but he feared that the hour of the Angel with the flaming sword, the dismal hour of expulsion, must be near ; and he ended his little speech with a sigh.

"It shall be as you wish, George," she answered, smiling at him. "His Majesty has bitter need of all the money we can spare."

She always addressed him by his Christian name, and he fancied sometimes she had a pleasure in pronouncing it. Her voice would linger on the sound, and she would look at him with a strange sadness. Once she called him Charles, and started as if she had been shot, then burst into tears, rose suddenly, and left the room. Was it the King's name that had come unawares to her lips ; and were her tears for the Sovereign's sorrows? He thought not ; and that the name must have a sadder association.

And all this time Mistress Geraldine was growing handsomer, and more womanly, more arrogant, more wilful—yet with intervals of melting kindness—a beautiful, fitful creature, to whom life was sometimes earnest and sometimes sport.

In her sportive moods she loved to tease her tutor,

and would often upbraid him for not being with the King.

"I have more important work to do here. When your education is finished, I may join the royal army."

"My education will never be finished. I mean to go on learning all my life. I wish to be a remarkable woman."

"You are that already," he said, forgetting his usual reticence.

"As how?"

"The handsomest among a thousand. Is not that enough fame for a woman?"

"No, sir—beauty is not fame. I shall like to be great as Elizabeth was, who was far from handsome, though I fear she was somewhat vain."

"Somewhat is not the measure. Her vanity was egregious. She would have bartered all her greatness— and England's into the bargain—seen Spanish ships ride exulting in the Downs—only to be as lovely as her unhappy cousin, and to have had true lovers—not lying flatterers—at her feet."

"You do ill to disparage her, sir. She was a marvellous woman, and I revere her memory."

He had observed admiringly that personal vanity had no place in Geraldine's character. She was haughty and ambitious; she wanted to be first among the first, to excel in every accomplishment she attempted : but if she knew she was beautiful, she took no pride in the fact, but passed it by as of no account. She was careless of her attire, which was always rich and in good taste, for it was chosen by Lady Llanbister, who had an exquisite appreciation of form and colour, and loved to set off the girl's fresh young beauty. Geraldine paid but little heed to her clothes ; and this unconsciousness or calm disdain of her own charms gave something of queenliness to her air, as of a person superior to externals.

As, with each passing day, the pupil grew lovelier and more irresistible, the tutor drew further aloof, until his graver manner began to exercise a repressing influence, and Geraldine left off teasing him, and exercised all her malice upon her waiting-woman, Mistress Betty, who was tolerably pretty and exceedingly vain, spending every shilling she could scrape together upon finery, and cherishing the conviction that Mr. George Mountain was deeply in love with her, though he had not yet avowed his passion. She was, indeed, ever on the alert for that avowal, saw a proposal faltering on his lips when he asked her for a cup of chocolate, and took his fondling of her favourite spaniel for the sign of a tender passion for herself. His shyness kept him at a distance, she thought, and he took a romantic pleasure in caressing the creature she loved; while, could she have read him aright, she would have known that it was because he had not the faintest interest in the dog's mistress that he diverted himself with the dog.

Geraldine discovered Mistress Betty's secret, which indeed that young person took little pains to hide; but she was not able to divine George's feelings; and as he was now distant and cold towards herself, she began to suspect that he had fallen in love with her companion.

She said as much to her old nurse one evening, when she had quarrelled with poor Betty all through the business of the toilet.

"The simpleton is in love," she complained, "and cannot even put my gold comb straight on my head. Or perhaps she tries to make me hideous, lest her sweetheart should chance to consider me handsome. As if it could matter to anybody what he thinks of *me!*"

"In verity, dearest, you are too far above him for his opinion to count—any more than it would about Queen Henrietta."

"You think he is her sweetheart then?" snapped Geraldine, twitching away the arm on which Mrs. Hillyer was clasping a bracelet.

"Nay, madam, 'tis but likely. He is an honest youth, and when two young creatures of the same rank and station come together 'tis but natural they should make a match—though indeed, I believe she is better born than he."

"How so, pray?"

"Because Mistress Betty is a parson's daughter, and 'tis bruited in the hall the poor youth cannot put a name to his father."

"What then? Does that prove him low-born? His father may be a prince. There are state secrets—there are hidden children. 'Twas rumoured in Paris when the Dauphin was born that there were twin princes—one that saw the light three hours after his brother. No one outside the Queen's chamber ever saw that one. But a cry was heard—a newborn child's cry—after Madame de Hauteville and the Royal nurse had carried the Dauphin to another room, out of earshot. I heard Francis Mountain tell his lordship the story. I was playing my theorbo at the other end of the room, and nobody knew I was listening."

"Mr. Francis Mountain is a fabulous person who would decimate any vile inventions. But would you have it that Mr. George is twin brother to the French Dauphin?"

"Nay, nurse, for that would make him less than five years old. But I say again, there are state secrets in every reign; and for all you and I can tell, Mr. George might be a prince of the blood royal."

"He may be the Pope's nephew for aught I care; but he'll have to prove his princedom—or his Popedom— before he'll be allowed——"

"To do what?" asked Geraldine, as her nurse stopped in the midst of a sentence.

"To marry anybody better than a Shropshire vicar's daughter."

Mrs. Hillyer having centred all her affection upon her young mistress, was naturally jealous and quick to discover a rival; and she had for some time past suspected Geraldine of caring more for her young tutor than it was well for a lady of rank to care for a nameless youth. She had hinted as much to Lady Llanbister, who had heard her in a grave silence, and with a brow so clouded that Nurse Hillyer dared not press the question. Neither had she presumed to arouse his lordship's uneasiness by any hint or innuendo ; for though she met him frequently in the house and gardens, and he would often stop to talk to her, she had never lost that feeling of awe with which she had regarded him when she entered his service on the marriage of her mistress.

A crisis came at last in those two young lives which had been passing in monotonous tranquillity within the sheltered comfort of home, while the world outside had been so full of trouble and perturbation, while the best blood in England had been expending itself for the King, and raw recruits from the plough-tail and the counter had been flinging away their lives for the Parliament.

It was in that delicious season when spring melts into summer, almost unawares—since our capricious climate makes the date of the divine transformation a matter of uncertainty, whereby that exquisite morning when the sunshine and flowers blaze out in their fullest splendour, and the evening when the nightingales are heard for the first time in the perfumed dusk, have often the added charm of unexpectedness. Such a sudden awakening of summer came upon the groves and gardens at Isleworth in the middle of May, after a week of east wind and grey sky which had made the cuckoo seem an anachronism.

It was a morning on which only to live was bliss, provided no present and immediate sorrow came between poor humanity and the beauty of the world. Such a sorrow lay like a leaden weight upon George's heart as he walked up and down the broad gravel terrace before the open windows of the parlour where Geraldine sat at her desk, writing one of those exercises which he had devised for her. They had been reading Dante together ; and when she had translated a select episode into English with fluency and correctness, he had bidden her re-translate her English into Italian prose, and the measure of her success was to be the fidelity of this re-translation to the language and spirit of the poet.

She had been ever an aspiring pupil, and had flung aside elementary books—the horn-books of each language—in a huff, insisting on going straight to the poet or the romance writer whose repute she knew.

"'Tis as easy to learn Spanish from 'Don Quixote' or Italian from 'The Inferno,' as to drudge over such senseless trash as these petty story-books and baby sentences," she had told George ; and he had yielded to her whim. And so the first Italian words she had ever learnt were in the first line of the first canto of Dante's "Inferno"; and her acquaintance with Spanish began and ripened with her knowledge of the Wandering Knight—her tutor being very careful to keep from her every chapter in which the coarseness of an earlier century had left its mark upon the page.

How proud he had been of her progress! What pains he had taken ! what studious hours he had given to the mastery of those great books they were to read together, so that he might never fail her when she questioned him ; so that he might be critic and commentator as well as teacher. How he had loved the bright upward look, the eager question, the freakish impatience when the poet soared to realms beyond her reach.

To-day his heart was full of sadness as he walked slowly to and fro in the sunshine, passing very often in front of those open windows through which he could see the pretty head with its profusion of curls bent over the desk, and sometimes a small white hand thrust into the mass of bright hair, and clutching it, in an attitude associated with problems difficult of solution. He and his pupil had been growing farther apart for so long a period that he looked back and wondered at the time when they were close friends, when they played at bowls on the green yonder, beside the tall hornbeam hedge, when they played at battledore and shuttlecock in the low, wide hall in Aldersgate Street ; where sometimes it happened that their laughter, and the sharp sound of the flying cork upon parchment, became a little too boisterous for his lordship's patience, and a servant came with an expostulatory message—courteous, but crushing—perhaps desiring that they should withdraw to the nursery for the conclusion of their game, or suggesting that they should join King Edward's boys in the fields by Newgate. They had romped together like brother and sister, she chasing him at hide-and-seek in the great overgrown City garden, where the fresh north wind blew the scent of gorse and broom from the hills of Hampstead and Highgate. How happy, how innocent, it had been, that sweet companionship! He had been her master; for she submitted herself unquestionably to his teaching, and obviously esteemed him a paragon of learning. He had been her slave; for, once away from her lessons, she ordered him about as her lackey, hers to command in all things relating to her pleasures and amusements—and she could scarce choose a skein of silk without his help. He was her chief footman, groom, and gardener; fetched and carried for her all day long; washed and combed her dogs; trained and exercised her horses; physicked her falcons; planted and tended the wild flowers she ordered him to dig out of the meadow banks, or the choicer roots which her friends gave her for the parterres or the herb-garden.

For more than two years they had been such joyous comrades; and now, though the hours of study, the readings and translations, went on as regularly as of old, master and pupil were so much estranged as to seem almost enemies. The estrangement had been gradual, George putting a little more and a little more constraint upon his manner as his feelings deepened from admiring tenderness to passionate love. And now the gulf seemed impassable. He was ever cold, and she was absolutely uncivil, demonstrating her dislike in every way she could imagine; hardly ever joining in the conversation when he took part in it; passing him with her head in the air and a contemptuous lip when he opened a door or a gate for her; accepting his attendance as a thing of course, and with no more acknowledgment than she would have given to a footman; affecting to dislike everything he liked, and holding herself aloof from every diversion they had ever shared. "Bowls? I detest bowls! A game only fit for tavern wretches that are tipsy before noon!" "The river? Odious in the broiling sun!" "A ride in the dust on Hounslow road? I would as soon be hanged!"

And at the old lessons that had been so familiar and so dear, instead of the ingenuous hoyden, with her elbows on the table, and the ample satin sleeves falling away from the round white arms, like ivory flushed with rose, and her loose hair flung back with a careless hand in wandering curls that he longed to clasp and kiss, he now found a stately lady who had always prepared her lesson, and who sat upright as a dart, and looked at him with a frozen face, and was scarcely as civil as she would have been to a shoemaker's apprentice who came to measure her foot.

To this had they come ; and he was content so to live with her rather than to leave her. The cruellest look she gave him was ever so much better than that outer darkness where he would never thrill at the flash of those scornful eyes, that barren wilderness of the world where she was not.

Mistress Betty, whose light duties left her ample leisure in which to watch and listen, espied her lovely youth walking in the sunshine, and ran to join him, her fat spaniel waddling before her. She ran to him with the air of having a right to his company wherever he might be, such right as only sweethearts have, thought the young lady in the parlour, whose bright head was drooping over a difficult passage. She heard them talking and laughing as they walked up and down, their steps and voices now near, now far. How happy they seemed out in the sunshine ! That glum face of his could break into smiles in his sweetheart's company. Well, let them marry, and set up a school in Aldersgate, and rival Mr. Milton, whose dreaming face she had so often noticed, as he walked in the rear of his noisy pupils, abstracted, brooding upon deep things. George might become such another pedant and pedagogue as that Mr. John Milton, and go over to the Parliament and the Puritans. Let him speak out manfully and ask for Mistress Betty; and she, Geraldine, would give the girl a handsome dowry, and have done with them both. Was it not her duty to provide for her servants?

She gave a little laugh at that fancy of George in a small City house, keeping a school with Mistress Betty —but the laugh was like a sob; and she struck her clenched fist upon the open pages of her folio Italian dictionary, in a fury at not finding the word she wanted.

"Why are there moods and tenses?" she muttered. "What is this life worth, that one should take so much trouble to talk or write about it?"

The laughter out of doors had ceased five minutes ago. She looked up and saw George standing at the window, watching her.

"Is the passage harder than common?" he asked, with his dry-as-dust schoolmaster air.

She corrected her lounging attitude in an instant, and sat up prim and straight in front of her desk.

"Perhaps I am more stupid than common," she answered stiffly. "But you had best judge for yourself."

She scrubbed some faint trace of tears out of her eyes with her handkerchief, while he was coming through the hall, and felt herself safe in the iron mail of womanly pride when he entered the parlour. She handed him her exercise-books without a word—one containing her English translation, the other her Italian rendering of that English. The passage—her own choice—was the heartrending story of Ugolino and his famished brood, familiar to her in Chaucer's homely verse.

George read the page, standing by the open casement, —read to the end, but was dumb. It was full of faults, a worse Italian than her much earlier efforts had ever produced. Verbs, pronouns, adverbs, genders, idiom, all were confused and faulty. He knew not what to say to her, and stood staring at the page in mute distress, afraid of wounding her pride by the truth.

"Is it very ill done?" she asked sullenly, after an embarrassing pause.

"It is not near so well as other of your translations."

And then he took her pen and pointed out the errors, putting a cross against each, till the page was scattered with crosses. "This should be the subjunctive; the adjective here should be feminine: *annunziava* is wrongly spelt."

His voice hurt her like the water-dropping torture. She did not suffer him to finish, but snatched the book from his hand, tore out the leaf, crushed it into a ball, and flung it through the window, where his lordship's Spanish pointer came galloping across the lawn to pounce upon it.

"There is an end for to-day, madam!" said the tutor, taking off his hat and making her a bow, as he moved towards the door.

"I think it had best be an end for ever!" she answered, with a trembling lip, and whiter than he had ever seen her. "I have no mind for more lessons—indeed, I am too old for schooling. And you are too much taken up with your courtship to be a good master. Well, 'tis only right young people should marry, when they are fond and true, as you and Betty are. I shall ask my grandfather to give my gentlewoman a dowry, and charge it to my future fortune. So you need not begin the world penniless—and you can turn schoolmaster, sir, like——"

She stood erect, a fever-spot high on each cheek, the hectic of a brain on fire. Her lips quivered so that a word broke here and there, and her voice shook like the tremolo in music.

"Good God!" he cried, before she could finish her sentence, "what lunatic talk is this? Mistress Betty— your gentlewoman! A dowry—courtship—fond and true! Are you mad, Mistress, that you dare pronounce such words to me?"

It was he who was furious now, and on his face the angry blood spread its crimson from cheek to brow. He looked as if he could kill her.

That she could suppose him in love with Betty! That she could think that simpering piece of vanity good enough for him!

"Dare!" she echoed. "Dare is a grand word! I pray you pardon me, sir. I thought you would perhaps stoop to a schoolmaster's trade for the woman you love!"

"I would stoop to the lowest—would turn trencher-scraper—for the girl I love, or would be a wayside beggar and beg for her. But I am cut to the heart that you should link me—but in a moment's thought—with your gentlewoman!"

"Oh!" she cried, beginning to laugh, a light, airy laugh at the first, "poor Betty is not good enough then, though you are so sweet and fair-spoken to her. Yet you must like her better than you like me, to whom you are ever harsh and unkind, and distant, and proud, and hateful, hateful, hateful!"

She laughed, betwixt broken sentences, all through her speech; and now the laugh grew loud and hysterical, and she sank in a heap on the stool on which she had been sitting at her lessons, and flung her arms upon the table, and hid her face in her clasped hands, sobbing heart-brokenly.

This made an end of her lover's fortitude. He fell on his knees by her side, and drew her hands away from her tear-stained face with a gentle resoluteness.

"My own adorable girl," he murmured, covering the struggling hands with kisses, drawing nearer and nearer to her, till his head was leaning against her shoulder, and their flowing curls were mingled, dark and fair, gold and brown. "What! You who are so shrewd and all-seeing, could you not read the riddle right? I was discourteous, hateful, only because I loved you with an over-mastering passion, because I could scarce trust my voice to speak the commonest words, lest my love should cry its cherished secret aloud, and I should be flung from the threshold of this dear house, as now I must be; or must rather go of my own free will into banishment."

She had recovered something of her composure by this time. She drew herself from his embracing arm, and that intermingling of gold and brown tresses was ended. She stood up before him like a queen, and bade him rise from his knees.

"After all, I am not Queen Bess," she said, "though in the days we were friends you used to tell me I was just such a termagant."

Her face was radiant. Joy never spoke more divinely from shining eyes and lovely lips.

"And are you really fonder of me than of Betty?" she asked, with a sweetly childish coquetry.

"Than of Betty? Don't talk to me of Betty!"

"Oh, but I love to talk of her, now I know that you are not her sweetheart. Poor Betty! It is hard for her; but she is silly enough to forget easily. But oh, how grave you look, George! when I am so merry."

"Ah, dearest, should not a man be grave who has broken the spell that held him in Paradise?"

"What spell?"

"So long as I was silent—so long as my secret was faithfully kept—I could stay here. I could see you every day—all day long."

"And be as uncivil as you chose; and make me think you hated me," she interjected, pouting.

"While you thought I hated you I could stay, and not feel myself a traitor. But now you know that I love you——"

"You can stay all the same," she cried insistently, "and we can be good friends instead of ill friends; and you may be as civil as you like to Betty, so long as you are civil to me too, in a different way. We can be true friends; master and pupil; and friends; sober, civil friends. Not brother and sister, as we used to be. I am too old for that—and not sweethearts, till his lordship gives his consent."

"He will never give his consent. My dearest girl, there is no choice for me. I have broken the spell. We have plucked a golden apple from the tree of knowledge. I will not wait for the angel with the flaming sword—to wit, your grandfather's just indignation. I will take my fate upon me like a man. Some day, perhaps, when you are married to one of the greatest gentlemen in England, and we are a quarter of a century older, I may come back into your life, and teach your daughter the modern languages—as I have taught you."

There was a sound of tears in his voice at the last. She stretched out imploring hands to him.

"George, George, George!" she cried, "as I live, I will never marry any man but you."

She doubted if he heard her protestation, so quickly had he vanished out of her sight ; and, frank, impetuous child though she was, pride forbade her to follow him. She gathered up her dictionary, and grammar, and Dante, and exercise-books, flung them in a heap on the floor, and stamped upon them.

"How can he be so cruel?" she cried. "He has a heart of stone. I will try to forget every word he ever taught me."

It was ever so long afterwards that she began to appreciate the heroism in his cruelty, and to understand that love which goes hand in hand with honour is the one true and perfect love of all.

Not for an hour did George palter with fate. He went straight to Lady Llanbister's parlour—the small, panelled parlour with one broad, deep-set window that filled the south side of the room, while all its diamond-paned casements opened—a wonder in those days—to let in the odours of roses and rosemary, thyme and gillyflowers, violets and chamomile, sweet and bitter, spicy and aromatic, from the beds and borders in her ladyship's physic-garden. He had spent such happy hours in that room ; keeping Lady Llanbister's accounts ; helping her in the preparation of those herbal remedies which, in conjunction with a good deal of faith and occasional money aid, had proved so efficacious among the cottagers at Isleworth ; reading to her as she sat at her spinning-wheel, ever choosing the poets they both loved—Chaucer, Spenser, or those sunny comedies of Shakespeare which chime in tune with summer gardens and happy, innocent lives—*Twelfth Night, As You Like It, Midsummer's Night's Dream.* He had read them all to her, and she had taught him how to read poetry as well as how to feel it, inspiring him with her enthusiasm for all that was loftiest and best in the pages he read.

Coming into that room to-day, braced for self-sacrifice, his heart sickened at the sight of his beloved patroness seated by the sunny window, her wheel idle beside her, and the folio copy of the "Faëry Queen" open on her reading-desk.

"Is your lesson over so soon? Have you come to read to me, George?" she asked; and then she looked up at him and saw the change in his face, so firmly set, so deadly pale.

"I have come to bid you farewell," he answered, in the deep, grave voice of despair.

"What?"

"I am going to leave this happy home, where I have received such bounteous kindness from you and his lordship."

"George, what has happened? Have you offended my husband—that good man, who has treated you so generously? No, I cannot think so ill of you."

She had started to her feet, almost as agitated as he was, and taking no trouble to restrain her feelings.

"Do not think ill of me, dearest lady. No, I have not yet offended; but were I to linger here but another day I should offend. My very presence in this house would be an injury to my benefactor."

"What have you done?"

"I have disclosed a secret that I ought to have kept locked in my breast for ever. Geraldine knows that I love her, fondly, despairingly, love her and renounce her with the same breath. You see that I must not stay here."

"Geraldine! Why, she is a child—almost a child."

"Seventeen on Valentine's Day last year."

"Seventeen! The years roll on so fast when one has come to my age—the smooth, quiet years, that can bring us nothing. We thank God when they take no precious treasure away. Geraldine! I have thought that some day, some far-off day, you might perhaps—

she might—but she was still a child, or I thought her a child, only caring for foolish things, changing her whims and fancies a hundred times in a year."

"She is a woman, and I love her."

"And she gives you love for love?"

He made a little sign of assent, and turned his face away from the sunlight, and from those anxious eyes that were watching him.

"Come here, George," she said, resuming her seat, and pointing to the window-bench beside her. "Sit here by me, and tell me your troubles. We have talked enough of the King's troubles, in these latter days. Tell me yours—the sorrow of a young heart, which is to itself a kingdom, and holds as much of joy or grief as the big busy world outside. Ah, dear heart, if I could set things right for you! If any power or prayer of mine could give you all you sigh for——"

"I know—I know how much you would do for me. I have loved you and looked up to you as a son might look to his mother—if one who never knew a parent's love dare conceive a son's feelings."

"Nay, George, it does not need experience to teach what filial love is like. You have been to me—almost —as the son I lost."

"The sweet flower that withered so early. His lordship has talked to me of that so lamented heir."

"As the son I lost," she repeated, looking at him fixedly, with dreamy eyes.

And then she won him to talk freely of his unhappy passion, to pour out his heart to her. She told him that he did wisely to leave them. It was not possible for her to propose him to her husband as Geraldine's suitor. The gulf between them now—while he was untried by life, and had done nothing for fame—was too wide. But later his chance might come. This dreadful war, which was mowing down the flower of English youth, might reduce his lordship's ambition. And in troublous times distinction may be quickly won. His chance might come.

He shook his head despondently. He would not

suffer himself to hope. For the first time, he was almost angry with her. He had thought her wisdom personified; and now she was talking to him like a silly woman who would rather live in a fool's paradise than face bitter truth. He cut short all ambiguous consolations, and told her what he meant to do when he had packed his trunks and left her house. Francis Mountain was in London on one of his flying visits, a secret Mercury between Henrietta and the French Queen, and was going back to Paris immediately.

"He will take me with him if I ask him. His kindness is unbounded."

"But alas! he is so ill a companion."

"Nay, dear madam, you wrong him. Except for an extra bottle of wine now and then, he has not a vice."

"And for you to live with a sot!"

"His excesses are only on occasion. He is generous, open-hearted, fearless, a great, good, careless man that has never left off being a boy. His worst taste is for conspiracy, and I shall strive hard to keep him out of that mischief. He has a yielding temper, and will suffer me to hector him as if I was the elder. You do not know how good he is."

"Not good enough to be your companion, George. I hate to think of the dangers and temptations of your life with such a man."

"You forget that I leave my heart at Isleworth, and that I carry a talisman against danger and temptation."

He held out his hand with her sapphire ring upon his finger.

"To look upon this ring will be to keep in that straight path the Puritans talk of so often," he said.

The dinner-bell rang loud in a cupola above their heads. It was half an hour after noon. Her ladyship's two gentlewomen and a page came trooping in, ready to attend her to the dining-room.

"You will sit at meat with us once more, George?" she asked, giving him her hand.

He bent down to kiss that exquisite hand, but answered only by a negative motion of the head. He

could not speak to her. He had carried himself stoutly
while he discussed his banishment, but was near breaking
down all the time. His eyes were cloudy with unshed
tears, and he could scarcely see the kind face he looked
at. He left her without another word, went straight
to his room, packed his trunks, left them to be carried to
London by the waggon, and made his exit quietly by
a side door, while family and household were at dinner,
meaning to walk to Chiswick, and there take boat for
London.

There was a small park on this side of the house,
adjoining the larger domain of Syon, and opening into
a lane that led from the great Bath road to the river.
George followed a beaten track between the massive
trunks of old oaks, and walked slowly towards a turnstile
which afforded a short cut to the lane.

He was within a few yards of the turnstile when he
heard the rustle of a woman's silken gown upon the
long grass behind him, and turned, flushing crimson,
and his heart beating furiously.

No, 'twas not she of whom he had thought in that
moment of ecstasy. It was my lady, with her sweet,
sad smile, and sober grey satin gown.

" I heard you leave the house," she said, " though you
were so stealthy. George, I must say some words to
you before we part,—God knows for how long. I shall
pray for our speedy reunion ; but my most fervent
prayer will be that our Father in heaven may keep your
heart pure and true, and your life free from sin."

"The thought of your prayers will sustain me in
my darkest hour. Oh, dear lady, how shall I thank
you for your angelic kindness ? Your bounty has given
me all that Fate denied, all my boyhood lacked."

"There is no question of goodness or bounty. I have
loved you. That is all you need remember. I shall
go on loving you while our lives are parted. Remember
that in the hour of temptation ; and think of the heart
that would bleed—as mothers' hearts bleed for their
firstborn—for your sin, for your dishonour."

"Your image will be with me wherever I go. And

for temptation—none can ever assail me so fierce as that I have conquered to-day : the temptation to linger under your roof, knowing I had lost the right to live here."

"You have done well, George. And now go your ways, my dear adopted son. Be careful to avoid ill influences. Beware of bad company. Be thoughtful, industrious, temperate, as you have been here ; civil to all the world, but not quick to make new friends. Write to me sometimes in your leisure hours—a long, long letter, with the history of your life. And however long our parting may be, do not abandon hope. I am not without power to help you in the right season. Be patient, be true to yourself, as you have been to-day, and hope for all best things this life can give."

She had laid her hands lightly on his breast when she began her sermon, looking at him fixedly all the time with tearful eyes. When she had spoken her last word she kissed him on each cheek in the pretty foreign fashion, and turned and walked slowly back over the thick, flowering grass.

CHAPTER X.

THE WOMAN'S REIGN.

CHANGES had come over the city of Paris since George had trodden its streets ; and France and her people had passed through one of those transitions which begin new epochs. Richelieu was dead. In the December of 1642, while the City of London was in a panic, lest the King's troops should surprise and surround it, the people of France were counting the last hours of the Minister whose iron hand had ruled them. Those who were in Paris at that time tell how men were almost afraid to speak of the great Cardinal's death, lest that implacable spirit should flame up again, Phœnix-like, from its ashes—lest that marble form should rise from the bed of Death, ghastly in its grave-clothes, to convict them of a lie. They remembered the time when he who had ruled France with a whip of scorpions lay sick at Lyons, and the Queen Mother, far away, in foreign exile, was glad, and the hearts of men beat bolder with the hope that the iron bands were soon to be loosed, and the hand of the despot Minister was soon to lie in clay-cold stillness under the splendour of velvet and gold, clustered plumes, and jewelled insignia. They remembered Cinq Mars, and his brief span of glory—his daring attempt to overthrow that autocracy of intellect, and how swift had been the sick man's vengeance, how irresistible the force of that unyielding will which the consciousness of approaching death could not soften.

"I have had no enemies but those of France," the Cardinal had replied to the priest whispering into his dying ears, and urging the Christian's duty of pardon; but for a Minister who had made himself, as it were, the incarnate spirit of his country, the work of the headsman and the slow death of the dungeon must have had something of a personal flavour. Armand Richelieu's foes were in very truth the foes of France; but they were also the foes of Armand Richelieu. That disdainful and insolent *noblesse*, which had spurned the priest Minister's pretentions and conspired against his authority, had been sacrificed, one after another, in the interests of King and people; but they had earned the hatred of Richelieu long before they were ripe for the executioner; and the velvet shoe with the golden cross trod on many a stubborn neck that might have escaped the axe had it bent to the imperious churchman's yoke.

Richelieu was dead, every wrong avenged, and every foe vanquished; and the parasites who had trembled at his frown and espoused all his quarrels, hating whom he hated, loving whom he loved, were now the flatterers and sycophants of Anne of Austria, the widowed Queen; since before winter had changed to summer, Louis, surnamed the Just, had followed his Prime Minister to "the land where all things are forgotten," after a lingering illness, the slow ebbing of a life that had been always feeble, and which was worn to the thinnest thread at forty-two years of age.

From the gloom of that death-chamber at Saint-Germain, whence Louis' dying eyes had looked towards the towers of Saint Denis, the sepulchre of kings, the Royal widow had emerged a new creature. She had risen from the obscurity of a down-trodden Queen Consort, under the abiding shadow of suspicion, to the almost autocratic power of Queen Regent, the proud mother of an infant King; and the iron hand of Richelieu had given place to the affectionate subservience of his pupil Mazarin. The sleek Italian, papal legate in the dawn of youth—for some time a Cardinal, but not yet, if ever, a priest—handsome, accomplished, still in the prime of manhood, trained in Richelieu's service, at once his *protégé* and his tool, had already begun to acquire an influence, more subtle, but not less powerful, than that of the great Cardinal. Richelieu had ruled Anne of Austria by fear. She had plotted against him, and trembled before him. She, the Queen, had bent before him, the subject. She had been a prisoner without visible bonds, a slave with impalpable fetters.

After a few days at the old lodgings in Westminster, where Mountain gave him a hearty welcome, George accompanied his friend to Paris, and arrived there with a very imperfect understanding of the business that carried his master to the capital. That Mountain's secret mission had some bearing upon that troublesome question whether England was to remain heretic or return to the fold of the faithful, was all he had ever been told ; and he had to content himself with this limited confidence. It seemed to him that a time when England was rent by Civil War must be of all seasons the least favourable to the growth of religious enthusiasm, or the stirring up of the embers of the old fire—to have stirred which had made Archbishop Laud a prisoner in the Tower. But that Mountain had friends in Paris—and they among the most powerful—was made obvious to his page and servant by his happy *insouciance* and his well-filled purse.

" If business has brought us to Paris, George, pleasure shall keep us there as long as we have spending money," he said gaily. " I am as glad to leave the gloom of London, and the ever-darkening shadow that hangs over Charles and his fortunes, as an escaped bird to fly up into the blue."

George's only answer was a sigh. To him it was as if they had left all that is best and fairest in life behind them, in that unfortunate country. He thought of the grave old garden in Aldersgate Street, the flowery lawn by the Thames at Isleworth, with a sick longing, and it needed all the elasticity of youth to enable him to rally his spirits, and put on an appearance of interest in that splendid capital which his patron praised.

They had lodgings in the Court quarter, at the

Golden Crown in the Rue des Fossés Saint-Germain-l'Auxerrois, in the shadow of the church walls. It was a street of taverns—the White Rose ; the Eagle ; the famous Crab-tree, chosen resort of profligate wits, the guzzlers, as they were called ; and the Black Horse, where Madame Lagnet offered lodgings for persons from the country at thirty sols a night, with another thirty sols for meals. The stage coaches from Dreux and from Nogent le Roi stopped at the Eagle, and brought many travellers to the street, where there was accommodation to suit all purses. It was here, in all that remained of the Constable Charles de Bourbon's palace, that the Venetian comedians had acted when Henry III. was King ; and it was in the same building, later known as the Petit Bourbon Theatre, that Louis the Great was to dance, and Molière and his company were to act, in the golden age that was coming. Palaces and taverns, coach office and theatre, stood side by side in that narrow street, which has melted into the dark abyss of time past.

Francis Mountain established himself and his secretary in a large, double-bedded room at the back of the house, with a capacious fireplace, and three narrow windows looking on to a garden ; and after having supped in the public eating-room on the ground floor, made haste to open his saddle-bags and lay out his best suit, or indeed, his only suit save the leather jerkin and drugget hose in which he had crossed the Channel ; for it was this gentleman's practice to provide himself with the richest suit of clothes that his cash or his credit could command, and to live in it till it was threadbare, by which means, as he boasted, he wanted neither spacious coffer nor cumbrous cupboard, and was ever at the top of the fashion.

"To-morrow night we will to Court, George," he said, as he somewhat ruefully contemplated the tarnished lace on his velvet doublet. "I doubt my coat will look as well as the rest by candle-light. I have a letter for Queen Anne, from that harassed lady, her Royal sister-in-law ; and so we are sure of a welcome. You shall find yourself in a scene that excels Denmark House or Whitehall as the mid-day sun outshines a church candle."

The Queen Regent was still at the Louvre, whence she shortly afterwards removed to the Palais Cardinal— that newer and more elegant residence which Richelieu had bequeathed to his master. It was at the Louvre that George Mountain was admitted for the first time to the Royal presence, and where he was allowed to kneel and kiss the whitest hand in France, and to behold the arms and shoulders that had dazzled Buckingham, when Austria's fair daughter was the girl-wife of an unloving husband, and still a stranger in the land.

That Royal bust was more opulent now than twenty years ago, but the incomparable whiteness which courtly poets had praised was as remarkable to-day as in her Majesty's first youth, while the deep black of her gown and veil, relieved only by a magnificent *parure* of pearls, accentuated the transparent purity of her complexion, and gave dignity to her too ample figure.

Mr. Mountain and his page were presented to the Regent by that distinguished exile, Secretary Windebank, who, although a fugitive from England at the beginning of the troubles, was a favourite at the French Court; and her Majesty's reception was of a marked graciousness.

It was indeed a distinguished privilege for these two untitled Englishmen to be received in that inner drawing-room where the Queen Regent was wont to spend her evenings in a solemn *tête-à-tête* with her chief Minister, who was present on this occasion, a bland assistant at the interview.

The Queen asked many questions about her unhappy sister-in-law, and expressed an affectionate regard for that courageous and unfortunate lady.

"I wish my poor sister would leave your ungrateful country, where she has suffered greater sorrows and humiliations than ever a royal daughter of France endured, and has seen her creed insulted and her priests ill-used. Here she would have a cordial welcome and a peaceful asylum—a safe shelter from the cruelty of your barbarous people, who, by their late treatment of that poor lady, can be scarcely escaped from the savagery of the age when they painted their bodies and ran wild in woods."

"Your Majesty must not forget that there has been some intermingling of Gaulish blood in the English race since those aboriginal Britons cut the mistletoe in their primeval forests," said Mazarin, with that insinuating smile which lit his face with a sudden and almost dazzling brightness, but which his detractors declared he had learnt before his looking-glass, as a comedian learns his craft, rehearsing the play of features till he can assume an expression at will, however at variance with the workings of the mind behind the mask.

The Cardinal had his foot already on the steps of the throne, his hand already on the sceptre which he was so soon to wield with undisputed power ; yet no one had ever seen him angry ; no one had ever received a hard answer, even to the most audacious demand. The velvet glove had been in evidence on all occasions ; and if the hand of steel were underneath that silken softness, no one had felt the grip of it yet awhile.

The Regency began as a golden age. All the prison doors were opened : all the exiles were returning. Queen Anne, who had been pitied and praised rather because she had been slighted and persecuted than for any distinguished virtues of her own, seemed incapable of unkindness, even to an enemy. The Princes of the Royal blood, the Princes of the half-blood, the gallant Henry's titled grandsons and granddaughters, all alike rejoiced in the reign of universal indulgence. Richelieu, before whom guilty and guiltless alike had trembled— Richelieu whose assassination had been the desire of hearts that failed and hands that blundered, and against whose charmed existence treason had plotted and swords had been sharpened in vain, had succumbed to the common enemy ; and the reign of the Infant King was hailed as the beginning of the millennium.

Enthusiasm of this kind, an all-consenting approbation,

can hardly be expected to last long. The golden age was scarcely three months old when the plotters resumed their plotting, and the assassins' daggers were on the grindstone.

Cardinal Mazarin condescended to accompany Mountain and his page when they left the Royal presence, and conducted them through the more select circle of ancient nobility and Royal blood to the outer and largest saloon, in which a crowd of beauties and fops, dowagers and veterans, were assembled, many of them engaged at the card-tables, while others clustered in little *coteries*, or walked about, full of talk and laughter, and with that animated gesticulation which gave a factitious brilliancy to their conversation, and made the most insignificant speech seem full of point and meaning. George was the more struck by this super-abundant vivacity after his observation of English people, whose lack of movement and expression suggested a lack of wit, but whose discourse he had rarely found wanting in sense or humour. Here it was not speech alone that conveyed ideas. Eyebrows, shoulders, elbows, hands, were full of subtle meaning. A reputation died at the lifting of finely arched brows; a sovereign contempt was expressed by the turn of an elbow; a lover was reduced to despair by the airy motion of a delicate hand; and beauty's alabaster shoulders could blast a rival's character with a shrug.

Into this noisy rabble, but only a little way across the threshold, Mazarin accompanied the Englishman and his attendant, George standing respectfully behind his master while the Cardinal whispered in Mountain's attentive ear. There was a large Venetian mirror on the opposite wall, and George, glancing idly at the glass, caught his own reflection, and the reflection of the Cardinal's face looking at him with a startled expression, lips parted in arrested speech, eyes full of a sudden wonder.

George could but wonder too, for the faces had a curious likeness, allowing for the disparity between youth and middle age, and also for a considerable difference in colouring. Mazarin's countenance was dark with the glowing olive of Southern Europe, while George's complexion had the brilliant fairness seldom seen save in an Englishman.

Perhaps every one is familiar with that involuntary recollection of a long forgotten scene, which flashes with a startling suddenness across the mirror of the mind—a scene that has no relevance to the thought or the action of the moment, and which rises like an unbidden ghost before the mental vision.

Such a memory flashed across George Mountain's brain as he looked at the Cardinal's face in the glass; the picture of that one most awful scene in his childish experience; the deserted hall at Portsmouth; the dead form under the voluminous mantle; the dead face looking up at the ceiling, terrible in its ashen pallor, yet beautiful with all that humanity has of dignity and grace.

In after days, when he heard people talk of the resemblance between Mazarin and George Villiers, and how Cardinal Richelieu had speculated upon this likeness as an influence over the romantic Queen, George understood why that tragic spectacle had recurred to him amidst the buzz and glitter of so different a scene.

That sudden pause in the Cardinal's whisper had not escaped Francis Mountain, who had also noted the great man's look at the mirrored face, and from the glass to the man, and had interpreted his surprise.

"I am such a careless blockhead as never to have remarked your likeness to his Eminence till I saw him stare at you," Mountain said, as they walked from the Louvre to their lodgings; "but such resemblances are common enough where men are so lucky as to be living copies of the antique. I hope the accident may bring you into favour with one who, 'tis said, will soon be as powerful in France as Richelieu was last year."

George had too independent a spirit to curry favour with foreign greatness, or to desire the Cardinal's patronage. After three years' residence in England, and in a city overshadowed by the gloom of growing rebellion

and made distasteful to him by the judicial murder of
Strafford and the persecution of the Bishops, this gay
and light-hearted Paris seemed a new world, and he
could but note the happier atmosphere, albeit he had
left personal happiness behind him. True that here too
there had been tragedies as terrible as the doom of
Thomas Wentworth. Lives as noble had been snapped
short by the headsman, and Richelieu's rule had been
written in blood. But Frenchmen forget easily ; and
the new reign, the woman's reign, had begun in a burst
of sunshine.

George plunged into the Court vortex with a somewhat feverish alacrity. Having lost the tranquil gladness
of those gardens by the Thames, Geraldine's too dear
companionship, and the friendship of Lady Llanbister,
he would fain have drowned every fond retrospection,
every thought of his nameless birth, every anxiety about
his unprovided future, in the merry-go-round of Paris
dissipations. There were plenty of amusements offered
to a young man in that wonderful city—the fencing-
school, with its endless interest for a good swordsman,
the riding-school, founded by the famous Pluvinel near
the Place Royale, when Henry IV. was king, where the
Princes of the blood Royal were trained in the noble art
of riding the great horse, and where the education of
horse and rider was elaborated to a perfection unattained
in any other academy ; theatres ; puppet-shows ; the
evening ride along the Cours la Reine ; the modish
assemblies in Renard's Garden ; *al fresco* dances, *al
fresco* suppers ; festivals at which Majesty did not disdain to appear ; and most of all, that liberty to mix in
the nightly crowd of princes, peers, and commoners,
which the indulgence of the Queen Regent allowed to
throng her saloons, to babble its scandals and impertinences, and to whisper the ribald epigram composed
over the morning drink in some paid scribbler's garret,
printed by stealth in a cellar, and bandied from lip
to lip in the evening, almost within her Majesty's
hearing.

Under a rule so lax, it was easy for Francis Mountain

to obtain admission for himself and his secretary to the Court circle. It was not the first time he had carried a letter from Henrietta Maria to her sister-in-law, for he had served as messenger between those two Royal ladies for some years past, and had also been a prime agent in the secret correspondence of that much-persecuted heroine of romantic adventure, Madame de Chevreuse, during Richelieu's long day of power, when she had pleaded and plotted in vain for permission to return to her family and her estates.

Madame de Chevreuse no longer needed anybody's intervention. She had hurried back to France with other distinguished exiles, Madame de Hautefort, the Chevalier de Jars, immediately upon his Majesty's death. Indeed, Louis XIII.—dead in the prime of manhood, lying in a gloomy splendour of wax tapers and black velvet draperies, in his deserted chamber at Saint-Germain, with only the vulgar crowd to look upon his funereal state—while the wife who had trembled at his slightest frown ; the courtiers who had flattered him ; the brothers and sisters, and nephews and nieces, of the half blood, who owed all their magnificence to his generosity ; the ministers, bishops, sycophants, wits— had all hurried away to Paris to people those palaces in which he had so lately reigned supreme—might have furnished a theme for that austere sectary who said, " I cannot but look upon all the glory and dignity of this world, lands and lordships, crowns and kingdoms, even as on some brain-sick, beggarly fellow, that borroweth fine clothes and plays the part of a king or a lord for an hour on a stage, and then comes down, and the sport is ended, and they are beggars again."

Louis the Just had been carried at a smart pace along the road to Saint-Denis, as his son the great King was to be carried seventy-two years after, with as little reverence or lamenting love ; and the people he had hated, the intriguers he had banished, were dominant at the court of that wife whom he had never loved, and who had never loved him. A new era had begun ; the era of *laisser aller* on the part of the pious, self-indulgent Spanish Queen, and of a subtle policy in the person of Jules Mazarin, who, beginning with the silken subservience of an accomplished Italian diplomat, did not relax his efforts till he had made himself the supreme master of his Royal mistress, and almost as much the master of France.

Fortune had smiled upon the Italian minister in the very beginning of his rule. Swiftly on the gloom of that funeral train which carried the thirteenth Louis to his last resting-place came the fanfare of trumpets, with tidings of the battle of Rocroy, a victory that aroused a transport of joy, only to be measured by the knowledge of the disastrous consequences which must have followed defeat. From that golden afternoon of May when La Moussaye arrived at the Hôtel de Condé with the news, and thence, without drawing rein, rode on to the Louvre, all Paris was stirred with a wild rapture of exultation ; and later, when Chevers arrived with the trophies, and when fifty of the King's household troops and a hundred picked guardsmen scarcely sufficed to carry the glorious spoil of banners and standards, the great heart of Paris beat as the heart of one man. At the Louvre, upon the quays, at Notre Dame, Court, *noblesse*, people, were on foot in a tumult of joy.

It was said that the dying King had seen this coming victory in a dream. His son of four years old had reigned but four days when the battle was won, by a general still in the very morning of youth. For Mazarin the value of such a success was inestimable. It came at a critical moment, immediately upon that reconstitution of the state counsel which was the first stage in his progress towards absolute power ; and it helped him to hold his own against the daring ambition of the Vendômes, and their party, henceforth to be known as the " Importants."

The Importants were sulking in their tents now ; and the Duc d'Enghien's father, the Prince de Condé, and the fair-haired Duchesse de Longueville, his sister, were paramount at Court, and in the city.

While these royal argosies were sailing on the flood-tide of success, Francis Mountain steered his own modest barque along their wake, and took advantage of all opportunities with the cool audacity of an experienced adventurer. He speedily made his mark among the smaller fry at the Louvre, as a long-headed Englishman, who had been entrusted with important missions, and who was likely to be more and more useful to the unfortunate English Queen, since that poor lady stood in urgent need of trusty messengers and courageous servants on both sides the Channel, to help her in negotiations which might buttress her husband's tottering throne.

The favour shown to Francis Mountain was shown in a more liberal manner to the handsome youth who was always in attendance upon him. To be in the morning of life, and remarkable for personal beauty ; to have a melodious voice, and a manner at once modest and self-possessed,—constituted a strong claim to feminine approval, and it was chiefly among the fairer portion of the Court rabble that George found favour. He had soon more friends than he had ever had in his life before, and was embarrassed by having to refuse invitations to supper, and still more so by the disputes of rival coquettes who wanted his handsome person to adorn the dusty splendour of their windowless coaches on the Cours la Reine.

It was not to be supposed that the greatest ladies, the blood Royal of France and Lorraine, were rivals for so small a gentleman's favour, or condescended to invite Mr. Mountain's secretary to their houses ; but even among these, his fine person and elegant manners had not been altogether unnoticed. Madame de Montbazon had asked questions about him, and though those magnificent shoulders of hers had brushed past him with the disdainful movement of a goddess walking through a crowd of mortals with whom she had nothing in common, that noble lady had it in contemplation to order somebody to present the young Englishman

to her at the first convenient opportunity. Nor had
the Montbazon's fair foe, the flaxen-haired Anne de
Bourbon, Duchesse de Longueville, been unobservant
of the young foreigner ; so that there now needed but
some lucky accident to raise George Nameless from the
nether circle of Counsellors' and Colonels' wives, the
little *noblesse* of sword and gown, to that purer ether
where the highly born move at ease in an atmosphere
too rarefied for commoners to breathe with composure.

In one detail George's reception in the Royal ante-
chambers, flattering as it had been in a general way,
had disappointed his friend and master. The Cardinal,
who had seemed so startled at the resemblance between
the young man's features and his own mature countenance, had never exhibited the friendly interest which
Mountain had hoped for, as a consequence of that
likeness. It was a foolish expectation no doubt, as
Mountain told George one night, when they were
supping *tête-à-tête* at the Pine Apple, a favourite tavern
in the Rue de la Juiverie, in the shadow of Notre Dame,
where they met ribald wits and satirical poets against
whom the doors of the Louvre were shut.

"I am ever a sanguine ass!" he said, "and I was
an incorrigible ass to suppose that a man compounded
of equal parts of pride and selfishness would like you
any the better for reminding him at forty what a pretty
fellow he was at twenty. I dare wager he resents your
insolence in having brow, nose, and chin modelled after
his pattern. Those classic features are common enough
in Italy, no doubt, where the future mothers of the
race live and move surrounded by the masterpieces of
antiquity : but the French type is ruggeder, and follows
the aquiline of birds of prey rather than the delicate
lines of the Apollo or the Antinous—Francis I., for
instance, Henry IV., D'Enghien, a succession of hook-
nosed heroes. Well, you can prosper without help from
his Eminence, having caught the favour of the women,
whose liking is a surer road to fortune."

"I should be sorry to owe promotion to a woman's
help, unless——"

"Why that pause, and tender smile?   Unless——?"

"Unless that woman were Lady Llanbister.   No kindness from her would ever degrade or oppress me. I should be grateful, but not humiliated; and no service she could demand in return would seem too much or too low.   I would be her lackey, would wear her livery, if she bade me."

"Well, she may ask something perilous of you before you have done with her.   God knows when we shall see the end of the troubles that have begun in England; and in the meantime all schemes for the re-establishment of the old faith there must lie under, and wait for smoother times.   Now that the Royal standard is afloat, and the crop-headed troops are gathering all over the country, I question if Englishmen remember whether they are Papists or Protestants.   Rossetti has gone back to Rome; and Henrietta Maria has to think of transmuting pearls and diamonds into muskets and cannon. It is an ill time for Mother Church when her sons are cutting each other's throats.   And thus you will observe that Cardinal Mazarin sets little value upon your humble servant.   The use I may be to his mistress's sister-in-law counts for nothing now that I can be of no use to himself."

"You make him a monster of selfishness."

"Such monsters as most men are who push to the front rank, by elbowing aside all rivals, as he has done. Well, so far, he has not shown Richelieu's thirst for blood.   Monsieur de Paris complains that his office is losing all distinction, and that he has nothing to do but hang vulgar cut-purses, and serving wenches who steal their mistresses' finery to captivate the 'prentices on the quays."

It was on the following night that George found himself for the first time in the presence of a woman who was to exercise a stronger influence upon his fate than any of those ladies of the Court and about the Court who had hitherto favoured him with their smiles and hospitalities.   This new face flashed suddenly upon

him in that larger and thicker throng of the outer
saloon, where he stood behind one of the card-players,
watching a game at *hocca*, and impressed him at once
by its foreign splendour. He had by this time grown
familiar with the charms of all the Court beauties—
with Madame de Longueville's blue eyes and flaxen
hair, and Madame de Montbazon's more imperious
features, with Madame de Hautefort's severe and refined
countenance, coldly aloof from the frivolous society with
which she mingled, as it were, under protest. His eye
had learnt the trick of most of those faces which the
enamels of Petitot have preserved for an admiring
posterity ; but this dark and glowing countenance, this
rich carnation bloom on a surface like old ivory, these
eyes that flashed like sunshine on a river, were new
to him. The lady moved amidst a bevy of babbling
friends, who had flocked about her eagerly as she entered
the room, and who were offering loquacious welcome.

"Was not Rome insufferably hot ? " "And how
many days had she spent on the journey ? " "And had
she escaped all alarms or molestation from brigands ? "
"And how had she left the Holy Father ? "—with
innumerable questions of the same kind, to all of which
attentions the lady responded with a haughty carelessness, when she condescended to make any reply
whatever. For the most part she received this noisy
homage with the air of being stone deaf.

She was looking about the room for some one—those
dazzling eyes hurriedly exploring the faces of the
crowd, as one who seeks a single face among a thousand.
Then all at once those roving glances changed to a
long and earnest gaze, and George flushed crimson at
the idea that it was upon him the lady's attention was
fixed, and that he must needs have been the person
for whom she had been looking. It was strange as an
incident in a dream, and the strangeness of it took his
breath away, and set his heart thumping against his
ribs in a mixture of wonder and fear, as if some witch
had pierced him with a fatal glance from eyes that
shot death.

Before he could recover himself the lady had passed into the next saloon, still followed by her obsequious courtiers ; and he tried to concentrate his attention upon the game he had been watching, and to forget that too brilliant face.

"The Marquise is as handsome as ever, and not a day older," said one of the players, in an indifferent voice.

"Oh, those Italian women have tricks of the toilet that can baffle time—unguents to rub out wrinkles, and essences to revive the fire of handsome eyes. I should not like to see Madame de Lussac before she has made her morning toilet."

"She is far too wise to be seen at a disadvantage. Nobody gets admittance to her *ruelle* till near dinner-time. But I have explored her countenance closely, in the broad daylight at Renard's Garden, and I give you my honour, she owes nothing more to art than a wash of pearl-white. Her eyebrows and lashes are as genuine as Juno's—and the splendour of her eyes has a deeper source than the apothecary's shop."

George could not long doubt that he had been the object of the lady's glances, for while these gentlemen were discussing the new-comer, one of Mazarin's innumerable hangers-on came to his elbow, and whispered a startling message in his ear.

His Eminence desired to see him in the adjoining room. Such a summons conferred infinite honour on so obscure a person as Mr. Mountain's secretary ; for the next saloon, if not the holy of holies where the Queen generally sat alone with her Minister, was next to that august chamber, and within earshot of her Majesty. Those evening conferences were supposed to be devoted chiefly to affairs of state ; for the Italian was now almost as supreme in power as Richelieu had been, and the formal and elaborate " Declaration " of the late King, made upon his death-bed, reducing the Regency to a formula, had fared no better than the testamentary depositions of later monarchs—Louis XIV., George I., for instance—and had been cancelled by Act of Parliament.

Mazarin was of an age and of a type to gain the heart as well as the confidence of the Royal widow; and there were sentimental reasons why he should be preferred, which Richelieu had foreseen, in his likeness to that splendid Englishman whose audacious passion had made the one brief romance of Anne's life. Who could doubt that the lonely lady cherished the memory of a too daring love, and that Mazarin's likeness to George Villiers was a passport to the Queen's immediate favour, and a reason why that favour should ripen into a warmer feeling than the common friendship of a sovereign for her prime minister?

Of the woman's feelings the world knew little. A strict and solemn etiquette guarded the Royal daughter of Spain, even in the midst of a frivolous and adventurous Court. The Queen was never known to converse with her Minister within closed doors; but it was certain that all her evenings were spent in his company, and in a *quasi tête-à-tête*; certain also that, supple, insidious, many-sided, past-master in the art of making others serve him, Mazarin's progress towards the position of a second Richelieu had been as rapid as it was unobtrusive.

The change from that outer assemblage of small nobility to the room where the princes and magnates of the land were gathered, impressed George as if he had come into a new world. Here were the same amusements—the card-tables; the musical instruments lying about on tabourets, to be taken up by some casual performer, and flung down again after an air had been played, or a snatch of song accompanied; the groups of whisperers and titterers; the shoulder-shrugs and disdainful elbows. All things were in form the same; but the spirit was different. Here there was a grandeur that awed him in spite of himself; here he saw a splendour of gold and gems that was subdued and harmonised by the exquisite adjustment of fabric and colour in the costumes alike of men and women; and here, most of all, there was a beauty of face and form which subordinated the richness of dress to the brilliancy of the wearers. The voices, the laughter, the movements, were like, yet different. Here were the supernal forms, the celestial ideals, the archetypal charms and graces of which all others seemed but tawdry imitations.

True that amidst this assemblage of handsome men and lovely women there were some forms more remarkable for ugliness or eccentricity than for ideal grace ; Condé, the unheroic father of the popular hero, a small, mean figure, ill clad, unclean, with greasy hair tucked behind his ears, yet the mark for everybody's adulation ; Angoulême, last of a vanished race, offspring of Charles IX. and Marie Touchet, elderly, gouty, basking in Court favour during an interval of release from the Bastille, where he had spent the better part of his life. Even the unbeautiful figures had a distinction in the young adventurer's eyes ; for here every figure was momentous in the making of history, and almost every head was carried in peril of the axe.

The courteous gentleman who had summoned George threaded his way discreetly through this elegant assembly, and led him to an alcove formed by the deep embrasure of a window, in which recess Madame de Lussac and Cardinal Mazarin were sitting apart, the lady in one of those ponderous, high-backed armchairs which are more comfortable than they look, the gentleman humbly accommodated on a tabouret—that modest, armless and backless seat, the right to occupy which in the presence of the sovereign was ever a burning question among the greatest ladies of the French Court. Some there were, indeed, among those magnificent personages —those Junos of the Louvre—who aspired to and claimed this honour for half a century, and went down to their graves unsatisfied. The tabouret was not for them.

" You are Mr. Mountain's secretary, I think, sir," said the Cardinal, looking up in the midst of an earnest conversation, as the young man drew near, and surveying him with a careless friendliness.

" Yes, your Eminence."

"This Mountain is one of the innumerable slaves and partisans of Madame de Chevreuse, and is devoted to the good cause," said the Cardinal. "I am pleased to make his secretary known to you, Marchesa, and hope that he too may be serviceable by-and-bye, when King Charles has put down the rebels, and England is calm enough to think of spiritual things. The English Catholics have need of all the help we can give them; and you have been ever a devoted daughter of the Church."

"I have but little else to live for," answered the lady, with a disdainful melancholy that struck George as the saddest note he had ever heard from the lips of a handsome woman.

That profound sadness was out of harmony with Madame de Lussac's beauty, which was calculated rather to dazzle and intoxicate the senses than to melt the soul. He stood before her in more embarrassment than he had felt since he had known the Queen Regent's Court, wondering why he had been presented to her, and suspicious of the Cardinal's motive in making the presentation.

Mazarin rose and left them, with a courteous inclination to the lady. He passed through the throng of notabilities, pausing here and there, now to murmur a sentence into the ear of the Duchesse de Longueville, lately married to a husband twice her age, but a model of all the virtues; now to buttonhole Marsillac, afterwards La Rochefoucauld, who was generally to be found in Madame de Longueville's vicinity; saluting princes and princesses of the blood Royal with the calm assurance of one who knew that any notice from him meant honour. The great Cardinal, he who lay asleep in his grave in the Church of the Sorbonne, had moved among them as a shape of fear, surrounded in the imagination of some men by the spectral forms of those whose judicial murder had helped in the making of his new France, Marillac, Montmorency, Chalais, Cinq Mars, De Thou. The trivial courtiers of a frivolous Court had quailed and shrunk within themselves before that quiet presence—the thin, crafty face, the look of mental power lighting the attenuated clay. Few in that splendid throng but had known bitter cause to hate the Red Cardinal, in the bloody death of kinsman or bosom friend. But this new master was of a milder temper. Sleek, handsome, courteous, accomplished in diplomatic evasion, rich in promises that were never to be kept, he glided past them to the bower of his Queen ; and the worst the common herd thought of him, at this early period of his power, was embodied in a licentious epigram, or jingled in a vulgar ballad.

The Marquise fanned herself languidly in a listless silence, while George stood by the empty tabouret, lost in wondering admiration, and awaiting her speech. He told himself that she was handsomer than Lady Llanbister ; but of a beauty as different as night from day. The lovely calm of the English matron's countenance was wanting here. Passion had set its fiery brand upon the low, broad brow, and about the full, ripe lips. There were lines which told of a passionate youth, an adventurous womanhood, of love, and hate, and fear, and the deep craft that comes where woman's life is a series of great risks and petty stratagems, the trivial, pitiful arts that recall the plover's ruses when she tries to lure the sportsman from her nest.

" And so you are one of Marie de Rohan's great army of martyrs," she said. " She will be here presently, I doubt, the centre of a bevy of antique admirers, but with her eyes ever on the door of her Majesty's *salon*—waiting to be summoned, and assuming all the airs of an adopted sister, the Queen's *alter ego*. How strange that so clever a woman should ignore the influence of time, and should return from banishment expecting to find Queen Anne as fond of her as she was eighteen years ago, when they intrigued with Buckingham, and fooled Richelieu with false hopes ! She comes back to find her old friend devoted to pious works and meditations, and only caring for one person's society. And she is short-sighted enough to plot against that very person, and to measure a worn-out friendship against a dawning love. She is still handsome, is she not? Are you one of her ardent admirers?"

"Nay, madame, I have never been in the Duchess's company."

"But you have had a finger in her plots? Your master is one of her emissaries."

"Any plotting in which my master has been concerned has been of an innocent kind, and for a good cause."

"Every cause is good till it fails—and then 'tis rank treason ; and the next step is to the scaffold. You have a good face, sir, and I should not like to hear your head had paid forfeit—as it surely will if you ally yourself with *that* lady. She is a born conspirator, and never easy save when she is the central spinner in a web of intrigue. She will spin such fetters about you as only the axe can loosen. The Cardinal never showed himself so much Richelieu's inferior as when he cancelled the late King's veto and suffered the return of that firebrand."

"You speak harshly of a lady who has at least been faithful to her religion and to her Queen, madame, and who has suffered cruel hardships and reverses."

"You are young, sir, and apt to believe that a handsome woman must needs be a persecuted saint. I know what value to set upon Marie de Rohan's affection for that kind, weak lady whom she once ruled, and whose maturer wisdom would fain keep her at a distance. I cannot say more in this place," she added hurriedly, as she rose to meet a lady who had newly entered, and who was approaching her with the smile of pleased greeting. "Come to my house to-morrow morning before eleven. You may chance to find me alone at that hour, though my chamber will be crowded at noon. My own Marie, you are younger and lovelier by a decade than when we parted in Spain! I have been longing for your arrival, my soul," she exclaimed, as she and the new-comer sank gracefully to about half their height, in the perfection of Court curtsies, then rose again and kissed each other airily on either cheek.

"Dearest Héloïse, it would need the poetry of Voiture or the wit of Balzac to praise your charms. My scanty feminine vocabulary lacks words. Yet I can at least assure thee that 'tis a glimpse of Paradise to meet thee after such long separation. Was it at Rome or Madrid we last saw each other?"

"Who is that lady with the conquering nose and the rose-coloured velvet robe?" George asked a gentleman who stood near him in the crowd in the doorway, watching the meeting of these two splendid ladies.

"Do you not know her? She is the most famous woman in France—the heroine of a dozen romances: the Duchesse de Chevreuse."

CHAPTER XI.

BEING bidden to visit the lovely Italian lady before eleven, George, in his desire to obey, was at the door of the Hôtel de Lussac ten minutes after ten. The house was a palace on a small scale, and lay between the church of Saint-Germain-l'Auxerrois and the Seine, the gardens extending to the river bank.

A groom of the chambers led George up a broad oak staircase, with richly carved panelling, and massive newels surmounted by the escutcheon of the De Lussacs, a bastion tower *sable*, on a crusader's shield *or*—reminiscent of a De Lussac's prowess before the walls of Acre—and past a long line of dead and gone De Lussacs, whose pictured faces gloomed through the dimness of a gallery lighted by casements set in such deep embrasures and divided by such heavy mullions that the small panes of glass seemed to admit gloom rather than light.

One of Madame de Lussac's women was waiting for the visitor, midway between the staircase and her mistress's apartments.

"You are before your time, monsieur," she said, "but Madame has taken her chocolate, and is willing to receive you."

The woman spoke French with a strong Italian accent, and her dark olive complexion, blue-black hair, and deep-sunk eyes under heavy black brows, suggested a Southern lineage. She was short and thick-set, richly dressed in black brocade, her lawn kerchief fastened with a large single diamond, a gem that seemed alive in the broken light of the gallery. She kept her sombre eyes upon the young man, with a severe and, as he thought, unfriendly, scrutiny, as she walked beside him to her lady's door.

"Here is your visitor, Marchesa," she said, pushing back the tapestry *portière* and entering the room before him—"impatient and in advance of time, as hot-headed youth ever is."

"Come hither, Monsieur Georges," said a languid voice, from the distance of an immense bed, mounted on an *estrade*, and of an architectural solidity that would have sufficed for a church, "and do not heed my woman's surly speech, who takes the utmost licence accorded to an old servant."

Madame de Lussac's bedchamber was even darker than the gallery, for the casements here were shadowed by voluminous velvet curtains, and the splendour of a Florentine toilet table, crowded with gold and crystals, glittered across a prevailing twilight. The bed was curtained as heavily as the five narrow windows, and George could only faintly divine the pale face of the Marquise, and a pair of flashing eyes looking at him earnestly, as she supported herself upon her elbow, in a reclining attitude, the fashionable posture in which to receive morning visitors.

Two young women were seated at a distant window, both working upon the same satin robe, engaged in scrutinising and repairing the embroidery, which had cost years of labour, and had but just escaped spoiling in the mob at the first performance of Corneille's new tragedy, at the Hôtel de Bourgogne.

"Take your work into the next room, Louison," said the Marquise; and the two girls rose, curtsied to the ground, and disappeared through a door near the window by which they had been sitting. "And you, too, Signora."

The elder woman did not obey, but walked to the bedside.

"Madame will be wanting her smelling-salts, or her pillows shifted," she said. "I had better stay."

"Madame desires nothing but to be alone with this young gentleman. Go!"

The slender white hand pointed imperiously to the door through which the two girls had vanished. The Signora gave an angry sniff, and marched out of the room, her shoulders drawn up to her ears in a sullen shrug, her high heels pattering on the polished floor with a rapidity which indicated mental irritation.

"Sit down, sir," said the Marquise, pointing to a tabouret on the *estrade* between the wall and the bed. "There is no worse tyrant than an old servant. I recommend you to change yours once in three years."

"I serve my master, madame, and have no servants I dare call my own."

"They will come in due time. You will have your own establishment perhaps sooner than your modesty anticipates. The Cardinal is interested in you."

"He has been slow to exhibit his interest, madame; and indeed, I know not why he should be interested."

"Do you not know that you are like him?"

The lady's haughty indolence had changed to an almost feverish intensity. She was indeed a woman in whom the light and fire of life burnt fiercely, and her speech was energetic, and her manner keenly earnest, whenever she deigned to be herself, and to throw aside that assumption of languid insolence which she maintained as a part of her splendour. This morning, in the gloom of the airless *ruelle*, in an atmosphere heavy with Oriental perfumes, leaning upon her elbow in a *déshabille* of lace and cambric, her form half buried in a large down pillow, the Marquise was intensely herself. Seldom had eyes so ardent and so searching fixed themselves upon the young man's countenance; and he felt his own eyelids fall under that feverish scrutiny.

"Come," she cried impatiently, "you must have discovered that you are like him—as like as a son might be—if he had a son."

"I caught our faces reflected in a mirror, Madame la

Marquise, and I noted a resemblance—but such a likeness between strangers is a common circumstance, and no ground for the Cardinal's liking."

"I said nothing of liking; but I say that he is interested in your career—and that he can push your fortune. He can, he must! He is not wholly adamant, not compacted, head and heart, of impenetrable self-love. And now tell me something of yourself. I know that your master is an adventurer—and dangerous, like all adventurers, a man of the Campion breed. But I want to know what you are. *Imprimis*, how old are you?"

"I do not know."

"Not know your own age? That is strange."

"There are other things that I do not know: the place where I was born; the name of the mother who bore me. In a word, Madame la Marquise, I am one of those unhappy creatures who have no history."

She drew a deep breath, and her face glowed as she looked at him.

"I thought as much," she said. "You do not look like common clay. If your past is a blank, so much the better for your future. You have to be the beginner of a great race. I hope you are ambitious."

He sighed, and was slow to answer, remembering his conversation with Lady Llanbister, and how in that discourse he had forsworn all vulgar ambition, desiring only to be worthy of that revered lady's friendship. But this woman had the power to kindle fiercer fires. She breathed her own passion into him, as she bent over him, with flashing eyes, and lips tremulous with excitement.

"Surely you are ambitious! Young, handsome, intelligent—why, you would be but a dull clod of earth if you did not hunger for fame and fortune!"

"I am nothing, Madame la Marquise, and must needs desire to be something."

"I will help you. I will be your lucky star. I am a childless woman. My husband is a great soldier —old enough to be my father, and loves the camp better than his fireside. I am always lonely—yes, in the midst of the crowd where you saw me last night—lonely, and an alien, and sometimes very wretched. I will be your guiding star. But you must tell me the story of your childhood. Were you brought up in France? You speak French like a Frenchman."

"I came to France when I was a child—and have lived but a short time in England. I have been a wanderer, for the most part, with my friend and master, Francis Mountain, with whom my fortunes are closely bound. If you are to help me, madame, you will have to help him."

"You begin to dictate to me already. Well, I will do what I can for your friend. You came to France while a child, you say. But where did you live before you came to France?"

"In England, madame, like an English peasant's child."

She was silent, and seemed surprised at this statement.

"In England, reared in England—as an English peasant's child. But surely you were not born in England—you have no British blood in your veins?"

"I have told you, madame, that it is my misfortune not to know my parentage. But my earliest memories are of England; and I have ever thought myself an Englishman."

"That cannot be," she answered, in her quick, eager way. "You have no quality of that phlegmatic race, which produces genius and beauty only once in a quarter of a century, and succeeds a Villiers, modelled in the likeness of a Greek god, with a heavy-featured provincial like Wentworth. Believe me, you are no Englishman. A child's memory reaches not further back than his third year; and what vicissitudes may you not have passed through before your infancy awoke to consciousness! You found yourself in England—in a peasant's cottage. You had been carried there by those who had custody of you. You understand, do you not? You were carried there, over land and sea. You were not born in that dull island, under that leaden sky!"

She leant over him as she spoke, and laid a feverish hand on his; and the fire in those Italian eyes held him like a witch's charm as she bent her eager face nearer, till he felt her breath upon his cheek. Was there not some touch of lunacy in this strange eagerness, some hallucination hanging to a troubled history which he knew not, and thus lacked the key to her strange conduct?

"Truly, madame, I know not how I may have been buffeted about in those years of unconsciousness. I may have been saved from the sea like Shakespeare's Marina, or suckled by a wolf, like him who founded Rome, and who, doubtless, remembered not his brute-foster-mother; but I know that I love the dull island you despise, and have friends there who make it the dearest country on earth for me, and so shall ever deem myself of English birth, till I receive proof positive of another origin.

The Marquise had sunk back among her pillows, and answered him with the languid air of one whose interest in his affairs had been but a caprice of the moment.

"Oh, you have friends in England? That makes a difference. A sweetheart perhaps."

"No, madame; the lady I most honour, and from whom I have received most kindness, is a lady of mature years, the wife of a noble gentleman, who resembles the Marquis de Lussac in being his wife's senior by over a quarter of a century."

"And the lady is as unhappy as I am, I'll warrant, with her ancient tyrant and jail-keeper."

"Indeed, no, Madame la Marquise. My dear lady's husband is no tyrant, and his wife honours and loves him, and has ever been contented with her lot."

"Contented? Ah, she is an Englishwoman, and phlegmatic! So long as she can eat three heavy meals a day, and is not too asthmatic to waddle to her coach, or too fat to squeeze herself into it, she is content. Why do you laugh, sir?"

"At your fancy portrait of an unknown lady."

"Have I hit her off so exactly?"

"You have described her very opposite. Lady Llanbister is tall and slim, and has a step as light and as quick as if she had seen but twenty summers."

"Llanbister! I have heard her name from the Queen. Is she not a friend of Marie de Rohan's?"

"She is a devoted servant of Queen Henrietta, and interested in all that concerns her Majesty."

"That means that she is deep in the Catholic plot. Let her take good heed lest she hazards that beautiful head of hers. Holland tells me your Puritan rabble in England are growing ever more dangerous."

"Alas, madame, religion has become but of secondary import in England since the King and the Parliament have been at war. It is no longer a creed that is in danger, but a Crown, and the question is whether that country is to remain faithful to the last of its long line of kings, or is to be ruled by a little knot of demagogues, the disciples and successors of that master spirit, John Pym, whose fiery soul was suddenly called away last December, following swiftly on his murdered victim, Strafford."

"I have heard of your demagogue leaders. This Pym was of the great Cardinal's temper, and trusted to the headsman's axe to hew down abuses."

"The execution of Lord Strafford was a judicial murder, madame, so remorseless and determined that one would fear for the most sacred life in England in the power of that ruthless faction, who pretend to strive for a people's rights, yet would be worse despots than the Indian Emperor, had they the upper hand."

"Your King should be able to deal with a single parliament, assembled over against his own palace. Our late King had to deal with many parliaments, and with provincial governors, each of whom was a king in little. Had Strafford been as great as Richelieu, Pym and his confederate would have cumbered the scaffold."

A clock on the chimney-piece chimed the half-hour.

"*Au revoir*, friend," said the lady. "I shall have all the world here presently. Come at supper-time to-morrow—ten o'clock—and I will show you my fine friends. They sup with me of a Thursday night, when they leave the Louvre."

"I shall be pleased to come, madame, if I may bring my friend and master, Mr. Mountain."

In spite of Madame de Lussac's gracious permission, George went to her supper-party unaccompanied. Mountain had business for that evening.

"And were I free to choose, I confess that I prefer a night at the Pine Apple or the Crab-tree to the finest company in a great lady's house. I like to hear the sound of my own voice, which I should not do there. I like to drink out of a deeper tankard than her lackeys would fill for me. I like to stretch these long legs of mine under a tavern table, and to laugh and argue with some of the cleverest men in France—all of which I can do without being beholden to Madame de Lussac."

"I fear you bear some ill-will to the lady."

"Not I. But she is ill friends with some whose liking I value, and I must not consort with her. For you she may prove a good friend, and I recommend you to make the most of your fortune in having won her countenance She is Mazarin's country-woman, and they have ever been close allies. So to know her should lead to pro-motion. There are hundreds of offices and sinecures at his disposal, any one of which would provide for the rest of your life."

"I do not look so far, Frank. But I confess myself curious about the lady. There was something in her speech and manner this morning which would have piqued any man's curiosity."

"Body o' me!" cried Mountain, with a broad laugh, "and was it the first time that a handsome woman of forty set you wondering why she was so civil?"

"Your speech and your grin are an insult to a lady

whose behaviour was innocent of all improper freedom. She talked to me of her childless condition, her solitary home."

"She may be on the look-out for an adopted son, and may think that you have a good figure for the situation. I have heard the lady's character, and am prepared for anything strange or romantic—a woman of vehement passions and sudden caprices; a restless, unsatisfied spirit, married to a man she hates, and who reciprocates her dislike; a wanderer at home and abroad—now buried alive at the Château de Lussac, in the desolate country between Marseilles and Montpelier, now living like a princess at Venice or at Rome, the friend of cardinals and ambassadors. She has been ever a dangerous woman, George; yet she has the power to be your very good friend!"

"Since when have you been so familiar with her character and history, Frank? You would tell me nothing about her when I questioned you last night."

"Would not because I could not, George. I have talked to-day with one who knows Héloïse de Lussac well."

"And hates her, as I guess from your discourse."

"Nay, George, who loves her just as much as one handsome, adventurous woman is wont to love another. Kiss and claw, George, claw and kiss! 'Tis the women's way."

"'Twas with Madame de Chevreuse thou wert confabulating; the woman against whom the Marquise warned me."

"Another of their ways, George. When a woman knows that her friend knows too much about her, she takes pains to spread the opinion that the said friend is a dangerous liar, and so lays a foundation of doubt beforehand."

"You are determined to make me think ill of this lady; but if your informant be Madame de Chevreuse, as I guess——"

"A man is no nearer the truth for guessing, George. 'Tis a cheap privilege, which I will not deny thee."

In his morning visit to the Hôtel de Lussac George had seen only the gloomy staircase and gallery, where the pictures and furniture had undergone but little change since that never-to-be-forgotten eve of Saint Bartholomew when the life-blood of a dying fugitive had splashed the outer door, and the massive oak had reverberated with the blows of savage pursuers, yelling threats of vengeance against the Papist household that dared to shelter a heretic. His evening view of the same house was a revelation, for he was now introduced to *salons* and *salle-à-manger* furnished and decorated with the elaborate splendour of the Italian Renaissance, and with a luxury of gold and colour and mosaic and inlaid work that surpassed the somewhat faded magnificence of the Louvre. Here taste had gone hand in hand with outlay, and the young man's eye, educated by the riches of the King's cabinet at Whitehall, was quick to mark the pencil of Raffaelle and Titian upon the walls, and the *chefs-d'œuvre* of the goldsmith's art which adorned the supper-table.

Dazzled by the brilliancy of the scene, and flattered by the infinite kindness of his hostess, George felt as one who has passed from the dull grey of life into the rainbow glory of a dream.

The party assembled at that exquisite table, in the light of a hanging candelabrum that held a hundred wax candles, was small and distinguished. Madame de Longueville and her young sister-in-law, the Duchesse d'Enghien, Richelieu's niece, still scarce more than a child, were present ; and they alone would have sufficed for distinction. Beaufort, young, handsome, popular, and arrogant ; De Retz, the Coadjutor, newly elevated to a dignity for which his habits and ideas were curiously unfit ; the Duc d'Angoulême ; Bassompierre, radiant after release from the Bastille, leaning across the table to compliment Madame de Longueville on her brother's victory.

"'Tis the first time in history that a battle has been won for a king of four years old on the fourth day of his reign, and by the youngest general in France

Ah, friends, 'tis youth now that throws the double sixes. We of a bye-gone generation, we who have danced and drunk with the Bearnais, and touched glasses with the lovely Gabrielle, may draw down our night-caps and blow out the candle."

Even among men of the oldest blood in France, the most distinguished guest was the Italian Cardinal, who came in late as the company were finishing supper, a brilliant figure in his scarlet robe, veiled by a *rochet* of Venetian lace, and exhaling an atmosphere of perfume from his flowing garments as he moved along the room. His moustache was curled as carefully as that of the youngest fopling in Paris, but the handsome face had a languid look. He came straight from his evening *tête-à-tête* with the Queen, and had the air of not having greatly enjoyed that privilege, which, in spite of open doors and Court ceremonial, was the subject of many a slanderous insinuation and many a malignant epigram. He would eat nothing, nor would he take wine. He sank wearily into the gilded chair which the lackeys brought for him from a daïs under a canopy at the end of the room, where Royal guests were wont to sit, and he took a bunch of grapes and a glass of water from the fair hands of his hostess, while the assembly hung upon his words. He had a civil speech for each of the more distinguished among the party—a compliment for the fair-haired Duchess, a jest for old Bassompierre, a friendly nod for De Retz, whom he patronised, and for Beaufort, whom he hated and feared ; but there was the languor of exhaustion and low spirits in his voice and manner, and the hand that lifted the heavy crystal goblet was faintly tremulous. George watched him wonderingly from his place behind Madame de Longueville's tabouret, that lovely lady having condescended to take particular notice of the untitled youth whom her hostess had presented to her.

" I love strange faces," she told him. " The world we live in at Paris is so stale that a new face is almost as welcome as a new volume by the inimitable Scudéri."

Madame de Lussac's violins struck up in the adjoining

salon, and played the first movement of a favourite coranto ; and the folding doors were flung open, revealing the perspective of brilliantly lighted rooms full of company. The great world of the Louvre had followed the Cardinal to Madame de Lussac's "night," as they would have followed him to the wickedest or the meanest house in Paris, self-interest pointing the way.

"Do not wait for me, gentlemen," said the Cardinal. "Your partners are on tip-toe for the coranto. I'll warrant my fair Duchesse d'Enghien has learnt by this time how to dance upon a polished floor with safety as well as with grace."

"Indeed, your Eminence, it was not the floor but my petticoat that made me fall," cried the Duchess, with a piteous little grimace, amidst the laughter of the company. "And I wonder how long impertinent people are going to remember an accident that happened when I was a child ? "

"Your Grace is taller by half a head since your marriage," said the Cardinal. "And I'll wager you can walk a coranto as gracefully as your husband, who was ever first in the ball-room, as he is first in the field."

"If he were here, no one would venture to laugh at me," pouted the Duchess.

"Let me be his deputy," laughed her sister-in-law, looking round at the company with a serio-comic defiance, her beautiful head, with its aureole of pale gold hair, flung back in that proud attitude which so well accorded with her Royal lineage. "I challenge this company to show proper reverence to my brother's wife, who was thirteen on her last birthday, and who is vastly offended that anybody should be so ill-bred as to remember that she tumbled down in the opening dance at the Palais Cardinal on her wedding-night."

"You are as bad as the rest of them, sister," cried the little Duchess, as old Bassompierre led her off, with the stately air of one who had been trained in the art of motion when Henry IV. was king.

Madame de Longueville followed with Marsillac, and

Beaufort with Madame de Liancourt, whose company poorly atoned for the absence of his latest divinity, the magnificent Madame de Montbazon, the handsomest and most audacious of the Court *houris*, whose quarrel with the Duchesse de Longueville had agitated all the great world of Paris, and whose exile from the Court Beaufort deeply resented.

The dance began, and the Cardinal remained seated at the head of the table in the *salle-à-manger*, from whence he could watch the dancers, while he conversed with the Marquise, who sat on a tabouret at his side.

"You look ill and weary," said Héloïse, when they were alone.

"How should I be otherwise? Do I lie on a bed of roses? Look at all those smiling faces. Note the subservience of your friends. Observe Beaufort's frank, manly air. I have reason to know that he has been plotting my death for the last month, thinking that were I underground he might recover his influence over the Queen, and become to all intents and purposes Regent of France. The stakes are high, you see; and Gabrielle's grandson has always been a bold player."

"You have the Queen on your side—your devoted, your loving friend—whose affection must be your strong rock," urged Héloïse, with a smile that betrayed the bitterness lurking behind her speech.

"Her affection," echoed Mazarin. "Her affection my strong rock! My shifting sand, rather, Héloïse! The one thing in this world of which I am least certain is the Queen's favour. I know that Beaufort hates me. I know that Marie de Rohan is capable of planning my death. Nay, that bold, adventurous witch who rode *à califourchon* to Spain—a beardless cavalier in black velvet—ready to fling aside doublet and hose, and exchange the handsome *hidalgo* for the beautiful *bacchante*, at any stage of her journey—would as lief hold the knife herself, as trust it to a hireling. I know that she has the two Campions in her pay—one her lover—both her slaves. All this I know. But whether the Queen values or loves me ; whether, when she seems to yield to my counsel, to defer to me as a pupil to a master, to look up to me as a novice to her Abbess, she is but using me as her tool—the living rampart between her and her foes ; and whether, if the hour of failure came, and she saw me weak and beaten, she would fling me to the wolves ;—is a riddle that I dare not answer. I dare not say I am sure of that woman."

"Is she so vile a creature? Do you so loathe the being you are said to love—your mistress, your adoring mistress?"

"That is a lie, Héloïse, and you know it."

"Is it a lie? To-night, perhaps! But will it be a lie always?"

Mazarin's brow darkened, and he sat silent. The lively music of the twenty-nine violins, and the animation of the dance, were loud enough to prevent the possibility of any speech of these two being overheard, however energetic ; and Mazarin's denunciation of the lady's slander had been intense rather than vehement.

"There was a time when you thought yourself invincible," Héloïse said, searching his brooding coutenance with her brilliant eyes, rapping his listless hand sharply with her fan, as it lay languidly upon the arm of the chair, to recall his attention. "But perhaps you feel that the age of *boudoir* victories is past, and that, with the Cardinal's robe, you have assumed a more venerable character. If I count myself an old woman you can scarce consider yourself a young man."

"Your adorable sex ages earlier than our ruggedness —as delicate flowers wither in the frost which leaves the oak unscathed."

"But you must feel that youth is past—youth which alone is invincible. Forgive me for slandering the Queen. I can believe that there is nothing but a stately friendship in her regard for you. Beaufort is as handsome as Apollo ; a bold, reckless devil, too, as you say, with all the gallantry and romance of his Royal grandfather. If the Queen is human enough to entertain a tenderness for any man living, Beaufort must needs be the man."

"Your lively wit ever hits the mark, *chère âme*," answered Mazarin, in those dulcet tones the courtiers knew so well. "If Buckingham has had—or is to have—a successor in Anne's lukewarm affections, Beaufort is the man. Yet she is so profound a dissimulator, so apt a pupil of that arch-hypocrite, the late King, that I should not wonder if, half a year hence, the world, and even you, Héloïse, may think that I am the favourite ; should I live so long, *bien entendu*."

"Why do you move about Paris with only a couple of lackeys behind your coach? Why go from the Louvre to your house on foot and alone, if you fear assassination ? "

"I do not *fear*, Héloïse. I no more fear death to-day than sixteen years ago at Casal, when I rode between the cross fire of adverse armies, bareheaded, a messenger of peace."

Her face flushed, and her eyes sparkled at the recollection his words evoked.

"Ah, you were a soldier, then, Julio, not a diplomatist. That was a glorious day ! Dieu, how the time comes back to me ! And all you were then—and all I was ! Sixteen years ! What has the interval made of us both ? "

"It has made you a woman of the world, and me the inheritor of Richelieu's policy, and Richelieu's enemies. If I talked of the dangers that hem my path, it was not because I fear the men and women whose servility is only a mask for their hatred—any more than the great Cardinal feared his inexorable foes. But it is harassing to have to reckon with a company of traitors ; to clasp hands that are itching to pull the trigger or thrust the poignard home. It is harassing to walk through streets where a dozen trained murderers may be standing in the shadow of projecting gables, pistols cocked, swords unsheathed."

"Why not ask the Queen for a guard ? "

"Never ! She shall offer one. Till she does I will

take my chance. She would be sorry, perhaps, if she heard that her faithful servant's mutilated corpse had been found behind a buttress of Saint-Germain, within a stone's throw of her palace. Enough, Héloïse! I talk to you as I dare talk to none other—except my secret journal—and even there I never trust myself to write in French, for fear of broken locks and prying eyes."

"I am glad you honour me with your confidence," said the Marquise, still with the same sub-acid tone and ironical smile, "even though every other feeling is dead."

"Time and death are synonymous, *chère*. Something of us dies every day we live. You must not be angry with me because I am mortal. Across that long perspective of past years, since we fought for the Valteline, think how many brilliant figures have passed—how many and how powerful reasons the lovely Héloïse de Lussac has had for being somewhat oblivious of an old friend in a black robe!"

"I have been what the world, and you, have made me."

"You have not hidden your beauty in the wilderness, with Mary Magdalene, or sought escape from life's allurements behind a convent gate. My dear Héloïse, you have done well to enjoy life's too brief summer. There is plenty of time for the woollen habit and the scourge. I see you have brought that young Englishman into your house. Was it wise, do you think?"

Her cheek flushed angrily as she retorted, "Where was the unwisdom?"

"On his account, I think, you have been ill-advised. To bring him into a circle so far above him is to inculcate discontent. He has already a fearlessness that would soon become insolence. He is not likely to make friends among your visitors ; and he is more than likely to make enemies."

"How can you talk of him as if he were some low-born wretch who ought to be in the kitchen, scraping trenchers ?"

"Better in the kitchen, than where he may give umbrage to one of your noble friends, who would refuse to fight with a *roturier*, and might order his lackeys to wait at your door and horsewhip the offender. Do you think that Marsillac, or Beaufort, or De Retz, would show much forbearance to a youth without friends or pedigree?"

Héloïse rose from her seat with a movement of uncontrollable impatience.

"He has one friend who would go through fire and water to serve him," she said, trembling with angry feeling. "Oh, you have a heart of ice—you—to talk of his pedigree—you, who ought to be proud, enraptured, to have found——"

"To have found what? An English adventurer of twenty-two years old, or so, who happens to be like what I was at the same age. I regret my folly in calling your attention to an accidental likeness."

"He is not of English birth—and the fact that he has spent his infancy in England helps to identify him. He speaks French as no Englishman ever spoke."

"Would that prove him of Italian lineage? I have made myself acquainted with his history. This youth is a cosmopolitan, a hanger-on of that half-gipsy adventurer, Francis Mountain—who in turn is a hanger-on of La Chevreuse. Had I thought you would take this business so seriously, Héloïse, I would have let that young man perish sooner than challenge your interest in him."

Her eyes flashed sudden fury.

"You would have let him perish—yes! If he is the man I hope—the man I believe him to be—it is by no merit of yours that he is still upon this earth, and not under it. You would have liked that better, perhaps."

"You do ill to upbraid me because I held your good repute higher than any other consideration. But you were ever a creature of violent caprices, and no man could prophesy from which quarter the wind of passion would blow. If he is the man you think him, what then? Two-and-twenty years ago you had but one prayer—that your son's existence might not disgrace you. Do you want to invite disgrace now? Remember that though the world we live in may seldom reckon the number of a great lady's adorers, it will be less indulgent to the woman who dares to acknowledge a nameless son, unless she can father him upon a king."

"Acknowledge him! You know that I could not acknowledge him. You know that De Lussac's heart is hard as the nether millstone. He would have no mercy. Two-and-twenty years ago! True, I prayed only that I might be saved from the world's contempt —from a father's cruelty. The future was before me— a great marriage—a brilliant career—to be the mother of a noble line—brave sons—lovely daughters. Now I have only the past. God's curse was upon my marriage—and on my offspring. The daughter I worshipped withered in my arms—faded on my bosom —and no other child came to fill the vacant place. My husband's heart hardened against me. I am a desolate woman, loveless, friendless, solitary in the midst of fine company. I have no hope for my old age, except the hope of finding the child whose birth was my despair."

The suppressed passion in her voice, the heaving of her bosom, threatened hysteria, and the Cardinal dreaded a tragical scene. He laid a restraining hand upon the arm that was lifted in an impassioned gesture.

"*Carissima mia*, is this a place or time for emotion? Since you have set your fancies upon this friendless— and, as I believe, low-born youth, we must do the best we can for him. Cherish him as you please—have him about your person—make him your page, or your secretary. Be sure he can be bought from his present master by an offer of better wages. Only, as you love me, let there be no scandal about him. If you are scornful of a world that wearies you, I am still a humble dependent upon the world's favour; and, since I have always been mindful of your interests——"

His glance seemed to take in all the surrounding

splendour in one swift sweeping survey, as he said those last words; and there was a significance in the look which might be interpreted, "Since my purse has furnished the means for your almost Royal state."

"Yes, yes, I know," she answered fretfully, the tide of passion ebbing, and a pale weariness creeping over the face that had flamed with anger. "You have been generous. Without the help of your purse I must have buried myself in a convent ten years ago—driven there by rapacious creditors. But I am sick of it all—the splendour—the struggles—the triumphs. If Marie de Rohan—who has had more adventures in a year than I in a lifetime—if she was as tired of her existence as I am of mine——"

"She knows no weariness. She will never tire. She is the incarnate spirit of intrigue—and while that splendid frame endures—though wrinkles come, and grey hairs—that unresting intellect will plot and conspire, flatter and betray. She has the Queen's ear still, though she has outworn the Queen's affection. They talk of Buckingham together, perhaps; and of the garden where Anne walked with him in the dark; and of that audacious hour when he found his way to her chamber and grovelled on his knees beside her bed; but I question if even those romantic memories can rekindle the old affection. Two women of mature age—one a born adventuress, the other the very pattern of piety—dwelling on the memory of an early intrigue! Faugh! It is not a pleasing picture."

"How you hate the Chevreuse!"

"Hate her! No more than I hate my antagonist at chess. We are playing an intricate game—our stake the Queen—and I think I shall checkmate her; if——"

He left the sentence unfinished, as he rose from his chair.

"If what?"

"If she does not spoil my game with Campion's dagger! There is always that risk. Come, Héloïse, take me to this wonderful youth, and let me discover if he has any higher recommendation to my favour than a handsome face and figure."

The second dance ended as the Cardinal moved slowly along the room, with the Marquise at his side, through a lane of salutations ; lovely ladies sinking almost to the ground in slow and solemn curtsies, with a stately subservience ; lofty heads bending before the minister who had power to give or to refuse ; abject smiles upon lips that nature had made for scorn rather than for humility ; necks, that hereditary pride should have stiffened, bending gracefully to the yoke of a foreign adventurer, an alien who could boast neither Richelieu's noble lineage nor Richelieu's far-reaching intellect.

George had been honoured with the hand of one of his fair patronesses, a handsome young widow who had caught sight of him standing modestly in the background, and had claimed him as her partner, pleased to find her untitled *protégé* in such an aristocratic company.

He had but just handed the lady to a seat when the Cardinal approached and stood for at least five minutes conversing with him, an act of condescension at which the surrounding company wondered, not without a touch of malice.

No matter how banal the great man's speech, how trivial and automatic those civil inquiries as to the stranger's business or pleasure in Paris, the intended length of his residence, his liking for the things he saw —the mere fact that Cardinal Mazarin stopped to talk with this good-looking nobody was enough to set a hundred tongues wagging.

Why had he been so favoured, and how came that arrogant woman Madame de Lussac to notice the hanger-on of a foreign adventurer like Mountain, a man of whom nobody knew any good ?

CHAPTER XII.

IN acting over again the scene of that evening, as he lay feverishly wakeful upon his pallet at the sign of the Golden Crown, listening to the chimes that told the hours, and half, and quarter hours, from that neighbouring tower whence had sounded the tocsin of murder—George hardly knew whether to be proud or humiliated at his experiences in Madame de Lussac's assembly.

He had received much hospitality from those smaller gentry of Queen Anne's outer circle ; but to-night he had mingled with those of the inner circle, the privileged by birth or elect by Royal favour ; and in the faces that had looked at him he had seen more than once the freezing smile, or the scornful wonder, which tells a man he is an intruder, or at least an unexplained presence. And yet, though the memory of such looks stung him to the quick, he could hardly help being gratified by the marked kindness of his hostess, and by the Cardinal's signal favour.

Late as George returned to his lodgings, Mountain was later, and as the elder man ever made up next morning for the sleep he sacrificed over-night, his comrade had little hope of conversing with him before dinner—a meal they took at noon in the public room, in company with other lodgers, and a good many droppers-in, and at which there would be small chance of private talk.

George awoke earlier than usual after his sleepless night, and, having no better use for his time, went off to the riding-school near the Place Royale, the school founded by Pluvinel, that great master of the *manège*, whose traditions were still carried on, though Pluvinel had been dead a quarter of a century. Here he tried to calm his spirits by a morning's active exercise, vaulting, leaping, passaging, caracoling, on horses that gave their rider no leisure for consciousness of his own existence. A young man mounted on a destrer of full blood had to be all muscles and sinews, a mindless being with an iron wrist, and a frame sensitive to the slightest movement of the beast under him. There was no pity in that arena for the bad rider; and to see a gallant cavalier sprawling on the sand with his spurs in the air was the surest incentive to mirth among the flock of fine gentlemen who spent their mornings at the famous school.

George was master of all the manœuvres of the ring, the *terre-à-terre*, or forward jump, the *demi-volte*, *courbette*, *cabriole*, and had at once secured the approval of Pluvinel's successor and his numerous assistants, whose sole estimate of a man's moral and physical value was grounded upon "hands" and "seat." A handsome rider on a handsome horse was the riding-master's idea of an archangel.

"You ride as well as your countryman, Lord Herbert," he told George, "a gentleman I should have admired more had he been less of a braggart. But he rode next best to the old Duc de Montmorency. And you are near as good with the foils as he, though he was always wanting to kill somebody, which you are not."

George smiled a bitter smile at this praise. Would any of those fine gentlemen, who aired their idleness at the riding-school, have deigned to cross swords with him, who could show neither patent of nobility nor witness of gentle birth? He had noted the contemptuous good-nature with which these Frenchmen talked of his friend Mountain; and he knew how little consideration he had to expect from them. He had secured their forbearance, and even their respect, by

an unobtrusive manner and a somewhat stately reserve ;
but he carried himself carefully on his guard against
unmerited insult.

To-day he discovered an altered tone in some of the
men he had met at Madame de Lussac's assembly, and
who were inclined to compliment him on his hostess's
favour, and the Cardinal's notice ; but he opposed to
these compliments an icy reserve, which was set down
to his insular stolidity.

"I wonder that a man can talk such good French,
and yet remain so thoroughbred an English pig," said the
Comte de Nanglois, to his cousin the Baron de Mauprat,
when George had turned his heel upon a cluster of
petits maîtres, and had sprung on to the back of a fine
Normandy percheron, which was to be broken for a
charger, and of which the master had offered him the
first trial.

The percheron had his head on the ground and his
heels in the air before George's feet were in the stirrups,
and then, while his rider settled himself in his saddle, tried the effect of walking round the ring on his
hind legs, like a demon cat ; and finally, finding this
manœuvre fail in dislodging the unwelcome burden,
accomplished a rapid succession of buck-jumps, which
the old riding-master applauded as the prettiest thing
he had seen that morning.

"The fellow can ride," muttered the Baron to the
Comte. "I believe he must have been groom and
horse-breaker to the Marquis of Newcastle when
Mountain picked him up."

"No, *mon ami*, Mountain picked him up as a baby,
asleep on a gun-carriage at Pormous. I heard him
tell the story the other night over his cups at the
Pine Apple, after this sober young gentleman had gone
home to his lodgings."

Francis Mountain had a constitution that a pro-
fessional gladiator might have envied, and an appetite
that neither mental anxiety nor deep drinking could
impair. He ate as heartily as usual of the wine-soup

and the stewed beef, and demolished a chicken afterwards, leaving nothing but the bones, which he threw under the table, for the dogs and cats to fight for. But he was much less loquacious than usual at dinner to-day. He asked George a few careless questions about his evening's entertainment, at long intervals in a thoughtful silence—and was obviously inattentive to the young man's answers.

"Your own business kept you later than usual, Frank," said George. "I hope it was a pleasant business."

"No, it was not, George. It was d——d unpleasant."

"And it was a secret business, I take it; for you are generally more ready to tell your adventures. And I have seldom seen you with so gloomy a brow— even when our luck was at the lowest."

"Oh, 'tis nothing out of the common, George. A man must think sometimes, you see—even as scatter-brained a scoundrel as I. There must be serious moments, when black Care jumps on to the back of the saddle. I have taken to thinking of late."

"I am sorry for it, sir, since I, who have been ever a slave to dark thoughts, have found my chief comfort in a light-hearted master."

"You will be leaving me, belike, if I grow gloomy. You will take service as gentleman usher to Madame de Lussac."

"Never while you want me, Frank. I owe you too much."

"Don't make it a question of debt," interjected Mountain pettishly.

"And I love you too well."

"That's better. But you are no longer the lad that tramped the world's highway with me, and had no other friend or counsellor. You are Lady Llanbister's pupil ; and she has stuffed your brains with high notions, and taught you that this is honourable, and t'other thing is shameful, and that a young man must never consult his pocket or his inclinations, but must remember how King

Arthur or the Chevalier Bayard would have proceeded in the same circumstances. Oh, I know these preaching women, and their fanciful morality, and their monstrous ignorance of the world they live in."

"You know Lady Llanbister to be the most admirable, the most honourable of ladies, as she is the kindest."

"Oh, I admit her honour and her kindness; but I bear her a grudge for stealing my boy. You have never been quite the same to me since you knew her. You have taken a questioning air; and I'll warrant if I were entangled in some business that your scrupulousness could not stomach, you would turn traitor and leave me."

"Never while you needed me, Frank. But, indeed, I fear from your speech now, and your manner of late, that you have been beguiled into some perilous companionship. I am too young to lecture or to counsel; but oh, my dear master and benefactor, I entreat you to keep aloof from all plots and plotters—even from that great lady, Madame de Chevreuse, whom you call your friend."

"She is my friend, and has been yours too, George, in the days that are gone. She has filled your maw when you were nigh upon starving. You did not know who helped us in our worst vicissitudes."

"I remember that you had a mysterious friend—and that when luck was lowest an unseen hand was stretched out to succour us."

"Marie de Rohan's hand, George; and there is no more liberal hand in Christendom, as there is none more beautiful. She is a woman who will always be poor, because she can never be otherwise than generous."

"It is Madame de Chevreuse I fear. Her life is a history of conspiracies."

"She has no further occasion to conspire, George. She is restored to her home and her friends. She has the Queen's favour. There is no greater power in France than hers. She can make and unmake ministers."

"Is she a match for Cardinal Mazarin? His power is growing—hers waning. If she will but submit to take the second place—and not struggle for ascendency over the Queen—all may go well. But if she opposes her puny power to the master of France——"

"Nay, George, never addle thy brains with politics. Nature has fitted thee for Courts, to twang a theorbo, or to teach a young lady Latin. Make the best of life while thou art young and handsome, and thank God thou art privileged to live in this gay city, and not among sour-visaged sectaries in London."

"I have but two troubles here, Frank—fears for your safety——"

"Dismiss them, and have done with trouble number one. What is t'other?"

"The thought that my place is a sinecure. I am no longer of any use to you; and I am not earning my bread, as I did when I was Mistress Geraldine's tutor."

"Who says you are no use? Did you not brush this doublet, and polish this sword-hilt, and furbish a hat and plumes that have seen better days, while I lay snoring? And will you not sit by my bed to-night and put vinegar on my head, if I come home with my brains on fire with their vile Burgundy wine? What more can any gentleman want of his squire?"

"Alas, that you should ever need that last service!"

"Oh, thou Puritan! What is it the old fat knight says in the play? 'Because thou art virtuous, are there to be no more cakes and ale?' I grant you I drink more in Paris than I used to drink in London; though we had some famous nights at the Devil Tavern. I have livelier friends here, and move in higher company," he said, taking up the cloak which he had flung upon his bed. "Prythee, adjust my cloak, George, and see that the buckles of my sword-belt are safe. I have a visit to pay in the Marais. You can amuse yourself as you will, 'twixt now and midnight; but if you are playing page to Madame de Lussac, remember to keep a silent tongue about me and my business. And never talk of sinecures—or of earning your bread. My purse is not empty yet! and when it is, I know those who will fill it. You are as dear to me as the son I never had—dearer, perhaps ; for his notion of filial duty might be to lecture me—which you must not do."

Tone and look gave significance to the last sentence ; and George felt that his master meant it as a warning against a too-officious solicitude.

Mountain went out immediately after, and his squire had nothing to do but wander about the streets, or to beguile the summer afternoon by a swimming-match in the adjacent river, were he so minded. He was too wise to begin this sport soon after the solid mid-day meal, and so sauntered in the streets and gardens and open places of the gayest city in Europe, meeting several acquaintances of the Louvre and the riding-school in the course of his wandering, but carrying with him a heavier heart than his friends suspected.

He was disturbed by his late conversation with Mountain, for he told himself that were his master not involved in some perilous enterprise, some treasonous plotting against authority, there would be no need for such reserve. He had never pried into his master's secrets ; but never before had Mountain failed to give him some inkling of the business that engaged him, being, indeed, a sanguine and somewhat loquacious soul, always seeing gold, fame, and happiness, in any incipient enterprise.

It was the first of September, and there was that keen freshness in the air which comes with the first breath of autumn. After an hour's exercise in the river, George found plenty of amusement for his idleness in the gardens and along the quays, loitering with the crowd on the Pont Neuf, watching a company of *saltimbanques* or listening to a ballad-singer, at the risk of having his money stolen by a cut-purse, or his cloth mantle snatched off his shoulders by a *tire-laine*, cloak-snatching being then a common practice of the Parisian rogue. Then there was Tabarin's theatre on the quay, hard by King Henry's bridge, where there was always some laughable farce, or some quack-salver's facetious tirade to waste an idle man's time, and extract a few sols from his pocket.

For all refreshment, being still of a boyish sobriety, George treated himself to a cup of chocolate at Madame Servant's in the Place de l'École; and he loitered, listening to the talk of a group of card-players at the table near where he sat, who filled the pauses of their game with a discussion of the Regent and the Cardinal —the little Richelieu, as one of them called him scornfully. They were among Beaufort's partisans, and were eager for change, careless whether change meant Paris in arms, churchmen preaching rebellion, and a repetition of that terrible Day of Barricades, which old people could remember.

He had been seeking distraction from those gloomy forebodings, caused by Mountain's enigmatical behaviour; he had courted noisy company and trivial amusements, comedians and quack-salvers, all the afternoon; and it was sundown before he turned his back on the busy quay, and strolled westward, past the steep slate roof and conical turrets of the Louvre, past the Porte Neuve, flanked by the Tour du Bois, whose twin peaks over-topped the Palace roof—past the Tuileries gardens, to the carriage road beside which benches had been placed for the accommodation of the humbler citizens of Paris, who came here of a summer evening to see the fine company.

Across the river sparkled the lanterns on the quay, and in the shadowy background solitary lights in convent windows showed dim through the evening grey, and the carillon of the Samaritaine, the great clock of the Waterhouse, on the Pont Neuf, rang clear in the still air.

Between the river and the bench where George seated himself, carriages and horsemen were passing thicker than he could count or distinguish them; for this broad highway was the famous Cours la Reine, the carriage road from the Bois de Boulogne to the Tuileries, made by Marie de Medicis in her day of power—a promenade the most brilliant that history has on record, perhaps, if it be remembered what manner of mortals passed between Palace and wood in these golden days of Condé's conquests and Anne's indulgent rule.

George stood up to see those ponderous gilded coaches, those spirited horses, splendid cavaliers, plumed hats and flowing hair, smiling faces radiant in a cloud of dust, jewels less brilliant than the beauty they adorned, throats that outshone the pearls that circled them, gold and silver, satin and velvet, all the glory of this earth that patrician blood can inherit, or vulgar money can buy. All these things were passing in swift procession before his eager gaze; faces he knew, faces that were strange; the women craning out of their coaches to smile on favoured admirers; the men reining in their horses beside the carriage-doors, leaning half out of their saddles to talk to the lovely occupants.

The grey light of evening was full upon the young man's face as he stood up to watch the glittering train, and he was startled presently by an imperious voice calling to a postilion to stop, and the sudden halt of a great white-and-gold coach with six horses, three postilions, three footmen hanging on behind, a pair of outriders, and a group of attendant cavaliers, which unprepared arrest threw the triple line of carriages into confusion.

It was the Marquise de Lussac's coach that blocked the way.

"What are you doing there, Mountain?" she asked. "You had better ride with me than stand staring like Jacques Bonhomme. Open the door for Monsieur," to one of the lacqueys, who had alighted when the cavalcade came to a standstill.

Madame de Lussac was alone in her coach; and when George would have seated himself with his back to the horses she ordered him to the place beside her. The gentlemen who had been riding in attendance upon her looked at each other curiously, shrugged their shoulders, and dropped into the background as her coach turned towards the Bois and that large space of market gardens through which Queen Marie's drive had been made.

"I am glad of this meeting," said the lady. "I wanted to talk with you last night; but from the time Mazarin appeared there was no chance. He was very kind, was he not? Did you not feel that your fortune was made, when he stopped to converse with you? If you did not, be sure others did, and you will have to reckon with their envy as well as their surprise."

"I was honoured by his Eminence's notice, Marquise; but I know 'twas no spontaneous beneficence moved him, and that I am more in debt to your kindness than to his. And as to fortune, I would sooner owe it to my friends in England, who have known me well for these three years last past, than to the Cardinal."

"To Lady Llanbister, you mean? You would rather owe all to her than to me."

"I said rather to my old friends—Lord and Lady Llanbister—whom I know and honour, than to Cardinal Mazarin, whom I do not know——"

"And do not honour. Why not finish the sentence?"

"Indeed, Marquise, I meant no disrespect to his Eminence, who is a man of great gifts—and a most noble presence. But to an Englishman's mind the despotic power which Richelieu held so long, and to which his successor is said to aspire, is ever intolerable. The English people cannot brook a one-man government; not even when the man is as great as Strafford."

"I see you have learnt your lesson from Mazarin's enemies. Their name is legion; for they include every greedy courtier to whom he has refused a place or a pension."

"I swear I have learnt no lesson, Marquise. I am old enough to have opinions of my own."

"And thinking so ill of the Cardinal I doubt you would stand by and see him murdered, were his enemies lucky enough to accomplish what they have been plotting for the last six weeks."

"My sword would leap from its scabbard to defend any man against an assassin."

" Even if the assassin were a friend of your own ? "

" Yes, were that possible ; which it is not."

" You do not know ! Your master—your friend—is in league with Madame de Chevreuse ; and where she is there is treason. He has been seen at the Angel in the Rue St. Honoré with the two Campions. He does not take you there perhaps? That tavern is the rallying-point of traitors ; and I doubt he fears your simplicity too much to let you into their schemes. You can judge yourself how he is occupied, and whether he has dangerous secrets."

George's brow clouded. He knew too well that his master was working in the dark ; but he could not believe him involved in any plot that might culminate in murder.

" Why should any one seek the Cardinal's life ? "

" For the same reason that Richelieu lived all his later life in peril of assassination. Under a king who was but a shadow the Prime Minister was absolute master, and was hated as kings are hated. Every vainglorious schemer who thought himself a great man was at war with that real greatness. And now, merciful, generous, indulgent as Mazarin has been, he is already almost as well hated as Richelieu was. They see him climbing to the summit—see the King's long minority before them, and France at the feet of a ruler who will humble those haughty heads, as Richelieu humbled them, or lay them as low as Richelieu laid others. Beaufort, Chavigny, Gondy, Marsillac, they all hate him because they all fear him."

" You speak as if you had secret knowledge of a plot against the Cardinal, madame ? "

" I know that there is such a plot—by indirect evidence rather than actual proof. Beaufort's troops have been drinking in the taverns about the Cardinal's house, night after night, for the last fortnight. I believe it is only since Madame de Montbazon's disgrace that the plot has become imminent. Mazarin's movements have been watched and followed, and Beaufort's men have been lying in wait for him—ready to strike the fatal blow. So far they have missed their opportunities; once, in the Faubourg Saint-Germain, when he was on his way to the Luxembourg, to visit Monsieur; again on his return from Maison. Had he been alone in his coach on either occasion, he might have been murdered. While ostensibly selling his horses, Beaufort has been secretly buying double the number. No one who knows these facts can question that these men mean murder."

"If they do, my master is not of their party. I would pledge my life that he would have no hand in so vile a business. He is brave, generous, kind—and he is a gentleman."

"Was not Cinq Mars a gentleman, and Chalais? Yet either of these would have slain Richelieu with his own hand, or by a hireling's, and would have thought he did a noble act. If you care for your friend —if you would prevent murder, worm yourself into his confidence, find out with whom he is in league, and bring the intelligence to me without an instant's delay. While we are riding here, in this peaceful scene, in this soft evening hour, the assassins may be getting ready for their work."

"Turn spy and betray the man who has been to me as a father?"

"*He* shall not suffer. His name shall not leak out —I pledge myself to that. And remember, it is to prevent a murder, and the worst kind of murder."

"I will not betray my benefactor."

"You are not bidden to betray him. You are urged to save him from a crime for which he might be broken on the wheel. If you have any influence over him you may make him withdraw from the plot, and help to save the Cardinal. And remember, George, it is your duty to save Mazarin—if you have power to save him—even at the hazard of your life. It is your duty!" she repeated, with all the intensity of which her fiery nature was capable.

"It is every honest man's duty to prevent a crime,

at any cost to himself. You have no need to tell me that, Marquise!"

"It is *your* duty. There may come a time when you will understand the full force of these words—as you cannot now."

George hardly noted the significance of this speech at the moment, though he pondered over it later. His brain was on fire. His heart beat thick and fast. He knew that there was a change in his friend—that Francis Mountain's mind was bent upon some business more serious, more agitating, than anything that had occupied him in the past. To save that good friend from being implicated in a murderous scheme—the tool of high-bred villainy? What would he not do, what would he not venture, for such a purpose? But he felt himself powerless as a child. He could only trust to the urgency of a child's appeal to a father whom he saw on the brink of a precipice.

"Will you stop your carriage, madame? I must go back to Paris," he said.

"My coach shall carry you there."

She gave the order, "To the Louvre as fast as you can;" and the ponderous coach turned, the postilions cracked their whips, and the leaders cantered along the now deserted road, while the four horses in the rear kept up with them in a sharp trot.

"I will do all that Heaven will help me to do, Marquise. But I know nothing of my master's movements when he leaves our lodging. I know not where to look for him."

"Try the traitors' rendezvous. Try the Angel."

The remaining distance was travelled in silence. The street lanterns and the lights of the Louvre were soon in sight. The horses were reined up on the quay near the open space in front of the Palais Cardinal, and George sprang lightly to the ground, lifted his hat in brief salutation to the Marquise, and hurried almost at a run to the Rue St. Honoré, where he slackened his pace, composed his features, and assumed the saunterer's air, while he debated within

himself how best to surprise his master among the associates whose company meant deadly peril for Francis
Mountain.

In spite of Madame de Lussac's vehement appeal, it
was not of the Cardinal he thought. It was of his
benefactor, the man who had picked him up on Southsea Common, fatherless, nameless, friendless, homeless.
Not for worlds would he have this cherished friend
the accomplice of murderers—himself ignorant of their
ultimate aim ; for he could not believe that Mountain
would knowingly consort with assassins. It was of
the reckless, happy-go-lucky, dare-devil Mountain he
thought. To be broken on the wheel! Yes, for the
untitled conspirator that would be the sentence of the
law. Not for him the dignity of headsman and block,
the fate of Chalais and Cinq Mars. For him the lingering death of the common felon, merciless, disgraceful,
excruciating agony, for which a crushing blow from the
executioner's iron staff was a stroke of mercy. To step
in between his master and those fatal associates, to save
Francis Mountain from being implicated in murder,
or the attempt to murder, was the purpose that gave
resolution to his step and fire to his mind.

The Angel was an obscure-looking tavern, overshadowed by the pavilion at the corner of the courtyard in front of the Hôtel de Vendôme. The entrance
door was in a vaulted passage at the side nearest the
Hôtel ; and the single window on the ground floor was
thrown into shadow by the projection of the upper
storey, sustained upon ponderous oaken beams, and
of the deep gable above that. It was a house made
for secret meetings and the hatching of evil deeds,
George thought, as he looked at it from the opposite
side of the narrow street.

The casements were open, for the night was warm ;
but the wooden shutters had been drawn together, and
there was only a thin thread of light shining between
their edges. The shutters may have had the effect of
a sounding-board, since the voices within were audible

to George on the other side of the street in the summer stillness.

He heard several voices, none of them loud, and among them recognised his master's well-known accents, subdued to a cautious undertone.

It was not possible to hear more than occasional words at this distance ; but George could make out that the conversation was no common tavern talk—no quick interchange of repartee, no fiery discussion of public affairs, such as he had listened to many a night in London, at the Devil or the White Lion. There was danger for somebody in that cautious speech.

He crossed the street and stationed himself in a deep recessed gateway next the tavern, a little in the rear of it, and from that concealment he could both watch and listen, with little fear of being observed. Such sentences as reached his ear were, however, of a nature not to be easily understood by the uninitiated. There was no mention of the Cardinal or any other name, but there was frequent and excited reference to some personage who was invariably spoken of as the Lady ; and George did not question that this personage was Madame de Chevreuse.

One man asked, " Will she pay us for all we hazard in serving her ? "

" Pay ? She will load you like a pack-horse with gold, if you win the game."

" But if she is deep in debt as they say ? . . ."

" She ! Does your geography not reach to such a place as Madrid ? Play the winning card, and the money for your reward will not be wanting."

There was further talk, in which the names of Court cards represented the people spoken of.

" Will the King of Hearts be here to-night, think you ? "

" He will come to let us know when to begin the suit. He is to be in his place in the pack till 'tis time for the game to begin ; but we do not budge till we see him."

Rapid footsteps sounded on the rough stone *chaussée*

as the man spoke, and George saw a cavalier come swaggering along the street, his broad felt hat slouched over his face, and a voluminous cloak wrapped round his figure; but the diamond buckles and chain that flashed in his hat, as he passed across the lantern light, and the high heels that clattered on the stones, indicated a fine gentleman, for whom the Angel would not be a likely resort.

It was to the Angel he came, however, for he rapped with his knuckles on the shutter as he passed, and then turned quickly into the entrance passage. When he was gone George stole from his hiding-place, and crept on his hands and knees along the wall under the window, and, crouching there, could hear the speakers inside as well as if he had been among them. His head was so close to the narrow opening between the shutters that his agitated breathing might have been heard in the room, had not those within been too much absorbed by their own business to be on the alert for sounds outside.

Peering through that narrow opening in the shutters, he could see the occupants of the room, who had risen at the entrance of the cloaked cavalier, and were grouped round him; five in all, Francis Mountain and four others, all wearing their swords, and with pistols in their belts, arms which would be concealed by their short round cloaks when they were out of doors.

The new-comer pushed back his hat and revealed the handsome features of Gabrielle's grandson, Beaufort, already a popular favourite in the city of Paris, and later to be known as the King of the Markets. His cheeks were flushed and his eyes gleaming, and he talked in short, spasmodic sentences that betrayed a feverish excitement.

It was not easy for the listener below the window to follow the meaning of that breathless speech. There was no word of bloodshed, no hint of the deadly purpose for which those pistols had been loaded. The Duke was giving instructions to his followers—instructions about the details of a journey which was to be begun within the next hour—whether some plan, not named, succeeded or failed. In either case the men were to leave Paris; but the circumstances of departure were to be different—the destination of each man different.

Beaufort cross-examined his men as to the streets and stables where horses were stationed, saddled for a journey; reminded each man of the road he was to take. Each was to leave Paris by a different gate—there was choice enough among the sixteen gates of the city—and even those who had to travel in the same direction were not to join company till they were at least ten leagues beyond the walls. In the event of failure the destination of one was to be Jersey; of Mountain and Campion, Anet, the Duke de Vendôme's château; of another, Avranches; of the fifth, Dieppe, on his way to London. All this George gathered from Beaufort's breathless speech, some of his instructions being repeated more than once, in his anxiety to be understood.

And the nameless enterprise, the thing that was to be done, was to be done possibly within the next half-hour.

"I had a hint that she has the *migraine*, and that he may bid good-night earlier than usual. Get to your posts at once, friends. There is not a moment to spare."

The Duke was moving towards the door as he spoke, the others following him, Mountain in the rear.

He was going with them, going to take part in that deed of blood, to be picketed in the shadow of a projecting wall, pistol primed and cocked, ready for his victim! His might be the bullet which was to rid France of a too-powerful minister. He, George's friend and benefactor, was to stain his conscience with the ineffaceable stain of deliberate murder.

Against this hideous possibility George flung every other consideration to the winds, or, indeed, never paused to weigh the chances of what he was doing. An irresistible impulse moved him, and reckless, resolute, he flung open the shutters, scrambled through the casement, which was but just wide enough to admit him, and leapt into the room in time to clutch Mountain's cloak as he was disappearing through the doorway.

"Not you, not you," he gasped thickly. "You shall take no part in their bloody work. Mountain, Frank, friend, father! For God's sake, stop."

They were wrestling together like foes, one in his eagerness to escape from a detaining grasp, the other in his passionate desire to hinder the man he loved from an unpardonable crime—equally matched, the breadth and weight of the elder balancing the supple strength of the younger man.

"What devil! Hands off, George, or your life may answer for it. Hands off, boy! Let me go! Are you stark, staring mad?"

"You must be, if you join hands with those murderers."

The whole company crowded back into the room, and in the next instant swords were drawn, George was held in the grip of two strong hands, a man on either side, and another standing in front of him with a dagger pointed at his throat.

"A spy!" shouted Beaufort. "Is this your English treason, Mountain?"

"No, Duke, 'tis but a foolish, impetuous lad, my page, who, happening to pass the window, peeps in and sees his master in what he takes for rough company, and so, thinking I have fallen into a *guet-apens*, jumps into the room to my rescue. There is no harm in him, your highness."

"No more harm than a knife can settle," said Beaufort fiercely. "Slit his throat, Campion, and he'll tell no tales."

"Your Highness forgets that I am not a common assassin," said the man who held the dagger. "We can find some less troublesome means of silencing this young gentleman. You are an interfering, officious jackanapes, sir," he went on, addressing George. "Had you used your eyes with better judgment you would have known that your master was among gentlemen, and in no peril of life or limb. Folly such as yours must be punished as troublesome children are punished. Can anybody spare me a strap or a scarf?"

The Duke loosened the silk sash from his waist and handed it to him. Aided by the men who had been holding him, Campion wound this sash round George's arms and tied them behind his back, taking pains to make the knot fast.

"Satisfactory so far, Duke," he said. "Now the next room has but one narrow window, and that guarded by a solid iron grating. The Bastille contains no securer chamber. Come, sir, you must be prisoner for the rest of the night. Your master will send some one to fetch you out of custody to-morrow morning. 'Tis a very lenient chastisement for your impertinent folly ; and if his Highness and the rest of us had any unlawful enterprise in hand you may be sure you would have fared a good deal worse !"

Held between two men and with his arms tied behind his back, George was powerless, and made no futile attempt at resistance. He was thrust somewhat roughly into an adjoining room, and the door bolted behind him, leaving him in unknown darkness. But even in that brief transit he had found time to turn a beseeching look upon his old friend, and to cry in piteous entreaty : "Mountain, for God's sake, stain not your soul with blood !"

It was lucky perhaps for the speaker that he uttered this impassioned appeal in English, a language which none of them understood.

CHAPTER XIII.

TO PREVENT MURDER.

HE was groping in an unknown darkness, fettered, impotent. He walked the room across and across, stumbling against a heavy table, knocking over a stool, and he could at least discover that it was a room of about twelve feet square. Gradually out of the darkness there grew the shape of a window, a faint glimmer of grey showing behind a grating of hammered iron. At right angles with the window, as the grey glimmer grew upon his sight, he could just distinguish the lines of a deeply recessed hearth and hooded chimney. He was there, a prisoner, while Madame de Lussac's worst forebodings were being realised. He understood too well who it was who had the *migraine*; who it was would leave her earlier than usual to-night. He heard a clock strike the third quarter after ten. The Cardinal had left the Louvre already perhaps, attended only by a couple of footmen ; and in the brief distance between the Palace and the Hôtel de Cleves the assassins were lying in wait, each ready to snatch the favourable moment, each with finger on trigger, and eyes straining through the dark.

Maddened by the thought of what might be done, he kicked the heavy oak door furiously, making a noise which might have been heard in the street as well as in the house. But there was no answer, no sound of footsteps in the next room.

What could he do ? Nothing, while his arms were pinioned. He could not even examine the fastening of the door. He could only ascertain, by rubbing his shoulder along the wall from angle to angle, and feeling the ground with his feet, that there was no other outlet. With his shoulders, too, he tried the casement bars, and found that the whole weight of his body, flung violently against the grating, made not the slightest impression upon its solidity. No yielding bar proclaimed a loosened rivet, or a rotten spot in the oaken beam that held the iron. The window was open, and he could hear the sounds of the city, the cry of a watchman, the muffled thunder of far off carriage-wheels.

To get his arms free, and then to escape out of that den in time to warn the victim without betraying his friend! To youth and strength that have never known sickness or failure, there is no such word as "impossible"; and now began the agonising struggle of arms and hands that had been bound with no feeble bandage, and which tasked his utmost endurance, strained every muscle, and swelled every vein almost to bursting, before the stout silken scarf yielded ever so little to his efforts.

Energy less desperate—any minor consideration than the thought that life or death was in that struggle— might have resulted in failure: but George's feelings had reached a point in which his own agony or his own death seemed as nothing compared with the prevention of a dastardly crime.

"He saved me from starving to death on the high road. I owe him all I have ever known of happiness and prosperity. He shall not—he shall not do the assassin's deed—or die the assassin's death. He shall not! He shall not!"

He repeated the words aloud in his agony, between set teeth, and his voice was strange and shrill in his ears, for the words were in truth more the scream of unendurable pain than articulate speech, so intense was the anguish of his backward-strained shoulders, every nerve wrenched, every joint twisted almost to dislocation.

But the thing was done! A petty ordeal, perhaps,

he thought with a shudder, compared with the agony of the hapless wretch *roué vif*: the unspeakable torture of the wheel. Yet it seemed to him that his lacerated muscles had experienced something of that agony, and that he knew better now what breaking on the wheel meant. He was free. The cold sweat rolled down his face. His arms hung at his sides, trembling as with Siberian cold. His swollen hands throbbed and burnt. But he was free.

He felt for the fastening of the door. The clumsy iron latch moved freely up and down in his bruised fingers. But the door was fast bolted on the other side. No chance there. None at the grated window.

There was one chance only—the chimney. It was vast and roomy enough at the bottom, but God knows how it might narrow near the top, or what unsurmountable barriers of oak or iron might bar his way.

He heard the clock of Saint Eustache strike eleven. That agony in which he had wrestled with his bonds had lasted less than fifteen minutes. And what of the wretch upon the wheel, agonising for endless hours, dying by infinitesimal stages of torture, dying a thousand deaths before the stroke of mercy parts the fainting spirit from the excruciated flesh?

The thought of that hideous punishment flashed across him, even in his feverish hurry to get himself out of that silent darkness into the free air of night. He lost no moment after he had made up his mind as to the one chance. He was on his knees on the hearth, looking up through the black throat of the chimney.

God be praised! He could see the stars shining far above the darkness. That meant hope. His bruised hands explored the sides of the chimney. The bricks were loose and uneven, there must be foothold for an agile climber. Booted as he was, the ascent would be difficult; and he must carry his sword so that it should not hinder his movements. He felt the unnatural calmness of a brave soul in a deperate extremity. He had done plenty of climbing in his day, among the ruined fortresses of Burgundy, in the woods round Isleworth, in the Aldersgate garden ; but it had been for sport. He was climbing now to save men's lives.

From projection to projection—with the help of an angle here, a jutting stone there, a beam, an iron brace —inch by inch, as it seemed to his impatience—he neared the top, and squeezed his head and shoulders out into the open air, sending down a cataract of mortar and a loosened brick or two, in that last struggle through an orifice that would have been impossible had it been an inch narrower. He had been obliged to dislodge a bit of crumbling brickwork with his bare nails before he emerged upon the steep slope of the tiled gable, from which he let himself slide down to the gutter, and thence by easy stages, on the projections of the half-timbered upper storey, to the massive iron bar that carried the sign of the inn, a winged angel in hammered iron.

He dropped lightly to the ground, forgot his wrenched sinews, his bruised and bleeding hands, and ran as fast as his feet would carry him to the gate of the Louvre. That older front of the Palace, facing the church of Saint-Germain-l'Auxerrois, had still the aspect of a fortress, the wall flanked with towers, the gateway guarded by a drawbridge ; but it was to a smaller gate in the new buildings that George applied for entrance, a gate opening on a vaulted passage, bridging over the moat that surrounded the Palace on all sides, and leading to a door through which Mr. Mountain and his page had been admitted among the more privileged of the Regent's visitors, on the strength of the English Queen's intro- duction. He was well known to the man in charge of this gate, and, after some scruples as to the lateness of the hour, was allowed to pass through. All Court ceremonial had grown laxer since the punctilious and melancholy King had vanished from the scene over which it had been his privilege to cast an abiding gloom. The Regent was kind to everybody ; and although imperious after her own fashion, was incapable of sustaining an isolated grandeur. That proud spirit had been broken by a quarter of a century of ill-usage, as child-bride, hated wife, insulted Queen.

"Has the Cardinal left the Palace?" George asked breathlessly.

"His Eminence is still in her Majesty's apartments."

"I carry a message from the Marquise de Lussac. I must see his Eminence before he leaves the Louvre."

This was the statement which he repeated to one functionary after another, progressing from the lacqueys in the outer hall to the Captain of the Queen's Guard at the head of the grand staircase, and to the gentlemen-in-waiting in the first *salon*, very much in waiting, and yawning in the dreariness of a deserted room, whence the brilliant crowd had melted half an hour before.

In the light of a hundred wax candles the applicant for an immediate interview with the greatest man in France presented a sorry aspect. His face had been cut and scratched in his ascent of the chimney, and broad streaks of blood had trickled from brow to chin. His clothes were grimed and torn ; his hands were swollen out of all human shape ; lace and cambric of collar and cravat hung about him in rags. Yet it was this tatterdemalion appearance which won him the attention he might have otherwise sought in vain. The gentlemen-in-waiting knew him as Mountain's page, and knew that it was no common adventure which had brought him to his present condition.

"*Le diable me prend!* You look as if you had been hunted by assassins!" exclaimed the first gentleman.

"Or by a jealous husband," laughed the second,

"There are assassins about, but not for me. For the love of God let me see the Cardinal!"

A bell rang silver clear through the lofty rooms, as he spoke.

"Impossible! Her Majesty's bell! His Eminence is about to retire."

"And he will leave the Louvre with a single servant, perhaps?"

"A lacquey with a lantern. He does not affect state ceremony. Richelieu had a Royal Guard."

"I tell you, sir, I must see him. Her Majesty's

presence would not stop me. If he leaves the Palace unprotected, he goes to his death!"

He had spoken with increasing vehemence as he went on pleading, and the full, ripe tones of the young voice resounded in the lofty saloon.

"Is this a guard-room, gentlemen, or can you find no other place to start a brawl in?" said a voice at the end of the room, a voice whose level tones were in marked contrast with George's impetuous speech.

The Cardinal was standing in the doorway, a picturesque figure in his scarlet soutane and beretta, his handsome features fixed in an almost unnatural calm, while the hand that trembled ever so slightly as he fingered his moustache betrayed the emotion under that statue-like repose.

"I implore your Eminence to accord me one minute's private speech."

"Not to-night, sir. I am on my way home."

"It must be to-night—now—or it will be too late. For God's sake, give me a hearing, Monseigneur. Look at me!" stretching out his swollen, blood-stained hands. "Do you think I would come on a fool's errand thus? It is in your service these hands were bruised and torn —there is not a bone in my body that has not suffered for you. If I were an old servant you would not refuse to hear me—and God knows that among your oldest servants you will find none to serve you better than I have done to-night."

Mazarin scrutinised him with a searching look.

"Is this a Turlupinade, a farce to set all Paris laughing to-morrow at the way the Cardinal was caught? Is that blood or red paint upon your face? I think I know that comely countenance, stained and scarred as it is. Are you not the youth I met last night at Madame de Lussac's?"

"The same, Monseigneur!"

"For that lady's sake I will hear you," said Mazarin, laying his hand on George's shoulder with something more of kindness than he had shown him yet. "This way, sir!" motioning him to the inner room. "Say your say, and make an end of it."

The room was empty. It was the Queen's cabinet, that sacred apartment to which Mountain and his page had been admitted once only, when they delivered Henrietta Maria's letter. The Royal bedchamber opened out of this room, and even amidst the excitement of telling his story George heard the stealthy turning of a key, and noted that the door of communication had been opened for the space of an inch.

He was careful not to betray the friend he loved, and, to shield him, avoided all mention of names. He had heard some men talking in a tavern. He knew that there was a plot to murder his Eminence that night, between the Palace and the Hôtel de Cleves, the assassins counting on his being attended by a single servant, or at most a couple of unarmed lacqueys.

Mazarin pressed him hard. Surely if he had seen the men's faces he must have recognised them—some of them, at least.

No. He affected a sheepish stupidity. He knew of nothing but the plan of murder. His Eminence must not pass unguarded through the narrow streets that led to his house. The danger was imminent.

"There has been no hour of the last three months in which my life has not been in danger, sir—and I know not this moment if you, with your hypocritical simplicity and pretence of an impossible ignorance, may not be playing into the hands of my enemies."

"Your Eminence has but to take a sufficient guard——"

"Let me look at you, sir, eye to eye. I have had too many dealings with scoundrels not to know one at sight."

He held George by both arms, with delicate white hands that gripped like steel pincers, and wrung a scream of pain from him.

"Pardon me, Monseigneur. My body is one bruise."

"I am sorry I hurt you, friend. I believe you are honest. I thank you for your warning. I knew the crisis in this conspiracy was drawing near, and I am glad it has come. If you have suffered in my service you shall be lavishly rewarded—yes, lavishly!" repeated the Cardinal with conviction, after a moment's thought. " And now get you to your lodging, and let no mortal know of this interview from your lips. The names you conceal are known to me: the head and front of the conspiracy, Beaufort; the instruments, Henri and Alexander Campion; the witch that sits in the middle of the web and guides the threads, Marie de Rohan. Your reticence is of no moment. You could tell me nothing that I do not know."

George bowed low and retired, relieved to find that Mountain's name had no place in the Cardinal's black list. He withdrew, as he was bidden, and left the Louvre; but only to wait and watch in the street outside.

It was on the stroke of midnight when the gate of the vaulted passage was opened and a glare of yellow light streamed out upon the darkness of the street, and the steady tramp of soldiers' feet sounded on the stone floor that spanned the moat.

A company of the Queen's Guard, carrying torches, three abreast, marched out of the gate; and in the midst of them, vivid in the torch-light, gleamed the scarlet of the Cardinal's robe and the diamond cross on the Cardinal's breast. Thus surrounded, his Eminence traversed with his most leisurely footsteps the distance between the Louvre and the Hôtel de Cleves, the narrow street through which he went glowing like a brasier in the flare of twenty torches. And murder, lurking behind the angle of a stone bastion, or hidden in the deep shadow of a corner turret, bit its fingers and gnashed its teeth at the knowledge of ignominious failure.

Still waiting and watching, and stealing from one dark street into another, George saw four horsemen ride off, creeping out of narrow alleys or from under low-browed archways, their heads bent over their horses' necks. Slowly, cautiously, he saw those armed horsemen ride away, no two of them taking the same route. He heard the hoofs of slowly moving horses echoing along those labyrinthine streets and dwindling to silence ; but he did not see the one man in whose escape he was interested, and he dreaded the re-appearance of the Guard that had accompanied the Cardinal, apprehensive that Mazarin might send them to hunt down the baffled assassins.

To his great relief, the soldiers did not re-appear, nor did he meet any one that looked like a secret agent of the Cardinal's. There was ample time for the little band of conspirators to vanish into unknown distance. Not thus would Richelieu have acted in such circumstances, George thought, thanking Heaven for a mild First Minister. Swift would have been the search, implacable the pursuit, if the great Cardinal's life had been in question ; and the warning meant to save Francis Mountain from a foul crime and its deadly consequences might have served only to hasten his doom.

There was a long bar of pale light behind the towers of Saint-Germain-l'Auxerrois before George relinquished his watch. In his anxiety about that life which his own act might have jeopardised, he had been scarcely conscious of pain or weariness ; but now, making sure that Mountain must have got himself safe beyond the gates, on foot or on horseback, he began to feel the aching of bruised limbs and strained sinews, and to long for the repose of his pallet at the Golden Crown.

He passed the Hôtel de Cleves on his way home, and heard the steady tramp of a sentry in the court-yard, and saw the gleaming of breast plate and helmet beyond the *porte-cochère*, whereby he perceived that his Eminence had retained the escort Queen Anne had furnished for his protection when he left the Palace.

Among the lodgers at the Golden Crown there were several night birds, for whose convenience the door was left on the latch from midnight till morning. The darkness in the narrow passage and on the corkscrew staircase reeked with stale wine and coarse tobacco, and

the rank after-fume of yesterday's dinner ; and George,
who was wont to leap up the stairs too quickly to note
foul odours, dragged his tired limbs so slowly as to be
painfully conscious of the loathsome atmosphere.   It
brought back the memory of the wide staircase in
Aldersgate Street, the polished oak wainscot, the scent
of dried rose-leaves and lavender, woodruff and lemon
thyme, the freshness and purity that prevailed throughout
the house, where every detail was supervised by that
great lady for whom nothing that concerned the welfare
of others was too trivial.

He was surprised to see a light shining under the door
of his bedchamber, and still more surprised on opening
it to see his master standing in front of the old
Normandy press in which their garments were kept,
engaged in packing a pair of saddle-bags.

Mountain started and turned at the opening of the
door, and stared, round-eyed and open-mouthed, as if
he had seen a ghost.

"What devil! How in Satan's name did you get
out ? "

" By the use of my own wits and my own limbs ! "

" You were able to force that door—fastened with a
bolt as thick as my wrist? Pshaw! What does it
matter now? You got out—and 'twas you who betrayed
us to Mazarin, and made fools of us. It would serve
you right if I killed you."

He made a threatening movement, and drew his sword
half out of the scabbard, then dropped it back with a
laugh.

"I am not the killing sort," he muttered, "and you
are a bit of my heart. But I tell you, George, you have
cost me a long step on the highroad to fortune by your
interference this night. My friends will never trust me
again. I shall be known as a blundering spoil-sport.
You have lost me their favour for ever ! "

" And I have saved you from taking part in a murder
—cold-blooded, deliberate murder."

"Cold-blooded—deliberate ! Why, our blood was at
fever heat—our veins ran fire. Cold-blooded murder !

No, George, 'twere not murder, but patriotism, to rid France of this tyrant. This man is grinding the faces of the poor, and undermining the noble and the gifted. This man is the public enemy—a crafty Italian schemer, sleek and subtle, trading on a handsome face and a plausible tongue—luxurious—avaricious as the miser in Plautus, for all his pomp and splendour. This act 'of ours—which your cursed interference has hindered—was a blow for France, and would have done her better service than Condé's finest victory."

"You, Mountain, you! The brave and honest friend I have loved—you turn paid assassin!"

"No, no—'twas no question of gold that tempted me. 'Twas for no sordid motive I joined them. 'Twas for a woman, George—a woman who could win the stars from their spheres if she wanted them—the incomparable jade! The splendid, audacious, seraphic, diabolical she!"

"Ah! I knew 'twas her influence. The witch in the centre of the web! Madame de Chevreuse! 'Tis strange that faded beauty can put so strong a spell upon you."

"Faded beauty! You see her in her decay. I worship her for what she was. Faded beauty! Youth has such insolent phrases. Yes, she has passed the apogee of woman's ripest charms. She is on the downward slope. There are crows' feet at the corners of the finest eyes in France. But while she lives she will be beautiful. Women who have only the *beauté du diable* when they are young are devilish ugly when they are old; but her face is cast in that perfect mould which only death can spoil."

"Mountain, you must not linger. It is morning, and the Cardinal may order a house-to-house search for his enemies; and you, if you are known——"

"I am not known—unless *you* have betrayed me."

"Can you wrong me by such a thought? I warned the Cardinal, entreated him not to leave the Palace unguarded—but I was no traitor. He could extract nothing from me except that there was danger for him between the Louvre and his house."

"I am glad your superior virtue did not give me to the hangman. If you have not peached, I doubt I am safe enough for the next hour ; and I shall be forty miles away from Paris before night, if my horse be as good as they tell me."

"Where is your horse ?"

"In the Rue Saint-Antoine, five minutes' ride from the gate."

"What if the Cardinal has ordered all horsemen to be stopped at the gates ? There has been time enough for him to do it. Your friends all made off two hours ago. Why, in Heaven's name, did you linger ?"

"I had business in the Faubourg Saint-Germain. There was one I had to see before I left Paris. I could not be such a sneak as to think more of my own skin than of her disappointment."

"A woman ! The witch in the web, *sans doute !*"

"Ah, lad, when you know what it is to love a woman —and she as far out of your reach as the stars are—you will smile less scornfully at my folly. Yes, 'tis the enchantress in the web, and she has spun her gossamer round my heart. This head of mine is a poor stake in such a game——"

"Your head ! Alas ! 'tis every limb and every sinew you hazard for her—'tis the risk of being broken on the wheel. The axe is for our betters, Frank."

"I would risk the wheel to please her. 'Tis not the first time I have set my life upon a die. Do you remember in 'thirty-seven how I left you at Carcassonne, in charge of the landlord of that wretched hovel they called an inn—deserted you for three days and nights? 'Twas to ride to the Spanish frontier with her, George, her page and purveyor—to ride at her saddle-bow, she riding *à califourchon* in her impudent doublet and hose, her narrow foot and Arabian instep in a boot that a man might have kissed. The boldest rider, for a woman, that man ever saw ! I rode beside her through the mountain passes— hand locked in hand sometimes, when the road was perilous—and be sure I made the most of the danger. These arms received her when she sprang from her saddle, and once—'twas the end of our last stage, mark you!—I snatched a kiss. She fetched me a cut of her whip across my cheek that showed red for a month. But the kiss was worth the smart, George, for her lips clung to mine before she remembered that she ought to be angry, and it has been a memory to dream of."

"You are foolish to care for an intriguing wanton!"

"S'death! you shall call her no names. She sent me off with the fiery brand of her whip on my face, though I carried letters that would have been my death-warrant had Richelieu's spies caught me. But she knew that I was her slave, and had no more choice than the tides have when they obey the moon."

He was packing one of the saddle-bags while he talked, folding, thrusting, squeezing bulky garments into the narrowest possible space, his hands moving as fast as his speech, which was wild and feverish, keeping time with his throbbing pulses.

George helped him to strap the bags, and did all that could be done to hasten his departure.

"Have you eaten anything since you left the Angel, Frank?"

"No, nor since dinner yesterday. Men don't eat when they are concerned in a business that carries the fate of a nation: but I drank enough last night to furnish me against a week's sobriety. Alack! boy, were I a Frenchman, I could never forgive what you have done. If you knew what hung upon our design! . . . We should have been the saviours of France had we succeeded—we should have prevented civil war ; for, believe it or not, George, if Mazarin remains at the helm, there will be civil war. There is a volcano of hate under the smooth surface of Court and City, that must explode before we are much older. He has been at the head of affairs less than a year, and he is worse hated than Richelieu was in a quarter of a century. He is so much the meaner villain—will use a willing tool and not reward him, while he lavishes gold on the men he fears ; gold which he loves as good Catholics love the Mother of God. He is worse hated than Strafford was, and you know how London clamoured for his blood ; and Paris is a crueller foe than London. I tell you it must come—another day of barricades, Paris in arms, Frenchmen cutting each other's throats. The Princes hate him. The Parliament knows it has been bubbled by him—tricked into quashing the late King's will, and so making this Italian intriguer omnipotent. Well, I am ready !"—as he tugged at the last strap—needlessly, since George had made all the fastenings secure. "Good-bye, lad, and God bless you. I know you meant me no harm."

"Nay, dear friend, I meant to save you from a crime."

"Crime! Was that a crime which would have saved these streets from running blood ? Was Brutus a murderer, think you ? See, here is half my fortune "—taking half a dozen gold pieces from the purse that hung at his waist. "Before that is gone you will have found powerful friends. Mean as the Cardinal is, he must needs reward you."

This was said *sotto voce* on the stairs as they went down together, George following close upon his master.

"I will take no reward from him !"

"Nay, but punish him, George. If you love me, punish him ! Take his money—the thing he loves dearest. For my sake make him smart. Once more—adieu !"

Mountain had opened the door, and they were standing on the threshold. The street lay before them cold and grey, with the lights and shadows clearly defined in the dawn, and above them swinging sign and gabled roof were touched with the gold of sunrise.

"You will have a fine morning for your ride," said George. "God grant you meet no hindrance on your journey. Have you far to go ?"

"To Anet, Vendôme's château. I have a rendezvous there with Campion ; and once there I doubt we shall both be safe. Don't look so scared, George! I have very little fear of being hunted down for last night's business. This Roman knows 'tis wise to let sleeping dogs lie. He knows that for such as he—the men who scramble to the summit upon the necks of their fellows —there is hatred that never sleeps ; knows that the foe who waits and watches is a hydra the headman's axe cannot kill ; and knows that his best policy is to conciliate his enemies and make believe that the nation loves him."

He stopped, wrung his *protégé's* hands, and would have parted with him on the threshold.

" I will see you mounted and safe through the gate," George said, following him with one of the saddle-bags, which Mountain tried in vain to wrest from him.

" Nay, that you shall not. I will not put your head in peril !"

" Why, but this moment you swore there was no danger !"

" None that a hardy ruffian like me esteems worth his concern. But for you 'tis different. You have your fortune to make. Let Mazarin make it for you, if he will, while he is in power. Go back, lad—I will not have you wreck your chances to carry a bag and hold a horse's bridle for me."

" And I won't leave you this side the gate !"

The young man's resolution prevailed, and he went with Mountain to the stable of a great house in the Rue Saint-Antoine, where they found a strong hackney saddled and bridled, waiting for him, in the care of a groom who grumbled sorely at the ill-usage of himself and the horse—both having waited for nearly three hours.

Master and page only parted at the gate, where Mountain's pass-word was received without comment, making it clear that his Eminence had taken no pains to keep his enemies within the walls.

" I shall come back to you when this has blown over," were Mountain's last words.

The sun was high and Paris was astir when George

walked slowly back to the Golden Crown. Perhaps it was only when he saw Mountain's stalwart figure vanish through the gate, whip hand on hip, legs straight and stiff, broad shoulders yielding easily to the movement of the horse—it was only then, perhaps, that he knew how well he loved his comrade and master. What was his life to be like without him? Alone in Paris, without trade or calling; penniless when the few gold pieces in his purse were spent; friendless, since he counted a fine lady's notice at not a groat's value; alone, and without a friend on this side of the narrow sea, and severed by an impassable barrier from those cherished friends in England, of whose kindness he had never doubted, but whose dear company he must needs shun.

He had washed his face and hands, and brushed the worst of the soot and lime from his doublet while Mountain and he were talking; and he made use of his morning leisure at the baths on the Quai d'Ecole, which Marie de Medicis had provided for the citizens of Paris, and, having wasted some hours thus, returned reluctantly to the lodging whose solitude he dreaded. True that there was no lack of company in the rooms below, company whose cheerfulness ran into riot; for there fops and duellists, the *rodomonts, fanfarrons*, and *spadassins* of the day, ate, and drank and gambled, and laughed and sang, and quarrelled and fought, from morning till night; but it was such company as his present humour loathed, and to which he preferred the dulness of the upstairs room, where the yawning doors of the great cherry-wood press revealed the empty shelf on which Mountain had kept his scanty wardrobe, and where the table was still littered with the latest Mazarinades, printed in clumsy type on coarse paper, and bought from the hawkers on the Pont Neuf. Mountain had been an eager purchaser of all such defamatory literature, though not so careful a collector as the Savoy Ambassador, who was known to buy and treasure every licentious ballad and virulent lampoon against the First Minister.

The warm bath had relaxed the stiffness of his bruised limbs, and lessened the pain of wrenched muscles, and he began to feel the effect of the night's exertions in a longing for sleep. He flung himself upon his bed, and soon sank into slumber so deep that the brawling voices and strident laughter in the rooms below had no more effect upon him than the rustle of summer boughs in the gardens that lay between his open casements and the Seine.

He had slept for nearly three hours when he was roused by a loud rapping at the room door.

"Come in, and the devil take you!" he cried, startled into sudden consciousness, and savage with his disturber.

"I thought I had come to the cave of the Seven Sleepers," said a woman's voice on the threshold ; and, starting to his feet, George recognised Madame de Lussac's waiting-woman, Signora Bianca, who stood looking at him with dark unfriendly eyes.

"Pardon me, *Signora mia.* I was fast asleep."

"Too fast even to find a civil tongue on waking, sir. But I deserved no better when I undertook an errand which any lacquey in Madame's service would have done as well."

"That your mistress has employed you upon an unworthy mission is hardly a reason for being angry with me, Signora."

"The Marchesa sends you this, sir "—handing him a letter. "Read it, and give me your answer by word of mouth."

"My hero! You have made me proud and happy : and you have made your own fortune secure. Come to me without an instant's delay.

"Thine till death,

"Héloïse de Lussac."

George's face crimsoned as he read the lines. The tone of appropriation vexed him ; the lavish praise for an act which he deemed simple duty almost disgusted him. Not to win a great lady's approval had he done this thing. Yet it was natural, perhaps, since the warning had come from her, that the praise should come from her also.

"Will you come?" asked the Signora curtly.

"Yes. You know the contents of this letter?"

"There is nothing which concerns my mistress that I do not know."

"That is a servant's duty, I suppose; in which case I am glad I have to make shift without a servant."

"There are servants and servants. I am the Marchesa's foster-sister. I was plucked from my mother's breast in order that she should thrive and grow strong and beautiful. I grew up rickety and stunted for her sake. I have been her slave all my life. I suppose you think that gives no rights—that all is done when I have drawn my wages."

"Indeed, Signora, I am not so hard of heart or dull of brain as to undervalue a lifelong fidelity. Yet I may suggest that you could throw a shade more courtesy into your treatment of a humble servant of your lady's, without derogating from your dignity as her trusted waiting-woman."

"You have a glib tongue, sir. Are you coming?"

"I shall delay only to change doublet and hose, Signora—an operation which requires privacy."

The woman turned on her heel, and departed without word or salutation.

Half an hour later George was ushered into the *salon* where Madame de Lussac awaited him. She was pacing the room as he entered, and she turned suddenly at the sound of his name, and advanced to meet him, with outstretched hands, and a radiant smile that took a decade from her age; or it might be that the vivacity of her movements, the spontaneous grace, the lofty carriage of her head, made her look younger and hand-somer than in her evening splendour.

It was no trick of subdued light, no cathedral dimness, which enhanced her beauty; for the room in which she received him gave upon the garden, and the mullioned windows extended from end to end of the wall, the light chastened only by the armorial bearings of the De Lussac family, and its allied nobility, blazoned in delicate colouring in the topmost panels. No, it was assuredly the soul within the woman which had put on this renewal of youth.

"My hero!" she exclaimed, clasping his hands, and kissing him on either cheek.

The kisses startled, but did not disgust him. Inexperienced as he was in the ways of fine ladies of this stamp, he knew instinctively that these were not the tainted kisses of an aristocratic courtesan, but the warm greeting of a woman who for some inexplicable reason had come to regard him with affection.

Gallantry demanded an acknowledgment of such an honour. He dropped on one knee and saluted the lady's hand with his lips.

"Dear Marchesa," he said, as he rose from that attitude of homage, "if 'tis for last night's work you thus honour me, you over-estimate that poor service. There was nothing heroic in it. I took some pains to warn his Eminence of a peril that allowed of no shilly-shally—but it was of another's safety I thought most, and the Cardinal owes me nothing."

She put her hand upon his lips hastily, and he saw her glance towards the tapestried wall, where the story of Theseus and Ariadne glowed in colours mellowed by time, a masterpiece from the looms of Tournay.

"Foolish boy, to make light of a service in which you risked your life. You must have put yourself in the power of a band of traitors in order to discover their scheme of murder—you, so young, so inexperienced in treachery and bloodshed, alone among a gang of assassins! And it was I who sent you there. If they had killed you, your blood would have been on my head —on mine. Yes, on mine!" she repeated passionately, and now her beauty assumed a tragic aspect, and he looked at her wonderingly, recalling the actress he had seen a few days before at the Hôtel de Bourgogne, in Corneille's *Cid*.

"For one untoward moment my life may have been

at stake, madame," he replied lightly, "but I should be a poor poltroon if I remembered so brief a hazard. If you would do me a kindness, tell me whether the Cardinal means to pursue last night's plotters with his vengeance—whether their lives are in danger."

"If they had their deserts they would be in the oubliettes under the Bastille by this time—and in the hangman's hands at sunrise to-morrow. But Mazarin is not like Richelieu. He does not love bloodshed—and as those two who are the heart and brain of the conspiracy are beyond the reach of justice I doubt his clemency will suffer their hirelings and vulgar tools to go unpunished."

"He will be wise if he refrain from discoveries which would but prove how bitterly he is hated," George began impetuously; but the Marquise interrupted him with an angry stamp of her foot, and a frown that darkened her beauty like a thunder-cloud.

"*Diantre!* I fear you are a most incorrigible block-head!" she muttered, under her breath.

The rustling of tapestry caught his ear while he stood gazing at her, bewildered by this sudden displeasure; and, looking at the opposite wall, he saw that the arras had been pushed aside, and that a man was standing in the opening—a commanding figure, clad in that picturesque costume which the princes and nobles of the Louvre had adopted from the solemn hidalgos of the Spanish Court, a grave and stately fashion which lends nobility to the portraits of Velasquez and Philippe de Champagne; a costume for which the bad taste of Louis the Great substituted the Dutch stiffness of buckram-lined coats and tall perukes.

The flowing mantle, broad-leaved hat, velvet doublet, and high boots, well became the shapely figure and classic features of the man who stood calmly contemplating Madame de Lussac and her visitor; and it was some moments before George perceived that the handsome cavalier, with his face somewhat shadowed by the droop of his hat, was no other than the Minister who ruled France. It was the Cardinal's habit on occasion to assume the secular dress which set off his fine person and reminded his enemies that he had once been a soldier, that he was still in the prime of life, and in all physical attributes the opposite of his great predecessor, whose later years had been a prolonged struggle with disease, the invincible mind warring against the frail and fading body.

"'From the lips of babes and sucklings!'" exclaimed the Cardinal, his eyes brightening with malevolent light as he looked at George. "My French contemporaries have refrained from telling me that I am hated by the people for whose welfare I have devoted the labour of my days and nights ever since I came to their ungrateful country. It remained for an Englishman, not three months in Paris, to give me the advice my friends feared to proffer."

He waited to see George sink to his knees, crushed by the great man's displeasure, and stammering a prayer for pardon. But the offender stood erect and unblenching, returning scowl for scowl.

"I did but echo the popular cry," he said. "Those who sit in taverns know more than the dwellers in palaces of the vulgar herd and of their thoughts and feelings. The taxes your Eminence has laid on Paris scarce touch your noble friends and advisers, but they fall heavily on the common people; and it is the common people who make rebellions."

"No, Mr. Jackanapes, it is the malignity of envious princes which stirs up the spirit of revolt. The common people will believe what they are told. They follow the rebel's flag, but they seldom initiate rebellion. Come, sir, I forgive you for saying I am hated; and since you saved me the risk of an awkward encounter at the cost of a spoilt suit—for which my tailors shall compensate you with the finest brocade and embroidery of gems and gold that their skill can command—I will treat your friend Mountain with a clemency for which my late revered master would blame me. His insignificance can go scatheless, and I will not even lodge a complaint of his perfidy with Sir Richard Browne, your

Ambassador, provided the scoundrel has the civility to put himself upon the other side of the Channel."

"Your Eminence may be assured that Francis Mountain has good friends on both sides of the Channel."

"And has good friends beyond the Pyrenees, no doubt; but he will find those powerful friends his worst enemies if he lets them entangle him in any more of their plots against my life. If I let them go this time, sir, remember it is because I love peace, and am not of a vindictive spirit; but were the game to begin again I might hold other cards, and play a different sequence. And in that case, however subordinate Mr. Mountain's part might be, he would find it not too low for the hangman."

Madame de Lussac had betrayed her impatience by various petulant shrugs and nervous movements, during this conversation; and she turned upon the Cardinal now with an angry vehemence which would have been a shock to any man with less self-control, and less experience of the lady's temper.

"Do you forget that this young man saved your life—and that it is of his courage and resolution you have to think, and not of his friend's treachery?"

"Oh, I am grateful; but since the gentleman has confessed 'twas for his friend he feared rather than for me, I may be excused if I settle the question of that friend's existence before I talk of payment for Monsieur——" he stopped, looking to George to prompt him.

"My name is Mountain,—George Mountain."

"The same surname as your friend's. He is your kinsman then?"

"No, Monsignore. I have no kindred."

"An orphan?"

"And a waif—nameless, did not the friend who gave me food and shelter lend me his name. But your Eminence spoke just now of payment—payment for my service of last night. You will, I hope, withdraw that word, and believe that I acted without thought

of reward—and, as your Eminence overheard just now,
that I had it nearer my heart to save my friend from
a crime than to protect the most distinguished life
in France."

There was ineffable pride in the speech and bearing
of the nameless adventurer, as he stood face to face
with the man upon whose lips princes and dukes of the
blood Royal hung for favours, strong in the power of
youth that has never stooped to a mean action or been
influenced by a sordid motive.

"Hear him, and look at him, Julio!" cried Madame
de Lussac, "and then doubt me if you can. But you
have a heart of adamant! God help man or woman
who looks to you for human feeling, for love, or pity,
or gratitude, or pardon! What is it to you that he
is what he is? What is it to you that you owe him
your life?"

"Let us have no tragedy, I entreat you, *cara Marchesa.*
We get enough of that from Pierre Corneille. This
young gentleman, whose cause you have taken up with
needless vehemence, has been pleased to flout my offer
of recompense for his services. He is hot-headed and
proud, as you see. Years—perhaps months—on the
streets of Paris may bring him wisdom. When he
wants my assistance he can come to me. *Addio, anima
mia !*"

He lifted the tapestry and disappeared through the
door by which he had entered. It was no secret passage, only a communication between one of the statelier
reception-rooms and Madame de Lussac's private apartments. Her bedchamber was on the floor above, and
from an adjoining turret an *escalier à vis*, with elabo-
rately carved balusters, a *chef-d'œuvre* of the unfortunate
Jean Goujon's, afforded a private access to that upper
storey.

The Cardinal's departure did not restore the lady to
calmness. She paced the room again, as she had been
pacing it when George entered. Her hands were clasped
convulsively; her rapid footsteps and heaving bosom
indicated an almost overpowering emotion. George

stood near the door, bareheaded, waiting to take his leave, when his hostess should have recovered sufficient calmness to acknowledge his parting salutation. For the moment he thought her unconscious of his presence.

After several agitated journeys along the whole length of the room she came to a sudden stop, and sank on a tabouret by the open window, pushing the casement wider, and turning her face to the summer wind.

"He is adamant!" she exclaimed. "Or he is something worse than a thing which has no feeling. His feelings are all evil. I believe he hates you. He sees you standing before him, generous, fearless, all that a nobly-born youth should be, and his eye grows colder as he looks at you, his lip more like iron."

"Dear lady, why are you thus distressed for my sake? I have told you once for all that what I did last night—no more perilous an adventure than a lover will risk to serenade his mistress—was done chiefly for my friend's sake. His Eminence rates my service quite high enough—but 'twas ill done to affront me by offering me a suit of clothes, or by talking of payment."

"It was a *parvenu's* insolence—the petty pride of the Sicilian peasant's son who has made himself the superior of princes. He hates you because you are young and handsome, and of a bold spirit, and have your life all before you. He hates you because you are what he has been, and can never be again. But I have done with him. He can keep his piled-up gold—the treasures his miserly soul dotes upon, his diamonds, which already outshine the Crown jewels. He blazes before the Queen—he, the creature her favour has made—more splendid than his sovereign. We want nothing from him, George. We are strong enough, you and I, to do without him!"

"Indeed, madame, I ask favours from no one, being, as you say, young, and with my life before me."

"Favours! No, no, you need seek no one's favour. But you are alone in Paris; friendless, except for those fine ladies who invite you to their houses, and carry you about in their coaches, and who will blot you out of their memory if ever they see you in a threadbare *juste-au-corps*, and a hat with draggled plumes. You carry yourself proudly, George ; but pray what are you going to do in Paris, now that your master is an exile ? "

" Paris is not the world, Marquise. If I cannot earn my bread in Paris I can go elsewhere. I am not a philosopher, like Mr. Hobbes, but I have some learning, and I have spent near three years as tutor in an English nobleman's family. I can seek a situation of the same kind in this country."

" You ! In the bloom of your youth ! When your life should march from triumph to triumph, from pleasure to pleasure ! You, a pedagogue, a pedant, a drudge, to teach unruly boys Greek and Latin, and physic their mothers' lap-dogs ! "

" If I find the schoolmaster's post irksome—as I might chance to do among strangers—I can carry a musket in Flanders. The field is wide enough for all."

" You distract me when you talk of it ! You, a mere soldier, one of the herd who are sacrificed by the hecatomb to swell D'Enghien's renown ! No, George, you are to stay in Paris, and my house is to be your home. You can revive my Latin, if you like, to keep your hand in. I was once a fair scholar, and could construe Ovid and Virgil as well as some collegians. This house shall be your home."

" Dearest lady, you load me with favours ; you overpower me with undeserved kindness. But indeed, the benefit you offer is impossible for me to accept. Had you sons I might be their tutor ; but you are alone."

" Yes, George, I am alone, and very lonely. It were Christian charity in you to share my solitude, to be the consolation of my waning years."

" Alas, dear Marquise, the world has but little charity ; and even the pious ladies who make their confession once a month have not Christianity enough to refrain from slandering a handsome rival. I have heard how the women of Paris talk of each other, and I would not for the wealth of the richest street in this city suffer my presence under this roof to invite slander upon its mistress."

"Let them slander me! I have been slandered, and have lived. Lies do not kill. I have no fear of what my friends can say. They said their worst twenty years ago, and I survived; and you have seen those same women fawn upon me as if I were an empress. They think I have influence with Mazarin; they know he rules the Queen: and they would kiss the rose upon my slipper as they kiss the cross on the Papal shoe, if I bade them."

"Be sure, Marquise, that I am grateful for your generous offer; but a sybarite's life in a lady's house would be as distasteful to me as it would be unworthy any man of my age and condition. I cannot relish bread that I have not earned; and I would rather live on the soldier's scanty rations, and lie under canvas, than sink to the state of a dependent on a woman's bounty."

"You should make no sacrifice of manly pride, or manly ambition. I would have you aspire to the highest place the world can give; you would be no dependent."

"If not a dependent, what am I to be?"

"What God made you—my son."

CHAPTER XIV.

BEFORE George had recovered from the shock of these never-to-be-forgotten words, Madame de Lussac was on her knees at his feet. He felt her tears raining upon his hands, which hers were clasping distractedly. He raised her from the ground with some broken speech that was meant to soothe her agitation, and she flung herself upon his breast, sobbing, " My son—my ill-used son ! "

He bent his lips over the rich masses of dark, silky hair, the rippling curls and airy tendrils arranged by the lady's waiting-woman with an artistic negligence which cost infinite pains, but now veritably disordered. He let his lips rest lightly, in the merest phantom of a kiss, on the burning brow under those love-locks, and it was bitterness to him to feel how little there was of filial affection in that kiss.

Was it true? Had he wandered over the world to find her here, that shadow and dream of his childish years, of his graver manhood, to find the sad and lonely phantom embodied in this great lady, beautiful exceedingly, but with a beauty which had never touched and charmed him as a less splendid face had done. Even in the profound agitation of that moment, the image of Lady Llanbister came between him and the woman whose dishevelled head drooped upon his breast, whose arms were about his neck ; and he thought of her whom he had always loved to consider his adopted mother.

The real mother had come upon the scene, asserting

the irresistible claim of motherhood; and if the claim were true, he would have no choice but to obey.

"Dear lady, are you not the victim of some delusion? Women are more credulous than we are; and your kindness—or some fancied resemblance—may lead you to see a long-lost son in one who has no drop of your blood in his veins."

"The evidence is strong enough for me, George. You will want chapter and verse, perhaps. You will want to fit the chain of circumstance together without one missing link. That may prove impossible. And you may deny me a mother's rights because I cannot give you legal proof of the tie between us."

She had unclasped her arms from his neck, and had allowed him to lead her back to her seat by the window. He knelt beside her there, looking up at her with infinite tenderness; but it was the kindness of a man who pities woman's weaker nature rather than any touch of awakening affection for the woman who had advanced the most sacred claim upon his love.

"Dearest lady, it is not a question of legality."

"No, it is not a question of legality," she echoed, with a defiant look, "for you were born outside the law. The law gives me no claim upon your obedience or your affection."

"Do you think I would withhold either because both are free? Ah, if you are not mistaken, if you have indeed that sacred right, I should hold the claim threefold stronger because the law cannot enforce it. But for your sake, dear Marquise, quite as much as for my own, I would urge you not to accept some womanly fancy for evidence of a stern fact. There is nothing— not one incident—in my conscious experience which can link my life with yours. I was reared in an English homestead. The only man whom I remember as having any power over my destiny was an Englishman."

"That is one of the strongest links in the chain!" returned the Marquise eagerly. "The son I —lost"— there was a slight faltering in the earnest voice at this point—"was given into the charge of an Englishman, to be reared in England. There were reasons why it had to be so, George. I was not the mistress of my own destiny. I might say that these eyes never saw my child's face, for I was in a raging fever—my wits wandering in a world of spectral shapes, hideous, threatening shadows, when he was taken from me. If I ever looked upon his infant face I have no memory of that look, the mother's first wondering contemplation of her firstborn—the smile of half-awakened love. I have seen mothers with their firstborn, and have envied them, recalling my misery."

"But what after-tidings had you of that child? Is his history a blank from the hour that he was entrusted to this—nameless—Englishman?"

"The Englishman was not nameless. He was a certain Captain St. George, a soldier, an adventurer, well born, but of ruined fortunes, who had fought in the Valteline, under the Duc de Lorraine. You were confided to him, to be reared as a gentleman and a soldier, his son by adoption, and you were to bear his name. Thus in your Christian name I discovered another link in the chain. You had but been privately baptised when you were given into his custody, and your baptismal name was not told him. You were to be brought up as an English subject, of gentle birth, and the sum of money which was given to your adopted father was large enough to provide for gentle rearing."

"And if Captain St. George, mercenary soldier and adventurer, chose to squander that fortune on his own uses, to waste it in taverns and stews, what of your child's rearing then?"

"*Mea culpa, mea culpa, mea maxima culpa!*" murmured Madame de Lussac, the tears streaming from her swollen eyelids.

She had not ceased to weep since she had dropped on her knees before the man she claimed as her son, and before whom this proud spirit suffered a humiliation rare in the history of high-born womanhood.

"You have an erring woman for your mother, George," she said, after a brief silence, "a sinner who can but ask from your pity what your love might refuse—forgetfulness of her guilt and of your wrongs. But you may—in your charity—consider that I was but eighteen when you were given into that stranger's keeping, that it was little more than a year since I left the convent where I was brought up in ignorance of all that there is of peril to woman's peace in the world outside convent walls. In knowledge and experience I was a child; a woman only in the power to love and suffer. Do not ask me to tell you more of that tragedy which left me in the dawn of womanhood lonely in the midst of flatterers, joyless, loveless, and compelled to accept wealth, rank, and a great place in the world, as the substitute for all that woman holds dearest!"

"Dear lady, I will ask no question that can distress you. Not for worlds would I urge you to lift the veil from an unhappy past. But I beseech you to arrive at a mathematical certainty before you admit a stranger to the place of a son. Consider how sorrowful a thing it would be, were you to find that you had lavished a mother's affection upon an alien?"

"*Dieu!* I begin to think you have a heart as incapable of feeling as that man of iron who was here just now. Is it nothing to you to be offered a mother's affection, that you begin to chop logic like Descartes, and to ask for mathematical proof of your lineage? In all the years of childhood, of youth, have you never thought that somewhere an unhappy woman might be weeping for you, longing for you, praying to the blessed Mother of God—the pure and sinless—to have pity on a penitent sinner, and to give her the one adorable reward of her penitential tears—the son lost in early youth— before she knew how divine a gift she had renounced?"

George felt shame-stricken at this reproach. Alas! there was no sudden kindling of filial affection in his own heart in response to that fervid emotion of hers. A woman, peerless among women, had revealed herself to him, had claimed him as her son, had wept upon his breast, and clasped and kissed his hands, and knelt at his feet in profound humiliation; and he remained cold. He told himself that it was the suddenness of the revelation which had shocked and startled rather than gladdened him. His heart would have responded warmly had he known the lady better, had he learnt to think of her as a valued friend before she revealed this sacred tie between them. Thus only could he excuse himself for his coldness.

"Dear lady, yes," he faltered, "the image of the mother whose face I never knew has haunted my thoughts and my dreams ever since I came to the dawn of reason—ever since I saw, in the happier case of other children, what maternal love meant. I have had strange dreams—strange, strange dreams," he repeated slowly, a faint, sad smile stealing over his face, and a look as of one who saw a vision of the past rather than the actual scene.

"And you never dreamt of one like me, I doubt. You thought yourself lowly born. Your dream showed you some peasant's homely countenance."

"No, no," he answered quickly, and his smile brightened as he spoke. "'Twas always the face of a lady—a proud and a noble face."

"The face was prophetic, though it was not mine!" the Marquise said eagerly. "It told you that you came of a patrician race. When you know me better, and know the history of my house, you will know that, on one side at least, you are descended from a line of princes."

And on the other side, he wondered? Was his father for ever to remain nameless; albeit, if this lady's belief were well founded, he had now a mother? It was not for him to question her. But there had been words spoken that suggested a parentage from which he shrank with loathing. That smooth-tongued, silken tyrant, that *parvenu* Minister, whose growing rapacity was making his name execrated through the length and breadth of France! Rather would he have had to own himself peasant-born, the son of the kind, homely "Daddy" on whose knees he sat in the winter firelight, by whose side he trudged in the dewy mornings. The vulgarest parentage would not have shocked him like the thought that the man who ruled France was his father.

"I esteem patrician birth as but a trivial boon compared with a mother's love," he said. "Be sure, dear friend, if I seem cold and dull, it is but because the secret you have told me is one that must needs benumb a man's faculties—for the moment. And I did but urge you to be very sure of what I am before you suffered your heart to go out to me."

"My heart *has* gone out to you. It went to you on the first night we met. And when you told me that you had neither name nor kindred, every word pierced this desolate heart like the thrust of a stiletto. You *are* my son, George. Nature does not lie. The mother's instinct in my breast would be proof enough for me, were there not other and more material proofs—your age, your rearing in obscurity in England, your name of George, from that of St. George who adopted you. Scoundrel that he was to hand you over to peasants, to cast you out upon the wilderness of the world while he squandered your fortune! There is proof enough, indisputable proof, of your identity. Your lineage reveals itself in every feature. But if your heart is shut against me "—a sudden change came over her as she said these words, and she became in a moment the imperious woman he had seen at their first meeting in the Louvre —"if you recoil from my affection, and would rather go motherless to your grave than own me for your mother, why then, sir, you know your way back to the street ; and when you have left my house, we can be strangers ever more."

The suppressed passion under her proud bearing, the withering anger that froze upon her lips and flashed from her eye, thrilled him with a vague terror. To be offered a mother's love—and to refuse it ! To have seen the mother's face in his dreams—to have stretched out his arms to a phantom in the dim labyrinth of sleep ; and now, face to face with a woman of noble birth, of generous temper, beautiful, rich in all gifts that lift a woman above the mass of womanhood, and to hesitate, to hang back, to be frost where he should be fire! He felt how mean a figure he made, as he faltered his protestations of gratitude, of esteem, repect, submission to her will.

"Oh, I am too exacting, I ask too much!" she said, her mood changing again, after a silence, and a long, weary sigh. "But life is so short, and I have wasted my good years. I long for the sunlight of one calm, pure love to shine upon my declining path. Youth is gone, George. Beauty is going. I have only grey hairs and loneliness before me. If you can be content to spend your life with me, I will not make your bonds too narrow. My cherished falcon shall have neither hood nor leash. If, as the years go on, and you live under this roof, sacrificing an hour or two of your youth day by day in my dull company—if a filial affection grow in your heart, ever so slowly, I will be thankful to God and **you**, and will deem that Heaven has used me better than I deserve."

"You would have me live under this roof?"

"Not as my son, George, but as my steward and secretary. It is more than a year since I lost the valuable man who managed my husband's estate, and wrote my letters, and kept my creditors at a distance. He was a man of good birth and incorruptible integrity. I treated him ever as an equal. A creature so precious was not easily to be replaced, so his post has remained empty; and neither De Lussac nor the world will wonder at my engaging another secretary, even though you are twenty years younger than my good Clerimont. I shall tell my friends that I discovered the wisdom of a sage under those boyish curls; and indeed, I believe you are clever enough to manage a large estate, if you will but give your mind to figures and account-books for an occasional hour."

George told her that he was not unaccustomed to accounts, and that he would work like a galley slave at her bidding; but after that assurance he ventured, as delicately as he could, to remind her that she was still handsome enough to provoke the slander of envious women and profligate men, and that the choice of so young a man as himself for a grave and responsible office in her household might give ground for calumny.

"Let me keep to my own lodging, dear Marchesa; and summon me here as your guest when you will. But to live under this roof——"

"You have promised to obey me," she interrupted, "and this is the first duty I ask from you—to sit by my hearth, to be within call when my dark hour comes upon me, when I am ill, and despairing, and sicken for the face of a friend. I defy slander! Am I to cry to all Paris, from the house-top, that I am not such a woman as the Chevreuse, or the Montbazon? Let my false friends say what they choose—so long as my son loves and respects me, and lives under my roof, and can judge for himself what my life is. I will not be denied, George. You have no excuse for refusing me. You are alone in Paris, without employment, without means."

"I will do as you would have me, dear lady," he answered, with a grave submission.

He knew he must never address her by the sacred name of mother, even when they were alone, lest the word should drop from his lips involuntarily on some public occasion. If he were indeed the son she claimed, he must enter her house as a masquerader, in the eye of her husband a paid servant; while every time she looked at him, his presence would recall the tragedy of her life, the secret of her erring girlhood. To his mind it seemed as if there must be misery for both of them in such relations; but she had appealed to him by arguments that were irresistible, and he had no option but to obey.

Paris had plenty to talk about during the next few days, for Cardinal Mazarin had been quick to avenge the baffled scheme of September 1st. It gave him an excuse for crushing the rival he feared and hated. The most popular man in the city, Henry IV.'s fair-haired grandson, the Duc de Beaufort, was arrested late one evening, on leaving the Queen's apartments at the Louvre, and conveyed to the state prison of Vincennes, that feudal castle in which the princes of the blood Royal and of the half-blood had too often suffered captivity.

The thought of Mazarin's peril, the attempt at assassination, had urged Anne to severest measures, and Beaufort, the golden-haired prince, the Phœbus Apollo of the Louvre, once her favoured ally, was the first to suffer her displeasure.

She had greeted him with smiles, and friendly inquiries, when he came to her private *salon*, after a long day's hunting ; she had let him kiss her hand at parting—that alabaster hand which everybody praised. And lo ! in the ante-chamber stood Guitaut, the captain of the guard, waiting to arrest him as he passed from that Royal presence.

The whole scene was like a bad dream ; but in that hour Mazarin attained a supremacy which he had not reached before, and France began to feel the strength of the hand under the glove.

Close on this startling arrest followed the banishment of the offender's family—the Duc and Duchesse de Vendôme, and Beaufort's elder brother, the Duc de Mercœur—to one of their country houses. Other arrests succeeded, and the beautiful firebrand, Madame de Chevreuse, disappeared from the scene, taking flight with her daughter to Guernsey, after a vain attempt to return to England. Bishops and priests, faithful servants, old friends of the Queen, were alike sacrificed to swell the power of the Minister who had made himself master of the heart or the mind of Anne of Austria.

Three days after that startling interview with the Marquise George removed to the Hôtel de Lussac, carrying with him a well-furnished wardrobe, and a choice stock of books which Lady Llanbister had given him from time to time—the books she loved and desired that he should love. These were all his possessions, save one thing, which he valued above them all : a miniature of his dear patroness, for which, partly to please him and partly in pure benevolence, she had sat to a shabby old artist in the city, who had painted Elizabeth's faded charms at Richmond in the last year of her life, when he was young and prosperous, and a Court painter. He had fallen very low in repute and in means, and was a teacher of perspective and land-scape painting, in which arts he had been employed to instruct Geraldine ; and her ladyship, seeing his pinched countenance, meagre legs, and threadbare suit, discovered the poverty he would have died sooner than acknow-ledge, and, in her bounteousness for all things that can feel, gave him a handsome fee for her portrait on ivory, which he executed *con amore*.

To George the gift was of infinite value ; and there was scarce a day on which he did not open the little shagreen case and gaze with melancholy fondness upon the pictured countenance. It was a spell to bring back the happy hours that were gone, to inspire hope of a happier time to come.

The major-domo ushered him to his room in a stately silence, but, having inducted him, condescended so far as to say, "The tapestried closet, sir, is for your study, and this inner room is your chamber. They were Monsieur de Lussac's rooms during the lifetime of his father, and have been ever allotted to the heir of the House. Monsieur Clerimont, the late steward, occupied a *grenier* in the roof. I hope you will find the suite to your liking."

"I have no choice in such matters, sir," George answered haughtily, flinging open one of the casements as he spoke, for the room lacked air.

He detected a sneer in the man's speech, and felt an angry flush mounting to his brow, and was vexed with himself for being angry.

That which the servant had called a closet was a room of ample dimensions, with two windows opening from floor to ceiling in the Italian fashion, and giving on to a stone balcony. The walls were hung with tapestry of a much older date than that in the reception-rooms below, and the bluish verdure and heavy colouring of forest scenes made a somewhat gloomy background to carved oak furniture of an antique and ponderous character, a gloom only relieved by the Venetian glass in a frame of chased silver that hung above a large ebony writing-table. The bedchamber was furnished in less sombre colours, and was more sumptuous than the study. The tall bedstead was draped with a rich azure satin, embroidered with garlands of roses, hanging from a gilded canopy; the wardrobe was of Italian inlaying, in many coloured woods; but the chief glory of the room was a huge Venetian coffer, a dower-chest of the previous century, with panels painted by Veronese, and having on one side the espousals of Joseph and Mary, and on the other the marriage feast at Cana in Galilee. The toilet service was of silver, the ewer richly worked in *repoussé*, and the basin parcel gilt.

Here, as in the study, the windows opened upon a small quadrangle, and the only prospect was of other windows in the opposite wall, and of a massive tower with a conical roof in one angle of the courtyard. Walls and tower shut out the afternoon sun, and the quadrangle was for the most part in shadow. To George's eye it was the dreariest outlook he had ever seen; and, in spite of the splendour within, the house seemed a prison rather than a palace.

The Maître d'Hôtel showed him a bell which rang in the corridor outside, and which would be answered by a servant, who was to be always at Monsieur's orders. Madame la Marquise would like to see Monsieur in the tapestried *salon*, when he had rested and taken some refreshment.

"I need neither rest nor refreshment," George told him.

"In that case I will conduct Monsieur to the *salon*."

"No, there is no occasion. I belong to the house now, and can find my way. You can go, sir."

He was glad to get rid of this stately personage, tall, lean, grey-haired, with deep-set Italian eyes glowing like live coals under bushy grey brows, a skin of dark olive without a glimmer of red upon the cadaverous cheeks, and a lip that seemed made for scorn. He opened all the windows in bedchamber and study; but even then the rooms seemed airless, for want of horizon and open sky. The luxury of these rooms stifled him. His soul sickened at all that pomp of satin and velvet, gold and silver, ebony and ivory, tapestry and painting. Things that had been provided for his delight only served to disgust him.

And was he weak enough to be stung by a servant's sneer? He had always hated that man's face—a servant with the stateliness and assumption of a Spanish hidalgo, slow and soft of step, his head in the air, with all the pompous self-consciousness of one who condescended to minister to masters he despised. George gave an impatient sigh as he remembered the honest faces in Lord Llanbister's household, and his own fresh airy rooms at Isleworth, with their outlook to Richmond Hill, and the scent of roses and gilly-flowers blown in from the garden; and those almost as pleasant garrets in Aldersgate Street, looking towards Highgate and Islington, across wide spaces of pasture and cornfield, broken by patches of woodland—rooms plainly furnished, but provided with all things needful for comfort and cleanliness. How different, how unspeakably different, life had been in those airy houses, open to all the summer winds, steeped in sunshine, full of the sound of swift footsteps and happy voices! Here all was airless, silent. The very breath of life seemed smothered in this gloomy splendour.

Madame de Lussac greeted him with a little cry of gladness as he entered the Ariadne room, so called in honour of the tapestried hangings through which the Cardinal had appeared so unexpectedly during George's previous visit.

She kissed him on either cheek, as Lady Llanbister had done in that unforgotten moment of parting.

"Now you are all my own," she said. "Henceforward you belong to me; your present, your future, your hopes, your ambition. You are mine; and I am content to be forgotten by the world. From this day my sole desire is to see you achieve greatness ; in arms, in diplomacy. Your own aspirations must direct your career. If you want to marry a princess, you shall win her. All I have of talent, tact, fortune, influence, shall be used for you, for you, George. You are all I possess in this world. You are all that life has left for me."

"Do not say that, dear Marchesa. Your husband has a stronger claim on your affection than I—whom fate has made so long a stranger—can ever have."

"My husband !" she cried, with scathing scorn. "A husband's claim ! Do you know what husbands and wives are to each other at the French Court ? The husband ? A name to sanction a wife's liberty. The wife ? The bringer of fortune—despised, loathed perhaps, from the hour of espousal—married as a child, like Richelieu's little niece, Enghien's baby-bride. Or, if dowerless, and chosen in some passionate freak, for her beauty, neglected and abandoned for another woman when that beauty begins to pall upon its master. My husband can claim nothing, and demands nothing. He married me for my beauty, and was proud of me, I believe, while I was in my zenith. But at the first sign of wrinkles and faded looks he transferred his affections to one of the ugliest women in Paris, who talks like a fish-wife and drinks like a fish. It is to her that he will carry his newly won laurels when the campaign is over. He will bring me withered leaves and sour looks. I never loved him, George, not even when he was at my feet ; I hated him when he abandoned me for that woman, and when Paris laughed and friends condoled. But hatred soon burnt out, and left only contempt. Never fear a rival in Godefroy de Lussac."

She had agitated herself by this angry retrospect, and took two or three turns up and down the room before she recovered that happier mood in which she had given George welcome.

"Do you like your rooms ? " she asked presently, seating herself by her favourite window.

All that there was of brightness was on this side of the house, commanding the garden with its straight walks, marble statues, balustrades and vases, its fountain, and *bosquet*, through which there flashed glimpses of the sunlit river, and above which rose the towers of Notre Dame.

"They are much too handsome for me. I am accustomed to homelier rooms and humbler furniture."

"You say that as if you liked the homely rooms best."

"I was more used to them. Pray do not think me ungrateful. I am deeply conscious of your goodness."

"Ungrateful, no," she answered impatiently. "But I may think you something worse than an ingrate. That is only common. I may think you one of those dull natures that cannot rise above the level where adverse fate first placed them; that, being bred among coarse companions, and accustomed to vulgar surroundings, you have a soul that cannot aspire, a mind dead to the beauty of the world—knowing no difference between an apprentice's garret and rooms upon which art and gold have been lavished."

"Your impatience wrongs me, Marchesa. I know how to admire the splendours of a palace, though I have slept soundly under a gipsy's tent. I have no love of coarse company or a squalid lodging, and for the last three years I have been lodged in a nobleman's house, and as commodiously as if I had been his son. But Lord Llanbister's houses are furnished with a Puritan plainness as compared with your sumptuous apartments; and I confess that I care more for a sunny outlook and a broad horizon than for the finest tapestry in Europe."

"You will learn to care for the work of great artists. We have artists of the needle as well as of the brush. Basta! I am foolish to be disappointed at your lack of taste; and I ought to commend your honesty. Now, as to your wardrobe. You must go to the best tailor in Paris. Tabouret is the man most esteemed. Order what you will, so long as it is of the richest material and the latest fashion; and bid him send his bill to me."

" My dear Marchesa, I have clothes to last me for a
year."

"Clothes suitable to Lord Llanbister's airy garrets,
not to my house—or to my son," she added, in an
undertone.

" I think in your bounteousness you forget my place
in your house," George answered gravely. " If the
world is to know me only as your secretary I should
but provoke the contempt of your friends and equals
were I to ape their splendour. I promise never to go
ill clad, or wanting in the things that become a gentleman. But if—if indeed I have any place in your
esteem——"

" ' If,' and ' esteem '! You have a heart of ice—like
your father's."

She started, and her face crimsoned, conscious of
having told too much in those impatient words. George
perceived her confusion, and was still more painfully
moved. His cheek blanched while hers reddened.

"Forgive me, mother," he faltered, and his lips
trembled at the name. " Forgive me, if I seem dull and
cold, while my heart aches with feelings I have no
power to express in speech. Think how your love—
your bounty—have come upon me like some angelic
vision seen in a dream—as suddenly—as strangely."

"Oh, I was wrong, impatient, exacting ! It is I who
should ask you to forgive. I have been longing for you
through these last barren years, with a desolate old age
creeping nearer and nearer. I had but to look in my
glass to see my fate coming. Grey hairs, withered
cheeks, and the world's contempt. What could life give
me so precious as the son I lost when I was young and
handsome ; when he was an infant, a child just like other
children ; before Heaven had given me a mother's heart ?
It came in after years, that sacred fire of maternal love,
when other fires were cold and dead. And then I saw
you, the re-incarnation of the man I loved when I was
young—and who has no existence now. No! *That*
man is dead ! "

"Let me be all that a son can be to a mother,"

George said tenderly, moved to deepest pity by all that was pitiable in a proud woman's self-abasement. "But for your honour and good name I must play my part in this house with discretion. I detected a touch of insolence in your groom of the chambers when he showed me to my apartment—an evident wonder at your indulgence in giving me such a lodging. If I am not to stand at your side as your son, I must fill my office as your servant so as to provoke neither question nor scandal, and by the sobriety of my costume and the reserve of my manners I must hold myself at a distance from the fine gentlemen who crowd your *salons*—even if it is your desire that I should appear among your company."

She listened with a gloomy brow, and gave a long sigh before she answered,—

"You are a model of wisdom, George. I doubt you judge rightly. I live in a circle of human vipers, whose fangs are primed with venom. You shall keep your sober olive doublet. You could look no handsomer in Candale's white satin birthday suit, stiff with gold and gems. You shall live in my house as you please. You shall dictate, and I will obey. Only let me see you in my dark hour; and bear with my moods and caprices; and remember that in a life the world would call prosperous I have known few cloudless days."

He knelt beside her chair, and kissed her hand.

"Since we must keep our secret before the world," he said, with a mournful earnestness, "will you think when my lips call you Marchesa my heart says 'Mother'; and in all things command me as the most exacting mother would command her son."

"No, no, I must not exact too much. I have to win your love."

CHAPTER XV.

NOT TO BE BOUGHT.

To be greatly loved, and not able to give love for love ;
to be loaded with benefits, and not to be grateful ; this
is of human bankruptcies the most painful : and it was
such a bankrupt that George knew himself in the house
of Madame de Lussac. He was true to his promise of
the first day. He obeyed and honoured her with all
courtesy and attention. He was at her beck and call
from morn till midnight ; sat in the perfumed atmosphere of her *ruelle*, talking confidentially, or reading to
her, for a quiet hour before her fine company assembled,
when he withdrew to a distance, and lounged in the
embrasure of a window, listening wearily to the fops and
fribbles, and the *précieuses*, whom Molière's biting wit
had not yet etched with the dry point of finest
irony.

He lived amidst splendour that he loathed, and mixed
with company he despised. There was no hour before
midnight in which he was his own master, no period
of the long day when he could be sure of being left
to read or write, or dream, in the room that had been
given to him for a study, or on the garden terrace where
he loved to sit alone, dreamily watching the traffic on
the river, or looking with unseeing eyes at the dome
and pinnacles on the opposite shore, where all that
there was of learning in Paris was concentrated in the
College of the Sorbonne, so lately restored by the great

Cardinal. George sighed as he gazed at the mighty dome rising above the Law Courts and prison roofs of the Cité, and thought how good a life must be that of a poor student, free to listen to the lectures in the College halls, to listen where Rabelais had listened, to tread the ground hallowed by the footsteps of philosophers and poets, grammarians and necromancers, in the dim, romantic centuries before printing and gunpowder.

Alas! if he stole into the garden, to his favourite seat on the terrace, or to some sheltered nook under the mulberry-trees, hoping for an hour's freedom, he had rarely been alone for fifteen minutes before he heard the slow footsteps of a lacquey, bringing him a message from Madame la Marquise, who desired the presence of Monsieur Georges in the Ariadne room.

The name of Mountain had been dropped, at Madame de Lussac's desire. She would not have him associated with that vulgar adventurer, that tool and minion of the Chevreuse. In vain did George plead that Mountain had been his adopted father when he was friendless and roofless. She told him that he might be as grateful as he pleased; but he was to bear no token of those past years. So he had now no surname, and was only Monsieur Georges.

He was installed as a superior kind of house steward, and Paolo, the old Italian major-domo, was ordered to give him all documents relating to household expenditure, and to the general management of the De Lussac income, which the Marquis had allowed his wife to administer, being alike reckless and ignorant in the use of money.

Accustomed to the plain and uncomplicated accountancy of a household in which ready money was paid for most things, and where no tradesman was ever kept waiting for his due, George was horrified, and at the outset almost bewildered, by the mass of bills, and pleading letters, and complaints, and threats of legal process, which Paolo brought before him on the first day of his new office.

His look of consternation was quickly interpreted by the keen-witted Italian.

" If Monsieur could understand those papers, he would be cleverer than Monsieur le Tellier, the Cardinal's financial manager—who is said to have the longest head in France. It is enough to distract the seven wise men of Greece only to contemplate Madame's embarrassments. Indeed, I believe that unhappy wretch Clerimont shortened his life by fretting over them. For myself, I have left off trying to understand. I give the creditors whatever funds I can scrape off the land, from farmers who are always groaning—a hundred crowns here, a hundred crowns there—and I wait with resignation for the deluge which is to swallow us all."

" Sit down, *amico mio*, and explain all that is explainable," said George, softened by the old man's frankness, having been prepared to meet with insolence and animosity.

Paolo shrugged his shoulders, and protested that he could not presume to sit in the presence of his mistress's friend and honoured guest. All his experience was at Monsieur's service as Monsieur's humble servant.

" First, then, for Madame's income, from all sources Before we reckon her debts it were best to calculate our means of paying them."

" *Ohime!* Think not to extinguish debts that have been accumulating for a score of years. Monsieur is young, and brave, and clever ; but he is not a saint, to make a roast fowl sit up on the dish and crow. He cannot take a bag of gold and invoke our blessed Lady to quadruple its contents."

" At least, let me understand the funds we have to administer."

Again Paolo shrugged his shoulders.

" He who can understand the shifting of quicksands or foretell the eruptions of Vesuvius, could perchance reckon the Signora's resources. They are as irregular as unexpected."

" But her estates? They must yield an income which cannot greatly vary," George said impatiently.

" Her estates? Oh, for estates—she has none. She was penniless when the Marquis married her. The Signora Bianca and your servant had to pledge our poor fields and hovels in the Campagna to furnish her *trousseau*. The Marquis was rich—*ricchissimo*; but they are both of an improvidence which would exhaust gold-mines. His estates at the present time furnish an income—of which he anticipates the greater part ; and for the rest, money is found somehow—peradventure a bag of gold—or a diamond on which to borrow a few thousand crowns."

" God help us, what a mode of living ! And with such letters as these—the prayers of ruined traders—the cries of widows, with hungry children, whose husbands died broken-hearted by a commerce that crushed them ! What sordid misery under all this regal splendour ! How can a woman of warm feelings and noble character, like the Marquise, endure such a life ? "

" Women do not think," answered Paolo, with conviction. " The Marchesa does not read those letters. There are too many of them. Or if she does sometimes look at one, she does not believe the writer. ' They all sing the same song,' she says, and flings me the letter. ' Keep them quiet, Paolo, keep them quiet. You are clever at that,' she says. And then I tell her that to keep peace for another year I must have a round sum. And the round sum is provided—somehow."

" The Marchesa sells some of her jewels, I doubt."

" *Chi sa ?* The money is found."

George examined the kitchen bills—the accounts of three French cooks and two Italian confectioners. The expenditure horrified him. He knew what a large household ought to cost, carried on upon liberal lines ; for at Lord Llanbister's there had been comfort for everybody, down to the meanest scullion, and unmeasured beneficence to the sick and necessitous.

" Waste alone could hardly account for such a consumption of provisions," he told Paolo, after a lengthened scrutiny of the purveyors' bills. " There must be dishonesty somewhere as well."

" There is dishonesty everywhere," answered Paolo. " Do you expect to find honest servants in such a house as this, with a master who is always absent, who is known to have his favoured home in the next street— with a mistress who never looks at a tradesman's bill, or asks the price of any goods she orders? They are arrant thieves, every one of them. They steal provisions enough to maintain half their kindred. I cannot stop them, for if I tax them with cheating they ask me for the wages I cannot pay. They pay themselves by robbery. They have a league of roguery with the purveyors—and most of those accounts in your hands are shameless fabrications, charges for goods half of which have never been supplied."

" And you, Signor Paolo, what is your part in the scheme of ruin?" George asked, looking fixedly at the Italian, of whose probity he was still doubtful.

The steward returned his gaze without flinching.

" Monsieur thinks that I, too, am a cheat? Well, it is only natural. But Monsieur is wrong. I do not cheat, because I do not want to be richer than I am. I have an orchard and some fields, and an olive wood, an oil-mill, and a cottage, on the slope of a hill near Albano. Such sunshine steeps that hillside as never warms this gloomy city. If I could buy sunshine with ill-gotten gold I might turn plunderer. To lie in my orchard and bask under that Italian sky, and dine upon a melon and a slice of black bread, or a bunch of my own grapes! That is the life I look forward to, Monsieur, when I am too old and feeble to wear the Marchesa's livery. And I have saved enough to provide for that modest existence—that serene old age."

" You are wise, Signor, to be content with so little."

" So little? The Italian sky; my own orchard and maize-fields, my olive wood and mill! So much! And again, though Monsieur may not believe it, I love my mistress. I served her when she was a child, a beautiful, wilful, daring child ; and when she came from the convent in the bloom of her girlhood—handsomer than those Italian nieces of the Cardinal's, of whose beauty people tell such wonders, and of whom he has so many—bright-plumed, beautiful birds that will peck this French soil bare before we have done with them. No, Monsieur, although I am a steward, I am not a thief."

"I am glad to know as much, Signor Paolo. And I take it kindly that you have given me your confidence, and do not resent my interference with your duties. You had a diabolical manner when you showed me these rooms—and I doubted we were to be enemies."

"I love my mistress, Monsieur; and love is ever jealous. I have been jealous of her greyhound, and kicked the brute on the sly before now. But if it please her to have your company and to entrust you with her affairs—well, it is not for me to object. She had ever curious fancies."

"I hope to serve her as faithfully as you have done—and to reduce this chaos to order, Paolo," George said, dropping the ceremonious prefix, and offering his hand to the Roman, who clasped it cordially in a skinny paw that was not scrupulously clean.

George lost no time in informing Lady Llanbister of his altered fortunes: but he did not enter into details, and dealt in the briefest manner with so portentous a change; telling her only that he had assumed the office of steward or secretary in the household of the Marquise de Lussac; that it was an arduous post, but involving considerable privileges, and a more sumptuous style of living than he cared for; but that he hoped to turn to good account all of household economy that he had learnt from his dear benefactress and friend, the loss of whose so cherished company he should ever lament.

Lady Llanbister's reply came as soon as winds and waves and his Majesty's post could bring it. Her letter expressed an affectionate regard of which he had long felt assured; but although she congratulated him upon his good fortune, he could divine that she was not pleased with the form it had taken.

"I must confess I would have had you in a great gentle-

man's service rather than in a fine lady's," she wrote,
" since from all I remember to have heard of Madame
de Lussac, in the days when the gossip of the French
Court used to make a considerable part of the conversation in our poor Queen's company, I fear she is a person
of a capricious temper, and renowned for neither religion
nor strict morals.   But I do wrong perhaps to write thus
harshly of an unknown lady, since it is but too common
for fine gentlemen to speak ill of a good woman, if she
chance to offend them ; and all the harm I know of
Madame de Lussac is but hearsay.

"Yet in this lady's sumptuous home and amid the
splendours and *fêtes* of Paris, which has been spared
the troubles that have fallen on our unhappy London,
I would not have you forget old friends and a much
meaner home, where you were ever esteemed, and where
your absence has left an empty place that nobody can
fill.   And, ah, remember, George, that in the days to
come, if by any chance I should alter the scheme of
my life, and choose to live soberly and aloof from all
noisy spirits in a house of my own, rather than to enter
a religious order, whatever home I make for myself in
England or abroad will be your home as well as mine,
and there will be no one more welcome there than my dear
young friend and pupil.   It may be, as you think, that
Fate will for ever refuse you the mistress of your heart,
and that we must submit to see the wife I would choose
for you given to another.   If this should be so, it shall
be my privilege to console you with all that friendship
can offer in the place of love, and to be your companion
till, with the passing of years, your faithful heart, cured
of the old sorrow, shall worship at a new shrine, and
under happier auspices."

George was grieved to think of Madame de Lussac's
name shuttlecocked on the malevolent Court battledores,
tossed lightly from one wit to another amid flying
arrows of scorn.   He knew how the Frenchmen in
London talked of their compatriots at home, and had
heard the peals of laughter and the malicious delight

at some outrageous anecdote of Madame de Chevreuse, or her youthful step-mother, the Montbazon. *The* Montbazon, whose reputation made sport for fops and witlings from whose sphere the woman herself was as inaccessible as the stars! Doubtless among those idle, jest-loving cosmopolitans at Henrietta Maria's lively Court, there had been some one to slander the beautiful Marquise; and he had no need to make himself miserable because the woman he was bound to honour had been lightly spoken of in a circle which would hardly admit the virtue of an archangel.

He dwelt fondly on the close of his dear lady's letter. Never before had she so urged her life-long friendship, never given him such full assurance of the future. Yet he sighed over those lines, remembering how he was bound by that stronger right of the woman who claimed him as her son. Her son? He had no evidence but her assertion of his identity; yet he could scarcely doubt a fact of which she was so convinced, since she must best know how the circumstances of his early years fitted into the history of her lost child.

After a laborious investigation of the house accounts, and of Madame de Lussac's persona lexpenditure, George took the first opportunity of laying a statement of affairs before the lady, and was shocked to find how lightly she regarded obligations which to his mind were appalling, and still more shocked at her scornful dismissal of piteous complaints from tradesmen who laid their ruin at her door.

"They are all cheats and sycophants," she said, throwing aside the letters he wanted her to read. "They bring me their goods, and cajole me into buying, always at exorbitant prices; and afterwards, when I can't pay, there comes this tragical chorus. It is Madame la Marquise who has ruined them—not their own waste and gluttony, their own finery and aping of their betters! Oh, I know them."

"But indeed, Marchesa, there must be truth in some of these complaints. Your tailor's widow was with me this morning—the tears raining down her poor pinched face. She declares it was starvation that killed her husband—the want of necessaries. Their goods had been seized by the silk mercer who supplied the stuff for your last set of liveries, and they had not received a crown piece from you on account of them, though the liveries are a year old."

"A year old! No wonder my men look shabby. I was ashamed of them last night. I saw the Montbazon looking at them with a curling lip. *She* has no year-old liveries. But then, she has so many purses to draw upon. You had best order a new set, George, from Tabouret, who is almost out of fashion, but who has a grand style."

"And the poor widow?"

"If her husband is dead, the business is at an end. Give her some money—as much as you can afford."

"Dear Marchesa, the treasury is emptier than King Charles's after a year's war. The servants are clamouring for their wages, and I can give them nothing. There will be no rents due till Easter."

"Then I doubt money must be found—somehow," sighed the lady. "Life is very troublesome, George. Give me that bottle of violet essence the Cardinal sent me last night. It came straight from the Certosa at Florence. Dear spot! The perfume wafts me back to that sunny hillside, and the garden the Carthusians tend so exquisitely."

This was a morning conference. The Marquise, with her head dressed for Court, and her shoulders covered with a rose-coloured satin *négligé*, was sitting up in bed, propped with pillows, to receive her before-dinner company. The bedstead, mounted on a daïs, and richly carved and gilt; the curtains of *frisé* velvet bordered with bullion fringe; the embroidered satin coverlet; the clusters of ostrich-feathers that crowned the tall columns;—were of an almost Royal splendour that stopped short only at the Royal privilege of a surrounding balustrade, or railed barrier, to keep off the crowd of visitors; a privilege which Mazarin was afterwards to usurp, in that later zenith of his power which marked the close of vicissitudes such as few but kings are subject to. Amidst all this opulence of gold and velvet and priceless furniture, sumptuous decorations, the spoil of monarchs deposed and palaces deserted, it seemed the irony of fate that there should not be a few crowns to stop the complainings of a starving widow; and George left his seat in the *ruelle*, heavy-hearted, almost despairing, and withdrew to his distant station in an oriel window, to make room for the gossips and flatterers, whose airy babble tortured his ear like music out of tune.

He was not ungrateful. He kept telling himself that. He was not ungrateful for love and confidence so freely given; but he hated his life in that palace as he had never hated it in his worst intervals of bad luck with Francis Mountain. The very atmosphere of the house sickened him, overcharged with those Italian perfumes which the Cardinal and the Queen loved better than the sweet breath of heaven—a house which had been so planned as to admit as little air as possible; a house where many of the finest rooms looked out upon a deep stone quadrangle like a dry well.

There was a reception at the Hôtel de Lussac that evening, and it would have been difficult to perceive a flaw in the splendour of the entertainment; for, in spite of the Marchesa's disparagement, the dress liveries of peach-coloured *camelot de Hollande* with silver *passementerie*, looked as good as new, their magnificence being of a solid kind that would stand the wear of years. Her servants, good or bad, had been sedulously trained in one article of duty, which was to put on the appearance of excellence before the world. They might steal, gamble, drink, fight, blaspheme, in their own quarters; but they must be equal to the best when the critical eye of courtly Paris was upon them; and thus, on Madame de Lussac's day and evening, the *chefs* and the *marmitons*, the *valets de pied*, and the grooms of the chambers, appeared the most accomplished servants that ever conducted a household. The supper was such as the most fastidious gourmet must needs praise ; the rooms were perfumed and lighted and warmed to perfection.

Mazarin was among the guests, but only vouchsafed a smile and a nod to the secretary. He was full of the troubles in England, and of some diamonds which he had bought from Henrietta Maria, more out of kindness to the poor lady than because he wanted the gems.

"She left them with the Prince of Orange when she set out upon that tempest-tossed voyage last February," he said. "I sent my jeweller, Lescot, to Holland, to look at the stones ; and 'twas on his report I bought them, paying a price that was measured rather by the lady's necessities than by the value of the gems."

A gentle smile circulated among the privileged group with whom his Eminence was conversing, since every one knew that of all traffickers he was the most astute, deliberate, and unyielding. From the day when he sprang into power he had been occupied in laying the foundations of that fortune which was finally to become the most stupendous ever possessed by a minister of state.

"It is good news to hear of your Eminence buying more diamonds, since it proves that France is rich," Héloïse said, with the faintest suspicion of irony.

"Say rather it proves that France may have need of money before long, Marchesa. Diamonds are the most convertible kind of wealth. The English Queen has changed hers into munitions of war ; and I may need to change them again into the same commodity, should France want soldiers. All that I possess is held for my master, the King."

When George paid his accustomed visit to Madame de Lussac's bedside next morning, she seemed in unwonted spirits.

"Sit there!" she said, pointing to the chair near her pillows. "Heavens! what a lugubrious countenance ! Has the tailor's widow been riding on your chest all night, like one of Urbain Grandier's hags ?

I never knew a man so take another's debts upon his
shoulders. Why, everybody of any rank in Paris is
in debt. Shopkeepers could not live if we were all
sober and cautious, and eager to pay our way. If we
did not cheat them now and then—by not paying them
—they could not cheat us always, as they do, by their
overcharges. Come, try to look cheerful ! Your starving widow shall eat herself into a tertian fever if she
pleases. Open that casket on my dressing-table, and
say what you find there."

He rose, looking at her wonderingly, and went to
the dressing-table—a broad expanse where an arsenal
of toilet implements, gold, silver, steel, with jewelled
handles, brushes, mirrors, essence-bottles, were set out
in glittering array for the morning parade. The central object was an oblong casket in tortoiseshell inlaid with gold—a kind of Neapolitan work which he
knew well.

He lifted the lid, and saw that the box, which was
about eight inches deep, was lined with copper, and
was closely packed with *rouleaux* of coin, wrapped in
white paper.

" Is this gold, Marchesa ? "

" Every coin of it. Is there enough there to satisfy
your widow and the rest of them, and give me a
twelvemonth's peace ? "

" Do you not know how much there is ? "

" Not I ! You can count it at your leisure. I told
a friend of my distress, and he sent me that casket
this morning—the casket by one messenger, and the
key by another. My friend is careful, you see. Come,
smile, George—if there be a smile in your composition.
I hate doleful faces ! "

" Dear Marchesa, I rejoice that there is wherewithal
to satisfy your most pressing creditors—to give something to all. Yes, I am heartily glad : and your friend
—is good."

He spoke earnestly, but without the smile she had
asked for. He was relieved at this way out of difficulties
that humiliated him for her sake, since he had taken

her errors upon his shoulders and held her honour as his own, and since there was ever in his mind a painful recollection of Lady Llanbister's words—"without religion and without morals." His heart was too heavy for smiles.

He began to count the money, going through every *rouleau*.

"*Dieu merci!*" cried the Marquise, "cannot you defer that plodding business till you are alone? I want you to read the *Gazette* to me—and not count those gold pieces."

"But I had rather you should know exactly how much money I have to pay away."

"I never know anything exactly. I hate exact knowledge. It is the bane of life. You are to buy me as long a truce as you can from my importunate creditors. I confide everything to your wisdom. You seem to have a genius for figures—but I pray you not to make me think you an arithmetical machine."

He submitted reluctantly to leave the gold uncounted, and sat in his usual place to read the news of the war in Flanders—and some brief notices of the troubles in England, where the King seemed still to have the stronger hand, and to hold the winning cards, did he but know how to play them.

Once in the seclusion of his own study, George applied his whole mind to the disposal of the contents of the casket, which he found amounted to two thousand of the new double louis ; and with this respectable sum he had enough to pacify all Madame de Lussac's creditors, but not enough to pay any of them in full, save in those exceptional cases, such as the tailor's widow, where justice demanded full payment. To do the very best with the sum at his disposal involved profound thought and calculation, and to this task George devoted himself with as much care as if he had been dealing with the finances of a bankrupt nation.

He locked the cash in the Venetian dower-chest, of which the key was a work of art that would have defied forgery; and he carried the empty casket back to Madame de Lussac's apartments. There was little need to wonder whence this wealth had been obtained, since the initials "J. M." in a curiously interlaced cypher appeared among the golden arabesques on the lid. It was to the Cardinal, who dealt at his pleasure with the riches of France, that the Marquise had appealed for aid. George thought of the whole transaction with an unconquerable aversion. He would have given much to be able to shut out of his mind all thought of Jules Mazarin and his relations with Héloïse de Lussac; and still more gladly would he have ignored the link between those two lives and his own life. But it was not possible so to forget, and never again could the world be to him as pleasant a place as it had been before that startling revelation which had imposed duties and fetters upon a life that had before been as free as it was lonely. He looked back and remembered his repining at that happy ignorance—his yearning to know the story of his birth and parentage.

Well, knowledge had come to him without effort of his own; and it had cast a deeper cloud over his days than that vague shadow of shame which had hung upon his nameless youth.

There were young men in Paris who would be proud of such a lineage, and who would have made it the stepping-stone to high fortune. But George felt that any favour from Mazarin would crush him; and it was with infinite pain that he thought of Madame de Lussac's easy acceptance of the Cardinal's money.

He was put to a severe test not long after the incident of the casket A letter from Mademoiselle Lescot, daughter of Pierre Lescot, the famous jeweller of the Parvis Saint-Barthélemy, on the Quai du Palais, invited him to an interview, the lady having an important communication to make to him. He knew that Lescot was the Cardinal's jeweller, and trusted agent in the purchase and selection of precious gems, and works of art of all kinds, making frequent journeys to foreign cities on such missions ; but he did not conjecture any link between Cardinal Mazarin and the lady's letter, which he took to be a common lure to get him to the shop, where he would be tempted to buy jewellery by some specious offer of a bargain.

He went at the time named, not as a buyer, but to waste half an hour in the shop, which was a favourite lounge of the fops of the period, although the jeweller's daughter and able representative was neither young nor beautiful.

Beauty was to be met there, though not in the mistress of the house—for it was a convenient place in which to interchange greetings that might have been impossible elsewhere.

George found the shop full of loungers ; but Mademoiselle Lescot left a customer who was cheapening unset emeralds to the care of her clerk, and came from behind her counter to greet the new-comer.

" Will you honour my humble *salon* by withdrawing there, Monsieur? I have to talk to you of a serious matter ! "

" With pleasure, Mademoiselle ; but I must warn you that if you are seeking a buyer for any valuable jewels, 'tis but waste of time to display them to me. I am a plain man, with neither taste nor means for gewgaws."

" My business has nothing to do with the shop. sir."

" Then I am at your service."

He followed her through a side door into a low, dark room, facing the river, and so crowded with works of art, busts, pictures, clocks, inlaid coffers, *pietra-dura* cabinets, and tables in Florentine mosaic, that it was more a storehouse than a sitting-room. There was, however, just space enough for two chairs and a small table in a recessed window. Here Mademoiselle seated herself, and invited George to take the other chair.

" I will not waste time on compliments, monsieur," she said, " but proceed at once to business. You have powerful friends in Paris."

"The plural is an error on Mademoiselle's part. I have one friend in this city—the lady whom I have the honour to serve as house steward."

"Oh, sir, you underrate your advantages. Madame de Lussac is a great lady, but she is a foreigner, and has never possessed much influence at Court. You have better friends—one of whom has entrusted me with a delicate mission. I have to tell you that henceforward you will be independent of the Marquise, who is capricious——"

"Mademoiselle will kindly remember that the lady is my benefactress and friend."

"Who is capricious," Madamoiselle Lescot repeated obstinately—"all women are capricious—and who is not rich. You will henceforth enjoy an income—not large, but enough to make you independent of feminine patronage, and which will enable you to choose your own career: arms, the Church, state-craft, law—whatever inclination prompts."

He saw, as in a flash of lightning, the figure of Mazarin behind this inviting offer. He saw again the eyes that had looked at him so coldly, the scornful lip, and heard again the intolerable irony in the measured accents of that melodious voice, made to flatter and beguile, to lull suspicion, and pass falsehood for truth.

"And pray, mademoiselle, where is the Jupiter who would let fall this shower of gold? and what have I done to merit this unsought beneficence?"

"That is your friend's business, monsieur. He may at some future time reveal himself. For the present he does me the honour to make me his agent. An income of five hundred louis d'or, the new coinage at twenty-two carats, will be paid to you quarterly by my father or me at this shop, or will be sent to you on your receipt, if you are at a distance. This income will be continued to you as long as you live, and do nothing—which I know in advance Monsieur will not do—to disgrace your name. Here is a receipt for a hundred and twenty-five louis—the first quarter. Will Monsieur be good enough to sign it, after he has counted the money?"

She offered him the receipt and a leather bag stuffed with gold.

"No, mademoiselle, I can have nothing to do with that paper—or that money!"

"You will not sign? You refuse the offer of independence?"

"No man could attain independence under such conditions. I accept no benefits from the unknown. You will be good enough to tell the gentleman whose agent you are in this matter, that I respectfully refuse his favours."

"But if he counted it no favour? If he were but fulfilling a duty—a sacred obligation?" Mademoiselle demanded eagerly.

"No unknown friend can have any obligation to help me. I have asked for nothing, and I can accept nothing."

"*Grace de Dieu*, Monsieur! you are more headstrong and foolish than I thought any man could be. To refuse a substantial income, assured to you for the rest of your life—and to depend on a lady whose extravagance is notorious, and whose humours are as fitful as the wind——"

"I know the lady, mademoiselle, better than you can possibly know her; and I cannot suffer to be instructed in her character by you or any one else. I wish you good day."

"*A la bonne heure!* You are a monstrous pig-headed youth; and I wonder his Em——I wonder anybody troubles his head about you!"

George was half out of the room before that slip of Mademoiselle Lescot's, but she was not the less angry with herself for having made it. She, the hard-headed bargainer with Jews and Alsatians, Germans and Dutchmen, who prided herself on her tact, and thought herself a little Richelieu in petticoats, had promised to carry this business through in the discreetest manner, and she had been baffled by a quality which she had never believed to exist in human nature—a complete indifference to money.

" Well, if the tie between those two be what I think it is, there never were a father and son less alike in disposition—however they may favour each other in feature," she said, as she put away the unsigned agreement and the unopened bag.

" Twenty-two carat," she sighed. " There are not many countries that have such gold in circulation. And yonder fool refused it as if it were dirt ! "

CHAPTER XVI.

AFTER the contents of the tortoiseshell casket had been judiciously distributed, there came a halcyon calm in the offices and ante-chambers of the Hôtel de Lussac. No more clamorous creditors battered the solid oak doors, passionately demanding audience with the Marquise, or at least with her steward ; no more pinched widows or anxious wives waited and wept in the ante-chamber where a Mater Dolorosa by Raphael, for which a princely price had been given, looked down sorrowingly on their less sacred sorrows. For the time everybody was satisfied, and even George felt his burdens lightened. And so the year waned, and a new year began, and the Marquis came home from the wars, not quite so dashing a figure as Bayard or Dunois, and indeed a somewhat rickety old soldier, whom a month at the Baths of Bourbon had failed to set up, and who, on the rare occasions when he honoured his wife with his company, drank copiously at dinner, and spent the afternoon in a great armchair drawn close under the projecting chimney-piece in the Ariadne room.

Here he sat and shivered, and flung logs upon the fire with the silver tongs, and grumbled at everything, praising only the days that were gone, the long-ago days at the beginning of the century, when Henriette d'Entragues was reigning over the great king's heart, and the wines of the Côte d'Or were worth drinking. The soil of France had soured since then. Indeed, since then everything had changed for the worse, and France, which had been glorious under Henry and Sully, was now a football to be kicked to and fro between an Italian schemer and a General scarce out of his teens, who had more luck than wisdom—to be governed by D'Enghien or by Mazarin, whichever should prove the stronger.

"One man has an insatiable avarice, the other an insatiable ambition," said De Lussac. "I know not which were the worse for France. One will creep over the land with stealthy, silent exactions, eating us up like the locusts in Holy Writ—the other will squander blood and gold to make his name famous, and will go blundering on to victory by a waste of life that will depopulate his country. The victories we win to-day are wasting the stored-up forces of our glorious past. It is the army Richelieu created that wins, not the genius of Henri de Bourbon. The infantry—our invincible infantry—'twas they won the day at Rocroy —not the boy Prince you all hailed with such insensate clamour."

"But sure, sir, you must needs deem his Highness a born soldier?"

"He is a born Bourbon, and I grant you there is a streak of fire in that blood which he may have inherited, though his father lacks it. And for the rest, he has luck, sir—luck, which is better than science, and which has nothing to do with a man's deserts."

The Marquis was civil to George, indeed, even friendly, seeming glad to have an intelligent listener to his complaints. But he spent the greater part of his life away from the Hôtel de Lussac. His wife's carriage sometimes passed another carriage in the Cours la Reine, a fine gilt coach in which the Marquis, wrapped to the tip of his nose in Muscovy sables, sat by the side of a mahogany-complexioned person who enjoyed a certain vogue as the ugliest woman in Paris. Her fierce black eyes glared at the handsome Marquise, as their coaches met and passed; but Madame de Lussac's only notice was a far-away gaze, as of one who saw not anything so near the earth as Madame Déprèz's gaudy splendour, or a smile which glanced in amused astonishment at so much ugliness. To George, sitting opposite the Marquise, there seemed something tragic in these brief encounters, albeit she took the outrage so easily. A husband and wife, living in ostensible union, yet utterly apart, hating each other perhaps, and the wife accepting public infidelity with indifference! Could anything in life be more painful? He recalled that happy English home he knew so well, the husband's devoted love, the wife's affectionate solicitude.

George observed with surprise that the Marquis had always some reason for absenting himself from his wife's receptions, and that he was nevertheless curious about her company, as he would seize any opportunity to ask questions when he and George were alone.

"Indeed, sir, I think last night's assembly was one of the most brilliant I have ever seen here. The House of Condé was in full force—Madame de Longueville, the Prince de Conti, the Duke and Duchess, the lady superb in purple and silver."

"Superb? Yes, I remember her when Charlotte de Montmorency was the loveliest woman in France, and when the greatest king France ever had put on a postilion's jacket and waited for hours in the wind and rain to get speech of her."

"Ah, sir, those were the days of romance. The world has grown older and duller," said George. "But I wonder Monsieur le Marquis should deny himself the pleasure of seeing Madame's friends?"

"I have two excellent reasons for being absent," answered De Lussac. "My wife receives a man I abhor—and refuses to receive a woman I love. When she shows herself as indulgent to my friendships as I have ever been to hers, she will see me at her assemblies."

The New Year began earlier by the calendar than in England. The year that was gone had been an eventful and adventurous year for both countries—a year that had seen the French King's death and the

elevation of his consort from insignificance to power ;
a year which had witnessed Mazarin's stealthy progress
from subservience to paramount authority ; a year of
conquest and aggrandisement ; while across the Channel
the Royal arms had suffered strange varieties of fortune.

All through spring and summer the King's men had
been in the ascendant, and that handful of peers sitting
at Westminster, that mere rag and remnant of a House
of Lords, must have felt that it were better to have
been charging with Rupert's horse on the Quantocks,
or bivouacking on the Cornish hills with Hopton and
Sir Bevil Grenvil and their gallant army of the West,
than to be sitting there, the minions and slaves of an
insolent Commons, with no flavour of romance or
chivalry to sweeten ill-fortune. Better to have perished
in the field like Falkland at Newbury, rushing madly
on his death, sick of a world where the time was out
of joint, and where he had no power to bring about
the Peace his philosophic mind so ardently desired.

Falkland was gone ; and Sir Bevil, the gallant
Cornishman, and Carnarvon, and many another dauntless spirit, had gone out into the unknown darkness,
content so to die for Church and King. And in the
bleak mid-winter that uncrowned leader at Westminster,
" King Pym," Strafford's inexorable foe, had surrendered
to the common enemy.

It was the second week in March, and the first soft
breathings of spring stirred among the evergreens in
the Tuileries Gardens when George received mournful
tidings in a long letter from Lady Llanbister written
at Isleworth, and sealed with black.

" A fortnight has passed, dear friend, since the tragedy
this letter has to relate ; but indeed I have not till
these last two days found courage to take my pen ;
and Geraldine, who has shown a brave spirit in the
hour of calamity, has written all indispensable letters
for me. To you I waited to write with my own hand,
for I can unburthen my heart to you as to none other ;

and there is a mournful consolation in writing of the husband I loved to one who loved him as well as you did.

" He is gone from us, George. We shall no more see that kind face or hear that beloved voice, in all the space of our mortal lives. God grant that we may meet him in the wider life that lies beyond this earth. I think my heart would break if I did not look forward to that meeting, if I did not hold fast to my faith in that better world where there shall be no more tears, no more death. He has been taken from us; and, in spite of all my endeavours to keep him in a safe haven, where the troubles of this distracted country should not touch him, his so precious life has been shortened by the cruelty of our time, which has made religion a rod to scourge us instead of a consolation and a defence in the day of trouble.

" You may have heard how that company of Puritan bigots, the Assembly of Divines at Westminster, has swollen in power since its establishment in the beginning of last year, and how it has proceeded from one act of tyranny to another, the last and worst being an insistence upon the signing of the Solemn League and Covenant by all English citizens of whatsoever creed, taking the acceptance of these Articles as a test of fidelity to their rebel Parliament.

" Although I was told what rigorous means were being pursued to obtain signatures, even in the remotest country parishes, and how the Commissioners were going about to force the hateful Covenant upon men of greater mark, I still hoped that the secluded life my dear lord had been leading, and his avoidance of all overt interference in the struggle between King and Parliament, would have saved him from these persecuting wretches, and secured peace for his declining years. But no, George—these men who murdered Strafford, and who have kept the old Archbishop Laud in a cruel captivity for these two years last past, and who have made their miserable Presbytery an engine of persecution, would not forego the delicate pleasure of torturing a weak old man, hoping to wring from his feebleness the renunciation of all that he held most sacred.

"The poor old Earl of Bridgewater, an invalid, and living in retirement since the beginning of the war, had been visited by Lords Rutland and Bolingbroke, and, after a feeble resistance and entreaty for delay, had been scared into signing away his honour. It was these same lords who appeared at this house—now, alas! hung with black—on the twelfth of last month, three days after Bridgewater's surrender, and demanded my lord's signature.

"On Llanbister's refusal to sign, they told him how Bridgewater had complied, after so brief a time for consideration as the Parliament would grant, which was but two days. 'Indeed, it is best and wisest to comply without hesitation, my dear lord,' Rutland urged. 'It is a bond of union which secures for us a certain peace and brotherhood at home, together with the love and good-will of our Scottish neighbours. In this tranquil retreat you know not how England is rent and harried by fanatical sectaries at home, and how undermined by insidious seminary priests from beyond the sea. Of the Independents or the Jesuits I am uncertain which are the more dangerous; but I know that if we do not join hands against them we shall have London in flames before the end of the year.'

"I recall his every word, and the smooth, insidious tones, and the persuasive smile; for I watched and listened with painful anxiety, knowing how severe a trial this marked in my dear husband's life. I was sure he would refuse to sign the Covenant; and I knew not how far the power of that tyrannical assembly might go, and whether those last years which I would fain have made so happy might be spent within prison walls.

"He heard Lord Rutland with a thoughtful countenance, and showed no trace of agitation in his reply. He had been ailing since the summer, and I had noted a sad decay of strength, which his physicians indeed admitted, though they comforted me by the hope that he might be spared for some years.

"'I am like Bridgewater,' he said; 'I must have time to consider these Articles before my pen pledges me to adopt them.'

"The Commissioners urged him to sign at once, but on his being firm in his refusal they consented to leave him till the next day, when they would return at noon for his signature. Bolingbroke added that he made this concession on his own responsibility, and that he would have to deliver the paper to the Parliament, duly signed, on the next afternoon. After this they withdrew to take some refreshment before remounting their horses, and took leave of my dear lord with cordial expressions of friendship. Little did I know that they had entered his house as his executioners, and that the paper lying under his hand was no less fatal than the axe.

"He was thoughtful and very silent for the rest of the afternoon, and his countenance was of so deep a melancholy that I had not the heart to question him as to his resolve. He retired to his chamber directly after supper, at which he ate scarcely anything, and he allowed me to sit beside his bed and read to him from one of those plays of Shakespeare which he ever loved. He bade me read from the third part of Henry the Sixth, though I chid him for choosing so tragical a theme.

"'Those troubles of poor weak Henry Plantagenet's jump with our time,' he said—and so I obeyed, and spent two hours by his side, in that melancholy reading; and looking back on those last peaceful hours it seems to me that the tall wax candles burning beside his bed were like funeral torches, and that the dark green velvet curtains were deepened by the shadows into the blackness of a pall.

"He lay late next morning, having passed a sleepless night, as his gentleman told me. It wanted less than an hour of noon when he left his dressing-room, attended by his gentleman, and passed through the white parlour where I was sitting with an anxious heart, on his way to his study.

"I went to meet him as he entered the room, but

he had a grave and preoccupied air that forbade conversation. We clasped hands in silence, and I lifted his dear hand to my lips, on which he looked at me with a mournful tenderness, and murmured a blessing in so low a voice that I could scarce distinguish his words. I would have gone with him to his study, but he stopped me, saying that he desired to be alone for an hour. I urged him to comply with the Commissioners, since what was expedient for Lord Bridgewater must be best for him, being in the power of those Westminster fanatics, so that a signature given under such compulsion could count for nothing in the eye of Heaven or of men. He made me no answer, but paused and kissed me as we parted on the threshold of that room he preferred to all others, with its smiling outlook to the Thames.

"It was later by an hour when Lord Rutland arrived, attended by his secretary, but without his brother peer, and delayed somewhat by his horse having cast a shoe at Turnham Green. I went with him to my lord's room, anxious to be at hand, should my dear husband need counsel or sympathy in this great emergency.

"Ah, George, there are moments in life that must remain fixed in the mind, like a picture graven upon copper, every stroke standing out with a pitiless distinctness. Such was that moment when I stood within the study door—Rutland and his man waiting behind me—stood looking across the February sunshine to the great armchair—the high-backed tapestry chair you must remember so well—and saw Llanbister sitting there, with his head leaning against the cushion, and one arm hanging loosely across the arm of the chair, and with so ghastly a pallor in his countenance that my heart seemed to stop beating, in that sudden agony of fear.

"He was dead, George! He had expired sitting there alone, unwatched, untended in that last moment; but I thank God his physician and our apothecary of Isleworth—who saw him daily—both assure me that death must have been painless. The heart, which had long been weak, must have failed suddenly, and he had expired in a sigh.

"The copy of the Solemn League and Covenant was lying on the floor, under his foot. I can but think that, sitting there, after a night of severe meditation, he had determined not to sign, and that, as he set his foot upon the hateful paper, resolved to suffer the worst that tyranny could inflict upon him, his heart beat high with that proud defiance, and, so beating, snapped the frail thread of life.

"To me that death appeared no less heroic than Falkland's wild charge at Newbury.

"Do not be unhappy about me, dear George. My sorrow is a deep sorrow, and must be with me till the end of life. But there are consolations and gentle pleasures that can go along with such a sorrow. Your fair young mistress has proved herself of a higher character in this day of our mutual grief than I thought her when we were happy; and I see now that I sorely belittled her merits, and that she is indeed a jewel which any man, were he the greatest in this land, might be proud to wear in his cap. You know who it is that I would choose for her, was I ever free to choose; and, knowing that, I doubt not you will set all your thoughts upon making yourself worthy to win so sweet a prize. If, after all, you miss that dear reward, you will be the better for the endeavour, and your life the nobler and happier for having aimed high.

"At present you have no rival. In these distracted times men's thoughts are not of marrying or giving in marriage; and many a handsome head has gone down in the blood and dust of an English battlefield. Ah, George, to think of it! This once so peaceful country one vast battlefield : cities besieged—noblemen's houses stormed and destroyed—a rolling tide of war over all the land, wider and more devastating than the wars of the Roses—for they had no Rupert then, to pillage and slaughter—no Puritan devils to defile cathedrals and riot in wanton mischief. You who are happily at a distance from those hideous scenes can scarce conceive how much of blood and treasure this miserable war has cost us, or although on both sides there is ever a pretended desire for peace, how the possibility of reconciliation seems to be further off every day we live. You can scarce conceive the changed aspect of London and its surrounding villages ; for though you saw the streets last winter prepared against attack, the city had nothing then of its present dolorous emptiness—a city abandoned by the best of its inhabitants ; shops closed, markets empty, a silence in the streets as in those mournful days of the pestilence that followed so close upon our heroic Queen's marriage.

"I look back at my girlhood and remember those long years of peace under King James, when the most we heard of war was a great talk of fighting for the Palatinate, and when the prophecy of hostile armies in our English lanes and woods would have seemed a bugbear to frighten children. God knows when or how peace and comfort and happy days will return to this distracted land. I would to Heaven our King were wiser in his negotiations with his foes, and they less exacting in their demands. All the good and orderly people in town and country are longing for peace, and the King declares that to be reconciled with his Parliament is the chief desire of his heart—yet, while he plays fast and loose with his people, looks now to raising an army in Ireland, and now to joining arms with Scotland, and is never steadfast in his adherence to any one party or any one course of action, what hope can there be of peaceable adjustment of these miserable dissensions? And while his Majesty hesitates and conspires, the best blood of the land is being spilt like water, and the country grows poorer every day. Heaven knows I would not make light of his difficulties, or misconstrue that obstinate resistance which has its root in kingly honour, yet, when I remember how he yielded Strafford's life to a clamorous mob while he might yet have kept the upper hand, I can but wonder at his stubborn claim for Prerogative now, when every shred of power has been torn from him.

" I travelled to Oxford in January to see my Royal mistress. Alas! how changed from that brilliant Queen I saw but a few years ago at Whitehall—that animated, sparkling creature, whose smile was like a light. The smile is brilliant still, but, oh! so rare—and the so admired beauty is now but a memory. She has a courage that defies fate—and a kind and tender heart. You will have heard how she ran back to her lodgings in the midst of the enemy's cannonade, to rescue her dog which had been left in her chamber. The key to her character is in that action—brave, generous, impulsive, counting no cost when her loving or liking is at stake. She has provoked the slander of the malevolent by her lavish praise of Jermyn—a man I have ever disliked, but who was her valuable ally in those months of perilous adventure between her landing in Yorkshire and her re-union with his Majesty at Oxford.

" For myself, dear George, I have made no plans yet. The bulk of my dear lord's estate, with the Castle in Wales, descends to Geraldine, as his only son's heiress. To me he has left a large sum of money, and the two houses in which the most of our married life was spent, this dear place and the mansion in Aldersgate Street. Our lawyer has entered upon the troublesome business of compounding for all this property, in Geraldine's interest and in mine, and a considerable portion of all we possess will go to the Parliament, and pay for shot and shell to be used against our King. It is hard, and we feel humiliated at thus having to kiss the rod; but resistance would but occasion a larger loss—and all we can spare from the expenditure of our retired and unluxurious life here will be conveyed to my Royal mistress. We are indeed now living in a kind of holy poverty, which would be a fit preparation for the cloister. For the rest, there is peace in this retired village, and here Geraldine and I intend to make our abode, though we know not how long it may be before the sounds of war may break upon our quiet, and force us to seek some other refuge.

" And now, dear George, let me hear from you soon;

and I pray you to tell me more of your own life than
your late letters have told.   There was a time when
you gave me the history of all you saw and heard in
Paris, and of all your occupations and amusements.
But since you have been Madame de Lussac's secretary,
your letters have been brief and disappointing.   Is it
that your days are too full of gaiety and pleasure in
that brilliant circle for you to find time for letter-writing ;
or is it that you are out of spirits and lack the energy
to depict the scenes in which you move, with that
spirited pen which produced pictures almost as vivid as
a painter's brush ? "

This sad news from Isleworth was a severe blow,
and George thought with deep sorrow of the kind old
man whose friendship had been so generously given
to him, and by whose fireside he had lived as in the
house of a kinsman.   He must needs contrast that
dignified bearing, the grey head and beard, the sober
life, the large benevolence and unselfish regard for others,
with the manners and appearance of Monsieur de
Lussac, who had his beard dyed and his face painted
by a barber whose grandfather had been chief valet
to Henry III., and who had inherited the secrets of
the Valois beauty. Plastered with paint and gaudy with
jewels and orders, the Marquis de Lussac, eaten up by
gout, hobbled off every afternoon to the not-distant
mansion where the ugliest lady in Paris expected his
attendance.   His wife knew if he spent an evening at
home it was only because his Medusa was in the sulks,
and had banished him from the light of her mahogany
countenance.

CHAPTER XVII.

THE year wore on to May, a mild and early season, and the orchards beside the Cours la Reine were full of perfume and white blossom, the ground between the brown trunks blue with violets or yellow with primroses and celandine ; and the coaches were driving three abreast.

George drove every evening with the Marquise. It was one of his duties, and one he never sought to avoid, knowing her lonely position in the midst of so-called friends, divining perhaps the deep melancholy of a woman who has touched the age when lovers are impossible, and the voice of praise rings hollow, and who is forsaken by the one man upon whose devotion she has a sacred claim. An unloved wife, childless, sitting alone in her carriage to see the garish crowd go by ! He could conceive no sadder state, and his heart ached for her sometimes as he sat by her side, and suffered the monotony of this life which she had been leading for years, and which had palled upon him after the experience of a few weeks.

His heart ached most of all perhaps because, though he compassionated, he did not love her. He thought of her as childless ; since, whatever the link between them, he knew that he could never be to her all that a son should be. Obedience, duty, he might give, and meant to give her ; but love cannot be commanded. He had lived in her house for half a year ; he had accepted her kindness, been cherished and praised by

her as sons are by doating mothers; and yet felt no
warmer affection for her than in the dawn of their
acquaintance, when he had admired her beauty, and
had divined the passionate nature that had written its
record of storm and suffering upon that splendid face.

They were driving together on a balmy evening early
in May when the low sun shone golden on the grey old
city and its girdle of towers, the Temple, the glistening
steeple of the Sainte Chapelle, a shaft so delicate and
aerial that it suggested a pinnacle in some mirage city
rather than a thing of stone and iron. The Royal
promenade wore its most brilliant aspect, and almost
every other carriage they met showed the colours of a
duke, or a prince of the blood Royal.

Yonder young lady, with the vivacious smile and
quick movements, was the Grande Mademoiselle, the
richest woman in France, just now resident at her father's
palace of the Luxembourg, but as likely as not to be
banished in a week or two to one of her numerous
country seats—a spirited and adventurous young
princess, for whom no husband had yet been found,
since nothing less than a reigning sovereign would
have satisfied her ambition. Had not Anne of Austria
sportively suggested that she should marry her child-
cousin, the King, making light of their disparity in
years? Some people said Louise de Bourbon had set
her heart on being Queen of France, and meant to wait
for the young Louis.

Other equipages there were, almost as brilliant as
this, with its emblazoned *fleur-de-lis* on panels and
housings. Madame de Longueville, the young Princesse
de Conti, Madame de Bouillon, the Princesse Palatine—
one after another the gilded coaches, with velvet and
brocade coverings and coats-of-arms in bullion and
jewels, went by, while gracious salutations and friendly
words were exchanged from coach to coach. Madame
de Lussac's peach velvet and silver carriage was scarcely
inferior to the best, and her new liveries shone in all
the glory of *passementerie* that was fresh from the
makers' hands. She was looking her handsomest, too,

in a black velvet gown, and a wide-brimmed white felt hat with a bunch of flame-coloured feathers, and a solitaire diamond of surpassing size and brilliancy shining in the triangular opening of her Genoa lace collar.

"I love to astonish my envious friends with a new jewel, even if I only borrow it for the occasion," she said, when George looked curiously at this pendant, which he had not remarked before. "This was last worn upon a Royal neck."

"You mean it is one of the Crown jewels the Cardinal bought in Holland?"

"Yes, it is one of Mazarin's bargains. He thrives upon Royal vicissitudes."

"I wonder that you can stoop to borrow his gewgaws."

"Stoop? Oh, there is no favour in it. For him the diamonds are but a mode of hoarding money. They would lie hidden in a strong box if I did not give them an airing. Jewellers tell me that pearls sicken with such treatment; so I shall be obliging enough to wear poor Henriette's necklaces now and then. She had ropes of pearls, which her complexion was vastly too brown to set off. Orient pearls only look their best on a neck that has a purer white than their own."

"I wonder"—George began again, and stopped, thinking he did ill to cavil at a display of vanity which was but natural in a fine lady.

The coach was nearing the gate—most of the coaches going back to Paris at this hour—and the western sun was shining in their eyes, and painting golden light upon the roof of the Tuileries and the long gallery of the Louvre, when in the midst of the crowd at the gate a tall, slovenly-clad man, with his hat slouched over his face, leapt forward and flung a paper into Madame de Lussac's lap.

"A ballad for the Cardinal's——"

The final word cannot be recorded. It turned George's blood to ice—yet flushed his cheeks with the hectic of fever. He sprang out of the coach—not waiting to open the door, but dropping over it—intent upon seizing the wretch who had committed that outrage. But the crowd was thick here, and the man had disappeared. The coaches had all stopped in the throng at the gate. He heard subdued tittering as he went back to Madame de Lussac's carriage. She was sitting more upright than usual, looking defiance at the gaping crowd on the footpath, but her cheeks were ghastly under the metallic bloom of her rouge. Never of late had he so distinctly noted the paint upon her cheeks and lips.

A footman was holding the carriage door open. George got in and resumed his seat beside the Marquise.

"The madman who insulted you was not to be found for the moment, Marchesa," he said ; "but I shall know how to discover him later."

She held the paper crushed in her right hand. He tried to take it from her.

"No, no, no!" she muttered. "You must not—for the love of God!"

"Nay, but I must, dear Marchesa," he urged in an undertone, with a tenderness she rarely heard in his voice. "It is for me to punish those who outrage you —and I must know——"

She had been making a great effort to keep herself from fainting, and her power of resistance was at its lowest, or she would have done more to withhold that paper from him, apprehending the malignity of a libel so launched at her.

He thrust the paper in his breast, and turned to her with a smile.

"It is the common fate of great people to be libelled," he said gently, laying his hand on hers, his face white with suppressed passion.

They drove home as fast as the postilions could steer their way through the press of carriages all hastening homeward. It was to be a gala night at Renard's Garden, though the year was yet early for an *al fresco* entertainment. The Queen had promised to appear, and had lent her trumpeters to swell the orchestra, and Mademoiselle's violins were to perform in another part of the gardens. All that there was of beauty and of rank in Paris would be gathered in the lantern-lit groves and alleys.

George wondered whether the Marquise would be in spirits to appear in a crowded assembly after the atrocious insult she had suffered, within the hearing of the Court ; for he had seen, as in one flash of searching light, the faces of the Princess Palatine and of the Grand Mademoiselle, peering out of their coaches in the block at the gate, and he knew not how many more might have heard that foul name, flung like vitriol in the face of the Marquise. Would she have the courage to meet false friends and open enemies within an hour of that affront ? Would it be her best policy to show herself and defy slander ?

He had not long to wonder about her intention, for while alighting from her carriage she told her people to be ready to drive to the Garden at nine o'clock.

" What are you going to do with that paper, George ?" she asked, when they were in the vestibule.

" Read and destroy it."

" But it concerns me rather than you. It is for me to read the slander, and judge how I may best punish the slanderer."

" If it resembles those Mazarinades that are printed daily in defiance of the Cardinal's police, it is not fit for a woman's eye. Dear Marchesa, your honour is more precious to me than my own. You may believe I will not suffer your wrongs to go unavenged."

" To avenge such a wrong means to make a greater scandal—to widen a pool to an ocean. I abhor clamour about my name. I hold myself high enough to defy slanderers."

" To defy slanderers, but not to submit to slander. Trust yourself to me, Marchesa. Be sure I will do a son's duty."

They were alone on the staircase when he spoke these last words. She turned from him with a smothered sob, and went slowly upstairs.

George read the ballad in the seclusion of his study. It was about as vile a specimen of the libellous literature of Paris as he had ever seen. It was a rhyming biography, not without a certain caustic wit, but reeking with unutterable foulness, and picturing Madame de Lussac as a modern Margaret of Burgundy, who was only less criminal than her Royal prototype because she lacked power and opportunity for murdering her lovers when she was tired of them. Mazarin's name was interwoven throughout this slanderous farrago ; and he and Madame de Lussac were stigmatised as a pair of penniless adventurers who had descended from the seven-hilled city to devour and pillage Paris. And lastly he saw his own name—*ce jeune fanfaron Anglais, ce meurt-de-faim Georges*—as the latest and most contemptible of the lady's caprices. From princes and dukes she had descended to a nameless *petit maître*.

He had seen too many such libels to give a moment's credence to the accusations in this one. He knew the horrible slanders of the Queen that had been scattered broadcast in Paris. He knew that no vice of the most debased Roman emperor was too loathsome to be ascribed to the Cardinal. Yet it wounded him to think that the woman he was bound to honour could be subject to such an outrage. Had she lived like Lady Llanbister, at the Court, but not of it, ever preferring the serene atmosphere of home to the glare and noise of crowds, such slanders could scarce have been coupled with her name. But it was not for that restless, impetuous spirit so to have lived, nor had she enjoyed Lady Llanbister's domestic blessings.

He locked the hateful paper in the coffer where he kept all important documents, hoping, by a careful comparison of type and paper with other such libels—at the head office of the Cardinal's police—to discover, first the printer, and then the writer of the slander.

He attended the Marquise at the garden concert, and saw her shining among the most brilliant of the Court beauties, and distinguished by the friendly notice of the Queen ; but while watching her from the outer edge of the circle, he was hurt by hearing more than one cynical allusion to the *fracas* at the gate. He felt a rage of impatience until he should lay his hand upon the perpetrator of that outrage ; and he was in the streets of Paris soon after daybreak next morning, on his way to the headquarters of Mazarin's police, that secret band whose members pervaded Paris, whose ears were ever open and eyes ever on the watch for the Cardinal's foes.

Here the name of Madame de Lussac acted like a charm, and the head official was ready to assist George to the uttermost of his power. The scene of last evening was known, having been witnessed by one of the officers, who had not, however, been able to identify the ruffian who flung the paper. Here, after a close inspection of the file of Mazarinades, the official selected one particular printing-press known to him as the source of the foulest libels, and undertook to obtain the printer's confession.

"These wretches live in hourly fear of the wheel," he said. "Yet because this despicable work is paid double, there are always scoundrels enough to do it. The utmost rigour has not even reduced the number of his Eminence's slanderers. But in the event of this printer denying his work—the means of identification being but weak—it would be well if Monsieur could discover whether the Marquise happens lately to have made an enemy, and his name and person."

George acted on this suggestion, and in his morning *tête-à-tête* with Madame de Lussac—both being too preoccupied to pursue the adventures of Polexandre, in a fashionable romance of eight volumes—he asked her if she had any suspicion as to the author of the libel.

"I can hardly know whom to suspect, unless I read the thing," she said.

"That you shall never do if I can help it," George answered resolutely ; and then he urged her to think of any likely person to inspire or to perpetrate such an injury as she had suffered.

"Behind every libel there is a foe," he said. "Your foes cannot be many."

"Can they not? They are as many as the friends of Madame Désprèz. She hates me—not because she fears my rivalry in the affections of her antique adorer, but because I refuse to live on familiar terms with her, or to recognise her in public. She would like for us all to live in this house—which is much handsomer than her own—as a happy family. No doubt it would be more convenient and more economical than our separate establishments, as De Lussac has often insinuated; but she shall not cross this threshold while I live. Her friends are my enemies, for they know the surest way to please her is to injure me."

"And she patronises the wits and pamphleteers, the duellists, the guzzlers and topers—the men who hold their nightly orgies at the Pine Apple!" cried George eagerly. "I'll warrant the libel was inspired by her."

"'Tis monstrous likely," assented the Marquise, yawning, as she sipped her chocolate out of a gold cup, "but by all the gods I wish you would burn the loathsome rag, and forget it. The outrage was abominable; but the wretch may have been drunk, or mad. And you saw last night that his malice has done me no harm. The Queen was never more friendly."

"And the printed slander, circulated all over Paris perhaps?"

"Mazarin's police shall hunt it down, and suppress it. And you may be sure it is no more than has been printed about every woman of mark in Paris."

"There are women who could scarce endure such an insult and live."

"Then they are women who have never lived in Paris. *Mon ange*, how solemn you look! Do you want me to poison myself because a blackguard has been uncivil?"

"God forbid that you should distress yourself! Yet there are occasions when we do well to be angry; and this is one. But you have given me a clue. I ought to find this scoundrel."

"George," she cried, lifting herself up among her pillows, and seizing him by the arm, "George, you must not fight him. I will not have your life imperilled for my—good name. No, no, no! You hear! You must not provoke a duel."

"I must do my duty," he answered sternly; and before she could reply the double doors were flung open, and the groom of the chambers announced " Madame la Duchesse de Longueville."

The fair-haired daughter of Bourbon princes, cousin of the King, came sailing in, tall, graceful, in the zenith of her charms, and was followed almost immediately by the witty Prince de Marsillac, always to be seen in her train—and in a few minutes Madame de Lussac's room was full of the finest people in Paris, a larger crowd than usual, all curious to see how she took the incident of the previous evening, an incident which might possibly develop into as serious a business as that of the famous love-letter dropped from Coligny's pocket, and falsely attributed to Madame de Longueville.

George was too agitated to endure the babble of that gay crowd. He hurried out of the house, and walked the whole length of the Rue Saint-Antoine, and out of the gate to the bleak heights beyond Paris, where, from the rugged ground above the quarries of Chaumont, he looked down upon the crowded roofs and chimneys of the walled city, and thought with bitterness of the vice and folly within that stone girdle. The long walk and the fresh air quieted brain and nerves, and he was able to think more collectedly as he walked back to the Court quarter. It was past the dinner-hour at the Hôtel de Lussac—and even if he had been earlier he would fain have avoided meeting the Marquise ; so he dined at the ordinary, in his old lodging-house of the Golden Crown, knowing that, of all resorts in Paris, this was one of the likeliest at which to obtain information about bullies and reprobates.

He seated himself next a man with whom he had been on friendly terms when he lived in the house—an out-at-elbows poetaster and political scribbler, who wrote occasionally in the *Gazette*, and was said to be in the pay of the Parliament, and who ranked as fairly respectable among men of letters—literature being, at this time, represented by two distinct sets of men, the famous poets and *savants* who basked in the sunshine of Royal patronage, cherished and petted by the finest company in Paris, and the hack writers who lived as they could, and passed the greater part of their days and nights in taverns, with only occasional admittance to the outer edge of the Court circle.

George's acquaintance, Jellifort, belonged to this latter set, a person likely to be received by Madame Désprèz.

" If I know her !" he cried, on being questioned. " I have no better friend for a dinner or a supper. It rains not gold in the Hôtel Désprèz. It is no El Dorado ; but Madame has a genius for her cook, a fellow she stole from Madame de Lussac, before she stole the Marquis. Perhaps it was the cook De Lussac followed, rather than the lady, who is ugly enough to scare birds, but who has a fine figure, the handsomest hand and foot in Paris, and the tongue of a Seine boatman."

" And she is kind to men of letters, like yourself ? "

" To many a worse man than myself, more's the pity. Half the thorns that stuff Mazarin's pillow are grown *chez la Désprèz*."

" I have been told as much. There is one rascal, a tall, bony wretch with a scarlet beak, like an unclean bird."

Jellifort flung himself against the wall—the bench on which they sat having no back—and laughed long and loud.

" Dolroy !" he cried, " Dolroy to the letter. It costs Madame Désprèz a fortune in burgundy and cognac to colour that vulture beak. But then, she has the most virulent pen in Paris—the greatest master of *ordure*—at her service. Villon was decent, Rabelais restrained, compared with Dolroy in the vein. No one dares make light of a woman who keeps such a champion. The boldest satirist in Paris will hardly venture so much as an epigram upon her wide mouth and East Indian complexion."

" With such a talent Dolroy is doubtless rich ? "

" *Pas si bête !* Dolroy enjoys ; he does not save. He drinks his last crown. He counts upon his venom lasting as long as he, and that while he can bite he will be fed."

" A pretty gentleman ! "

" I own the character is detestable. Yet if there were no market for such filth, these literary vipers would bite their own tails for very hunger, and die of their own poison. Frankly I sometimes wonder that the wits and poets at the Pine Apple can stomach Dolroy's company ; but men who loathe him and his trade will yet laugh at his most obscene jests, if he strike hard enough at the Cardinal."

Eleven o'clock had chimed from the tower of St. Jacques, and the tide of revelry was at the flood when George made his entry in the crowded room where the patrons of the Pine Apple took their pleasure, and where the wits and poets of Paris met their patrons and admirers of the *noblesse* and the *bourgeoisie*. There only perhaps in all the city might be found a forecast of the Liberty, Equality, and Fraternity, which the coming centuries were to bring to all Paris. In this jovial rendezvous the gentleman of the *vieille roche* rubbed shoulders with the man of yesterday. Under this smoke-blackened ceiling the princely blood of Bourbon scorned not to touch glasses with the out-at-elbows poet or the hireling wit. The common room of the Pine Apple was a republic of disreputable letters, an academy of gutter philosophy, where the Socrates of the night was ever he of the deepest swallow and the dirtiest tongue.

George wore his oldest suit, and a slouched beaver hat, that had braved wind and weather, so as to approximate as much as possible to the *habitués* of the tavern. He had put on his trustiest rapier, having a shrewd suspicion that the night might end in blood ; and indeed, there was that in his eyes which might have sent a thrill along the nerves of some of those careless topers, had not the menace of that look been shadowed by the breadth of his beaver. His entrance passed unchallenged, and he

was able to take a searching survey of the company—
passing to and fro among the tables, as if in quest of a
friend—and so to convince himself that Dolroy was not
yet upon the scene, before he took his seat near the
hearth, where some burnt-out logs were smouldering on
the accumulated ashes of many fires.

The nights were chilly, and the guests of the Pine
Apple loved warmth ; but the room, being now over-
heated by the press of company and the reek of coarse
tallow candles, the wood-fire had not been replenished.
George called for a tankard of Beaune, and sat silently
sipping his wine, amidst a tempest of voices, for there
was a group at every table, and in every group at least
one loquacious member. He heard them without heeding—though the names of Queen, Cardinal, Beaufort,
Montbazon, Enghien, were bandied about upon every
note in the gamut of abuse—since the man he wanted
was not among the speakers. The chimney was like
that one in the Rue Saint-Honoré, which George had
climbed on the memorable 1st of September. There
was the same penthouse slope overshadowing the hearth ;
and in that shadow the stranger remained unnoticed by
the boisterous topers and talkers clustered round the
tables, their animated faces lighted fitfully by the flare
of the candle which burnt in a tall iron candlestick on
each table. He sat thus amidst the babble and
laughter, the calls for wine, and rough jests between
customers and attendants, each of whom was addressed
by some nickname, the inspiration of a drunkard's
happy moment, which, from a casual jest, had become
the man's only appellation. He sat unheeding, deep
in painful thought, resolved to sit there waiting for his
enemy till the weary landlord drove the last of his
customers out of the door, to blink at the morning sun.
It was nothing to him to sit there all night if necessary,
so long as the slow hours brought the encounter he
longed for.

Presently he heard Dolroy's name from a man at
a table near him. Some one had commented on his
absence.

"Oh, he will be here before 'tis much later," said another man.

"*La mère* Désprèz is giving a supper, a snug little assembly—not more than half a score of the most disreputable women in Paris, with their favourite cavaliers—the kind of company old De Lussac loves."

"Can De Lussac be poltroon enough to sup with Dolroy after the rumpus in the Queen's drive, t'other night, when that scroundrel flung his filthy song into Madame de Lussac's lap?"

"De Lussac *is* a poltroon."

"Come, that's hard measure for the man who fought at Rocroy."

"Oh, he can face the enemy's guns—or scale a wall under a hail of bullets, with a jewel in his hat, and a smile on his lip, to the tune of Enghien's fiddles, in the Spanish manner. But he can't face a low-bred Zantippe like Madame Désprèz. The devil only knows by what charm the ugly witch holds him; but she has got him, body and soul: and he is too much her slave to rebel even when her paid bully puts a public affront upon his wife."

"He may not know of the affront yet."

"Not know—when all Paris is talking about it! Ah, here comes the scoundrel—between two wines, I can see, by his walk, and in a savage temper."

And then the speaker bawled out the first quatrain of a *moyen âge* drinking-song, in a voice somewhat thickened by wine.

> " Beau nez, dont les rubis ont cousté mainte pipe
>   De vin blanc et clairet
> Et duquel la couleur richement participe
>   Du rouge et violet."

The man with the vulture nose came slouching across the room, halting here and there by one of the tables to speak to an acquaintance. His long, lean figure was clad in a suit that had once been fine, but the frayed and tarnished gold lace and the stained satin testified to hard wear and slovenly habits—the prodigal's one suit. He wore his hat with the true *spadassin* tilt, slant-wise over his right eye, while the left glared upon the company with an angry gleam in it—a large black eye, *à fleur de tête*.

"Your May midnights are colder than December," he grumbled, making straight for the hearth. "There is a wind blowing up the river that might come straight from Muscovy. *Coquin de Dieu!* Nothing but ashes in the chimney! Here, you scoundrel," calling to the host, who was serving a flagon hard by, "bring some logs and kindle a fire."

"We'll have no more fire to-night, Dol," protested a young man sitting in a little knot of well-dressed company at a table in front of the hearth. "The room is as hot as a furnace."

"*Sang de Dieu!* It shall be hotter than hell if I choose, pig," said Dolroy, kicking about the burnt-out logs, and scattering a cloud of grey ashes over the fine gentlemen's white boots and satin ribbons.

"'Pig' is scarce civil to an old friend, Dol," remonstrated the youth.

"Do you suppose I meant to be civil? You come to the wrong shop when you expect compliments from Jacques Dolroy. But if that's Beaujolais you're drinking I've a throat that can be civil to a draught of good wine."

Dolroy's brutal manners were familiar to the company, and nobody ever took offence at his speech; so he was seated presently, clinking glasses with the little knot of courtiers; while mine host, who knew his customer, and hated a row, brought a couple of pine-logs from a basket in the corner, and made a feint of relighting the fire, which served his turn, for Dolroy was warming himself with deep draughts of the hoarded sunshine on the Côte d'Or, and took no further heed of the fireless hearth.

He absorbed his wine for some time in a moody silence, in spite of his modish friend's endeavours to provoke those ribald sallies and profane jests which constitute the chief attraction of low company. To slip

away from the Louvre, where wit walked on stilts, to
the Pine Apple, where wit wallowed in the filth of
profligate Paris, gave zest to appetites that were sated
with refined pleasures.   From the Hôtel de Rambouillet
to the Pine Apple!   The contrast was refreshing ; and
Dolroy's frank brutality was a thing to be cherished
with choice wine and even gratified with gold.

"Thou hast the wine sad to-night, Dolroy, and art as
gloomy as the Cimetière des Innocents," said Vallançay,
the young man who had been called " pig," and who was
still young enough to feel a perverted admiration for the
corrupt scoundrel whose coarse satires could make
princes of the blood Royal smart and pay, and who had
an air of conferring a favour when he drank at a gentleman's expense.

Dolroy's only visible eye stared at him with freezing
severity.

" And if I am sad, dost think thou hast wit enough
under that hay-cock of frizzled hair to enliven me ; or
that this Piquette, which yonder cheat calls Beaujolais,
is the stuff to fire my brain? Bring me a flask of
brandy, rascal, to wash out my mouth after your
verjuice.   Monsieur de Vallançay pays the score."

" 'Twere ill if I had to look to the Sieur Dolroy for
payment," grumbled the host, as he put a bottle of
brandy and a pair of long-stemmed Dutch glasses on
the table.

Dolroy filled and drained his glass three times before
that evil light within him which he called his mind
kindled into speech.   And then, Great Heaven, what
speech it was that poured its foul torrent from that
raucous throat! what hatred of the rich, what scorn of
the poor, what vilification of all that is holy in heaven,
all that is sacred in the affections and joys and sorrows
of earth!   And the jests which larded that long diatribe
against a society that would have none of him—jests
that had all Rabelais' coarseness, and little of Rabelais'
wit, but tickled jaded ears as highly spiced viands tickle
jaded palates!

The fine gentlemen gave him the *réplique*, knowing

how to draw him when he was in the humour to be drawn.

George sat unobserved in his corner, behind the reprobate's back, listening to every word, and waiting for that one word—the first mention of Madame de Lussac's name, which should give him the cue for action. So far there had been no allusion to the scene on the Queen's drive, or to the scandalous ballad. The man's talk had been in the air, a series of tirades against the Court and the men and women who shone in that palace from which he had been violently ejected more than a score of years ago, when Louis the Just was young, after having sparkled there for a brief season as wit and poet, before the inborn foulness of his nature had revealed itself by speech and pen. He had never forgiven that expulsion from the paradise of princes ; and under his blatant scorn of noble birth and high places, stars and ribbons, there rankled the gnawing regret of the banished, the envious spirit which exaggerated lost privileges, and hated all who enjoyed them.

The sin that had exiled him had been an epigram about the Queen and Buckingham, which he had circulated widely, in the pride of authorship, and in the hope that those four stinging lines would prove a passport to Richelieu's favour ; but although the great Cardinal laughed at the epigram, and was even heard to call the author a clever dog, he did not *want* Jacques Dolroy ; whereby that long-headed gentleman won neither fee nor favour from his Eminence.

Weak as Anne of Austria was in those days, she was strong enough to get the man who had insulted her a public caning in the great quadrangle of the Louvre, with a promise of a cell in the Bastille should he ever venture to pass the drawbridge under the Royal gate. Had an insult to his *Eminence Rouge* been the offence the Bastille would have been a certainty, and the period of his imprisonment indefinite. It was well for him that he had insulted only the first lady in the land.

From that hour Jacques Dolroy had cherished an

implacable hatred against the Queen—and it needed but a certain amount of alcohol to set that smothered fire flaming. Vallançay and his companions winked at each other as he swallowed the third glass of brandy, and one of them gave the cue. They were all four sworn friends of Beaufort's, and had their grievance against her Majesty.

"'Tis pity thou canst not be among us at the Louvre, Dolroy. 'Twould amuse thee to see the Queen and Mazarin bill and coo—a pair of middle-aged turtle-doves—remembering what it cost thee to have turned a rhyme upon Buckingham and the scene in the garden."

"Buckingham!" cried Dolroy, his one visible eye brightening with the rapture of hate. "Buckingham is the history of the world before the flood. Buckingham is chapter the first in a long book. And the scene in the garden——"

"When she shrieked because he infringed Spanish etiquette, and kissed her hand with too much vehemence," interjected Vallançay.

"She has long since learnt that 'tis idle to make scenes. A succession of lovers have taught her wisdom," said Dolroy.

And starting on this note he ran up the whole gamut of malignant obscenity, piling up evil words, revolting similes, the flowers of Latin epigram steeped in the filth of the Parisian gutter—Martial mixed with Villon ; and this of a woman, a devout Catholic, Royal daughter of Imperial Spain, mother of the reigning King! And this tinsel *noblesse*, the friends and followers of the Importants, laughed louder and louder, gratified to hear that Royal lady reviled, pleased with an invention fouler than their own.

'Twas when the laughter was loudest that George started from his low bench, and sprang out of the shadows like a tiger leaping from the jungle. Here was his opportunity—to strike for that Royal lady, to punish her traducer, and so keep the Marchesa's name out of the business. Springing up behind Dolroy, he gripped the neck of his doublet with one hand, while he clapped the other over his mouth, and so held him pinioned and dumb for a moment, while the other men started up amazed, as at an apparition. There were plenty of sudden brawls in that room ; but the suddenness of this silent attack was out of order.

"Thou foul-mouthed devil ! he said, after a brief and breathless pause. "If there is not a Frenchman in all this assembly to punish the slanderer of his Queen, there is an Englishman that will stop that obscene mouth of thine for the honour man owes to woman. Down, beast, down among the dust and ashes, and swallow some of the dirt thy soul lovest. Would to God there were a pig-stye handy to receive thy wine-soaked carcass !"

His hat had fallen off as he sprang up amongst them, and he stood there in the flare of the tallow candles, his breast heaving, his face radiant with a splendid fury, handsome as a Greek god. The little *noblesse* remembered him. Madame de Lussac's *protégé*—an adventurer, a young profligate, no doubt ; but, *pardieu*, he knew how to tackle a man.

Dolroy struggled in his clutch, roaring behind the hand that stifled him, with a deep, muffled roar like a wild beast. The vulture beak assumed a fiercer dye, and glowed like fire ; the great black eye seemed starting out of the purple face. He had been leaning forward with his elbows on the table and his stool tilted upon two legs. George took stool and man and hurled them crashing on to the hearth, where Dolroy lay on his back, smothered in the soft depths of heaped-up ashes, choking, spluttering, blaspheming, as the light wood-ash filled his mouth and eyes.

The little *noblesse* laughed till they cried. 'Twas pure sport to them to see this sudden fracas. The room was full of eager faces, all turned towards the chimney. This was the kind of thing for which one came to the Pine Apple ; a row, swift and sudden, perhaps even a spice of bloodshed, to enliven the long sitting over doubtful wine, and cards that were not always kind, or dice that had a devil of bad luck hidden in the heart of the ivory.

"What's the quarrel about?" said one; and, "He deserved it," said another. "'Twas his old game of abusing the Queen, and those *freluquets* yonder, friends of the Importants, encourage his beastly tongue."

And then a young man in Court dress jumped upon a table, took off his white-plumed hat and waved it, shouting, "*La Reine! Vive la Reine!*" And half the company took up the cry with boisterous vehemence, while the other half cried, "*Vive Beaufort! À bas la catin!*" It was a chance that the excitement did not rise to fever heat, and culminate in a free fight all over the room; but the *fronde* had not come yet, though the fever of it was in the air.

It cost that drunken brain and those slackened limbs of Dolroy's a painful effort before he was able to scramble up from the hearth and stand facing his enemy, grey from top to toe, head and face and garments coated with wood-ash. Only the vulture beak showed scarlet through the grey.

"Behold a poet's ghost!" cried Vallançay, amid the general laughter.

"Is it Virgil or Dante? It lacks the laurel crown; but it has a scarlet nose instead."

Fury braced the drunkard's nerves, and steadied his legs. He looked round him glaring, with eyes that shone like a tiger's, seeking his assailant. Then suddenly, with a wild beast's roar, he sprang upon George, gripping him by the throat with both hands, and flinging all the weight of his long limbs against him.

"What, was it you?—the Italian witch's gallant—the last on the roster?" he cried, while George wrestled with him, grasping his bony wrists, suffocating under the pressure of unclean hands, sickened at the drunkard's fiery breath, puffing fumes of coarse brandy into his face. He was conscious of that loathsome odour even while he struggled for his own breath.

"I have a good mind to kill thee," roared Dolroy.

"We'll have no killing here," cried a man in the crowd, everybody in the room being on foot by this time, and eager to intervene in the quarrel. "Loose your hands from his neck, Dolroy, or you'll strangle him."

"That's what I want to do," gasped the ruffian, as George flung him off, and sent him reeling into the arms of the bystanders.

Once free of that murderous clutch, George stood like a rock, gasping, but calm and collected, with his hand on the hilt of his sword. Those in the company who could admire courage, youth, and manly beauty, looked at him with friendly eyes.

"Who is with me among all you rabble?" Dolroy demanded savagely, scowling round the crowd. "Who will stand up for an old drunken man assaulted by a sober, fish-blooded jackanapes?"

There were plenty of offers, and George had as many. It might have been an engagement of half the room against the other half, so eager was everybody to fight somebody, for something; but after a wild confusion of tongues, and a hot dispute, the riot gradually subsided, and the combatants and place of meeting were chosen : and George, who had meant to settle his own account with Dolroy as quietly as the nature of the quarrel would allow, found himself one in an engagement of four against four, to fight with swords and pistols, on horseback, in the wood of Vincennes, an hour after sunrise, just when the light was clearest and steadiest.

"But how to get out of the gate," asked one of the combatants. "They are quick to smell gunpowder, since the law has been so severe against duelling ; and eight men riding out so early——"

"We need not all go by the same gate," said De Chancy, one of George's seconds, who seemed on fire with eagerness.

"That's easily settled. We shall be a hawking party," said Dolroy. "Some of you can carry a falcon, and you are going to fly your birds t'other side of the wood. I keep no bird save a bald-headed jackdaw that I have taught my own language—and would not sell for a thousand crowns."

There was the chill of dawn in the air and the pallor of dawn in the sky when George let himself in at the postern door in the tower where there was a corkscrew staircase leading up to a passage that communicated with the gallery on which his rooms opened. Madame de Lussac had given him the key of this postern door, which saved him the fuss and ceremony of the main entrance, and enabled him to go in and out at any hour of the day or night. Before going upstairs he went through a long corridor in the basement, which led to a door opening on the stables, where he roused one of the grooms from his straw pallet in the barrack where the coachmen and grooms had their quarters, and bade him saddle Sully, a horse he had ridden much and schooled to his liking, and have him ready and waiting in the lane behind the stables upon the stroke of four.

This done, he went to his room and wrote a letter to the Marchesa.

"I am going straight from this house to meet the man who insulted you—and it may be that either he or I, or both of us, will never see the setting of the sun that now shows red behind the wood where you and I have driven so often.

"It was in the Queen's cause I challenged him, but those who saw you insulted may guess that it is for your honour I fight. I go gladly, and, if Fate wills, I shall die gladly for your sake, since so to die is perhaps the only witness this poor life of mine can bear to my gratitude for all the bounties you have heaped upon me —the first and chiefest being your affection, of which I feel myself so little worthy."

So little worthy. Yes, for he could not pay love with love, and he knew that all other payment is but base coin. He thought of her gratefully, as he sealed the letter—thought of her sorrowfully, knowing that she would grieve for him should the event go ill; but he could not think of her tenderly. All his love, all his longing, went to others; to the kind protectress, the low-voiced, sweet-faced woman who had treated him as a kinsman and friend,—with no demonstrative affection, no overwhelming warmth of feeling, but with a pensive regard, as of one who cherished the memory of a lost friend, and loved him for his likeness to the dead. The tie had been so fragile that bound him to Lady Llanbister, but it held him faster than that passionately asserted relationship of mother and son, which he had been constrained to accept, reluctant even to the last.

And so, as he examined his weapons and arranged his dress for the encounter, there were two faces with him all the time : the fair girl-face, with the brilliant eyes, broad, low brow, and exquisite mouth, where pride was tempered by generous feeling ; the thoughtful woman-face, full of a pleading tenderness, lovely in the passionless calm of a life lived for others. It was of these two he thought, the beloved of his happiest years. They would be sorry if he fell in the fight that was so near. He could not go to meet death without leaving some token for his first—and, alas ! dearest, benefactress.

He sat at his desk again, when his preparations were finished, and wrote to Lady Llanbister.

" Beloved friend ! these lines may be a last farewell to you and that dear girl for whom, in sight of death, I dare acknowledge my passion—a love which neither years nor absence can lessen, and which can but cease when death stills the heart where Geraldine reigns paramount.

" Honour constrains me to fight a ruffian ; and I doubt the chances of a happy issue are against me. Receive, dear lady, this last avowal of an affection which words are too weak to express. Living or dying, I revere and admire and love you.

" GEORGE."

He placed the two letters in the Italian coffer where he kept his richest clothes—laying them on the top of the neatly folded garments, so that they could not fail to be seen by any one who opened the coffer, and yet

would not be likely to be discovered till the news of the
morning's business reached the Hôtel de Lussac, when,
if he were killed, there would doubtless be some exam-
ination of his rooms. As he calculated upon this, the
image of Héloïse de Lussac flashed upon him—frantic,
tragical, pacing those sumptuous rooms in a wild agony
of grief; and again he was sorry for her sorrow; and
again he hated himself because he could not feel for her
as a son should feel for his mother.

He was riding to the Porte St. Antoine presently,
with a hooded peregrine on his wrist, his horse fresh and
eager in the keen morning air. Horses and falcons,
greyhounds and spaniels, all toys for which youth cares
had been lavished upon him by the Marquise; and it
had been with the utmost difficulty that he had restricted
her money gifts to the amount which, as her steward
and book-keeper, he might fairly have received as
wages.
   There was no trouble at the gate.
   " Have my friends ridden ahead with their birds ? " he
asked the sentry, in a cheery voice.
   " Yes, monsieur, two cavaliers went through ten
minutes ago. A fine morning for a flight."
   And so, with jaunty touch of hat, through the gate,
past the grim towers of the Bastille, a great bulk of
masonry, dark under the pearly light, and along the
level road, between long rows of poplars, grey with
dust, to that other fortress, the prison-house for princes,
where Henri de Beaufort fretted in captivity, to the
wonder of all Paris.

Three hours later a cart came along the same dusty
road at a footpace, entering Paris through that same
Porte St. Antoine—a cart in which George Mountain
lay on a mattress, his garments soaked in blood, and his
countenance livid as death.

CHAPTER XVIII.

BETWEEN LIFE AND DEATH.

LONG days and nights of suffering, of delirium, of semi-consciousness, succeeded that eventful morning in the wood at Vincennes. The irritation of his wounds, treated by the imperfect lights of a seventeenth-century surgeon, kept the patient in a high fever, while the copious drugs prescribed by a Court physician sapped his strength and protracted his suffering.

It was a time of torment which George remembered for the rest of his life, an existence in a vague world that he took for Purgatory, or for Hell, according to the measure of his pain. Strange forms stalked there ; an old iron-grey man who plagued him perpetually, forcing him to drink nauseous medicines, dressing his wounds, and seeming only to intensify his agony, a man whom he took sometimes for a malignant fiend, and sometimes knew for the old Roman servant Paolo. Sometimes Paolo vanished, and a woman's dark face—uglier than Paolo's—watched at his bedside.

And sometimes there came a vision of imperial beauty, a woman who kissed him and cried over him, and implored him to live for her sake, but who never stayed long ; for though Héloïse de Lussac loved the sufferer, she did not love a sick-room. She who was so strong in pride and daring had all a fine lady's horror of suffering, and sickened at the sight of the blood-stained bandages, and shrank with something of aversion from George's altered countenance, pinched and cadaverous after a month of suffering.

"Make haste and get well, *mon ami*," she pleaded, "and let me have my handsome Georges again. As soon as you can bear the journey I will carry you to the Baths of Bourbon, and there you will soon recover your strength and good looks."

She visited him every day, and sometimes came to his room late at night—straight from the Court, shining in her evening splendour of diamonds and velvet, when if he were inclined to be light-headed, he would take her for one of the phantoms that haunted him in the night season—Melusine—Gabrielle d'Estrées, Diane de Poictiers, Joan of Arc. He had a hundred names for her ; and she would smile at him, and lay a cool hand on his brow, and bend over him to press a tearful kiss on his burning lips. But she never stayed with him ; and the dull hours in which he saw no face but those two dark faces of Paolo and Bianca weighed upon him like a funeral pall, and he abandoned all hope of ever going out into the sunshine, ever knowing the brightness of life and pleasant companionship, again.

The Court physician had ordered that his room should be kept dark ; that there should be as little difference as possible between night and day. There was no compromise with sickness in those days. A fever patient was not much better off than a state prisoner in one of the darkest cells of the Bastille. In the matter of air and light the prisoner had the best of it.

And while he lay in that darkened room, Paris was rejoicing at the conquest of Gravelines in Flanders, which had surrendered to Gaston d'Orleans after a protracted siege, an event celebrated by fireworks and coloured lanterns, by balls and collations, and dances in the open air on the terrace of the Palais Royal. Mademoiselle de Montpensier's violins were playing *corantos* and *passe-pieds* all over Paris in that week of jubilation, and all good citizens forgot for the nonce that arbitrary taxation of their houses which had so lately stirred them to revolt.

One stage there was in George's illness when, the

pain of his wounds being lessened, his hallucinations took a milder form, and his consciousness drifted away from the actualities around him to a shadow-picture of the past. He was at Isleworth again, sauntering on the river bank with Geraldine, or wading in some cool backwater to gather lilies for her. Or they were on the slope of the hill towards Highgate, in a meadow golden with king-cups, looking back at the city—the Cathedral, with its long line of roof and massive tower ; the fortress prison where Strafford had died, and Laud had pined in a prolonged captivity. Or they were in the Aldersgate garden, listening to unwonted sounds in the street within the gate—the beat of drums, the feet of the trained bands marching westward to guard the Houses of Parliament. Many a scene of that so-cherished past was acted over again in this later stage of delirium, when weakness, and not acute pain, was the cause of the fever. The dear phantoms were with him night after night ; and those beloved shadows came between him and the Marquise when she hung over his bed ; and he turned his face to the wall petulantly, muttering the names of his friends in England.

The fever burnt itself out at last, and the consciousness of every-day life and its obligations came back to him with an unspeakable melancholy and disgust. He lay like a log upon that sumptuous bed which had been his place of torment, and he felt that the world outside his windows was as colourless as the cold grey light of the quadrangle, where the sun never shone. Now that he was pronounced out of danger, the physicians had allowed him the light—but not the air of heaven. "*Pour l'amour de Dieu* not an open casement."

The days and nights passed now with a dull monotony, but he was too weak to feel the desire for action or change of scene, or to take the faintest interest in the great drama of life from which he had been so suddenly withdrawn. He had not even asked the issue of the duel—who had fallen, and who had survived. With that black melancholy which clouded his mind there went a supreme indifference to all the joys and

cares, hopes and ambitions, of earth. It was in vain
that Madame de Lussac tried to rouse him from his
apathy. He was no longer able to simulate interest
in her conversation, or pleasure in her society. He
lay languid and silent, with a face of marble, out of
which his haggard eyes looked at her with an unspeakable sadness.

"Have they given you the water of Nepenthe among
your medicines, *mon ami*?" she asked piteously, after
trying to arouse his interest in her gossip of the Court
intrigues. "You look at me as if you had forgotten
who I am—as if a stranger were sitting at your pillow."

"No, no. I have not forgotten. But everything
seems so far away, so long ago. Tell me, Marchesa,
how long have I been lying on this bed? A year, or
more than a year?"

"*Mon ami*, why, it is not three months yet, since
that dreadful morning."

He looked across the room at the great coffer,
wondering if his letters had been discovered there, and
having only this instant remembered writing them.

"Not three months? Then it is still summer.
Great God! I thought I had suffered a long winter on
this bed—ice, and snow, and storm—a winter of darkness,
and horrid shapes and sounds ; endless nights of cold
and gloom ; and then came burning days, and I thought
I was in the Americas with Raleigh, and the Incas had
made me a prisoner, and I was to be sacrificed in the
temple of their god—and I saw the knife at my throat.
Dreams—only dreams—but dreams that were like
years."

"*Pauvre cher ange! Hélas!* it was dreadful to hear
you raving. But it is over now—and we shall be at
Bourbon in a few weeks, you and I."

Then, for the first time since he dropped, head down-
wards, from the saddle, he began to think about the scene
in the wood at Vincennes.

"Is that brute Dolroy still alive?" he asked.

"He is dead ; but not by your hand. De Chancy rode
between you when that devil was rushing at you to give

the finishing blow. While you swayed in the saddle,
fainting from loss of blood, powerless to parry another
stroke, De Chancy wheeled his horse, and dashed
between you, and shot that evil beast through the brain.
It was one of the wickedest and cleverest brains in
France, people say; but there is nothing left of it now—
and the body it belonged to is lying in the *Cimetière
des Innocents*—and the hand that held the pen will give
no more trouble to anybody. He had accused Madame
de Chancy of an intrigue with Monsieur, and her
husband of being over-indulgent to his wife and her
Royal lover. 'Twas truth in both cases; but such
vilifiers should not be suffered to live. You owe your
life to De Chancy; and your liberty to the Cardinal."

"Indeed?"

"The other survivors in the fight are in the Châtelet.
They were arrested before they could leave the wood—a
sentinel at the Château having heard pistol-shots, and
guessed what mischief was on foot. Happily for you,
my faithful Paolo heard your step upon the tower-stair
in the early morning, and followed you—saw you go
out at the door, and then, seeing a light at the end
of the passage, went straight to the stables, questioned
the men, and you and Sully had not been gone half
an hour before Paolo and one of the grooms—Laurent,
who is staunch and trusty—were riding after you."

"How did they know where to look for me?"

"Oh, there is a fashion in these things—and of late
Vincennes has been the *mode* for duels. The boldest
scarce venture to meet in the Place Royale so soon
after Coligny's death. By reason of your choice of
Sully 'twas thought you had to ride some distance—and
as you would hardly fight before broad daylight, the
hour indicated as much. Paolo has a subtle brain for
finding out secrets. He rode on to the ground while
you were lying senseless in the dust, where Dolroy lay
dead. The rest had ridden off—and your good horse
was cropping the grass peacefully within half a dozen
yards. Paolo sent the groom to Vincennes to hire
a cart and a mattress, and he being lucky in falling in

with a good-natured farmer on his way to the village,
there was no time wasted, and you were brought here
in safety, past the guards who would have arrested you
had not Paolo sworn you were a dying man, which
indeed you looked, *pauvre ami*, when you were carried
to this room. That you have escaped being arrested
later you owe to the Cardinal, to whom you might owe
many valuable favours were you not too stubborn to
let him oblige you."

" I want none of his favours."

" But surely you are grateful for your liberty ? "

" I shall be—when I am free ; but so long as I have
to lie here I shall feel all the oppression of a prison
cell. There is a weight upon my soul which I cannot
fling off."

"Impatient ! Ungrateful !"

"Yes, I know I am an ingrate, and that is the
heaviest burden of all," he said, with a sigh.

"Well, I too am weary of Paris. The heat is suffocating in the narrow streets, and there is scarcely a
breath of air along the Cours ; the river mists reek
with foul odours. The Court is at Fontainebleau. Condé
and his Princess are at Chantilly, *fêting* their victorious son, and their Court is more brilliant than her
Majesty's."

"And what of unhappy England, Marchesa ? Have
the King's arms prospered while I have been lying
here ? "

"We hear rumours so various that one knows not
what to believe. In June we were told that King
Charles and his nephew were victorious on every side ;
and that the Parliament must speedily submit : in July
came the news of a fatal battle, at Mester-mow, I
think 'twas called, where Rupert's invincible cavalry
went down before clod-hoppers and city 'prentices, and
where the Prince lost his cherished dog, Boy, for which
he has mourned no less than for his slaughtered troops.
Your Queen has returned to France, and is sick and
solitary at the Baths of Bourbon, after giving birth
to a princess in one of your English cities, the child

of sorrow, born in poverty and mischance. This hapless infant was left behind, and I doubt mother and child may never meet again."

"Alas, poor Queen! And has no English letter come for me while I have been ill?"

"None. I see you hanker after your English friends, who have most likely forgotten you in the confusion of the times."

"I know them too well to fear that."

"You are young enough to believe in the fidelity of friends," answered the Marchesa, with a sneer.

It was one of her bad days. She was out of humour with herself and with the world. The Queen had gone to Fontainebleau without any intimation that her company would be desired there. Nor had she been bidden to that other Court at Chantilly, where Madame de Longueville was the reigning star. But she had been invited to join the princely circle at Blois, where Gaston d'Orléans was reposing on his laurels, with his wife and children, and where she knew that her presence would be welcome to Monsieur, although perhaps looked coldly upon by Madame, who had too frequent occasion for jealousy of beautiful visitors, or of fair young maids-of-honour, whose youthful innocence was ever slow to take alarm at the ardour of Monsieur's admiration.

George was allowed to leave his bed for an hour or two on the next day; and he was shocked at the aspect of his pallid countenance in the looking-glass, and at the feebleness of his limbs, which would scarcely carry him from the bed to the large armchair, even with Paolo's aid.

"Shall I ever be a man again?" he questioned despairingly, as he sank into the chair, and looked down at his shrunken and bloodless hands.

"Yes, Monsieur Georges, and a strong man, able to lay about you in a *mêlée*, if you will but eat beef and drink Burgundy," answered Paolo. "See! in the teeth of the doctor, I open the casement, and give you a breath of air. This room is a furnace, and the courtyard is not much better in this sultry weather. And now I must go to the Marchesa, who sent for me half an hour ago. Monsieur has a bell there on the table at his elbow, and Jean sits in the corridor, at Monsieur's service."

"Oh to be in England, in the meadows beside the Thames!" cried George, when he found himself alone.

His heart ached with longing and regret when he recalled that summer of two years ago, and heard the dear music of the Richmond bells floating along the river, out of the heart of the sunset. How often had he seen Geraldine's face, irradiated by that glory of the sinking sun! How kind she had been, or how capricious! But in all her humours, how lovely and how dear! To be the lowest servant at Isleworth or in Aldersgate Street ; to run errands or scrape trenchers ; only to see her now and then as she flitted past a window in the sunlight; to be anywhere near her, under the meanest conditions ;—were happier than to stifle in the gaudy splendour of a house he hated. Yes, hated! He was grateful to the woman who loved and cherished him ; but he hated the house he lived in, and the miserable dependence of a life without effort or ambition.

He yearned for England and the friends he had left there, as he sat with dull eyes fixed on the dead blank wall across the courtyard, broken only by the shuttered windows belonging to the rooms of Monsieur de Lussac, who was at Fontainebleau, where Madame Désprèz had a hunting-lodge which the Marquis had given her, and where they held a disreputable little Court of their own, a *tohu-bohu* of wits and adventurers, in open opposition to the Queen's stately circle.

"Oh for a touch of a friend's hand!" he thought, "for an honest grasp of an English hand!"

It was England and his English friends he longed for, with a yearning affection which seemed part of his very flesh. England! English friends! What had he to do with England and English ways, if his lineage were what he had been told it was? Italian! Italian to the marrow of his bones—a son of that beautiful, that gifted, that terrible people, in whom craft was an instinct, with whom revenge was a religion, and murder an elegant accomplishment. An Italian! He recalled those scathing denunciations of Jules Mazarin which made the common talk of taverns—his avarice, his invincible hypocrisy, velvet footfall, smiling lips, speech akin to music.

Footsteps in the corridor—the quick, resolute tread of one who walks the world without fear—startled him from that black melancholy. He could have sworn to that strong yet light step anywhere. His breath came thick and flutteringly as he stared at the door, waiting for it to open and show him the face of a friend.

"Francis, I knew 'twas you! God, how I have wanted you!" he cried; and then he let his face sink on the arm of his chair, to hide the rushing tears.

"Dost weep, sirrah! *Diantre!* is this a welcome for a man who has ridden six-and-thirty miles since sunrise, and through the hottest day in a pestiferous summer? *Jour de Dieu*, did you think I could stay away while you were ill, and in need of a friend? I only heard of your narrow 'scape of death three days ago, from a lieutenant in D'Enghien's infantry, whose servant has a brother in this house."

"But 'twas madness to enter Paris, Mountain. The Cardinal swore he would have you hanged if ever you set foot in the city. Great God! that you should hazard your life for my sake! You must be on the road again as soon as 'tis dark, and on your way to a safe harbour. Why should you not cross to England, where you would find friends, in spite of the troubles?"

"I have friends everywhere, *mon brave*; and I am not going to your beggarly England. As for the little Cardinal, I snap my fingers at him and his *fourches patibulaires*. I fear neither the gallows nor Montfaucon, nor the wheel in the Place de Grève. I have trailed a pike in Flanders with Monsieur's army since we two parted. I was all through the siege of Gravelines, and his Royal Highness will give me a character for courage in the face of the enemy. As for the Jesuit in red,

I doubt he is too wise to revive the story of Beaufort's attempt, and Beaufort's arrest. It has ever been his policy to let sleeping dogs lie ; and the dog Beaufort is a dangerous dog, that is ever tugging at his chain and will break it sooner or later, and head a pack of hounds that may hunt his Eminence out of France. Enough of my own fortunes, George. 'Tis of yours I come to talk."

He had seated himself opposite the invalid, and was leaning forward, clasping George's shrunken hands, and gazing into his face with a severe scrutiny—not unkindly, but deadly earnest.

" My fortunes are fixed. I am the servant of Madame de Lussac : gratitude and duty are bonds which I cannot break—were I ever so desirous of a freer life and a wider world."

"Gratitude, duty, to Madame de Lussac ! The lad raves. George, I am here to take you out of this Gomorrah, this house which it is your dishonour ever to have inhabited. If you have strength to sit in that chair, you can bear to be carried in a litter to our old quarters at the Golden Crown. I looked in on my way here, and left my horse in the landlord's charge. Our old room is at liberty ; and I bade them prepare for a lodger who would need more than common comfort."

" I esteem your kindness, Frank, and I fondly re-member those careless years I spent in your company : but I cannot leave this house, nor can I suffer you to speak ill of its mistress, to whom I am in debt for protection, and the love of a mother for an adopted son."

" *Sang de Dieu !* An adopted son! Do you know what Paris says of your sonship ? "

" I know but of one slanderer, and that dog will bark no more. When I discover another as malignant, I shall know how to silence him."

" Poor child ! Thou wouldst need a hundred lives to fight Madame de Lussac's slanderers—if that which is for the most part gospel truth can be called slander. Come out of this den, George. Wert thou to talk in an assembly of men as thou didst just now—of filial feeling towards the lady of this house, thou wouldst be greeted with a burst of Homeric laughter. In sooth, if you talk of adoption, I have a higher claim than the Marquise, for I adopted you when you were a helpless morsel of humanity that must have perished had no man fathered you."

"Generous friend, I have not forgotten. I shall be your loving debtor so long as I live; but I will not hear you malign a lady who has honoured me with her affection—the sacred affection which mothers feel for their children; a love which the difference in our ages justifies."

"George, are you fooled by a consummate wanton; or are you trying to fool me?"

"I will not hear——"

"You must—you shall hear. It is I, your father by adoption, the man of the world, who warns you that you are in danger of sinking deeper and deeper in a morass of guilt and shame. Maternal affection, forsooth! You are the woman's latest caprice, and she waits but the hour to throw off the mask. Must I tell you her history? Must I recite the catalogue of her lovers? Must I tell you of her intrigue with Bassompierre, with De Longueville, with Gaston d'Orléans? Shall I tell you of Count Hector de Lionval, who loved her passionately, sacrificed wealth and Court favour, broke his young wife's heart for her sake—and died cursing her, not without suspicion of poison?"

"Lies, slanders, the venom of paid libellers! You shall not repeat these hellish calumnies. I have lived in her house for a year—I have seen all that is noble and generous in her nature: a woman ill-used by the world; slighted and betrayed by her husband; a woman of surpassing beauty and commanding mind, hated by the ugly and the dull. You must not, you shall not, belie her. There are reasons for my presence in this house, for my allegiance to that lady, which I dare not explain, even to you, without her permission.

But you, who know that I am not a fool, may take my word that there never has been, there never could be, the shadow of dishonour in my affection for that lady, nor in hers for me."

"Oh, what a spell it is—the glamour of beauty, even on the wane. Poor lad! The sorceress can make you think what she wills. But I tell you that for such a man as you, young, nameless, without rank or fortune, to live under this roof, to drive about Paris by that woman's side, to depend upon her bounty—is dishonour such as I, Francis Mountain, soldier of fortune, adventurer, what you will, could not stomach; and I warn you that the stain of suspected infamy will darken all the rest of your life, unless you cast off your disgraceful bondage."

Mountain was pacing the room as he talked, fevered with vexation, caring more for this companion of his adventurous years than he had ever cared for kinsman or friend. But he forgot that he was talking to a man newly risen from a sick-bed, till he saw the sweat-drops break out upon George's pallid brow, and the last vestige of colour fade from his ashen lips.

"*Tonnerre de Dieu*, you're near swooning! Here "—hastily selecting a bottle of strong drops from other medicines on the table by the invalid's chair, and pouring out a dose—"swallow this! I was a brute to urge you beyond your strength. We'll wait for a day or two. But remember, I came from Flanders to pluck you out of this Tophet, and I will not be denied. I'll not leave Paris till you have said farewell to the Hôtel de Lussac."

"I swear, Frank, you cruelly wrong that unhappy lady. But, whatever thread of truth may run through that fabric of falsehood, for me there is no choice. I am here in the house of a woman who has the strongest claim upon my affection. Were she the wanton you describe, heartless, audacious—nay, were she guilty of that darker crime you talk of—my place would be at her side,—my duty would be to save her from the penalty of sin, to persuade her to repentance and atonement."

"Well, for the poison, 'twas but the common talk that follows every sudden death ; most of all when a man and woman quarrel, and the man dies while their wrath is hot. I'll not go so far as to accuse her of murder, though the women of her country are skilled in the use of anodynes that send troublesome people to sleep. But for the rest—for a life that has never known the shackles of religion or morality ; for adventures as daring, passions as capricious, as can be charged against Ninon or Marion—for so much I will answer."

"Oh, I know how men talk of women. I can believe you have heard vile stories of the lady I honour. A beautiful woman, proud of soul and fearless of speech, is ever the mark for calumny. In every rejected lover she has an inveterate enemy. And you, who know of what baseness men are capable, can swallow the fabrications of tavern slanderers, who have never crossed Madame de Lussac's threshold, perchance have never seen her face. I know the lady ; and nothing you, or any man on earth, can allege against her, will lessen my attachment to her."

"And you do not fear the world's verdict ? "

"I fear no judge while my own conscience approves. Look you, Frank, there is but one reason which could justify me in leaving this house. If it were indeed true that the Marchesa's good name can suffer by my presence here——"

"So far as the Marchesa's name is capable of damage, you may be sure 'tis the blacker for your friendship. Nay, more, by your presence in her house, by your companionship out of doors, you have brought upon her that which she can less endure than reprobation, for she is less used to it—the world's laughter. You have made her ridiculous. An elderly Helen, sunning her faded charms along the Cours by the side of a boy lover ! Think what a mark for the wits and song-writers ! Do you suppose there is but one Dolroy in Paris ? Why, lad, wherever you two are seen together scornful laughter follows you. But come, I have pressed you too hard to-day, while you are weak and ailing. God knows 'tis love makes me troublesome. We'll talk of my fortunes since that September dawn—near a year ago—when I left Paris. A chequered page, George. But before I begin my story, I wonder whether, amid all this splendour of Flemish tapestry and Italian inlaid work, one could happen upon so vulgar a thing as a tankard of Burgundy?"

"Forgive me, Frank. I ought to have been more hospitable," George answered hastily, ringing the hand-bell which summoned his attendants; and then, with a troubled look, he said, "But if the Marquise should find you here—you who have so cruelly reviled her— I beg that you at least offer her the civility of silence."

"I hope I know how to behave to a lady, George. Were Jezebel herself to enter, in all her bravery of painted cheeks and bedizened head, I would remember first that she was a woman and then that she was a Queen ; and she might talk with me for an hour without discovering that I thought her something less than a saint."

"Bring a bottle of your finest Burgundy, and as good a supper as you can contrive for this gentleman," said George, as the lacquey appeared at the door.

And presently, when Paolo spread a supper-table and lighted a cluster of wax candles in a tall silver candelabrum ; and when Francis Mountain drew his tabouret to the table and began to eat and drink, with a cheerful jingle of glass and silver, while the lowered curtains shut out the grey evening, George felt as if all that had happened since his last parting with that jovial comrade were but a dream from which he had awakened.

"God knows how sorely I have missed you, Frank !" he exclaimed by-and-bye, when Mountain handed him a brimmer of Burgundy, and they drank together and touched glasses, with a mellow note that rang true as their friendship. "You have been the something wanting in my life for this long year, and I have been the dullest fellow on earth without you. To spend an hour in your company is to live and to be merry again."

And then, remembering Mazarin's threat, he urged his friend to leave Paris at daybreak. But he could not awaken that reckless spirit to the consciousness of danger. Mountain persisted in his assertion that the little Cardinal was too shrewd a diplomatist to revive the story of Beaufort's conspiracy. Had not his policy since the arrest of that powerful foe been one of universal conciliation, his manners more ingratiating, his promises more lavish, than ever? while all his efforts had been directed to the task of amassing such treasures of pictures, statues, bronzes, tapestries, books, jewels, as constituted in themselves alone one of the greatest fortunes ever acquired—together with such accumulations of specie and such concessions of real estate as made the personal wealth of kings and emperors seem but a dignified poverty.

"My father had something of that accumulating genius," said Mountain, with a cynical laugh; "but in him the Parliament called it robbery."

He swore that he would stay in Paris till he had seen George shift his quarters.

"I give you a night to sleep upon my arguments," he said, "and if by to-morrow you are not resolved to break through the silken net, and be your free self again, I will say you are not the lad I reared on the highways of Europe, but some vile changeling, that loves splendour and luxurious living better than honour."

"You had best leave me to manage my life, while you take care of your own neck, Frank," George answered gravely, whereupon Mountain promised to keep out of the way of any one likely to remember him as an agent in Beaufort's plot.

There were, indeed, few who knew of his association with the Cardinal's enemies, and those few were far off. Madame de Chevreuse was living in strict retirement at one of her country houses; the Campions had left France. The conspirators and the conspiracy had melted into thin air.

George had put away all thought of Madame de Lussac during that last hour with Mountain. Not till

he was alone in the night silence did he look his fate
in the face. Sleep was out of the question. His brain
was on fire; his heart was beating with a feverish
rapidity. Over and over again the words that he had
to speak to her who had the strongest claim to his pity
repeated themselves in his mind. However kindly
spoken, they must be words of farewell. He could
live no longer under that roof. Whatever appeal she
might make to him, whatever obligation she might urge,
he must escape from that house, where every object
he looked upon was tarnished with the dishonour of
her who owned it. To live amongst splendour and
sicken at it is a worse penance than dry bread and
water. He had never loved those sumptuous surroundings; but now they had become loathsome to him.
The atmosphere of the house suffocated him.

Those lines upon the Marchesa's face! Guilty
passions had written them. Mountain's categorical
statements would have failed to convince him, had he
not his own dark surmises—had he not recoiled often,
with a sudden, sharp agony, at some chance revelation
from her lips whom he was bound to honour.

He could have revered grey hairs blanched by care,
wrinkled hands hardened by toil. He could have loved
a peasant woman, had such an one, honest, pious,
simple-minded, claimed him for her son. There should
have been no recoil from rustic ignorance and lowly
birth. But to know himself the son of a wanton; to be
called upon to respect a woman who had never respected
herself, whose beauty had furnished the loose talk of
vicious lips, a prize and a spoil for the boldest assailant,
a ribbon to wear on a profligate's sleeve! That was
bitter!

Finding sleep impossible, he rose, re-lighted his
candles, and paced the room till he sank into a chair,
almost fainting with exhaustion. He had forgotten
how lately he had risen from a sick-bed. He took
pen and ink, and tried to write his farewell; but the
fitting words would not come. He so feared to wound
her. She had loved him, and been generous to him.

She was a woman, beautiful and highly gifted. It was hard to shape the phrases which should excuse his conduct without insulting his benefactress.

No, a letter would not serve. He must meet her face to face, must discover, if he could, how much or how little truth there was in Mountain's indictment. He flung himself upon his bed towards daybreak, worn out in body and mind, and fell into a deep and dreamless slumber, that total oblivion which follows exhaustion, and so slept till noon, when he was roused by the great bell of Saint-Germain-l'Auxerrois tolling for a funeral. Paolo was standing by his bedside, having brought a warm morning drink in a covered silver cup, for his refreshment.

He took the warm drink, and ate a small wheaten roll, while Paolo expatiated upon Monsieur's prolonged slumbers. He had entered the room more than once since eight o'clock, and had found Monsieur as fast as the Seven Sleepers: though he feared, from the evidence of the candles, and the scattered papers, that Monsieur had been afoot in the night.

George dressed as quickly as he could, with Paolo's assistance, and sent, while he was dressing, to inquire if the Marquise would allow him to wait upon her before dinner. The answer was, Yes, Madame would receive him in the Ariadne room, if he were strong enough for the journey downstairs.

He had put on his plainest suit, of dark blue cloth, with a narrow braiding of gold, and the Venetian glass showed him hollow cheeks and a marble pallor against the cold colouring of his doublet: a face to frighten a sensitive woman, he thought, so gloomy was the expression of eyes and mouth.

Paolo ushered him to the tapestried *salon*, where he found Madame de Lussac walking to and fro as she had been on that fateful visit of his, nearly a year ago, when she revealed the tie that bound them. She came to him with a smiling welcome; but at the sight of his face she stopped suddenly.

"You bring troublesome news!" she exclaimed.

" Bad luck is written in your face. *Sang de Dieu !* What can have changed you thus, since yesterday ? "

" 'Tis not so much bad news, Marchesa, as a painful argument with myself that has made my looks sadder than they were yesterday. I have been meditating upon both our lives ; and I do entreat you not to be angry, and not to deem me ungrateful for all your kindness to me, when I tell you my resolve. I must live under this roof no longer. For your reputation and for my peace it is needful that we should part ! "

" Not deem you ungrateful ! " she cried, with her eyes flaming, and her tall figure seeming to put on an extra inch or two, as it always did when she was angry. " Why, if you were to desert me now—after the affection I have lavished on you—I should think you the most ungrateful hound that ever bit the hand that fed him. No, no, *mon enfant*, you could not do so vile an act as to abandon me."

" Nay, dear Marchesa, on that one point my mind is fixed. I must go back to the old free life, must be again the soldier of fortune, depending on such poor talents as I possess for my daily bread. But go where I may—live how I may—I shall still be your grateful debtor and servant ; and should you ever need the service of kinsman and champion, I will come at your bidding."

" I will accept no such service. I will have you here —here—here in this house," stamping her foot upon the polished floor, " my friend and companion, close at hand when my dark hour comes upon me."

" That cannot be, Marchesa. If you can live under the shadow of a lying accusation, I cannot. Your un-acknowledged son can have no place in your house."

" Cruel, to taunt me thus ! When you know I dare not acknowledge you."

" Would it be to create a worse scandal than any that has ever shadowed your life—a darker story than the death of Hector de Lionval ? " he asked, looking at her with a mournful seriousness.

He felt that the utterance of that name was cruel,

but he wanted to test her, to give her a chance of refuting that hideous slander. The result appalled him. A passage in a play he loved recurred to him in the midst of his agitation. It was verily

> "As if that name,
> Shot from the deadly level of a gun,
> Had murdered her."

She recoiled from him a few paces, clutched at a high-backed armchair, the first she could reach, and leant against it, staring at him with features convulsed by her agony of horror or of fear. Her lips moved rapidly, as if she were speaking, but no sound came from them—only a faint white foam, which she wiped from those pale lips with her handkerchief.

"How dare you?" she gasped at last. "You, you, you—my own flesh and blood! How dare you echo the malignant whispers of wretches who accused me of a hideous crime, only because De Lionval's death was sudden, and his fatal illness seized him in my house. I had loved him, sir. I would not have hurt a hair of his head ; though he used me vilely—gave my letters, the out-pouring of a heart that adored him—gave them to one whose esteem was life or death to me, and made me the friendless, desolate woman who thought she had found succour and consolation when she found you, ingrate!"

"No, Marchesa, not an ingrate! You have given me affection for which I must be grateful to my dying day. Should calamity overtake you, test me then ; try me in the hour of your sorrow, and you shall find I will not fail in my duty as man to woman, as son to mother. But I cannot stay in this house. If De Lionval's had been the only name slander has linked with yours, I might believe you the innocent victim of malevolence. But there are others—Gaston, that coward, fop, sybarite, profligate, whom it were shame for any woman to love——"

"Cease your indictment, sir, and come to the verdict. Guilty, guilty, guilty, if you will have it so. 'Tis the old Roman story reversed—not the father who sentences his son, but the son who judges his mother. I will suffer no further interrogation. Think as vilely of me as it pleases you. Condemn me on the evidence of one of Dolroy's ballads—or an epigram by Bussy. Did I ever tell you I was a good woman? I told you I was an unhappy one. I would have told you more had you asked me for my confidence—had you ever opened your heart to me, and made me feel that I had indeed a son, who would love me in spite of my sins, whose pardon would be infinite—like Christ's. But now—now that you tax me with my past life—it is well you should know under what auspices my womanhood began."

"Spare yourself, Marchesa, I entreat you. I seek to know nothing of the past—unless you can tell me that there is not one grain of truth in the scandals that blacken your name."

"Oh, my name! My name is much of a colour with other noble names at the Regent's Court. I have been more reckless of consequences than meaner women. I come of a race born to rule and not to serve. I have never schooled myself to the petty hypocrisies that pass for virtue. Shall I tell you the tragedy of my girlhood? Yes; since you have begun to question, it is right you should know all. Shall I tell you what I was in my seventeenth year? Motherless, newly released from the convent where I had grown from child to woman, absolutely ignorant of life outside convent walls; neglected by my father, who was squandering the remnant of his fortune among male and female reprobates at Rome, while he left me to the care of servants at his villa near Frascati. Paolo, the steward, son and grandson of former stewards, was my friend and counsellor, the only being who took a fatherly interest in my welfare. My nurse and foster-mother was the household drudge at the villa, and her daughter Bianca was my only companion. From my fellow pupils at the convent, the girls of my own rank, I was cut off as completely as if that abandoned villa, with its mouldering walls and garden wilderness, had been in

an Arabian desert. My father told me that he was too
poor to keep an establishment befitting my rank either
in Rome or at Frascati, and that I must be content to
live in seclusion until he was able to arrange a marriage
for me. He, himself, was living in a corner of his
Roman palace. It was all squalid and miserable ; but
I could have been happy if I had been allowed but one
of my convent friends to keep me company. That
happiness was denied to me."

"It was a hard lot for the morning of life," George
murmured compassionately.

He went to her and took her hand, and led her to a
chair near the fire, and seated himself beside her, with
a grave tenderness that softened her to tears. And
her angry mood changed to an appeal for his pity.

"Yes, it was a hard lot. How the time comes back
as I tell you that cruel story—that first summer of
womanhood and liberty! How I had dreamt of it,
longed for it, pictured it, in my convent prison! And
what had freedom brought me? The right to roam
from morning till night, a solitary creature in a deserted
garden. You, who have led an adventurous life, have
never known what such solitude means."

"I can imagine all it has of sadness, Marchesa, and
can pity you."

"Yes, I have a right to your pity—most of all when
the scene changed, and my garden-wilderness became
a paradise of flowers and birds, a place of sunshine and
of moonlight, where every hour and every change of
light and shadow seemed more beautiful than the last.
I was no longer alone. A young soldier-diplomatist,
who had fled from the heat of a Roman summer to the
seclusion of a lodging at Frascati, had discovered my
garden in one of his evening rambles, and had made
himself my companion. He claimed to be my father's
friend, and assumed the right to be my visitor ; and as
the garden was a spacious solitude, and Bianca and
Paolo hardly ever left the villa, there was no one to
question his right or to interfere with our friendship."

She was looking at the logs smouldering on the

hearth, and her eyes had the look of a dreamer whose inward gaze sees the things that are not.

"He was but two years older than I ; but in every accomplishment that can make manhood famous, he was a master. It was as if he had been born of Olympian gods, and had inherited all the arts that the earth-born can only master with time and toil. He had all the gifts that win love and honour. Reared in the Colonna Palace, the playfellow of princes, the favourite pupil of the Jesuits, he had escaped from their influence, had shone like a star in Roman society—a gambler and a profligate, as I know now, but with all the qualities that can adorn vice. For me he was the solitary student, whose heart was set upon lofty things, for whom mean ambitions, the love of place or of gold, had no existence. I loved him, George—loved him as a girl loves her first lover. Think of my helplessness— my trustfulness—with the innocence of a child and the passions of a woman. And I know that he loved me, whatever wickedness that young life had known— he was all mine, mine by a love that knew no memory of the past, no care for the future, in that summer wilderness, under those Italian stars."

She paused in her torrent of speech, and breathed a deep, sobbing sigh.

"When I recall that enchanting solitude, where I heard no sound but the beating of my lover's heart amidst the song of the nightingales—music that seemed to repeat our own impassioned words—I look back and remember the woman I was, the man he was, in that paradise of unreasoning love, and I know that both have long been dead. There is a death that ante-dates the coffin and the grave ; there is a change worse than corruption and the worm. Well, the dream was sweet ; but there was a fearful awakening. My lover had to leave me ; he was sent to Madrid on a diplomatic mission, and I was alone in the dark autumn days, when the bleak north wind came tearing down the mountain side, and the old grey olive woods bent under the storm—alone, and awakened to the knowledge of the bitter penalty that women have to pay for sin. And while that horror of a fast-coming shame was new, my father summoned me to Rome. The suitor had been found—a Frenchman, noble and rich, the latest companion of my father's orgies, and my senior by twenty years."

The agony in the strained features, the deadly pallor that crept from chin to brow, indicated the pain that went even with the memory of her girlhood's tragedy.

"What could I do, think you? What friend had I, what counsellor? My foster-mother discovered my secret, and, while she made light of my sin, she was aghast at the peril I had to face. Do you know what Italian fathers are? You have heard the story of the Cenci, perchance. They are not all such devils incarnate as that hellish tyrant. My father was not. He would not have been cruel for sheer love of cruelty; but he would have been pitiless to a daughter who dishonoured his name. My faithful nurse told me that my secret must be kept at any cost; it meant life or death. 'He will kill you,' she repeated, not once, but many times. 'He will have no mercy. By cruel words or by cruel acts he will be your death. If he discovers your situation, you will not escape alive out of his hands.' At any cost of lies, at any suffering, physical or mental, my shameful secret was to be kept all through the coming winter; and when, a betrothed wife, I returned to the villa, it would be the business of those three faithful servants to carry me safely over my time of peril, and to dispose of the child whose birth none but they must ever know. They would have had even the father of that foredoomed one kept in ignorance of my state; but to this I would not submit. My letters told him of all my suffering, the anguish of separation from him, and the horror of my fate, unless he came to my rescue, and offered himself as my husband. My father would have scorned such a suitor; but I would have gone to the end of the earth with him, content to live obscure and in poverty for his sake."

"Was he so great a villain as not to offer marriage?"

'Do not call him villain! He was only the most

accomplished gentleman of his time, who commanded
admiration and favour wherever he went ; and while
I suffered that long agony of fear and shame he was
leading a life of pleasure at Madrid, and narrowly escaped
a plebeian marriage with the daughter of a money-
lender who had helped him to pay his gambling debts.

"*Dieu*, how I hate that heartless villain !" cried George.
'Twas instinct made me loathe him from the hour we
first met."

" No, no, you must not hate him !   Use him, *mon ami*,
use him as he uses the world. Basta ! I obeyed my
father's summons, and was received with favour by him
and by his friend De Lussac, who affected a passionate
admiration for me. Our betrothal was celebrated with
Roman pomp, *feux-de-joie* in the courtyard, and angry
creditors in the vestibule ; all that was Royal and
princely in the city assembled to witness the signing
of the contract. I was prostrate in body and mind
after this ordeal, and Bianca took advantage of my
wretched state to obtain my father's consent to my
leaving Rome for the villa, where quiet and the pure
air would restore me to health. I had played my part
bravely, George. Not you, nor any man living, can
know how hard a part a woman has to play when shame
stares her in the face ; what sickening fears rack her
brain while she carries herself like an empress ; what
pangs of heart and body she suffers under the heavy
folds of velvet and sable, the burden of gold-embroidered
damask, the princely robe that hides the deforming
change which, once revealed, would blast her name
for ever. I suffered that ordeal, George ; and when
the fatal hour was past, and I lay weak and helpless,
alone in that desolate villa, can you wonder that, when
my lover came to me, my first prayer was that he would
hide my dishonour and save me from my father's fury.
Of the son that was born to me—that son who, to a
happy wife and mother, might have seemed fair as a
spirit from Paradise—I had but one thought, the desire
that his origin should remain for ever unknown. I
accepted the first plan his father offered. I saw him

carried from my chamber without one pang. Think
of me if you can, George, as I was—not eighteen years
of age, and with a father who had never given me one
word of love, who had measured me from head to foot
with the cold eye of the merchant, and had said, 'You
are handsomer than your mother. I must find you a
rich husband, to whom you will doubtless be just as
faithful as your mother was to me.' Never can I forget
those cruel eyes that scanned and appraised me, or the
malignant scorn of that cowardly speech. Think of
all this if you can, and try to forgive me. And do not
wonder if I have followed the stream down which other
women drift to old age and death. Do not wonder
if I have been no better than they. But in you—in you
—I hoped to find my redemption. From the hour in
which I saw your face, in the ante-chamber at the
Louvre, my mind has known no thought that has not
been of you. And now, if you forsake me in my
misery——"

She broke down at this, and covered her eyes with
her handkerchief—those proud eyes which had seldom
known tears.

"I will never forsake you," he said earnestly. "I will
remember and respect your claim to my affection—but
it will be for the happiness of us both that I should leave
you. Be sure that if I stayed, the scandal would go
further—it would reach the ears of your husband."

"My husband! He has ever made light of scandals.
But yes, he might make your presence an instrument of
torture, were he to put his own foul construction on our
friendship. And he must never suspect the truth. He
would have no mercy on you or on me. He would be
your death. Not by his own hand ; he is too clever for
that. He would pay one of his *spadassins* to pick a
quarrel with you, and if the first failed, another and
another. He would hunt you to a bloody grave. I
know the revengeful heart under his cynical indifference."

"Indeed, dear lady, it were best and wisest that you
should live at peace with him, and do nothing to provoke
the world's malice."

" Ay, it were best. I had a dream of something better than the best, when I brought you under this roof. But you have never been happy here—and you do well to go. I will think of you as a friend at a distance."

" Never too far to come to you in your sorrow."

" My sorrow is all my life. What have I left? Grey hairs and the world's contempt! They go ill together."

" Nay, you are beautiful still."

" To-day, perhaps ; but to-morrow is at the door bringing wrinkles and old age. But, George, for the love of God never believe that I had act or part in De Lionval's death. 'Twas an awful death : stricken with sickness in this house—carried out of it after midnight, to die before the dawn. 'Twas an awful, mysterious doom, and I can scarce wonder that those who hated me said 'twas my doing. But you—despite of all the ill you know of me—could not believe *that*!"

" No, no! Oh, forgive me for having uttered his name. I wanted to hear your denial. Thank God you have spoken freely!"

He knelt by the side of her chair, as he had knelt once before, and kissed her hand, which burnt with fever ; he murmured a loving farewell, linked with a prayer for her peace of mind, a promise to be with her at any time of trouble ; and then he rose and went quietly out of the room, leaving her with her head bowed over her knees, in profound dejection.

She heard the door close behind him, but did not look up. She had been hotly indignant when he announced his intended departure ; but she was almost resigned to it now. He had not been happy. He had attended her as her slave rather than as her son. No love that she could give him could win back the lost years in which they had been strangers.

" Could I have had him with me from his childhood, my plaything, my petted page, to fetch and carry for me, to lie at my feet when he was idle, he would have grown up to adore me," she thought. " He would have known no law of right or wrong but my will. All I did would have been justifiable in his eyes. He would have been a part of myself, thinking as I thought, loving those I loved."

She dismissed the *maître d'hôtel* when he announced that dinner was served. She was ill, and would not dine. Should he call the Signora Bianca? Bianca! No, no; she desired only to be alone. Her fevered cheek paled at the name of her faithful attendant.

Bianca! Oh, the horror of De Lionval's name on her son's lips—a name to conjure up the one most tragical memory of her life, a scene of terror indescribable. She looked back at that fatal hour now, sitting there by the lonely hearth, in the vast splendour of those tapestried walls, where in their boldness of design and brilliancy of colouring the classic forms seemed to live and move. Her life had been black with sin—bold, unscrupulous sin; and she had held her head high, deeming herself no worse than her contemporaries— a Diana compared with the Montbazon—and only less judicious in her amours than the peerless De Longueville, who was but at the beginning of her career. But murder! A deed of darkness—treacherous, cruel! Of that she had been incapable.

She looked back and lived again through that dreadful scene, as she had lived through it in many a dark hour. No, *she* had not been capable of murder, even in imagination; but there was one of a harder nature, of stronger passions, one who cherished her with an unreasoning love, and was ready to risk the gallows or the wheel for her sake, to be revenged upon her betrayer; and it was from that hand, Bianca's hand, he had met his doom.

She had loved De Lionval passionately—an intrigue of years—and had wearied of him, as she did of most things on this earth, and had urged him to marry, and to forget her—for the lover of her youth had come back to her, after years of severance—the lover to whom fidelity meant duty, and whose affection, if it were equal to his protestations, might yet redeem her life, as she believed, her marriage being a nullity, and make her that which she had always longed to be, a good woman.

And then De Lionval, married to an innocent girl, had sickened for the old love, and had tried to renew the old tie, and, discovering his rival, had turned traitor and sent those burning letters to the great Cardinal's *protégé*, the Italian diplomatist, newly risen on the Court horizon, sudden and brilliant as the evening star. Then had followed a cruel scene between Mazarin and the Marquise ; and she, who had hoped to ascend to a higher level by the resumption of that old tie which time seemed to have hallowed, saw herself scorned and abandoned. And Bianca had known all that her mistress had hoped, all that she had lost—her sufferings, her hatred of the lover who betrayed her ; and when, in his infatuation, De Lionval had entreated for one last interview, believing in his power to win pardon and the renewal of love, it was Bianca who planned the meeting, urging the necessity of keeping terms with him. It was Bianca who led him to the Marchesa's chamber in the late evening, by the winding stair from the Ariadne room, and it was Bianca who brought the supper and the wine, and who waited on them with her own hands, while both were too agitated—one by suppressed anger, the other by passionate love—to remark her movements, or know what they ate or drank.

He was stricken with illness while he sat at table— one of those horrible seizures so common in Italy, common even in Paris. He was huddled into De Lussac's sedan chair, and carried to his own house in the Rue St. Thomas du Louvre, where he died in less than three hours. That mysterious disease had been kinder to him than to the lovely Gabrielle d'Estrées, for whom the agony of dissolution lasted three days and nights, changing beauty to a thing of terror. No inquiry was held. No one knew where he had spent that fatal night. In some haunt of profligates, his family thought. His heir seized the estate. His young wife carried her dowry back to her own people. It was only afterwards —when the story of a midnight supper at the Hôtel de Lussac got abroad—that malignant tongues linked Madame de Lussac's name with that mysterious death.

She knew of the slander, and bore it in silence. Not even to clear herself from so horrible a suspicion could she betray the wretch who loved her, and who, by this hellish revenge, had done her more harm than her worst enemy had ever done. And from that hour, Bianca, the foster-sister, the faithful ally who had helped her to hide her shame in the dawn of womanhood, when guilt and shame were new, this devoted slave became a ghastly presence, for ever recalling a deed of horror. Sometimes, looking at the peasant's rugged features, the deep-set eyes, black as night, under lowering brows, the low forehead and heavy jowl, the something animal in the countenance, it seemed to her as if all that was wicked in her life was embodied in this woman—a monstrous presence, a haunting horror, which she must suffer till death divided them.

And her first lover, the father of her firstborn, what had he been to her since the reconciliation which followed within a year of De Lionval's death?

Well, he had been Mazarin! Selfish, calculating, cold as marble, grudging those large sums of money which she demanded from him, complaining of her extravagance with the same breath that swore to an undying love, proud of her beauty, and of the splendour with which his taste and his wealth had invested the grim old mansion of the De Lussacs, yet careful to remind her that the tapestries and bronzes, the pictures and porcelain, the Italian cabinets and parcel-gilt candelabra, were hers only at his pleasure, and must ultimately adorn that palace which the architect Mansard was building for him on the site of the Hôtel Tubœuf, that house which was to surpass the magnificence of kings, and was to suffer strange fortunes, and narrowly escape ruin. He had been Mazarin! He had parted unwillingly with that which he loved best of all things betwixt earth and sky—his money. To no one else had he been as prodigal of gold ; but if love had ceased to rule him, there was another influence, which grew stronger with his advance in the Queen's favour.

That influence was fear. He knew Héloïse de Lussac's ungovernable temper and reckless tongue too well to offend her. The higher he climbed upon that dazzling peak where the climber is ever an easy mark for poisoned arrows from sharpshooters below, the more did he desire to keep on good terms with the Marquise ; and if an occasional appearance at her assemblies, a few soft speeches, and, *ohime!* a few thousand louis d'or, could keep her civil and friendly, the sacrifice must be made.

CHAPTER XIX.

"LIKE A STAR FIXED."

GEORGE went straight to his old lodgings, after packing the two portmanteaux which he had carried to the Hôtel de Lussac, and which were large enough to contain the least sumptuous and most useful of his clothing, and all his necessaries. Those finer Court suits which the Marquise had insisted upon ordering for him he left in the Italian coffer ; nor did he carry with him the *nécessaire* in tortoiseshell and gold, presented to him at the New Year, the costliest gift which he had accepted from those lavish hands, since he had rigidly refused the jewels she pressed upon him.

He wrote to Madame de Lussac on the same evening, begging her to dispose of these splendours, which were unfitted for his present fortunes.

He found Francis Mountain in the public room at the Golden Crown, drinking with the *habitués* of the place, an imprudence against which he remonstrated earnestly.

"Believe me, it is to risk your liberty, if not your life, to be discovered here," he said, "and unless you love a cell in the Châtelet better than the high-road and the free air, you will slip out of Paris at sundown. I shall never forget how great a risk you ran for my sake."

And then he told his friend that he had left the Hôtel de Lussac for ever.

"I am moved to do this by the respect I bear Madame de Lussac, by the gratitude I owe her," he said, "and not in any wise by a lessening of that affection which but poorly repays her kindness. I know of how base a stuff men's minds are made, and that for a man and woman to think kindly of each other, and to live in each other's company, is to provoke ribald jests and filthy imaginings."

"Thank God for that wise resolve of yours, George," cried Mountain, with a swinging slap on his *protégé's* shoulder. "Why, now the sky is clear again, and I will never more breathe a disrespectful word of your Marquise. Let me but see you master of your own life, tied to no fine lady's petticoat, and I am content. Will you come to Flanders with me, and fight under D'Enghien, the greatest captain the world has seen since Cæsar?"

"Nay, I have no military fever—though I would turn soldier to-morrow if duty called on me. I love books—and tranquil days. I was never so happy as at Isleworth, teaching Mistress Geraldine, and keeping accounts for my dearest lady."

"Your dearest lady? What, is Lady Llanbister still your dearest, despite the mysterious tie that binds you to Madame de Lussac?"

George's cheek crimsoned, and his eyelids drooped.

"Lady Llanbister was the first woman who ever cherished me," he answered after a pause, "and I had no claim on her kindness—none! Her love was a free gift. And as she was the first to love me—so must she ever be the first in my love ; even before the Marquise," he concluded, with a curious deliberation, as if he were answering his own thought rather than his friend's question.

"*Mille millions de tonnerres!* I believe you were born to be a schoolmaster, like that Mr. Milton of Aldersgate Street, who writes republican pamphlets, and teaches a starched prig nephew the rudiments— doubtless with some aid of an ash-twig. But how do you propose to earn your bread?"

"Perhaps as a schoolmaster. I know Mr. Hobbes, who has influence with his old pupils, and who would,

I doubt, recommend me to a place in some noble family."

The friends bade farewell that night, as Mountain meant to leave Paris at break of day ; but they promised to keep each other acquainted with their fortunes and whereabouts, whatever fate befell them.

"Schoolmaster or scrivener, or what low thing it pleases thee best to be, thou wilt ever be my gallant, handsome George—the favourite of beautiful women, the envy of meaner men."

Paolo appeared at the tavern early next morning, bringing a letter from his mistress, and full of affectionate regret at Monsieur's abrupt departure ; full also of horror at beholding him in so rough and comfortless a lodging, where, being yet barely recovered from his long illness, he would be likely to fall ill again.

Madame de Lussac's letter was only a few words of chiding at his having left his handsomer clothes, and the *nécessaire*.

"You know not when you may be summoned to the Palais Royal," she wrote, "for there is one there who should take an eager interest in your fortunes. Think not, *m'amour*, I shall forget thee, and grow careless of thy welfare. To see thy face across the crowd of faces, to know that thou art prosperous and happy ! Those are the only joys that remain to me. I leave Paris to-morrow for Blois, where Madame invites me. Indeed, I only stayed in this pestiferous city—after every one of my rank had left it—that I might be near you."

A *fourgon* belonging to Monsieur de Lussac brought two capacious trunks containing all of his property which George had left in his rooms : clothes, books, and swords. He piled one trunk upon the other, in a dark corner of his room, and thought no more of them. Life was now too serious a matter for frippery.

He dined at the ordinary of the Golden Crown, in

all the noise and bustle of a full house, and ate with
a better appetite than he had known since his illness.
That black Saturnian humour of the last three months
had left him.   He walked Paris with a light step,
rejoicing in his liberty, and the narrow streets and open
quays seemed beautiful to his eyes.   He did not miss
the throng of coaches on the Cours la Reine, nor find
life dull because Renard's Garden was closed for the
season.   He went about Paris in search of employment,
and, having succeeded in finding the philosophical
Mr. Hobbes, was courteously received by that gentleman, who had been acquainted with the late Lord
Llanbister, and who promised his good word in the
English colony, which included several families of rank
and fortune, fugitives from a land devastated by war,
and from cities where the homely sounds of daily life
were drowned in the roar of the besiegers' guns.

And now he found himself walking the streets of Paris
with three louis d'or in his pocket, a heap of finer clothes
than he cared to wear in his present precarious fortunes,
and for stock-in-trade some little book-learning and a
head for figures.

In these circumstances his thoughts turned naturally
to England, and to her who had offered him a home
there.   How ardently he longed to accept that generous
offer.   But to live under the same roof with Geraldine ;
to see her courted and won by a lover of her own rank ;
to stand by penniless, obscure, the man she had once
loved, while that happier suitor sauntered by her side
along the familiar pathways, or hung over her as she
sang to her lute in the twilit parlour !—this were a
martyrdom of which he knew himself incapable.   Sooner
or later the imperious passion of youth would burst its
bounds, and he would be sobbing out his love at her
feet, or drawing his sword upon her betrothed.   No, it
could but be in the grey after years, when his dearest
lady was growing old, and Geraldine had left her to rule
another household, that he could dare to resume that
dependence which had been so sweet.

He had waited on the English Ambassador, and had

paid a second visit to Mr. Hobbes, who was busy about the printing of his first philosophical work ; so far without result. He spent a considerable part of his days at the Sorbonne, listening to lectures and academical disputations, and his evenings were mostly studious, for he had no love of the riotous company in the neighbouring taverns. His books were the dearer to him because of the difficulty he had suffered in snatching an hour's reading while under Madame de Lussac's roof. She had ever some employment for him which made study impossible, and had been petulant and offended when he showed a liking for books and solitude.

As the days wore on without bringing him the promise of employment, he began to think seriously of following Francis Mountain and trailing a pike in Flanders. He would have turned soldier, perhaps, but for the restraining thought that while he remained in Paris he was within call of Lady Llanbister, and had frequent chances of hearing news of her, and of Geraldine, from the English exiles. This consideration determined him to stay until he was starved out.

In his despair of obtaining a scholarly employment, he began to think of living by his muscles and sinews, and waited one October morning upon Monsieur du Plessis, the fashionable riding-master, to whom he offered himself as an assistant. He was known at Du Plessis' Academy for his fine riding, his handsome person, and patrician air, and the proprietor would have engaged him on the spot to break and school his young horses, and teach the noble art of horsemanship, after the manner of the Marquis of Newcastle ; but George begged a few days for consideration before he closed with the offer, which was a liberal one as to payment.

There could be no degradation in any honest labour that would give him a livelihood, he told himself ; yet the prospect of meeting the white boots and pointed beards, the *rodomonts* and *fanfarons* with whom he had lived on equal terms, as a paid servant of the school, galled him, and he waited till sheer want should compel him to take the offered wage.

More than once, in his perambulation of the narrow streets, he had been obliged to hug the wall, in order to give place for the Cardinal's coach; and the clear-cut Italian face had looked at him from the coach windows, without a sign of recognition. He was surprised, therefore, when, some days after his visit to Du Plessis' Academy, the coach was suddenly pulled up, as he stood in the gutter waiting for it to pass, and Mazarin's finely formed hand, with the sacred ring upon it, was laid upon his shoulder.

He took off his hat, and waited, bareheaded, silent, and grave even to sullenness.

"*Ecco!* the Marchesa's runaway steward has not left Paris!" exclaimed the Cardinal. "I thought you had sailed for the Indies, Monsieur Georges, to take service with the great Mogul, since the Hôtel de Lussac was not fine enough for your magnificence."

The two faces looked at each other, the elder with a light mockery, not unmixed with dislike, the younger with a proud reserve that savoured of hatred.

"The Marchesa's house was too magnificent for my habits or my inclination, Monseigneur; but I left it only because my presence there created a scandal, so unholy are the minds of fine ladies and gentlemen."

"You were right! Your presence was a scandal and a folly; and the most honourable thing I know of you is your surrender of a position that was founded on a woman's self-delusion. You have done wisely to cut yourself free from such an entanglement, and I think the better of you for your independence—as I did, some time past, when you refused a pension. But you may find yourself in need of a friend before long—indeed, you have already a haggard and careworn look—and in that case you can apply to me."

"Your Eminence is kind; but while I have thews and sinews for work I will solicit favours from no man, however exalted."

"Ah, friend, you are young, and youth is subject to a kind of vanity which it calls independence. A month in this city with an empty purse, and you will know what a unit in the sum of life is worth without the help of other units. Drive on, fellows. *A rivederci!*"

The postilions cracked their long whips; the four grey horses started at a walk; the two footmen who had kept guard on either side of the door sprang back to their places on the footboard; and his Eminence's coach lumbered along the stony street, a vision of scarlet and gold. And George felt that he had rejected help from the man who held France in the hollow of his hand—the man who had no second in power, except Enghien. While he had thought it no humiliation to ask Mr. Hobbes for a friendly recommendation, or to wait in the ante-rooms of English noblemen, in the hope of getting employment, he had rejected the help and the influence of a patron whose lightest word would command all that ambitious youth could desire. But he had made his choice willingly, and was prepared to suffer the worst that fate could bring.

It was a week later, and he had but the change of a crown piece between him and hunger. He had husbanded his coins with a rigid self-denial, had allowed himself only two dinners a week, and had lived for the rest of his time upon a morning meal of dry bread and thin red wine, and a supper of cabbage soup. He had given his landlord to understand that he was dining with his friends; yet, though he might have been sure of hospitable entertainment in several houses, he had been too proud to take his poverty into fine company, nor had he come to the idea of selling his bettermost clothes, or the tortoiseshell and gold *nécessaire*.

He had declined Monsieur du Plessis' liberal wages; but he had not even the promise of any superior employment, though everybody had been civil to him, and had sworn to keep him in mind, when a tutorship or any confidential post offered. Now, with those few small coins in his pocket, the prospect narrowed, and there was nothing but Flanders and the army of the Duke of Orleans before him. For choice he would have served under Enghien, whom he admired, rather than under Gaston, whom he despised; but he wanted to be with his friend, and it was in Mountain's regiment he meant to enlist. He had a long tramp on foot to look forward to, and must needs live on the charity of the towns and villages through which he passed. He looked back and remembered that tragic morning at Portsmouth, and the lonely nights that went before, and the pain of his aching limbs and wounded feet. How strange it would seem to be on the high-road again, after years of careless luxury —no better off than in his friendless childhood!

He was lying on his bed in the dull autumn afternoon, listening to the wind-driven rain rattling against the casement, and reading a book he loved so well that it could almost make him forget how pleasant a thing it is to dine when one is hungry, and what a strange, light-headed feeling comes to a man after a sequence of dinnerless days. He was reading "Don Quixote," in the Spanish, a book he knew by heart, and comparing the romantic knight's sufferings and deprivations with his own.

"There is nothing like a touch of madness for taking the sting out of misery," he thought. "I am too sane. Perhaps if I have to walk to Flanders and starve for the greater part of the way, I may fancy myself an emperor before I reach my destination. My brain feels as light as thistledown already."

It was three days since his last dinner, and he had flung himself on his bed because he felt almost too weak to stand. And in such a condition to contemplate tramping to Monsieur's camp! Well, the *nécessaire* would have to go, perhaps, to raise money for his journey. He felt unequal to considering ways and means ; and in the next minute he was laughing—almost hysterically —at the scene in the roadside inn which the demented knight mistook for a princely château.

He fell asleep before he had finished the chapter, the heavy sleep of exhaustion, and it was evening when he awakened with a start at the gentle touch of a hand upon his brow, and saw a face he loved looking at him in the twilight.

"Oh, I am out of my wits again!" he cried. "'Tis

the fever come back. No, no, no," with passionate
repetition, turning his face to the wall, "I will not be
fooled by dream-faces."

"George, dear George, you are not dreaming. It
is I, Lady Llanbister, your old and faithful friend. My
poor, poor boy. Your forehead burns like fire. The
people downstairs did not tell me you had been ill."

He had slipped from the bed, and was on his knees
at her feet.

"Dear God, it is real! 'Tis in God's truth my dearest
lady—the friend I have been longing for ever since
we parted. And you are here, in this poor room—my
friend and benefactor still! You have not forgotten
me."

"No, George—though you have found other friends,
you are no less dear to me. But why do I discover
you in this ill-favoured lodging, instead of at the Hôtel
de Lussac, where I heard of you as the adopted son
of the house, cherished and admired,—the spoilt child
of fortune ? "

"You heard of me—— ? "

"Yes. Do you suppose that all news has ceased to
travel between Paris and London ? I had a very choice
description of your appearance at Renard's Garden, in
Madame de Lussac's train. I was told how you attended
her everywhere, and the favours she lavished upon you ;
and, knowing you as I do, I could but think you must
have discovered some claim of kinship with this lady
before you would have accepted so much from her
bounty."

"Your ladyship has guessed the riddle. The favours
I accepted were forced upon me by the right of kindred.
And when I found that the world looked with an evil
eye at my post in the Marchesa's house, and made her
affection for me a subject for malignant slander, I had
no choice but to leave her and go back to my old
independent life."

"And doubtless she recognised your generous sacrifice,
and is still your devoted friend ? "

"Her farewell words were all kindness ; yet I doubt

she must think of me as an ingrate, and speedily dismiss me from her regard."

"That cannot be—if—if "—her voice faltered, and she looked at him searchingly, as she continued slowly —"if her reason for so favouring you was founded on a belief that you were her kinsman—perchance her close kinsman. Did she believe that, George? For God's sake be plain with me?"

There was a passionate insistence in her voice that startled him ; but he was not thrown off his guard.

" I cannot answer as plainly as I desire, dearest lady. My claim upon the Marchesa's kindness is her secret— not mine."

" You do well, perhaps, to be silent. And—if I have guessed the riddle—the rest is of no moment."

She spoke with profound despondency, and her speech ended in a sigh. A silence followed, George still kneeling, with her slender hand held against his lips. To him she appeared almost as an angel, quite as a saint, so widely did she differ from all he had known of womankind since he left her.

" Dear lady," he murmured at last, "how often has the hour-glass turned since we parted, and how slowly the sands have run for him whose life wanted your sweet presence ! "

" Flatterer ! You had a new friend and a kinder one."

" Never a friend so kind, never a friend so dear."

" You forget the claims of kindred, which must be paramount over mere friendship."

" Kindred can claim duty—it cannot compel affection. My greatest trouble has been not to love Madame de Lussac as I ought to love her. But tell me, dear lady, when you came to Paris, and what happy fortune has brought me such unlooked-for joy."

" Alas, George, England is no longer a pleasant place for two lonely women. Since my dear lord's death my heart has turned against the home he loved ; and there was little reason to remain in a country distracted by war, where never a month passes but brings the news of some proud head laid low. 'Tis said that on both sides there is a great longing for peace, but the insolent demands of the Parliament make reconciliation impossible. It is not alone that they would reduce the King to a cipher—their servant, whose sceptre would have no use but to pass their measures. They ask more than his own honour; they want him to sacrifice his Church, and to betray his friends."

" And he refuses? I doubt he remembers Strafford, and how poor a price he got for the greatest brain and boldest heart that ever served him. But after having yielded *there*, 'tis strange he should hold fast by the small fry."

" Ah, George, you do ill to jeer at him. He failed in that sad extremity only because he saw the lives of his wife and children in peril. He is not a coward. He has ever been careless of his personal safety. His Queen is now out of the enemy's power; and were his children as safe, I know he would cleave to his friends in the face of death. That being so, I see but scanty hope of peace in England for many a year. But for me Paris is the first stage on the way to a home of perpetual peace."

" Alas, alas! It is of the cloister you speak."

" Yes, George. These evil times—and the deep melancholy that fell upon my spirits after my lord's death—determined my choice. In the world I have nothing to live for. In the convent I shall live for a better world, which 'twere ill to enter without years of penitence and prayer."

" Nothing to live for! Dearest lady, I know that I have no claim upon you; but can you so abandon the lovely girl you have reared? Can you leave Geraldine alone and unprotected?"

" Geraldine will spend the next three years under the same roof with me. Those years will give maturity to her mind, and establish her in the true faith. Her education will be completed by the most accomplished women in France; and if, when she comes of age and into the possession of her fortune, she should choose the world rather than the cloister, she will be fitted to take her place among the noblest of her time."

"And if—subject to the subtle influence of minds stronger than her own—she choose the cloister, there will be two stars withdrawn from this base world, where purity and love are so sorely wanting. Oh, dear lady, that you can contemplate a living death for yourself moves me to wonder and grief. That you can think of entombing so bright a creature as Geraldine is more than my patience can suffer."

"You do but show a heretic's ignorance when you liken a convent to a grave. You know not how living and how sweet that cloistered life can be."

"Oh, I cannot be patient! I cannot endure so to lose you! Dearest friend, kindest, most generous mistress, I entreat you to pause before you commit your ripening years to a changeless captivity—the placid years of mature womanhood, which should glow and brighten with serenest beauty, like those summer sunsets we have watched and loved, ever loveliest towards the close. Think how fair the world is, and how dear a privilege the power to move from one pleasing scene to another; and then consider what it must be to wake every day in the same narrow chamber, to walk every day on the same path, to watch the shadows creep along the same panel on the same wall, the sunshine slant across the same square of turf— flicker on the same grey stone. Think of the same faces, the same dull habit, day after day and year after year! You who have the capacity to admire and enjoy; you who have lived at Court, in company with the finest gentlemen of your day; you who have been beloved and admired, ever commanding and never commanded;—can you submit to the irksome discipline, the iron rule of implicit obedience?"

"Stay, George. Again I say you prate of things you know not. Yes, I have lived at Court, and my heart has ached there! And what matters the unchanging order of outward things if the mind within be at peace? The loveliest scenes this earth can show are valueless to her who has lost the capacity for joy. I can recall the time when a meadow spread with king-cups could put me in a fever of delight; yet now I should look with a dejected eye on the most exquisite perspective of mountain, lake, and forest. But we will waste no more time on argument in this wretched chamber. If you will walk with me to my lodgings, on the other side of the river, you shall share my supper, and we can converse to our hearts' content at table."

"Yes, I can walk the length of the bridge," he answered, rising from his knee; "and the prospect of a good supper at the end of the walk will put strength into my limbs."

He broke into a laugh, which was half a sob, for his weak condition disposed him alike to laughter and to tears. The irony of the situation touched on the comic. In his rapture at re-union with this dear friend, he had forgotten penury and hunger; but the word "supper" reminded him how near he was to starving.

He lighted a candle-end in the tall iron candlestick on his table—such a morsel of tallow in such a monumental candlestick! He flung on his cloak and hat, and attended Lady Llanbister to the door, holding the candle to light her steps on the stone stairs, which were not over-clean. Indeed, to the English lady's fastidious senses, the tavern, with its discoloured wainscot and cracked ceiling, and its mixed odours of wine and garlic and tobacco and dirt, seemed a hideous den, a veritable *coupe-gorge*, which she had entered with a shudder, and left with ineffable relief. They went by the Pont Neuf, and to the Rue du Bac, where Lady Llanbister had lodgings in a house near a convent.

The door was opened by one of the old men-servants from Isleworth, whose homely visage was like a friend's welcome.

"What, Andrew? Is it you?"

"Yes, your honour; and right glad to see your honour in this heathenish city."

He opened the door of a large, low room on the ground-floor—a room that reminded George of her ladyship's parlour in Aldersgate Street. There were signs of womanly occupation all about—the embroidery-frame, the virginals, and the lute with the broad crimson ribbon he remembered so well ; and in the mild yellow candle-light Geraldine's sparkling countenance looked at him with an arch smile.

"What, have you brought the renegade home with you?" she cried, and sank almost to the ground in a mocking curtsy. "Welcome, Monsieur le Marquis— for that I presume has become your title since Madame la Marquise adopted you."

He tried to answer her, but his spirits were too much agitated by the rapture of this meeting, or the distance he had walked had been beyond his strength. He could but stagger to a chair, overcome by sudden faintness.

Lady Llanbister observed his deathlike pallor, and hastened to his side.

"Some wine, Andrew, or some brandy ! Mr. Mountain is swooning. My poor boy, how exhausted you look ! Alas ! I fear you have but just recovered from some serious indisposition, and I did wrong to bring you so far."

She was offering a glass of brandy to his pallid lips with a hand that trembled a little, in spite of her endeavour to be calm. The brandy, though he swallowed only a spoonful, revived him, and his colour came slowly back as she wiped the cold drops from his forehead with her cambric handkerchief.

"It was only a passing faintness," he said, "or but a sinking of the spirits from over-much content."

Geraldine had hurried to his side with a bottle of aromatic essence, and was watching his face with a compassionate tenderness, altogether removed from the mocking spirit of her first greeting. She noted his wan and hollow cheeks, and guessed that he had been unhappy, and loved him the better for looking miserable. It may be that she ascribed all his sufferings to the loss of her own company ; for, to come up to her idea of perfection in a lover, he ought not to have known one cheerful moment since they parted.

The table was ready laid for supper, and George being seated between the two ladies, Lady Llanbister carved a

capon and a carbinadoed ham with that practised skill
which was a part of a great lady's education ; and
although George restrained his ravenous appetite, lest
he should shock those delicate ladies, it seemed to him
as if he had never in his life eaten anything so delicious
as those daintily cut slices from the capon's ample breast,
or the spiced ham, that blushed rosy red amidst the
white. Even the agitating presence of those he loved
best on earth could not altogether subjugate hunger,
sharpened by a month of semi-starvation ; and Mistress
Geraldine was somewhat scornful at perceiving how
good a supper he was able to eat, amidst the agitation of
re-union with cherished friends.

Wine and food brought the colour back to his face,
and brightened his eyes ; and his life had known few
happier hours than that hour after supper, when he sat
between these two recovered friends in front of the
hearth, where the blazing pine-logs enlivened the low
panelled room, painted white, and decorated with
medallion portraits of the princely line for whom the
house had been built when Francis I. was king. The
autumn nights were chilly, and the fire-glow was welcome,
for comfort as well as for cheerfulness.

Lady Llanbister told him of all that had happened in
England in the year that was waning—of cities besieged,
and country houses, so lately the abodes of domestic
peace, turned into fortresses and girdled with cannon—
of the King's victories in the west, and of the crushing
defeat at Marston Moor, when Rupert's famous cavalry,
unconquered till that hour, went down like a little dust
under Cromwell and the horsemen of the Eastern
Association. She told him of Newcastle's white-coats,
and their heroic stand against overpowering odds, ready
to die for their honour and their King, and scarce a
handful of them leaving that bloody field alive.

"The Marquis left England directly after the battle,"
she concluded. "'Twas said he suffered more from the
blow to his own pride as a captain than for the loss of
those gallant fellows he had led to the gates of death.
'Tis a bitter trade, George, that of the soldier, whose

fault of judgment may cost the lives of multitudes. The Royalist losses at Marston Moor were computed at four thousand; and their loss ended not there, for on this disaster, the loyal city of York, which had made so heroic a defence, had no choice but to surrender. And so ended his Majesty's hold upon the north."

"I heard of Lord Newcastle in this city, and guessed his presence here was of ill augury. Indeed, I feared the day was lost when I heard of the Queen's flight," George said. "But since May last past I have lived in a troubled dream, and all I have heard of English news of late has been from gentlemen to whom I have gone as a suitor for employment, and whom I had no right to harass with importunate questions."

This evening was the first of many nights which George spent by the fireside in this most dear company. It was almost as if the old life in Aldersgate Street had come back; and sometimes, sitting with Geraldine in the firelight, he forgot that he was in Paris, and that the garden, on which one window of the *salon* looked, where the yellow chestnut-leaves were drifting down under the autumn rain, was the garden of a Benedictine convent, and not their old paradise in London. The convent garden stretched behind the houses on this side of the street, and they could catch glimpses of the nuns and their pupils walking on the trim pathways beyond a century-old yew-hedge, battlemented at the top.

Lady Llanbister persuaded George to exchange his room at the Golden Crown for a lodging near the Church of St. Sulpice—two airy upper rooms, with a pleasant outlook towards the gardens of the Luxembourg Palace; and he had scarcely shifted his belongings to this tranquil haven when he received a letter from Mr. Hobbes, bidding him call on Sir Nathaniel Burbery, a wealthy London merchant, who had retired from the turbulent alarms of East Chepe to a handsome house near the Sorbonne, where he had brought his wife and only son, a youth of fifteen, to whom he wished to give those advantages of foreign travel and foreign tongues which had been denied to himself.

"Sir Nathaniel is rich and liberal, and may prove a better patron than a greater man, if you can please him," Hobbes wrote in conclusion.

George waited on Sir Nathaniel without loss of time, and was cordially welcomed by the worthy citizen.

"Mr. Hobbes swears you are a 'varsal genius, sir," he said, after presenting George to his lady, a much more stately personage than the knight, and very disdainful of trade and the city, as the daughter of a small Wiltshire squire of ancient descent. "He says you are as good at the foils as at Greek and Latin, know French like your mother tongue, can jabber Italian and Spanish, when drove to it, and can ride like a centurion."

Lady Burbery gave her shoulders a despairing shrug, and tapped the floor with her high-heeled shoe. Sir Nathaniel *would* make these odious mistakes, instead of letting her do all the talking.

"You will teach my son how to wear a sword and how to use it; to ride and walk like a youth of good breeding; shoot with a pistol; and if you can make a dancer of him you will command *my* gratitude," said the lady. "And you will teach him to converse in French with all the newest words that are in use at Court and at the Hôtel de Rambouillet. Mr. Hobbes assured me that you have been at Court."

"Mr. Hobbes only told your ladyship the truth."

"Then I take it you will be able to make my son familiar with all those pretty turns of speech, and movements of the features and limbs, which are unfortunately unknown in East Chepe, where the poor child has been bred."

"You smoke her, sir? You are to turn the city lad into a fine gentleman, for which my lady will be your grateful servant; and if you can bring it about without teaching him to laugh at his father I shall be as much beholden to you."

"If he is to be a gentleman, Sir Nathaniel, one of his first lessons will be reverence for his parents; but I doubt he has mastered that already," George answered, with his grave smile.

He liked the jovial, rubicund knight much better than the pale-faced lady, who took too little trouble to hide her contempt for her husband. The young Nathaniel was presently introduced—a languid, overgrown youth of fifteen, who looked with scanty favour on his future tutor.

George was asked to name his salary ; and, the figure at which he valued his services being a modest one, Sir Nathaniel promptly agreed, with the promise of an augmentation whenever the pupil's progress justified such reward. The tutor's duties were to begin at nine in the morning, and continue till four in the afternoon, and he was to dine with the family, in order that his eye might be upon his pupil throughout that important function.

" I would sooner have my son a dunce at Latin than a sloven at the dinner-table," Lady Burbery told George. " And I hope your attention to his intellects will never make you unmindful of his habits in eating and drinking ; for what is the use of Homer and Virgil to a man who thrusts his knife half-way down his throat, and sops up his gravy with a hunch of bread ? "

A severe glance in Sir Nathaniel's direction gave point to this remark.

A new chapter in George's life-story began from that day. He had an employment that assured him a decent living, and he had his evenings free to spend with those dear friends so happily restored to him, and so kind.

To be bear-leader to a somewhat silly youth of fifteen, and to suffer the airs and graces of a petty squire's daughter, was certainly not the most congenial occupation for a young man who had roamed the Continent as a soldier of fortune with so bold and cheery a comrade as Francis Mountain ; but George had that sturdy spirit which prefers drudgery to dependence ; and he did not consider himself a victim because his morning hours were spent in teaching a dull-witted boy to speak French with something of the native accent, and his afternoons in the fencing-school or the riding-academy with the same slow pupil. Master Nathaniel was a warm-hearted lad, who loved his vulgar father, and made mock of his genteel mother ; and he soon took kindly to George, than whom he had seen no gentleman at London or Paris with a handsomer face or a grander manner.

"I shall never carry my sword like my tutor," he told his mother, when she complained of his awkwardness ; "and if I try to fling back my cloak as he does his, it gets round my neck and strangles me. He sits upon his horse all as one, and the wildest brute in the school can't kick him off. And the fencing-master swears there's not a man of his age could beat him with the rapiers."

Dull as the boy was, he made visible progress under a tutor he so greatly admired, and who laboured conscientiously to bring about improvement. The lad was no coward, and took kindly to the *manège* and the *salle d'armes*, and loved to ride with his master along the Cours la Reine in the short winter afternoons, where there were a good many carriages, though they no longer went four and five abreast, as in spring and early summer, and where George and his pupil sometimes rode beside Lady Llanbister's coach.

George would hardly have ridden daily along that familiar drive had he not known that Madame de Lussac was at Rome, whither she had gone for the winter, after a month's visit at Blois—a fact he learned from Mademoiselle de Montpensier, who always gave him a friendly greeting, and sometimes kept him at her coach-door in conversation for half the length of the Cours.

"I think all the handsome ladies like you, because you are so handsome," said his pupil. "But I know the lady *I* like best."

"La Grande Mademoiselle, perhaps, the King's cousin, who dresses finest and wears the biggest diamonds ?"

"Nay, I vow to God 'tis not she I like best—but the fair, pretty lady, with no jewels but a string of pearls round her neck, that sometimes is so smiling and kind to you, and sometimes as still and as mute as the stone figure you called Diurna in the Tuileries Garden. Your sweetheart, Mistress Geraldine, is the likeliest lady I've laid eyes on in Paris."

"You must not call the goddess of the chase Diurna, nor Mistress Geraldine my sweetheart, Nat. She is but my kind friend, and is vastly my superior in birth."

"I snap my fingers at your 'vastly.' I know she loves thee, Master Mountain, though she is not always civil. Her eye flashes like the sun through a chink in the shutter when she sees you ; and then she drops her eyelids, and pulls down her lips, and looks as proud and as prim as ever she can. But I knows what I knows."

"You must say 'I know,' Nat, not 'I knows' ; and you must not say foolish things about a lady," said George, who could have hugged the boy for the speech he reproved.

His heart beat thick and fast at the mere sound of her name, pronounced by his stripling pupil. Yes ; he knew that she loved him, with an affection as earnest as his own, that had stood the test of a year and a half of separation ; but, alas ! what could come of their love ? Could she, a fortune and a beauty, consent to marry one who was alike nameless and penniless, whose best hope of independence was in the schoolmaster's despised trade ? Had England been at peace he might have hoped, by Lady Llanbister's influence, to gain some post at Court, or some state office, which would have led to higher things, and so brought him nearer his mistress's level, or at least excused her for marrying him. But in the present disruption of all English society his dear lady's friendship could not advance his fortunes.

Yes ; she loved him. He had seen the same look in her eyes, had heard the same faltering in the full, sweet voice, of late in Paris, that he remembered two years ago in Aldersgate Street, when he began to feel assured of her love. Two summers had come and gone, and had left her unchanged. But then, in distracted England he had had no rival. All that was gallant and splendid in English youth was absorbed by the war. There was neither time nor opportunity for lovers. And so this lovely girl had lived in a seclusion almost as complete as the cloister towards which she had of late turned her thoughts.

But now that she was in the gayest city in the world, where all the days and nights were marked by entertainments and assemblies—the theatres for the afternoons, the drive for the exhibition of beauty, the Palais Royal, the Luxembourg, vying with each other in *fêtes* and dances, the Hôtel de Rambouillet offering a soberer but even more distinguished society;—how could he doubt that among the plumed hats and pointed beards, the red heels and long swords, Mistress Geraldine would find wooers enough to make her forget the tutor drudge whose richest clothes still lay folded and packed in chests that he had never opened since he left the Hôtel de Lussac? More than once of late he had been tempted to put on a suit of that courtly attire for his evening visit to the Rue du Bac ; but the idea of a tutor in *frisé* velvet and jewelled embroidery seemed incongruous, and he feared that Geraldine would be more disposed to ridicule than to admire him.

So far he had been fortunate, in that she had not appeared at any of the assemblies where her fresh young beauty could scarce have failed to hit the general taste. Lady Llanbister had avoided all fine company, and paid no visits except to her unhappy Queen, who was now lodged at the Louvre, and liberally entertained at her Royal sister-in-law's expense. Nor did George hear of any visitor except her ladyship's Director, who was with her every day, but whom he had never happened to meet going out or coming in, though on more than one occasion the Director had been closeted with her ladyship in her study or oratory, while George was in the *salon* with Geraldine.

" I doubt 'tis the same man I caught sight of once at Isleworth," he exclaimed petulantly, when the girl told him how Lady Llanbister was occupied. " I hate to think of his power over my dear lady, for 'tis he and he alone who has turned her inclinations from God's fair earth and all who love her on it, to the perpetual imprisonment of a cloister—and I can but wonder, madam, that you encourage her in so cruel a self-immolation—nay, that you can even think of sharing that gloomy life."

" What else should I choose, sir ? Do you think this world can be vastly attractive for an orphan who has not a friend in it that cares what becomes of her ? Were the convent gate to close on her ladyship and leave me outside, there would scarce be a lonelier creature living than I. Do you marvel, then, that I mean to follow her where there will be a holy sister-hood to receive me—where I shall be one of many happy souls who live to serve and worship God, and who have renounced all affection for a cold-hearted world ? "

"Cold-hearted ? Is the heart of the world ever cold to beauty and youth, think you ? Ah, Geraldine, were you but to appear for an hour at the Palais Cardinal, you would find yourself the dazzling focus of a throng of admirers. You would learn the supreme power with which nature has endowed you—the power to charm all hearts, and to make one heart ineffably happy."

A disdainful shrug was her only notice of this compliment. She turned from him with a sullen air, and looked out of the window by which she was sitting.

" You must know something of this man who has haunted my dear lady like the shadow of doom for these four years past," George said presently.

" I know he is a very disagreeable person, and that he keeps the keys of her conscience. I suspect he is an emissary from her brother at Rome. For my own part I have kept as much aloof from him as I could."

"Then it is not he who set you thinking of the convent ? "

" No, sir. You are monstrous dull this evening. Must I tell you over again that if I go to the convent, and live there, and grow to love the life well enough to adopt it for the rest of my days, it will be because I am a solitary creature, and that of all this throng of admirers your flattery promises me, there is not one I value at a penny fee?"

There was anger and there was also the sound of tears—angry tears perhaps—in her voice as she answered him, with her face resolutely turned towards the street, where the lanterns were being lighted in the gathering dusk of December. Before he could reply the door opened, and Lady Llanbister came in, looking white and weary, and stifling a sigh before she returned his greeting. He heard the outer door close as he went to meet her, and, glancing quickly towards the window, saw the man in black pass in the dusk—a cloaked figure, with a hat of clerical shape.

The evening meal was more silent than it was wont to be. Lady Llanbister had the worn and saddened look he remembered in Aldersgate Street, when she came late to supper after a conference with the man in black. Geraldine was in ruffled spirits, and enlivened the table with flashes of ill-humour which were at least better than mute despondency.

"There is one man in this world whom I hate," George said to Lady Llanbister on the next evening, when he found her alone: "that odious Jesuit—I'll warrant he is a Jesuit—who is at the bottom of your resolve to forsake those that love you——"

"Forsake! No, no, George! I shall love my friends as dearly as ever I did, when I am a cloistered nun!"

"Love them, yet leave them? That is not possible! Love them, and be satisfied to see them once in a way, when the Superior gives you leave, for ten minutes, in a convent parlour, perhaps behind a grate?"

"The Order I enter will not be so severe as to make friendship difficult."

"Will the Order let you live with those you love? Will the Order let me spend hours in your company, as I do now?" George cried. He had grown bolder than of old during this happy interval of re-union, and he thought of a lifelong severance with an angry despair. "Is the felicity I have enjoyed to end for ever when you pass the convent gate, when I see you kneeling before the altar, a penitent—you, who have never sinned——"

"Hush, George; you must not speak so. We are all sinners."

"It is that Jesuit's work—the slow and subtle process of years. He has haunted you like an evil spirit. First he would have you a Papist, and now he would have you a nun. He would strip you of the fortune which you have ever used with a divine discretion—in charity and kindness. At Isleworth you were a centre of happiness, and all the neighbourhood turned to you for comfort. In the dark city lanes your presence shone like a star. And this Jesuit would have you immure that sweet influence, that precious charity within four walls, to be absorbed in the mechanical virtues of a Sisterhood! Oh, it is shameful! I detest the name of Jesuit."

"Because you know nothing of that gifted, that sublime Brotherhood—or of the saint its founder. In your ignorance you must be pleased to keep silence about the gentleman who directs my conscience, or to speak of him with respect. He has long been my spiritual councillor, and knows my life as none other knows it; and it is because he believes there is but one safe haven for my declining years that he would have me take the veil."

"For your declining years! And you are still in the prime of womanhood—your beauty scarcely touched by time; you are still of an age to taste all the best pleasures of existence—travel, wise and amiable company, music, pictures, the theatre with its new and shining lights, Corneille, Molière. In a year or two, as I dare hope, the troubles in England will be ended, and you may enjoy your pleasant houses and estates there; and you have Geraldine, who should be to you as a daughter, whose husband would cherish you as your very son, whose children "—his voice faltered as he spoke the word—" would be to you as your own, and would renew your youth. All that long life of happiness, of simple womanly joys, lies fair before you, like one of those sunlit perspectives seen through a palace gate."

" And as false! Painted sunshine, unreal beauty ! "

" No, no, it is very real. It is the prospect to which every woman in your circumstances—not blinded by bigotry—would look forward. But because this fanatic prates of penitence, for you whose conscience is stainless ; of self-sacrifice, where to sacrifice yourself is to profit nobody, and to hurt all who love you—because of his persistence, his persecution, you shut your heart against Geraldine—against me, the nameless waif whom you have taught to love you. By Heaven, it was cruel to be so kind—to so possess yourself of my affection—if you meant to forsake me ! "

That reproachful appeal moved her. She looked at him for a few moments in silence, and then burst into tears.

" My conscience is my guide, George, and I must follow—though it may not lead me by pleasant paths."

" No, no, not your conscience, but a fanatic's teaching —a bigot's endeavour to absorb you and your fortune into the bosom of his Church. Do I not know what the Jesuits are, and what they can do? The grain of mustard-seed that Loyola planted has become a tree whose ever-extending branches blight all things their shadow falls upon."

" No, George, say rather a tree beneath whose shelter the weary and sin-laden may find rest from earthly cares."

" It is not rest, but death—to surrender thought and will, to forego all natural affections, to love the stranger of yesterday as well as oldest friends or closest kin, to be a cipher in the sum of life ! It makes me mad to think of so cruel a sacrifice."

" Because you are a heretic, George, and the love of God has never entered into your heart. The joys of heaven would be but weariness for a mind so out of tune with religion."

George was kneeling beside her, as he had knelt on

the evening of their reunion, in his room at the Golden
Crown. Her left hand, which lay upon the arm of her
chair, was clasped in his, but her face was still turned
from him, to hide her tears.

" If Geraldine were your daughter—if you had a son
like me—would this tyrant conscience let you leave
them ? " he asked.

" If I had a son," she repeated, " would God accept
maternal love as an atonement for——? "

She spoke in a low, dreaming tone, as one who looks
inward—rather questioning herself than replying to her
questioner ; and she left the sentence unfinished.

" Atonement ! " he cried, beside himself with impatience. " You talk of atonement !—you, whose saintly
life has been an example of all womanly virtue, a lesson
for all women——"

" Hush, hush ! You do not know me, George. He
who has been my spiritual guide for many years sees
me as God sees me, and knows my need of pardon."

" Your Jesuit confessor, who strikes through your
heart at your fortune. Curse him ! "

" Silence, sir, or you will irrevocably offend me,"
she cried, snatching her hand from his in sudden anger.
" The gentleman you so outrage is my brother."

" Your brother ! Oh, forgive me ! I knew not—
never suspected——"

" No ; for in England he could only visit me in
secret, by reason of the persecutors of his Order. My
brother's inclination ever turned to the old faith, and
he entered the Roman Church less than a year after
my father's death, who had himself been of the High
Church party. My brother was a saint from his
earliest boyhood, George, and over his severe temper
the pleasures and splendours of this world had no
power. From the day he was received into the Order—
after so long a trial of service and obedience as proved
an iron will and an exemplary patience—he has laboured
with a zeal and a courage that neither suffering nor
danger could shake. Under an untowardly manner
he has a great soul, and I must needs honour him."

"Alas! 'tis but natural you should listen to a brother's voice—that you should follow the leading of one you love."

"No, George, it is duty, not love, that leads me. It is one of my sins never to have loved my brother. From my childhood even, he lived in a world which I could not reach; his thoughts were given to higher things than my mind could grasp. But there came for me a time—of great sorrow "—the sad, sweet voice faltered, and there was a brief interval of silence before she continued the sentence—"a sorrow in which my brother was my only counsellor and friend. That sorrow made him the master of my life There was no other earthly guide to whom I could turn, for I had long been motherless, and I had forfeited my father's regard by one unhappy act of disobedience. Yes, George, I, whom you presumed but now to call sinless—as if any human life ever passed from cradle to grave without sin! We might doubt that Christ was very God, if humanity could so escape defilement."

"At least grant me one prayer," George pleaded. "Promise that you will do nothing hurriedly."

"Hurriedly! Why, this step has been urged upon me—has been the purpose of my mind—from the hour of my dear lord's death. Indeed, George, you know that it was my purpose before I lost him."

"Yes, I know—because, having lost that cherished friend, you thought life would be empty, so poorly did you esteem Geraldine's love and mine."

The door opened before she could answer him, and Geraldine came in from church, where she had been with Mistress Betty, who was in process of conversion to the Roman Catholic religion, following her young mistress into the fold, and who, in the dearth of suitors caused by the civil war, had serious thoughts of the cloister.

George went back to his lodging much disheartened. He could better understand the influence of that stealthy visitor, now that he knew the man in black was Lady Llanbister's brother, whose authority over her was the slow growth of years, and to whom she chose to believe herself indebted for help in a time of trouble.

She had spoken of some great sorrow in her earlier life. He could think but of one kind of grief—a love unhappy, or forbidden. Love for one who was her inferior in the world's esteem. Yes, that was the sorrow his imagination pictured. One who loved her as he loved Geraldine, and held himself aloof, and died perhaps of that hopeless passion, or flung his life away on some foreign battlefield, an unremembered unit in the sum of slaughter. Or it might be that, in her girlish ignorance, she had not measured the abyss between the Bishop's lovely daughter and her low-born lover, and she had secretly favoured his suit—and this was the act of disobedience which she remembered now, with penitential tears ; a soul so pure making much of so light a stain. And her brother, the Jesuit, striving for the aggrandisement of his Order, greedy to absorb her fortune into the maw that swallowed the revenues of kings, had worked upon a mind too sensitive, prating of atonement for this girlish error while enlarging upon the beatitude of a cloistered life. George hated that black figure only the worse for knowing that he was so near a kinsman, since he could but deem him the more dangerous tyrant because of that relationship.

The wintry days grew longer. January had brought bad news from England—the execution of the turncoat Hothams, father and son ; the judicial murder of Laud ; the losses at Abingdon, where Sir Henry Gage, Charles's faithful governor at Oxford, was slain. Lady Llanbister had reason for anxiety in her Royal mistress's cares, with whom she spent a sad hour from time to time, and who had so denuded herself by her remittances to the King as to already feel the pinch of poverty in her splendid lodgings at the Louvre, despite the Queen Regent's generous gifts.

George was a nightly visitor in the Rue du Bac, where a cover was always laid for him at the evening meal ; but a shadow of melancholy now brooded over the little party, and, save for an occasional outburst of gaiety or of spleen from Geraldine, supper would have been for the most part silent.

From Geraldine George learnt that Lady Llanbister had fixed upon Holy Week as the date of her retirement from the world. He heard, and sighed, and held his peace. He had reiterated every plea that affection could urge against an act that to his mind seemed fatal as self-murder. And so the days went on till the eve of Palm Sunday, and in less than a week the lodging in the Rue du Bac was to be deserted for the seclusion of an enclosed convent.

Never could George forget that Saturday evening, and the dull, aching melancholy that hung upon his spirits as he walked from Sir Nathaniel's house by the Sorbonne to the street he knew so well, through the windy gloom of a bitter March. The day was waning when he took leave of his pupil, and it was nearly dark when he let himself in at Lady Llanbister's lodgings, where the door was usually left on the latch till night.

He knocked at the door of the *salon*, and the sweet voice he loved bade him enter.

She was not alone. The only light in the room was the faint grey of the dying daylight from the low, wide window, and the flame of a pile of logs in the deep chimney. A man—the man in black—was standing with his back to the hearth, and the tall, dark figure made a screen between the room and the firelight, and spread its distorted shadow on the low ceiling.

" I beg your ladyship's pardon. I did not know you had company," George faltered, looking at the black figure, and making a movement towards the door.

" Nay, George, there is no need for you to withdraw. This gentleman was about to leave me; and we shall go to supper so soon as Geraldine comes in from the sermon at St. Sulpice."

The man in black did not move, but remained silent; and George felt that he was being scrutinised by dark, deep-set eyes, whose expression he could not see. A strange, dream-like feeling came over him as he stood waiting in that embarrassing silence.

"Has Sir Nathaniel received any further news from London?" Lady Llanbister asked presently.

"Yes, he had a news-letter this morning," George answered slowly, while he stared at the face in shadow, as if he could scarce find words for so simple a reply.

"Good news?"

"Nay, they were—ill news—or mixed news. Montrose has beaten Argyle and his Covenanters—but there is a new army forming for the Parliament—and I doubt——"

His speech grew slower. He could not take his eyes or his thoughts from that figure in black, standing straight and rigid in front of the flames, the pale face and dark brows but half seen in the fitful light. His words came with spaces between—as of one dropping asleep, and then he lapsed into silence, and stood fixed and mute, as in a cataleptic trance.

"George!" exclaimed Lady Llanbister, "what ails you? What are you thinking about?"

"Of that gentleman, madam. Surely, sir, I have seen you before?"

"'Tis not impossible, sir, though I have no memory of such a meeting."

"Oh, but I remember. Memory could not so mock me! 'Twas many years ago—when I was a little child. You were standing betwixt flame and shadow then, as you are standing now."

"Indeed, sir! 'Tis something of my habit to stand with my back to the fire—not an uncommon one, I believe. And pray where did this marvel—of your childish recollection—come to pass?"

"In a cottage within a day's walk of the Portsmouth Road."

Lady Llanbister looked white as a ghost in the sudden light of the brand that fell and flamed upon the hearth; but George had no eyes for his dear lady. All he had of sight and hearing, of attention and thought, was concentrated upon the man in black.

"That is not a precise description of any place," the man answered, in a sneering voice. "A day's journey from the Portsmouth Road might be anywhere in Surrey, or Sussex, or Hampshire. The road begins at London and ends at the sea. I cannot help your memory if you can tell me no more than that."

In a man who is always pale, emotion shows little change; but George, whose eyes were now accustomed to the half-light, detected an agitated twitching in this man's under lip, while his slower speech indicated a struggle to maintain his stately composure.

"My memory needs no help, sir," George cried impetuously. "Your voice is better known to me than your face—and both come back to me as though 'twas yesterday when you stood—as you were standing just now—your hands clasped behind your back, your head bent, and your eyes looking down at me, who was then no higher than the top of your boot."

"You have a wonderful memory, sir, a marvellous memory, to remember that which never was!"

"Oh, sir, it was, it was! It is your memory that fails. Perhaps you have paid for the maintenance of many nameless children in your life."

Had not all his thoughts been centred in the man he must have heard the low, agitated cry that broke from Lady Llanbister, as she leant with clasped hands against the great armchair from which she had just risen.

"And perchance you have branded many such with your mark, to indicate their dependence on your bounty."

"I fear, sister, that this gentleman, whom you so lauded a little while ago, has gone out of his wits since he was last in your company. You are talking like a lunatic, sir, and I have no taste for such extravagance of speech. I beg there may be an end to it."

"I swear, sir, I have all my wits—nay, more than I commonly have; for I feel as if I were all sight and hearing and apprehension, so earnest am I to discover the truth. Believe me, sir, I know you as I know my face in the glass. You came twice to my foster-father's cottage——"

"Your foster-father!" cried the priest, with sudden fury. "Your very father, you mean. What have stray sprigs like you to do with foster-fathers?—a bit of dirt in a peasant's hovel—a pretty gentleman to give me the lie!"

"Will you swear—before her ladyship—that you never saw me till to-night?"

He turned towards Lady Llanbister as he asked this question, and saw her leaning over the back of the chair, her face hidden, her frame shaken with sobs.

"Dearest friend, have I grieved you by my speech? Bid me be silent, and I will question this gentleman no farther. But no blast of his displeasure can shake me from my recognition of his person."

"Go on, George! I implore you to speak," she cried passionately, lifting her head suddenly and looking at him with eyes that flashed fire through her tears, and seemed to him to shine as he had never seen them shine before. "Go on, I beseech you. Yes; that was your first home, the house where you were born, the wretched, comfortless peasant's house—rough-handed people, yet not unkind. Yes; that was your foster-father—a peasant farmer; that was where you were born; that was where you were left. He willed it so"—pointing to the dark figure, the wrathful face—"left to thrive or to die! And God was good, and you are here to-night, given back to me as if by a miracle, for the felicity of my declining years."

"You are as mad as the lunatic you favour, madam," said her brother, in that chilling voice she knew too well. "You suffer me to be bearded by a fantastic stripling whom your womanish fancy cherishes because he chances to resemble one whose features you should pray God to blot from your mind for ever. You have fostered unholy memories; have sobbed and sighed over recollections which the penitent's scourge should have ripped out of your heart, leaving only remorse for your wanton folly."

"I was not a wanton! I will not have you call me so before *him*! You know I was no wanton. I trusted the man who besought me to be his wife—and whom I believed my Prince, my King that was to be——"

" A villain who told you a lie that would scarce have gulled a child. You believed the fable because you loved that profligate, and cared not whether he was true or false. You would have given yourself to the devil, had he come in as fair a guise. You stole from your father's house—a wanton before you were a woman —and would have brought everlasting dishonour upon that good old man, and upon me, had I not hindered you, and hid you from the world, and suppressed every evidence of your infamy, and so enabled you to marry a great gentleman, and to hold your head as high as the most immaculate she in England."

" Leave my house, sir. I have suffered your unkindness too long, and now it has passed all bounds of Christian patience. I will not submit to be upbraided and belied in the hearing of my son."

George ran to her, and fell on his knees at her feet, clasping the hand that hung at her side, kissing and crying over it.

" Dearest, dearest lady! 'Twas nature made me so honour, so love you, from those first days at Isleworth. Dear and revered lady! Can God be so good to me? Am I verily your son? "

" Yes, George, you are my son. It has been ever in my mind, as a strange chance that might become a certainty—since your likeness to the man I once too dearly loved inspired hopes which I tried in vain to stifle. You are my son—your recognition of my brother is proof enough for me."

" Nay, dearest madam, there is proof tangible and material which your brother can scarce gainsay—the brand he set upon my flesh, what time he doomed me to a farm-labourer's life. At least, sir, if you forget your speech—how you sentenced me to live obscure, and by the sweat of my brow—you can scarce forget the sailor you ordered to mark me—thus."

He tore open his shirt, and showed the letter V

tattooed upon his chest. Time had made no change in the deep purple of the charcoal stain.

"Will you deny that, sir?"

'Nay, I admit your identity, which it is for you to be ashamed of. You are the waif that disappeared from the farmer, Luke Scriven's homestead, in the year 'twenty-eight. I found the house deserted and the man lying in the nearest graveyard, in the November of that year. You have established your lineage, sir; and neither you nor this lady, who is so eager to own you, have any need to be proud of your pedigree. I leave you, madam, to your son's company, and your own after-thoughts, which I can scarce doubt will shortly bring your mind to a better state for that first step upon the heavenly road that you are pledged to take next Thursday."

"You are mistaken, Ralph. This revelation changes all things in my life. I have new purposes to live for."

"Oh, you are red-hot in folly! You will soon come to a better way of thinking. You, who have yearned for the peace of the cloister, cannot so surrender heaven. I know the natural piety of your mind, and that you but need leisure for meditation. I charge you, sir, you, who kneel and fawn there, not to stand in your mother's pathway to heaven. She has been a great sinner, vain, deceitful, disobedient to a pious father, clinging with unholy love to a liar and a profligate; but she may yet become as great a saint, if your evil influence does not hinder her."

He flung out of the room, casting a malignant glance at George as he passed him; but George was on his knees at his mother's feet, with her arms clasped about his neck. He thought for one instant of that other woman, who had wept upon his breast, and claimed him for her son. His heart had been marble then; but now it was as if he had found that one dearest and best to whom his arms had been outstretched since he was a little child—the mother whose love had been ever the something wanting in his life.

He left the house when Geraldine's foot was on the

threshold—at Lady Llanbister's desire, who was too deeply agitated to spend the rest of the evening in her ward's company.

"Come to me to-morrow afternoon, dearest, when we can converse freely, and I will tell you how much or how little of wantoness there was in my unhappy love."

"And you will think no more of the convent? You will give me your promise?"

"For the rest of my life I shall think only of my son. He shall be my counsellor and guide."

In the long *tête-à-tête* of the following day, mother and son sitting side by side, hand locked in hand, in the confidence of an affection which was at once the instinctive love of closest kinship and the gradual growth of happy years, Lady Llanbister told the secret of his birth to the son who could never bear a father's name.

Her sorrowful story was related in faltering accents, in speech broken by tears, and in a spirit of self-humiliation which ignored the guilt of her betrayer and the childlike innocence of his victim.

CHAPTER XX.

THE tragedy of Lady Llanbister's girlhood was but the common story of a woman's confiding love and a man's treason. It was only the seducer's exalted rank and the victim's noble character which distinguished the history of this case from the history of other women whose lives have been blighted before their knowledge of life began.

It was in the summer of 1620, when Lord Effingham entertained King James at his mansion near Southminster, that Viola Redgrave passed from the monotony of a joyless girlhood to the tempest and passion of a fatal love.

Evening shadows veiled the dark bulk of the cathedral when the Royal party rode in front of the Bishop's palace; but the setting sun shone full upon that pompous cavalcade, and to Viola, who had seen so little of earthly splendour, that passing picture suggested rather a vision of knights and ladies from Spenser's " Faërie Queen " than a procession of mortals fashioned in the common mould.

The dust of summer roads had spread a faint grey veil over velvet and satin, snowy plumage and jewelled embroidery; but that dim greyness, the cloud of dust under which they rode, only made the passing vision more dreamlike. The Bishop's daughter leant out of an upper window, with a basket of lilies on the ledge before her, ready to be flung upon the Royal roadway—

herself in shadow, the road below golden in the low sunlight. Her eager eyes roamed over the glittering train, but she had only time to distinguish three of the most striking figures in that Royal progress—first the old King, with bent shoulders, leaning somewhat wearily over his horse's neck, the feeble body jolted a little in the heavy saddle, the spindle legs hanging loosely against the gold and crimson housings ; next a lady, whose gaudy splendour, lurid in the sunset, reminded Viola of the wicked Duessa in the allegory she loved—so arrogant, so imperious, was her bearing, so magnificent her riding-habit of green velvet and silver, the bodice thickly studded with emeralds and pearls, her hat with its towering mass of ostrich feathers and *bandeau* of diamonds—a woman past her first youth, but still in the full bloom of a commanding beauty. This lady rode in the rear of the King, but a few paces in advance of a bevy of younger women, who had the air of being in attendance upon her, and, young, beautiful, richly dressed, and mounted on high-bred horses, looked but servants as compared with her, who as Countess of Buckingham assumed an almost regal state.

Only one of the courtly train rode his horse level with the Royal charger, and Viola's eager gaze, shifting in tremulous haste from point to point, suddenly concentrated itself upon that picturesque figure—the plumed hat, roped with jewels ; the crosses and stars that flashed many-coloured light from the white velvet doublet ; the grace of the tall form ; the slender hand that held the bridle with as light a touch as if it had been a thread of silk—the right hand resting on the hip. She had time, while the King and his companion approached at a foot-pace, to note even the deep bullion fringe upon the white gauntlet, as she leant out of her open casement, and dropped a shower of lilies in front of the Royal charger's hoofs.

As the flowers fell, the King jerked his bridle with a sudden clutch of his feeble old hand, startled himself, and fearing a movement of his horse. The cavalier at his side looked up, curious to discover whose hand had thrown the lilies ; and in one dazzling moment Viola met the upward glance of eyes that were like stars—at least to a girl's fancy: Royal eyes, with pride and laughter in their light, the eyes of her future King—for she never doubted that he who rode at James's bridle-rein was the Prince of Wales. How was she, the Bishop's daughter, bred in a seclusion as close as a cloister, to know the pinnacle to which a weak king's favourite might ascend ; or the splendid insolence of youth that has never known failure ; or the Royalty of consummate beauty in man or woman? This man came of a race predestined to conquer, endowed by Nature with the graces and gifts that belong to princes of fairyland, a race that walked this workaday world like Olympian gods, and seemed as certain of homage and victory. What if their enemies declared that the mother of these Olympians had once been a kitchen wench, and that the divine gift of beauty had filtered through the veins of peasants? It was that ruder race perhaps which gave strength as well as comeliness to the younger children of Sir George Villiers, and justified his union with his first wife's humble companion, or tire-woman, or kitchen-maid. Stories varied as to the exact depth of obscurity from which the most arrogant peeress in England had been elevated. Some measured the lowness of her origin by the altitude of her bearing, and swore she would never have been so arrogant had she not climbed from the kitchen to the steps of the throne.

The cavalier's upward-looking face, with its rich colouring and star-like eyes, appealed to Viola as the most perfect face her eyes had ever looked upon. She drew back dazzled, her cheeks crimsoning with a thrilling surprise that was new, and strange, and sweet—as if in very truth she had seen one of the elder gods, a vision of supernatural beauty materialised for a moment in the sunset. When she looked out of her casement again, they were gone—King and favourite, proud dame and girlish beauties, and the train of courtiers and statesmen. All had vanished in the dim perspective of the narrow street. There was nothing to be seen but her lilies lying trampled in the dust. They were gone ; and " Baby Charles," riding with the Lord Keeper, soberly clad in black velvet cloak and hose, and tawny leather jerkin, had passed unobserved by the Bishop's daughter.

Her father was to sup with the King at Lord Effingham's mansion that night. Viola heard him return to the palace in his heavy leathern coach after midnight, and she hoped he might give her some account of the Royal banquet when they met at dinner next day. But his lordship's brow was dark, and he ate his temperate meal in silence, and Viola, who called him " my lord," and never presumed to begin a conversation with him, sat silent also, though longing to ask questions.

Her life was as dull as the life of Danae in her brazen tower. She had no resources but her dogs, her aviary, and the one little cabinet of books which she read over and over again, till even those she loved the most made her heart ache with the burden of an indescribable melancholy. Books, life, the house in which she lived, the garden where she walked, the river that flowed beside the long terrace, the cathedral bells, whose deep-toned music was so old and so familiar that it seemed a part of her own being rather than of an outer world, as inevitable as the beating of her heart,—all things were steeped in the same dull grey, all things sickened her with their everlasting monotony. Chaucer, Spenser ! What a revelation of fairyland, of brightness and beauty, love, pride, chivalry, war, splendour, their old-world romances and picturesque allegories had once seemed to her !—but now, alas ! she knew them all by heart, and though she still loved them, they could move her neither to smiles nor tears. Indeed, she often found herself reading mechanically, while her thoughts were far away from the page, wandering in a world of vague surmises, longing for something—knight, dragon, angel or fiend—to break through the grey web that shut her from the world.

" I have been taught to pity the nuns in their convent

prisons; but was there ever a nun with less pleasure in life than I have ?" she said to herself.

Her education was finished. The various masters who had taught her Greek and Latin, to play upon the virginals, to embroider upon velvet and silk, to dance, and write, and cipher, had been dismissed. She was an accomplished young lady, who knew something of the classics, and the uses and properties of all the plants that grew in the physic-garden. She was fitted to take the head of a fine gentleman's household; but until any such gentleman—high-born, wealthy, and for choice noble—should appear upon the scene, matrimonially disposed—or, in other words, until Dr. Redgrave could find an opportunity of disposing of his daughter to the highest bidder—she was left to eat her heart out in an existence whose sameness was beguiled by no vision of future grandeurs. His lordship took the current view of parental obligations, and it never occurred to him to confide his schemes for his daughter's aggrandisement to the subject of them ; nor had he any fear that his daughter might sicken of her colourless life, and sigh for change and action, a world in which to expand those spirit-wings that beat so violently in the breast of youth. He looked at her with a critical eye, and saw that she was beautiful, graceful, gracious, with that innate air of high-breeding which would not misbecome a ducal coronet or the Royal daïs. For such a daughter, even with the restricted opportunities of a cathedral city, it ought not to be difficult to find a noble and a rich alliance.

The Bishop explained his views to his only son—the confidant of all his designs, clerical and domestic ; but the confidence was not too graciously received. Nature, which had been so liberal to the sister, had been churlish to the brother, who was a plain likeness of a plain father, the austere dignity of the Bishop's countenance degenerating into sullen sourness in the son, the features following the lines, but bluntly, like a bad copy of a face in a picture. Yes, Mr. Redgrave admitted the girl's beauty, and that she might please the eye of some

Court profligate, such as the man whose existence was the curse of England.

"I doubt there are a score of petty Buckinghams with the Villiers' insolence and greed, if not the Villiers' comeliness ; and my sister might find a mate among them—if you will pledge half your income to dower her," he answered moodily ; whereupon the Bishop assured him that, having so lovely a creature to offer in the matrimonial market, he counted on making a far different bargain.

Ralph Redgrave went back to Oxford immediately after the Royal visit to Southminster. He was a fellow of New College, and spent half his life within those venerable walls, taking his only pleasure in solitary visits to the Continent, where he had a few chosen friends living wide apart—at Paris, at Madrid, at Rome. He seldom stayed long at Southminster ; and he took very little notice of his sister. Viola had at least the liberty to do as she pleased at home, and had no one to interfere with her movements, so long as she was punctual at meals, and appeared with her duenna and sometime nurse at the cathedral services. Dr. Redgrave —ambitious, disappointed, angry with fate and with the world—spent all his leisure in his library, toiling at erudite pamphlets subversive of everything, one of which he occasionally printed at his own expense, dedicating it to the most discontented statesman he could hit upon—latterly to Lord Verulam—and which, though bristling with capitals and virulent adjectives, in long primer, made no more stir in the world of action than if he had dropped his manuscript into the Palace well. To be for ever abusing people and institutions, and never to provoke retort, is one of the states of life that tend towards untimely death ; and the Bishop was too unhappy a man to be a kind father. He had missed preferment under two reigns, having vegetated at Southminster since the year of the Armada. He was suspected of a hankering after the old faith, and even of having maintained a correspondence with more than one of the Roman Cardinals ; but those who were

in his confidence knew that these dallyings with the
Scarlet Woman were not of his own initiating. They
were inspired by a more restless spirit than his. The
ruling mind at the Palace—the active element of discontent—was not the Bishop, but the Bishop's son.
There had been mysterious visitors at the Palace at
long intervals, and always when Ralph Redgrave was
at home to assist in receiving them—olive-complexioned
gentlemen, sleek and supple of mien and manner,
whom Dr. Redgrave described as foreign merchants,
and who were closeted with him night after night.

While he held in reserve all schemes for his daughter's
establishment, and while her future of wealth and power
was but a splendid dream, interwoven with other visions
of personal aggrandisement, the girl herself was trembling
on the threshold of a dream more dazzling than the
fairest vision possible to the Bishop's duller imagination,
worn and blunted by the experience of hard facts. The
parterres and pleached alleys, the fountain and maze,
which Viola had ever loved, were now transformed into
an enchanted garden, where at each turn in the terraced
walks, at each arched opening in the high yew-hedges
she might meet a demigod.

Three of the gentlemen of the Court had their lodgings
in the house of a wealthy townsman, whose gardens ad-
joined the episcopal grounds, and whose upper windows
overlooked the pleasaunce; and thus it happened that in
the summer twilight Viola heard strange voices and the
musical jingle of sword-hilts and spurs, as these courtiers
amused themselves playing football on the citizen's lawn.

Even the sound of those unknown voices thrilled her;
but how overpowering was her surprise when, sauntering
by the river in the growing darkness, a boat was pulled
in suddenly to the bank, and a man leapt lightly on to
the terrace walk in front of her—a man in whom, even
by that faint light, she recognised the cavalier who had
ridden at King James's saddle-bow! He was less magnificent to-night, attired in ash-leaf velvet; but she saw
the star on his breast, and she had no shadow of doubt
that the Prince of Wales stood before her.

She had been brought up in the fear and reverence of kings, to think them gods, and to believe they could do no wrong, nor ever exact too much from their subjects. She sank on one knee, half swooning at this beatific vision ; but the intruder raised her to her feet with hands that were as strong as they were gentle—raised her till her face was near his own, eyes looking into eyes ; and then, in that dim solitude, began Viola's love-story, the passionate wooing of a high-bred profligate, the self-abandonment, confiding adoring, of an innocent girl, too chaste to fall an easy prey to the seducer, but simple enough to be won by an audacious ruse.

It were needless, in this later stage of that wronged lady's life, to follow the dream of her girlhood through all its phases. Her lover found means to pursue his secret courtship, and so far succeeded in his evil influence as to persuade the girl to keep silence, and so deceive her father. Quick to take advantage of her mistake as to his identity, Villiers told her that their union must be kept secret during the King's lifetime, but that when he came to his kingdom, she should be proclaimed to all the world as his Queen. When she argued that a prince should marry the daughter of a Royal house, that his future subjects would never accept Bishop Redgrave's daughter as their Queen, he laughed her fears to scorn. Kings could choose whom they would, so long as they could win and keep the love of their people. Had not Edward IV. married Anne Woodville ? and was he a less popular monarch because he had not chosen some foreign princess for his consort, with not a word of English to answer an English subject's petition, mute among her husband's people as a stock or a stone ?

"Be sure the lovely lady of my choice will please them better than the Spanish Infanta, or any Papistical princess living," he told her ; and so, beguiled by vows of lifelong devotion, by the fervid eloquence of one who knew how to strike every note in the gamut of passion, the confiding girl suffered herself to be led away from her father's house, and trusted her person and her fate to the man she loved.

It was but three weeks since the lilies she flung from her window had lain bruised and trampled in the summer dust, and the lovers were on the road, in a coach-and-six, travelling by easy stages to Buckingham's mansion and stronghold of Burleigh-on-the-Hill. Duchess Katharine was at York House, by the Thames, writing loving letters to her lord, telling of the baby-daughter's progress in baby graces, a wife almost as confiding as the girl who sat beside him on that journey of days and weeks through the pleasant highways of England, between south-west and north-east. He was her Prince still, Charles, Prince of Wales, her King that was to be, and she was his proud and happy wife ; for at their first halting-place at a nobleman's mansion on the borders of Wiltshire the Prince's chaplain had been in attendance, and had married them with all due solemnity, reading the marriage service of the Church of England, in a private chapel, by the light of two flambeaux held by the Prince's body-servants, who were the only witnesses of the ceremony.

Happy journey, happy dream ! She had the most accomplished gentleman in England at her feet, her devoted lover, skilled in every art, gifted with every grace that can win a woman's love. She had him in the pride and glory of his youth, romantically attached to the mistress whose unworldly simplicity made her seem more nymph than woman, whose every look and every thought was in marked contrast with the words and looks of the women of the Court, those indulgent beauties who challenged him to facile victories. Viola's freshness and purity gave him a new idea of woman ; and if he was her fairy prince, she was his fairy princess.

"When I drop asleep at your side, I sometimes wake with a shiver of fear, lest, on opening my eyes, I find the coach empty," he said. "You have an aerial look by torchlight, as of a creature that might vanish."

Outriders carrying torches accompanied their coach when the nights were dark and the roads difficult. There was a magnificence in their progress which sustained Viola's idea of Royalty. Who but princes would travel in such state, and with such a troop of servants? Her father, the Bishop, moved about with infinitely less pomp, yet he counted himself a great personage.

Her dream had lasted nearly two months, and she was at Burleigh when her brother burst in upon that solitude of two. The pursuit had been difficult, since there was no clue to the person of the seducer. Ralph Redgrave, hastily summoned from Oxford, found a distracted household, and the Bishop crushed by the calamity that had fallen upon him like a stone from heaven. Among a variety of speculations and wild assertions, Mr. Redgrave heeded only the positive statement that ten days after the Royal party had left Southminster, a coach-and-six, with a bevy of attendants, had been seen at nightfall in the road that skirted the north bank of the river, about a mile below the Bishop's garden on the south bank, where Viola walked every evening. It was surmised that she had stolen away by water, though no one had seen her leave the garden or land on the opposite shore. Ralph followed the scent like a sleuth-hound. But even his shrewdness and tenacity were slow to prevail, and the search lasted long ; for Buckingham had protracted that summer journey to a rambling progress among the houses of some of his patrician satellites, received everywhere with admirable discretion and sumptuous hospitality, by hosts who were either absent or invisible.

"How well your father's subjects love you," Viola said, when she praised the richness of their entertainment.

The journey thus conducted by capricious cross-roads had been difficult to follow, an ignorant peasantry giving little help to the inquirer ; but by a stubborn patience Mr. Redgrave at last succeeded in getting on the right scent—and, once his face set towards Burleigh-on-the-Hill, he no longer doubted that his sister's lover was either some creature of Buckingham's or the Favourite himself. The thought of this latter contingency infuriated him, for it was in his nature to hate any man who had sprung from nothing to superlative power, and he had long brooded with malignant envy upon the dazzling image of George Villiers, whom he had never seen until the late Royal progress, and whom he hated with a keener and more personal malice after the brief association of a festive evening at Lord Effingham's, during which Villiers had treated the Bishop's son with a magnificent carelessness—though not uncivil. Would an eagle be uncivil to a sparrow?

He had his revenge upon the Duke now, when, on the edge of midnight, he burst, booted and mud-bespattered, pale with fury, almost voiceless with passion and hard riding, into the saloon at Burleigh, and tore his sister from her seducer's arms.

There is no fortress so well defended that hatred cannot find an entrance. Redgrave had leapt the moat and found an unfastened door in the offices. Where there is a regiment of servants, there is always an open door. He had threaded the unknown labyrinth of that stately house and surprised the lovers in their bower, where the Duke had thought himself triply guarded from intrusion.

"Your Prince!" he echoed with brutal scorn, when Viola bade him respect the King's son. "What, has the villain put *that* lie upon you? Poor fool! Prince Charles is an honest man. The wretch who tempted and betrayed you is that venal slave, a King's Favourite—a dotard's pampered parasite—spawn of a kitchen-wench—exalted for a handsome face and a neat foot, bedecked with borrowed jewels—the curse, and shame, and ruin of England."

The Duke struck him across the face with the flat of his sword before he hissed out the last sentence, and in the next instant they were grappling each other, in a blind fury, more like beasts than men. Viola threw herself between them, her bare arms wreathing her lover's neck, her slender body flung against his breast, warding off the assailant. Duke or prince, traitor or true, she loved him, and in this desperate crisis thought but of his peril. She fell at his feet, swooning, and was carried into an adjoining room, whither her women were called to tend her ; while her lover followed his foe to the courtyard, where a bloody duel was fought by torchlight, without seconds, or any of the ceremony common to such encounters.

Both men were wounded, but Redgrave's injuries were the slighter ; and while the Duke lost a great deal of blood, and had to be carried to his bed, where he lay in a high fever, and passed from stupor to delirium, Ralph's were but flesh-wounds, which the surgeon dressed so as to enable him to leave Burleigh with his sister next morning.

For the better part of a year after that cruel night, Viola's life was spent in ignominious captivity. No cloistered nun, false to her vow of chastity, ever suffered a heavier expiation. For the deluded girl, who had fancied herself the wife of the second highest personage of the realm, England's Queen that was to be, whose path was to be strewn with roses, in the sunshine of a nation's love—for this innocent victim the strong, stern man was remorseless.

"I will save your father from the shame of an unchaste daughter, and will spare you the disgrace you have merited, if I can ; but to do this I must have your implicit obedience," he said, when his sister was at last in a condition to hear reason.

She was too unhappy to refuse submission, had the penance inflicted been a dark cell and a diet of bread-and-water. That innocent victim of man's perfidy was deeply imbued with a sense of sin. All the religious influences of her childhood were revivified by the misery and humiliation of her state. She submitted meekly to every kind of hard usage, except to hear her betrayer reviled. Her spirit rose against Ralph's sneers and disparagement. "A parasite—a venal slave!" That man who was like a god ; that creature of a nobler aspect than she had ever seen in living man, till her dazzled eyes looked upon him! A man whose thoughts were as noble as his countenance, whose voice was music, who spoke to the meanest of his attendants with an inimitable courtesy, whom his dependents served with an affection that verged upon idolatry.

"You do well to disparage him, for he and you scarce belong to the same species; you remind me of a monkey that snarls at a man: like, and yet unlike!" she said to her brother one night, rising from the supper-table at the obscure inn where they rested, trembling with passion, her eyes flaming, her head high.

All trace of the humble penitent had vanished, and only the indignant woman was left.

"You love your seducer better than you love your soul, mistress!"

"Aye, that do I, and would sell my soul to Satan if he would make me my Charles's true wife!"

"Charles! Oh, you abject fool, still to love the liar who tricked and dishonoured you!"

For eleven dreary months the Bishop's daughter endured banishment from home and kindred, comfortless lodgings, rough fare, and all the galling circumstances of a life hidden from the world. A lonely farmhouse in a pastoral valley between Hindhead and the Hog's Back was the scene of her seclusion; and no detail was wanting that could remind her of her degraded condition—waiting for the martyrdom of motherhood, and without one touch of pity or affection from kindred or friend to soothe her mental agonies, or help her through the ordeal to which she looked forward in her loneliness. Her only hope was that the peril through which she had to pass would end in her release from shame and sorrow. She could imagine no future happiness possible for her, except that Paradise of peace beyond the Gate of Death.

The people of the house served her with profound respect, tempered by a compassion which they dared not express; but in her inexperience of the lower classes, they seemed to her creatures of a coarser race, and she held them as completely aloof in her misery as she could have done had she been at the pinnacle of fortune. She was indeed haughtier in her fallen state than she had ever been in her stainless girlhood, and her whole nature had taken a sterner mould. Deeply as she felt her degradation, her grief expressed itself in no weak supplications to the tyrannical brother, whose occasional visits brought no consolation, and who made a favour of even such small mercies. She employed her loneliness in prayer and study, enlarging her little stock of Latin by a diligent perusal of Saint Thomas à Kempis and Virgil's Eclogues, two volumes which Mr. Redgrave had brought her grudgingly, in acquiescence with a reiterated request, and which he had given to her with a sneer at woman's mode of learning, and the remark that the Latin of one author would doubtless seem to her as choice as the Latin of the other. She beguiled the hours her limited supply of books could not fill with that exquisite and elaborate embroidery in which she was almost as accomplished as the unfortunate Queen who, half a century before, had lightened her captivity at Fotheringay by the same feminine labour.

The day of her release came at last, after a lingering illness, during which her wandering wits had taken little heed of the infant that lay for only a few hours at her bosom. When she recovered her senses, and asked to look upon the face of her child, Ralph told her that the nameless brat had been adopted by the woman of the house, and that its future fortunes would be his care.

"It will be happy for you if you can go through life without ever seeing him or hearing of him," he said, "and so may be spared the disgrace which your folly has deserved."

She was too weak and ill to contend for a mother's rights, and the maternal instinct moved her little for a child whom she was bidden to consider an embodied shame. She went back to the Palace at Southminster crushed and heart-broken ; yet she bore herself throughout the painful crisis of that home-going with a proud silence, which paralysed the officious pity commonly given to a penitent daughter. She knelt, pale and mute, at her father's feet, and bent her head under the hand that trembled as it blessed her ; but no word of repentance passed her lips. That attitude of submission was her only acknowledgment of her sin. Her dignity in sorrow impressed the Bishop more than the most passionate demonstrations of remorse. It was a year since he had looked upon her face, and he told himself that she was lovelier in her sorrowful womanhood than ever she had been in the gladness of unsullied youth, and that, if her secret were but faithfully kept, she might still attain the proud position he had reckoned upon as the price of her beauty.

It was three years after her return that, by her brother's influence—the influence of a man born for intrigue— the Bishop's daughter was offered the post of maid-of-honour to the new Queen, an offer which was perhaps inspired by the rumour of his lordship's Papistical inclinations. She would have refused a position so conspicuous, and one in which she must needs meet the beloved enemy whose falsehood had blighted her life ; but her father and her brother were equally insistent upon her acceptance of the proffered honour ; and Ralph, who was now frequently at Whitehall, assured her of a fraternal guardianship that would render Buckingham's approach impossible.

"If you meet him—and it may be impossible to avoid such a meeting—it will be in the broad light of the Court, and you will meet as strangers."

They did so meet, some half-dozen times before the murder at Portsmouth, and looked at each other with marble countenances and passionately beating hearts ; but they never touched hands again, or spoke words of love, or grief, or pardon.

Her marriage, which occurred a year after Buckingham's death, was a surprise to the Court, and a disappointment to the Bishop and his son. After refusing alliances of the highest mark, which would have furthered their ambitious schemes, she chose Lord Llanbister, a widower, of grave disposition and deportment, and old enough to be her father, having discovered in him a generous and sympathetic nature, and being able to confess to him, as she could have done to no other of her suitors, the sorrow and the shame of her first love. He had cherished her but the more fondly after the anguish of that humiliating confession, and had been grateful for the tender regard which her confidence indicated.

EPILOGUE.

TIME makes but little change in gardens whose verdure is the growth of centuries, whose fashion dates from a day long dead ; and the years between 1645 and 1657, which changed the government of England and the manners of Englishmen, made no perceptible difference in the old house at Isleworth, or the river that rippled past its lawns and *parterres*. April and May showed choicer tulips in those *parterres*, and some young cedars of Lebanon had been planted on the lawn, at the advice of Mr. Evelyn ; otherwise the garden in the year 1657 was very much the garden George remembered when his foot first touched the springy turf and his eyes first beheld Geraldine's girlish figure and flying hair.

Another Geraldine tossed her shuttlecock towards the blue sky—a smaller Geraldine, whose flying hair was of a brighter gold, and who had but lately celebrated her eighth birthday with a feast for the village children, and—tell it not in the austere society of Whitehall—a May-pole dance upon the lawn. Nor was this eight-years maiden in undisturbed possession of her garden kingdom, though, by right of superior years, she had a certain despotic power. Masters George and Charles, both active and clamorous, though George was but three years old, gave old Nurse Hillyer, and Mistress Betty, still a spinster, all the trouble that high-spirited and healthful childhood could give to its guardians.

England was at peace within its borders and powerful among the nations. The Protector reigned at Whitehall,

with a certain dogged tyranny which made London
a dull city, but ensured comfort of a humdrum sort
to the citizens, so long as they were content to forego
the Liturgy of the Church in which most of them had
been reared, and to abstain from bear-baiting, theatres,
cockpits, and other once-familiar pleasures.

It was a dull England assuredly to which George
Mountain and Geraldine, his wife (married at the chapel
of the Embassy in Paris, on the Feast of St. John the
Baptist, in the year '45), returned with their daughter,
and an infant son, after six years of delightful wanderings in southern France and Italy—from Montpelier
to Naples—always in the company of that beloved
friend and benefactress who shared every joy and sorrow
of their young lives.

George Mountain had given his allegiance to the
warrior-statesman who ruled England—not the less
deploring that unpardonable tragedy at Whitehall, but
too little attached to the monarchical form of government to set his face against a ruler who had made
England prosperous, and had kept within the limits
of constitutional law. A varied experience at foreign
Courts, and intercourse with the chosen spirits of great
cities, had educated him in the philosophy of life and
the policy of nations ; and he entered the arena of public
affairs better equipped for success than one man in a
hundred who offers himself for election. He sat in
Cromwell's third parliament as one of the Members
for Middlesex, and soon rose to parliamentary distinction,
and to an important post in the administration of foreign
affairs, which brought him into close relations with
Mr. Secretary Milton. In the year '56 he received
the honour of knighthood from the Protector, and, as
Sir George Mountain, became a personage of weight and
authority in the country, bearing a name that ranked
with the best names in the Republic.

For the titular King of England, that out-at-elbows,
pleasure-loving wanderer in the Netherlands, George
Mountain had but scanty reverence, having been too
familiar with that Royal exile's manner of life and

mode of thinking ; but he was careful to utter no word which could vex his dear Lady Llanbister, who maintained an occasional correspondence with Henrietta Maria, and who hoped to see the King established in his rights, than which establishment nothing seemed more improbable in the year '57, since the country had accepted a Republican government with a steadfast adherence which promised to be as permanent as the English soil. Liberties attained by such rugged and painful paths, at such sacrifice of men and treasure, would scarcely be surrendered for a sentiment of loyalty to an unknown youth, whose highest claim to the affection of Englishmen was his descent from those ancient Scottish kings with whom England's rulers had been ever at war.

George, who looked deeper into things than most people, saw the possibility of change in a government which, despite all show of liberty, hung on the life of one bold despot ; and when the Restoration came he was content to withdraw into private life—that blissful tranquillity of a home where love reigns supreme—and to await the hour when his services might be demanded under the new order. Nor was it long before the want of that clear brain and cosmopolitan experience was felt at the Foreign Office—and Sir George Mountain was again in harness when the Triple Alliance was signed. He was in favour with Clarendon and Albemarle—but he was out of favour at Court, because of a churlish disposition which made him withhold his handsome wife and daughter from the festivities of a Palace where Barbara Palmer reigned as Sultana, and where the Queen's ladies were more famous by reason of their adventures than renowned for their virtues.

His political career having only begun in '54, Sir George Mountain stood clear of all association with the enemies of the martyred King ; but the fact that he had served Cromwell with distinction, and that he preferred the unfashionable neighbourhood of Aldersgate to the Piazza, and the rusticity of Isleworth to the gaiety of Hampton Court, won him the reputation of a Puritan,

although his womenkind were strict adherents to the
Roman Catholic religion, and had their private chapel
and chaplain.

And if anybody inquired who was this Sir George
Mountain who had married Llanbister's heiress, and
upon whom Lady Llanbister had settled the bulk of
her estate, it was answered casually that he was one of
the Brewer's new men. The want of ancestors counted
for little in a man who had risen to eminence under
the Usurper Cromwell.

Sir George was not a man of many friends ; but those
whom he admitted to the happy circle in Aldersgate
Street and at Isleworth were among the choicest spirits
of the age. The friend most cherished, and ever certain
of being warmly welcomed—let him appear as often or
as suddenly as he chose—was the *débonnaire* gentleman
who found the nameless child on Southsea Common,
and on whose high spirits and happy-go-lucky temper
neither the passing years nor the change of governments
made any impression.

George's children called him Uncle, and adored him.
He was the boys' godfather, and chief instructor in all
manly arts, and the girl's admiring slave.

Once only after his marriage did George and Madame
de Lussac meet face to face. It was at a ball at the
French Ambassador's palace in Rome that he saw her
shining like a star among the most brilliant figures in
that patrician crowd. De Lussac's death, slain in a
savage duel with one of his mahogany-faced Circe's
vulgar admirers, had released the Marchesa from a
hateful bond, and she had exchanged Paris, where her
foes outnumbered her friends, for the Eternal City, where
she received all the honour due to princely birth and
powerful alliances. If she was not as rich as people
thought her, on the evidence of jewels that queens
might envy, she was to the last able to live in un-
diminished splendour, and to keep her creditors at bay.

There was weeping and gnashing of teeth among the

purveyors and usurers of Rome after this lady's death, which happened with appalling suddenness at a card-table in the Doria Palace, the worn-out heart swooning in a fatal syncope, amidst the buzz and gaiety of a crowded assembly.   Nor was the sorrow of her creditors unmixed with indignation when they discovered that the jewels which had startled Rome by their magnificence had never belonged to the wearer, but were a loan from Cardinal Mazarin, then an exile at Bruhl, to whom they were carried by Madame de Lussac's white-headed old chamberlain, Signor Paolo, attended by a Papal guard.

FOUR NEW VOLUMES OF

Hutchinson's Select Novels.

Each in crown 8vo, handsome cloth gilt, **3s. 6d.**

GRIF.

By B. L. FARJEON.

"A work of extraordinary interest."—*Nottingham Guardian.*
"A decidedly remarkable novel."—*Spectator.*

THE VILLAGE BLACKSMITH.

By DARLEY DALE.

"A clever and entertaining novel."—*Morning Post.*
"A novel of very high order, and sure to live."—*Liverpool Mercury.*

TATTERLEY.

By TOM GALLON, author of "A Prince of Mischance."

"An idyll such as Dickens himself might not have been ashamed to conceive."—*St. James's Gazette.*
"Exceedingly clever."—*Punch.*
"We could not recommend a better story." - *Academy.*

A STUMBLER IN WIDE SHOES.

By E. SUTCLIFFE MARCH.

"As a faithful picture of Dutch life, the novel is extremely interesting."—*Speaker.*
"A book of rare charm, originality and power."—*Pall Mall Gazette.*

LONDON: HUTCHINSON & CO., PATERNOSTER ROW.

F. FRANKFORT MOORE'S NOVELS.

Each in Crown 8vo, Cloth Gilt, 6s.

---

*The Fourth Large Edition being exhausted, a Third
Edition is Now Ready.*

THE MILLIONAIRES. With Illustrations by MAURICE GREIFFENHAGEN.

DAILY TELEGRAPH says:—" A powerful and brilliant novel."

PUNCH says:—"Unbrokenly brilliant."

WORLD says:—"Sparkles and crackles with humour."

DAILY NEWS says:—" Developed on brilliant lines; very amusing."

MORNING POST says:—"'I Forbid the Banns' was happily daring, 'The Jessamy Bride' fresh and picturesque, but Mr. Frankfort Moore has never before written so attractive a novel as 'The Millionaires.'"

THE JESSAMY BRIDE. [5th Edition.

WORLD says:—"'The Jessamy Bride' is so fine a conception that it seems cold criticism to describe it as Mr. Frankfort Moore's best literary feat, although this story claims such acknowledgment."

QUEEN says:—" Mr. Frankfort Moore's 'Jessamy Bride' places him at once on a pedestal. He has written many successful books, but most people would hardly have credited even him with being able to write a *tour de force* like 'The Jessamy Bride.' . . . Contains some wonderful dialogue . . . this brilliant, pathetic, and beautiful book."

DAILY MAIL says:—" This very delightful novel. The story alternately scintillates with wit, ripples with clever passages of intellectual talk, melts into tender pathos, and is always charming."

I FORBID THE BANNS. [9th Edition.

ACADEMY says:—"A novel which does not contain a dull page."

ATHENÆUM says:—"So racy and brilliant a novel. . . . At times there are positive flashes of wit. Most of the people interest one. . . . The women are, perhaps, even more cleverly done than the male characters."

DAILY TELEGRAPH says:—" A very remarkable novel. It is daring in conception, brilliant in execution, and altogether fascinating in treatment. Told with infinite delicacy and masterful skill. There is not an ill-drawn character in the book. There can be but one verdict on Mr. Moore's work, and that is distinct success."

LITERARY WORLD says:—" There is no question at all that 'I Forbid the Banns' is an uncommonly clever book. The subject chosen is an audacious one, but it is treated in a masterly manner."

LONDON: HUTCHINSON & CO., PATERNOSTER ROW.

F. FRANKFORT MOORE'S NOVELS (*continued*).

A GRAY EYE OR SO. [9th Edition.

ATHENÆUM says:—"One of the most amusing and taking of contemporary modern novels. The book is packed with vivacious cleverness of speech, sparkle of wit, and shrewdness of observation; it overflows with good things. There are, besides, passages that have charm, real charm, in spite of the very whimsical and biting irony."

PALL MALL GAZETTE says:—"Entertainment is to be had from 'A Gray Eye or So.' The book has some genuine wit. Not often do three-volume novels prove so profitable to the reader."

ONE FAIR DAUGHTER. [4th Edition.

LITERARY WORLD says:—"The plot is the cleverest Mr. Moore has yet conceived; . . . told with great cleverness."

GLASGOW HERALD says:—"This novel is undoubtedly clever—brilliantly clever. The novel will probably be as widely read as Mr. Moore's other stories; it has all the popular qualities of 'The Heavenly Twins' without its dulness."

PHYLLIS OF PHILISTIA. [5th Edition.

LITERARY WORLD says:—"For a reviewer to confess that he has read a book twice through, as I have Mr. Frankfort Moore's 'Phyllis of Philistia,' is equivalent to saying that the work is a production of extraordinary merit."

QUEEN says:—"There is hardly a page in the book on which there is not something worth quoting. The wit ripples off his pen from the very beginning of the book. . . . The book is uncommonly well worth reading, it is so full of thought and suggestion, though its style is so sparkling and airy."

THEY CALL IT LOVE. [2nd Edition.

DAILY NEWS says:—"The charm and passion breathing through the love scenes betray a master hand at work. Lily is a charming heroine."

WORLD says:—"A more laughter-compelling book than 'They Call it Love' or a more refreshing, it has not been our fortune to meet with for some time. Humour is a quality as precious as it is rare, and we feel the more indebted to Mr. Frankfort Moore. Seldom have we met fresher, fairer, or more wholesome girls than Lily Cosway and Mina Talbot, the two charming young philosophers in petticoats."

DAIREEN. [3rd Edition.

MORNING POST says:—"Remarkably original and well constructed. 'Daireen' is indeed a fine story, full of strength and manliness of spirit and style."

TO-DAY says:—"'Daireen' is well worthy of Mr. Moore's reputation. There are flashes of Irish humour in it worthy of Lever."

SHEFFIELD INDEPENDENT says:—"There is an air of freshness about this novel which makes it welcome, and not many who take it up will care to lay down the volume till they have read through to the last chapter."

London: HUTCHINSON & CO., Paternoster Row.

Marie Corelli's New Books.

A SIXTEENTH EDITION,

Completing 91,000 Copies, of

THE MIGHTY ATOM.

In crown 8vo, handsome cloth gilt, 3s. 6d.

A SEVENTH EDITION,

Completing 34,000 Copies, of

CAMEOS.

In crown 8vo, handsome cloth gilt and gilt top, with Title-Page
and Frontispiece by G. H. EDWARDS, 6s.

A SECOND EDITION,

Completing 17,000 Copies, of

JANE.

In foolscap 8vo, cloth, gilt top, with Illustrations by
G. H. EDWARDS, 2s.